A hard

"Do you mind if I ... your father's not about?"

"Mon Dieu!" Celene huffed in refusal and disbelief.

"I'd be glad to pay you the price of the meal," Cardwell cajoled.

Her eyes narrowed. She needed every sou if she and her son were going to have any kind of a life together. "How much is supper worth to you?"

"How much are you asking for it?"

"I think one plus is fair."

"One plus! One beaver pelt for a dish of stew?"

Celene was suddenly reluctant to give him dinner even at so exorbitant a price. "I suppose you could have a new iron hatchet for that, or a twist of fine tobacco . . ."

Cardwell was undeterred by her price, but seemed determined to cut a bargain of his own. "I'll expect a second helping, if you please, and perhaps some biscuits . . . And I expect I'll be paying for your company, too."

"You'll be paying for my company *at dinner*," Celene quickly clarified, though she could feel her cheeks get hot. She'd heard about women in New Orleans who sold a good deal more than their company at dinner, and she didn't intend to let Cardwell get any wild ideas . . .

BRIDE of the WILDERNESS

ELIZABETH GRAYSON

BERKLEY BOOKS, NEW YORK

BRIDE OF THE WILDERNESS

A Berkley Book / published by arrangement with
the author

PRINTING HISTORY
Berkley edition / January 1995

ISBN: 0-425-14531-X

BERKLEY®
Berkley Books are published by The Berkley Publishing Group,
200 Madison Avenue, New York, New York 10016.
BERKLEY and the "B" design
are trademarks belonging to Berkley Publishing Corporation.

PRINTED IN THE UNITED STATES OF AMERICA

10 9 8 7 6 5 4 3 2 1

Acknowledgments

Though writing is essentially a solitary activity, no author really works alone. During the months spent on *Bride of the Wilderness*, many people shared their time, their encouragement, and their expertise.

As always, I owe an enormous thank-you to Charles Brown, librarian extraordinaire, for his enthusiasm in meeting my many and outlandish requests for information. Charles and the St. Louis Mercantile Library Association are marvelous assets for which I am truly grateful.

In preparing this book, I could not have done without the expertise of my friend and fellow writer Eleanor Alexander, whose resources on and familiarity with Indian customs made the sections of the book that deal with the Chippewa far more meaningful and accurate.

I would also like to thank the many people who answered my questions about Ste. Genevieve and the French colonial period in the Mississippi Valley. They include Jesse Francis, Lucille Bosler, Judy Thurman, James Baker, Alma Hoelscher, and Molly McKindry. A special thank-you goes to Debbie Dirckx-Norris, who first suggested I write a book with a Ste. Genevieve setting.

On the writing side of this undertaking, I would like to offer my appreciation to Jill Marie Landis, Kim Bush, Susan Coppula, and especially Linda Hender Wallerick for her suggestions at crucial stages of manuscript preparation. Meg Ruley also earns a special salute for the sunshine in her voice—and so much more. And as always, I owe special mention to Eileen Dreyer, my personal common-sense fairy, who smacks me with her "wand" when I need it most.

As with any phase of life, there are people who give me friendship, love, and support on a daily basis. At the top of this list is my husband, Tom, who defines for me what romance means, and both the Witmer and Gow sides of my family. I also treasure my association with Debbie Pickel-Smith, whose enthusiasm for books and authors is a marvelous gift she keeps giving and giving. And finally I owe a debt of gratitude to the Missouri Chapter of Romance Writers of America for their unflagging camaraderie.

Thanks to each of you for all you've given me.

Author's Note

My husband and I discovered the town of Ste. Genevieve, Missouri, shortly after we moved to St. Louis in
1981. Its lovely French colonial homes, its rich history, and
its undeniable charm cast its spell over us on that first visit.
I have long dreamed of setting a novel there. It was, how-
ever, the publication of Carl J. Ekberg's excellent nonfic-
tion work, *Colonial Ste. Genevieve*, that gave me the
impetus to turn those dreams into reality. Using Mr. Ekberg's scholarship as my inspiration, I began to conjure up
characters that might well have lived and loved in Ste.
Genevieve during those bygone days. Researching *Bride of
the Wilderness* also led me to talk to a number of fascinating people who are dedicated to keeping French colonial
history alive in Mid-America.

In preparing to write this narrative, I studied a number
of surprisingly eloquent journals, memoirs, and letters left
by traders and trappers who plied the wilderness in search
of wealth and adventure. *Up Country: Voices form the Mid-
western Wilderness* compiled by William Joseph Seno, was
particularly informative, as was *The Voyageur* by Grace
Lee Nute. The journals of Alexander Henry—which I was
fortunate enough to read in an 1807 first edition—were
particularly helpful in determining Burke's character and
background.

Attending several Fur Trade reenactments similar to the
rendezvous at which Burke and Celene met was another
experience that enabled me to bring what I hope was a

strong sense of the period to this novel. Those at Fort de Chartres, Illinois, and at LaFayette, Indiana, were particularly fascinating. Each of them gave me a strong appreciation of what an eighteenth-century rendezvous might have been like: the smell of wood smoke and black powder, the taste of parched corn and jerky, the sounds of musketry and fiddles and Gregorian chant. I wish to thank the many reenactors who etched these vivid images in my mind and shared their expertise. For the historical novelist, being able to walk through an accurate reenactment is almost as good as stepping into a time machine.

In addition, I read several volumes of *The Book of Buckskinning*, which is a guide for reenactors put out by *Muzzleloader Magazine*. The well-researched articles in these publications explained many things the trappers' journals and letters did not and answered my questions of how and why things were done as they were by people who lived long ago.

All in all, researching and writing *Bride of the Wilderness* proved to be one of the most fascinating and enjoyable experiences of my career. I only hope that in inventing Celene and Burke, Antoine, Darkening Sky, Pélagie, and Jean-Paul and imagining their lives and adventures, I have lived up to the historical fact in Mr. Ekberg's fascinating book, and to the portrait of another era that is being kept alive by dedicated historians, volunteers, and reenactors.

I also hope that in writing *Bride of the Wilderness*, I have made this time in history live as vividly for you as it has come to live for me.

E.K.G.
P.O. Box 260052
St. Louis, Missouri 63126
August 1991

To Joyce Flaherty,
for your friendship, concern, and support.
And because I know this book
is your favorite.

BRIDE of the WILDERNESS

Prairie du Chien
Early June 1774

For Celene Peugeot Bernard being at this spring's rendezvous was a return to the world of the living after eight years of burning in hell. She drank in the crisp, cool breeze; raised her face to the brilliant sunshine spattering through the leaves; reveled in her sense of freedom. Around her the air seethed with the vitality of the men who had come to this tiny island in the upper Mississippi to trade their furs and enjoy the boisterous camaraderie after long, bleak months of solitude. It was filled with the scent of cooking venison and bubbling rabbit stew, with veils of filmy smoke rising from more than a hundred campfires, with the sounds of horses wickering, of drums beating, of joyous whoops and random gunfire.

Crouched on the lowest limb of a linden tree, Celene rested her hands on her buckskin-clad knees and looked out over the encampment. It sprawled in ungainly fashion across the broad grassy meadow between the river landing at the western edge of the island and the heavily forested slopes across the channel to the east. Along the muddy beach were all manner of boats, huge brightly painted *canots de maître* and slender birch bark canoes; dark, thin pirogues and bateaux that had fought their way up river a full eight hundred leagues from New Orleans. The dwellings hastily constructed in the meadow were no less diverse: tepees with mystical designs emblazoned on their

1

sides, domed wigwams of arching branches and rough-cut bark, tents whose sun-bleached canvas blazed white against the fluttering mat of prairie grass.

And moving between them were what seemed to Celene every kind of man God had seen fit to create. The voyageurs, like her father had been, were the easiest to recognize, dressed in their colorful knitted caps and long, flapping sashes. Thick-chested and broad-shouldered from months and years of paddling canoes through the convoluted waterways of North America, of carrying heavy packs over miles of portages, the voyageurs were a rowdy lot, given to endless singing, drinking, and storytelling.

The Indians were as diverse as the voyageurs were unified by their attire. There were Sioux, tall and regal with fans of feathers in their hair; strongly built Sack; and squat, wily Fox Indians come to trade the skins they had tanned during the long cold Northern winters. There were Chippewa, their topknots tinted red with a mixture of bear grease and powdered vermillion, dignified members of the Ottawa clans clutching blankets around their shoulders against the bite of morning chill. Her son, Jean-Paul, would have been fascinated by their presence, and she almost wished she had allowed him to accompany her to the gathering. But then, she thought, his turn would come. It would come in the years ahead when he would be less of a worry, more of a help.

Before their huge storage tents stood traders from New Orleans and Montreal, dressed in white shirts, colored vests, and woolen knee breeches. Both the bourgeois trading partners and their clerks had come to make their fortunes, to oversee the distribution of the goods spread in front of the tents in exchange for packs of beaver pelts.

Here and there among the Indians and the traders were *hivernants* and free trappers, white men who had wintered in the wilderness, trapping and bartering with the Indians until they had accumulated vast numbers of peltries to bring to trade. The *hivernants* worked and lived in groups under the auspices of a manager or bourgeois. But the free trappers were a breed apart, silent, solitary men who chose to live dependent on nothing more than their own initiative, choosing the freedom of the forest over the comforts and confines of civilization.

As Celene's gaze moved over the milling, thickening throng, it came to rest on one of these free traders as he stood deep in conversation with an Indian woman. Perhaps it was the man's extraordinary height that drew Celene's notice, or the brightness of his hair in contrast to the deep blue of his woolen capote. The twisted strands that tumbled from beneath his dusty, wide-brimmed hat and lay across the breadth of his back and shoulders were the warm, dark gold of buckwheat honey. As his conversation with the Indian woman continued, he turned, and Celene could see the straggle of his chest-length whiskers was only a shade or two darker than his hair.

Then all at once the tenor of whatever the trapper and the Indian woman were discussing changed. The woman's head came up. The trapper's heavy shoulders stiffened. From fifteen or twenty yards away, Celene could not make out their words, but it was clear their discussion was turning ugly. The man barked something and the woman responded, raising one hand toward the trapper's chest. But before she could complete the gesture, his hand slashed out to capture hers. The squaw's eyes widened as she tried to pull away, but the trapper held her fast.

His actions made Celene's stomach pitch, made bile burn a path up the back of her throat. She knew just how the bones in a woman's wrist would shift and grind together under the compression of a man's fingers. Even from where she was, Celene could sense the panic rising in the Indian woman's chest, sense that it would only be an instant before the trapper's ringing slap would fall.

Celene's perceptions blurred and her mind was filled with memories: the crush of another man's hand around her own thin wrist, an explosion of blinding pain, the taste of blood on her tongue. It was wrong for any man to mistreat a woman in such a way, wrong for this man to use his far-superior strength to subdue the struggling squaw. It was wrong for Celene to let it happen.

Goaded by the other woman's helplessness, Celene scrambled down the tree and raced toward where the trapper and the woman stood. She dodged around voyageurs and Indian braves, sprinted past several traders' tents. Splashing through puddles from the previous night's rain, she pushed through a throng of men that blocked her path and charged toward the place where the trader and the Indian woman were still locked together.

The trapper loomed before her, towering, massive, intimidating. Yet her outrage gave her courage. "Let her go!" she cried as she slammed her shoulder into the center of the trapper's back. The jolt of contact thundered through her. She knew a savage satisfaction.

The man gave a bellow of surprise and loosed his grip on the squaw. He struggled to wheel around, to defend himself. But the shove, with every ounce of Celene's strength and weight behind it, had knocked him off-balance. He teetered and went down, landing clumsily in a mud hole. He slid a foot or two from sheer momentum, splattering mud and water in every direction.

Celene fought to maintain her footing, to keep from following him down. When she had regained her balance, the Indian woman she had come to save had disappeared, leaving Celene alone to face the angry trapper. Fear of retaliation dawned through her, sending her pulse slamming in her throat, making her breath quiver and flutter in her chest. She had pushed this trapper down; she had humiliated him. As she looked into his smoldering eyes, she had never been more afraid—except for the eight long years when she had been forced to face her husband every day.

Sprawled hip-deep in mud and soaked to the skin, Burke Cardwell ground out curses in English, French, and several other languages. His assailant was small and slight, someone he'd never seen before. Burke couldn't think what he'd done to provoke this attack. But whoever this was and whatever his reasons, the fellow possessed a temerity that needed to be tempered. And Burke Cardwell was just the man, in just the mood to temper it.

Since late winter Cardwell's frustration had been gathering, thickening, festering in his chest and belly. He had been spoiling for a fight. Now he welcomed the prickling of venom in his veins. He liked the heat of it, the sting of it.

Cardwell became aware of the crowd gathering around them and used their laughter as a goad, letting the sound of their barbs push him closer to the edge. A faint red haze swam before his eyes as he focused on the fellow before him and prepared himself for a swift and satisfying victory. Though Burke would not have chosen such an obvious weakling as an adversary, he would not turn away now that the challenge had been issued. But before Burke could act, his attacker spun away.

With a bellow of rage, Cardwell surged to his feet bent on forcing the confrontation. But as the fellow turned, Burke had caught sight of the delicate angle of his assailant's jaw, the narrow shoulders, the gentle swell above and below the wide leather belt at the waist of the white capote. He stopped in his tracks as anger and confusion warred inside him. His fingers curled into fists with a force that made his muscles tremble.

Could his attacker be a woman—a white woman, dressed and behaving like a man? What the hell was a white woman doing here? Why in God's name had she attacked him?

Though some instinct warned that it would be wiser not to press his pursuit, Burke forced his way forward. Though at a casual glance she might pass as a fresh-faced youth, Burke had looked beyond the masculine clothes, noticing well-disguised curves and the beginnings of a streaky, white-blond braid tucked in to the back of her coat.

As he trailed her across the compound, his mind called up details of her appearance that he was not even aware he'd seen. Beneath the brim of her battered hat, there had been high color pinking the slope of her cheeks, and he had the fleeting impression that she was possessed of a strong chin and stubborn jaw. Though there had been determination narrowing the corners of her mouth, it had been soft and pleasantly bowed. If he put the features together, she seemed like someone to whom a man might well be attracted in other—more cordial—circumstances. Then, too, there was something about the sway of her hips and the bounce of her rounded derriere beneath the flowing skirt of her belted coat, that sent warmth stirring through Cardwell's blood.

Perfect. The thought skittered unbidden through Burke Cardwell's brain. Absolutely perfect.

A dozen yards ahead of him, the woman rounded the corner of one of the New Orleans trader's tents and snaked through the milling trappers and clumps of Indians toward the west side of the island. By the way she glanced over her shoulder, she knew that he was following her, and he wondered where it was she thought she would be safe from him.

Then, toward the northwestern perimeter of the camp, he saw a good-sized, wedge-shaped tent set up beneath a tree. A table made from wide pine boards stood before the open tent flaps, and on it were displayed the usual manner of trade goods. What made this trader different from all the rest was that in addition to the fire steels and the hatchets, the awls and flour and rum, a number of smoked hams were hanging in individual nets from the branches of the maple overhead.

By the time Burke reached the campsite, the girl had taken refuge at the trader's back. From the way she hovered there, it was clear she was counting on the older man to protect her. Instead he brushed her aside, intent on the two Indians fingering the objects on the counter. His actions left no doubt that his inventory took precedence over the welfare of his female companion.

Cardwell hesitated, wondering again what this white woman was doing at the rendezvous, and why she had come to this particular campsite for protection. The proprietor, for all his concern for his merchandise, looked more like a voyageur than a manager or bourgeois. He was broad through the shoulders and arms, though hardly taller than the woman at his elbow. A tuft of faded, light-brown hair was visible beneath the blue and white of his tasseled cap, and the face beneath it was dark and lined.

Finally, in response to the woman's prodding, the older man raised his head and looked in Cardwell's direction. As he did, a shimmer of recognition ran through Burke. The Frenchman looked years older than he had at last spring's rendezvous. Cardwell wondered at the change in him.

"Cardwell, *mon ami*," the man called out as their gazes met. "I didn't expect to see you here this year."

Ignoring the Frenchman's greeting, Burke closed the distance between them, staring instead into the blazing silver and green of his assailant's widening eyes. The sequence of emotions washing across the woman's face were telling ones. There was a flicker of shock, then one of fear that was quickly replaced by an expression of hopeless resignation.

"What is this woman to you, Peugeot?" Cardwell demanded when he reached the front of the makeshift table. "Why did you bring her here?"

Peugeot spared hardly more than a glance for the female at his side. "This is Celene, my daughter. What is it you want of her?"

A frisson of excitement rippled down Burke's spine as another part of his plan for revenge fell smoothly into place. Being Peugeot's daughter made her perfect for his needs. She would do what he said for the promise of gain and wouldn't balk at a bit of deception. He couldn't have planned this any better.

Burke drew a long, slow breath before replying. "I want to ask you for her hand, Peugeot. I want your daughter as my bride."

2

Bride? Celene sucked in her breath in a ragged gasp. The trapper wanted her for his bride!

Thoughts skittered around in her brain like mice scampering away from a swatting broom. Panic burned like live coals in the center of her chest. She would never be a bride again, never submit to another man. After eight long years, she knew what marriage was. It was total domination, it was cruelty without end. It was something she refused to endure a second time, and nothing in heaven or hell could change her mind.

The trapper must be mad to ask for the hand of a woman he had never seen until today, mad to want to marry a woman who had accosted him the very first time she'd clapped eyes on him. Certainly her father would not consign her to life with such a man, even if he had greeted this Cardwell like a long-lost friend.

Antoine Peugeot seemed nearly as stunned by the request as his daughter was. "Cardwell, *mon ami*," he repeated, gesturing impotently. "You are jesting. *Oui*?"

Cardwell shook his head. "No, Antoine, I meant what I said. Celene? Is that your daughter's name? Indeed, I want to marry her."

In spite of the man's determination, it was unthinkable that her father might accede to the trapper's demand. Celene tried to reassure herself, but the knowledge that Antoine had given her to Henri Bernard when she was barely fifteen destroyed any faith she might once have had in her father's judgment.

Panic thickened in Celene's throat as she stared at the trapper looming on the far side of the makeshift table. He was huge, broad-shouldered, solid, and incredibly tall. He was smelly, homely, and unkempt. She would not have Cardwell as her husband if he were the very last man on earth!

Determined to make her feelings about the trapper's proposal abundantly clear, Celene leaned closer to her father. "*S'il vous plaît*, Papa," she whispered. "Surely you wouldn't marry me a second time to someone I don't even know."

Catching his daughter by the wrist, Peugeot drew her around beside him, clearly intending to remedy that impediment. "Celene," he began, "this is Burke Cardwell, one of the finest trappers in all the Northwest."

Celene simply stared.

"Pleased to make your acquaintance, Mademoiselle Peugeot," Cardwell responded, touching the broad brim of his hat.

Celene drew herself up to her full height, which put her almost on a level with the center of Cardwell's chest. "I am *Madame* Bernard, to you," she spat. "My husband died of blood poisoning two months ago."

"Then please accept my condolences."

Cardwell's sentiments were precisely polite, yet they rankled Celene. Who was he to offer expressions of sympathy? And how was she to accept condolences when she was glad Henri was dead?

Before she could think how to respond, Cardwell stepped around the table, reached long, dirty fingers to grip her chin, and raised her face to his. His hand was hot against her skin, rough from the crust of drying mud. Celene shuddered at his touch.

As the trapper studied her with fierce and silent intensity, she glared back, furious that he seemed to be judging her as he might a mare for sale at a country fair. Months before she would have been cowed by his scrutiny, but now Celene returned his frank perusal. Her gaze passed over his ragged chin-whiskers to the full, pink curve of his lower lip, barely visible beneath the drape of his heavy mustache.

Her regard rose in a long, straight line from the tip of his nose toward the narrow bridge. His eyebrows were thick and fair, angling down over the outer corners of deep-set eyes. His lashes were every bit as bushy as his brows, long and a few shades darker.

It was the color of those eyes beneath the fringe of heavy lashes that took her by surprise. They were as turquoise as a summer sky, as clear and bright as a mountain pool shimmering in the sun. Against a sweep of sun-darkened cheek and forehead those pale eyes were unexpected, arresting, mesmerizing. They sent chills streaking down her spine.

The trapper's approval of her appearance registered in his face, and his fingers dropped away as he turned back toward her father. "Can I marry your daughter, then, Peugeot, now that I know her name?"

The air in Celene's lungs caught somewhere behind her ribs, wedged in a space too small for it. She had seen how Cardwell treated women, and it terrified her.

"*Merde!*" she spat at him, pride momentarily subduing her panic. "The devil take you, Cardwell. Go to hell!"

The trapper did not seem offended by her words. What might have been a smile seemed to lift one corner of his mustache. "I do admire eloquent cussing in a woman. You teach her that yourself, Antoine?"

Celene spun away as her father answered, shaking his head. "*Ah, non.* You would think that a proper wife and mother would have no need of language such as that."

"Mother?" Cardwell echoed. For the first time since he'd approached them, the trapper seemed taken aback.

It had not occurred to Celene that her motherhood might prevent the trapper from pressing his suit. Jumping into the breach, she turned to where the stranger stood. "Yes, I have a son, monsieur," she declared. "A five-year-old named Jean-Paul."

"A son," Cardwell muttered. His mouth disappeared from sight into the bush of scraggly beard as he considered this new bit of information. "A son. Well, a son would be all right, I guess."

"He's a most unruly child," Celene put in, hoping to scare Cardwell away and slandering her son in the process.

The trapper shrugged. "I like to see a bit of spirit in a lad."

Celene cursed under her breath this time. The trapper was as persistent as a swarm of gnats.

Since once again her father had not stepped in to protect her as she hoped he would and Cardwell seemed incapable of comprehending her refusal, it was up to Celene to make her position perfectly clear. "I don't want you as a father to my son, monsieur," she told the trapper. "I won't have you as a husband to me."

"But, *chérie* . . ." her father interrupted.

Celene's stomach rolled once and sank toward the soles of her moccasins. It always boded ill when her father called her *chérie*.

"Don't be too hasty in refusing Monsieur Cardwell's suit. He could provide for you and Jean-Paul as Henri could not. He would provide for you as you could never provide for yourself." Antoine's voice dipped conspiratorially. "Monsieur Cardwell is a very wealthy man."

Celene recoiled from the implied acceptance of Cardwell's offer. Eight years ago Antoine had forced her into a union with Henri Bernard, and in doing so condemned her to a life of subservience and cruelty. He had damned her to an existence where she was only half alive, where her son had reason to hate and fear his father.

Fury flickered through Celene's veins like a fuse burning toward detonation. She would not let Antoine decide her fate again. She would not be given to another man, especially one who would think nothing of abusing her. She was no longer a frightened fifteen-year-old. She was a widow, and widows had rights that wives and daughters never had. As a widow she could control her life, make her own way in the world, and she refused to give that freedom up.

"*Non! Non!*" she shouted at her father. "I don't care if Monsieur Cardwell has ten thousand livres a year, if he owns fine estates in England, France, and Spain. I don't care if he's a duke, a marquis, or an earl. I won't have him as my husband! He smells like a goat! He looks like a buffalo with mange!"

And I'm afraid of him.

Drawn by the sound of angry voices and the promise of excitement, people had begun to gather so that when Celene ended her declaration, there was a spattering of applause. Her cheeks went hot when she realized that someone besides the three of them had been privy to this humiliating discussion of her future. With a stifled cry she spun away and elbowed through the band of spectators.

Antoine and Cardwell watched her go.

"Looks like I've some courting to do," Burke observed. "It's been years since I've sought the favors of a lady. I just hope I remember how it's done."

Celene Bernard was right. He did smell like a goat. But then, wilderness living didn't exactly lend itself to maintaining a gentleman's toilette. Burke snorted in derision, remembering how at a different juncture in his life, he might well have expended a dozen linen neckcloths before he got the knot just so, that the cut of his coat had been of paramount importance, that it was imperative his boots be polished with French champagne. After living in the wilds these last eleven years, it seemed impossible to reconcile the dandy he had been with the ruffian he'd become. Nor had there been a reason in these past months to care about his appearance, at least not until he'd decided to court Celene Bernard.

A grin poked its way through Burke's shaggy growth of beard as he thought about the woman he was going to make his bride. Celene Peugeot Bernard was shabby, rough-hewn, prickly as a disgruntled porcupine. And exactly the kind of woman he wanted to take with him to England.

It was a pity he'd have to marry Celene to get her to play her role, but he knew Antoine well enough to be certain he'd never sell his daughter for anything less than a wedding ring. Marriage didn't hold much appeal for him anymore, Burke thought with a twist of regret, but it would be worth the inconvenience of taking a wife to see that everything went smoothly when they reached his family home.

Still, Burke reflected as he made his way toward the

Chippewa enclave at the end of the island, under her rough manners and masculine clothes Celene was a moderately good-looking woman. He'd taken his time studying her at Peugeot's camp and was far from displeased with what he saw. She had an open face, clear-featured and broad with a high brow and small straight nose. Her lips were full, dogwood pink, and they framed teeth that seemed in extremely good condition. Her hair was the only real beauty she possessed. It was blond, almost icy white where it had been frosted by the sun, with other shades blended into the heavy waving mass, everything from guinea gold to a honeyed tan. Celene was short like her father, and her lack of stature gave her figure a certain lush voluptuousness that any man would find appealing. But it was really only the green and silver glimmer of her eyes that marked her as her father's child. The color was most unusual; Cardwell could never remember seeing it on any but Antoine's offspring.

As Burke traversed the trampled grass encircled by the ring of dome-shaped wigwams, his Indian brother rose from where he had been sitting before his lodge and came across the circle to greet him. Lone Wolf moved with the easy grace of a seasoned woodsman, his long-legged stride closing the distance between them far faster than Burke would have liked. It was difficult to accept the warm welcome in the other man's face when the only emotion Burke could muster in answer was an unsettled, hovering dread.

"Greetings, Eyes Like the Sky. I am sorry I was away fishing when you arrived. Have you found a campsite of your own, or will you stay with Silver Dove and me?" Lone Wolf asked.

Cardwell shrugged. He had been deliberately avoiding this particular band of Chippewa for months, and Lone Wolf must surely be aware of it.

"With the pack animals to tend," he hedged, trying to make the excuse sound plausible, "it's easier if I keep a place alone."

The Indian nodded and frowned as if he understood Burke's reticence, even if he didn't approve of it.

"You will have a pipe and a drink before you leave us,

won't you?'' the Indian offered.

Knowing he owed Lone Wolf and Silver Dove at least that courtesy for keeping an eye on his mules and furs while he was scouting a camp, Burke nodded and followed the other man back to his wigwam. Like all the others in the temporary encampment, it was made of woven cattail mats with a roof of shaggy elm bark.

''Dove,'' Lone Wolf called out as they settled themselves to the left of the doorway, ''will you bring my pouch and pipe?''

A tall, handsome Indian woman emerged from the hut with the requested items in hand and smiled with genuine warmth at her husband's adopted brother.

''I had no chance to ask before. Are you well, Eyes Like the Sky?'' she asked. ''Have you been taking care of yourself?''

''Well enough,'' he assured her.

Cardwell could feel her gaze brush over his unkempt clothes and hair, saw her eyebrows rise in patent disbelief.

''I'll get you something cool to drink,'' she finally offered and ducked into the lodge before Burke could change his mind about accepting their hospitality.

Sitting in the baking sun, Lone Wolf prepared his wood and red-stone pipe with all the solemnity accorded this age-old ceremony. He feathered the twist of tobacco between his fingertips, packed the pungent weed into the bowl, lifted the pipe to the east, the west, the north, and the south, pointed it once toward heaven and once toward the earth. He lit a splint in the fire, touched it to the tobacco in the bowl, and puffed until it glowed bright orange.

As Burke watched, a kind of fatalism stole over him. Within moments these two well-meaning people would express their caring and concern and, in doing so, reopen excruciating wounds, only partially healed. For months he had managed to prevent a meeting with Lone Wolf and Silver Dove, managed to avoid their sympathy and solicitude, managed to distance himself from their lives.

But the moment Cardwell had dreaded was at hand. He must acknowledge his friends, accept their condolences, counterfeit emotions that were the antithesis of what he truly felt. His muscles tightened as he tried to prepare himself for what was to come, fighting to bring his emotions under even more stringent control. In spite of his efforts, he could feel the desperation rise in him, the aching loss, the mindless anger. He wished he was anywhere on earth but here.

Silver Dove emerged from the wigwam with two burl cups of maple sugar water and handed them to each of the men. Burke sipped from his and set it aside, letting the mellow, almost nutty flavor seep across his tongue. Dove disappeared inside again just as Lone Wolf handed the pipe across to Burke. He drew the pungent smoke into his mouth, exhaled slowly, accepting his part in the ancient ceremony of friendship and respect. They had repeated the ritual in silence three more times when Burke heard Dove push aside the blanket in the doorway. A shiver of premonition swelled from his scalp to his toes. He did not need to turn to know what she was carrying.

She moved around to his left and Burke could feel both Silver Dove and Lone Wolf watching him. He forced himself to meet their eyes.

Without a word, Dove lifted the object in her arms so he could see the sleeping child strapped in the ornate cradleboard. "This is our daughter, Morning Song," Dove said softly.

The name they'd chosen for the child ripped a raw, ragged hole in Cardwell's chest. His skin went cold as he fought for breath. The reality of seeing Lone Wolf's child for the very first time was far worse than his imaginings.

It took all his courage to look into the baby's face. For what seemed like an eternity he simply stared at the fans of feathery lashes beneath impossibly delicate brows, the faint red blush to her rounded cheeks, the rosebud shape of her dusky pink mouth. She was a wonderful child, perfect in every way, incredibly precious, and so very, very beautiful.

Cardwell swallowed hard. He knew exactly what was expected of him. He sucked air into his lungs around the knot that was lodged at the base of his throat. "May she grow to be as lovely and accomplished as her namesake," he finally managed to say.

At length, when Cardwell said no more, Lone Wolf waved his wife and child away and offered the pipe in Burke's direction. The Indian tobacco, laced with kinnikin-nick, suddenly seemed especially harsh, and the swirl of smoke rising from the bowl made Cardwell swipe angrily at his eyes.

As Burke passed the pipe again, Lone Wolf spoke. "Was your trapping successful this year?"

Lone Wolf's question was a merciful diversion from Burke's dark thoughts. Gratitude welled up in him. "It was fair," he answered. "Fair."

In truth it had been an extremely good year for trapping. He had eleven ninety-pound packs of peltries secured to his three mules' backs, and he knew that there were some groups of ten or twelve *hivernants* that would not have done that well. But Burke had applied himself to his task with relentless energy as the winter progressed. That alone had kept him sane.

"And how was yours?" Cardwell felt compelled to ask.

Lone Wolf nodded, indicating his satisfaction with this year's hunting. "The cold weather made the pelts especially thick."

Burke looked across toward the man who had grown as close as full-blooded kin and was painfully aware of the constraint that was suddenly between them. He saw the compassion in the Indian's eyes, the strain of frustration around his mouth. He stared at his companion's smooth chest, bare between the beaded panels of his vest, saw the dark brow stain of the bird-on-the-wing birthmark that marked the skin of Lone Wolf's inner arm. Cardwell stared long and hard at the shape and realized that whatever mystical bond had existed between them once had somehow dissipated. The magic that had brought and bound them together was gone, and neither of them could help what was happening.

Frowning at that thought, Burke gathered himself to rise.

"You're leaving?" Lone Wolf looked up from where he sat. "Without finishing your drink?"

"I have a camp to make," Cardwell told him. "With the animals it is so much easier if I set up near the water. If I wait too long, all the best campsites will be gone.''

Lone Wolf rose to stand beside him. ''You know you're always welcome here, my brother.''

Cardwell nodded and looked away. ''But I'm not content here anymore.''

Without waiting for further comment, Burke headed toward the corral where his horse and three mules were grazing with the Chippewa band's several dozen ponies.

Gathering the animals' leads in his hand, Burke turned back toward where Lone Wolf and Silver Dove stood together before their lodge. It was a pleasant scene, heartbreakingly familiar, imbued with abiding peace. It reminded him of happier days. But Burke didn't belong here at the Chippewa encampment anymore. If truth be told, he wasn't sure he belonged anywhere at all.

It was midafternoon when Antoine Peugeot finally made his way to Cardwell's campsite, and he was pleased to see the trapper already had his fire made, his animals tethered on the riverbank, and that he was nearly finished securing the packs of pelts at the very back of his deerskin lean-to. He and Cardwell had important things to discuss, after all, and though they focused primarily on Celene's betrothal, that did not prevent Antoine from quickly tallying the worth of the pelts in Cardwell's packs.

''It looks as if you've had a very good year, *mon ami*,'' Peugeot observed.

''The pelts are prime, too,'' Burke assured him. ''The severity of the winter will make rich men of us all.''

''Monsieur LaVallier will be most pleased.''

''And how well will LaVallier reward me for my diligence?''

Peugeot knew exactly how well Cardwell had been rewarded in the past and was secure in the knowledge that once again Monsieur LaVallier was going to be most generous. After dealing with Cardwell for the last nine years, Antoine also knew that Burke had a tidy fortune tucked away in LaVallier's care. It was one of the things that had made Burke's offer for Celene so fortuitous. When Henri died, what little money he'd saved had gone to pay his debts, leaving Celene all but penniless. Her desperate need for funds was the only reason Antoine had allowed her to accompany him to the rendezvous. It was a father's duty to see to the welfare of his only living child, and now Cardwell seemed willing to make that task an easy one.

"I suspect Monsieur LaVallier will offer you what the pelts are worth," Peugeot hedged. His years of experience prevented him from giving a trapper the upper hand in the coming negotiations—even if that trapper was about to become his son-in-law.

"Perhaps Monsieur LaVallier will give you a bonus on the furs when he hears that you've offered for my daughter's hand," Antoine added hopefully. "Celene's a good girl, and LaVallier has always been fond of her. He'll want to see her well provided for."

Burke joined Peugeot by the fire. There were Shawnee cakes baking on flat stones set among the coals, their tantalizing smell drifting upward with the ribbons of rising smoke. Cardwell bent forward to test one of the corn cakes with the tip of his knife. "I think a man could do far worse than to take your daughter for a wife," he said, his words officially opening negotiations between them.

"Do you?" Antoine asked, trying to get a look at the younger man's face. "Do you really?"

Burke continued to stare into the flames. "Indeed I do."

Peugeot had taken time to learn the particulars of Cardwell's meeting with his daughter, and couldn't for the life of him discern the other man's reasons for offering for her hand. "And just what is it about Celene that makes you think she'll make a good wife?"

Cardwell flipped the corn cakes to the opposite side.

"She's not a beauty," Peugeot ventured, curious when the trapper did not immediately respond.

"She's comely enough."

"Her husband did not leave her very well-off."

"I don't care about the money."

"At the moment Celene has no use for men," her father warned.

"Men are always useful to a clever woman," Cardwell said with quiet finality.

"Celene's clever; I'll give her that," Antoine murmured, not sure if the admission was a mistake or not. "She learned to read and cipher so she could help her husband with his business records."

"And did he appreciate her efforts?"

Peugeot thought back to how Henri Bernard had greeted the news that his wife had mastered something he could not. Antoine understood his son-in-law's reaction; any man would. But it was one of the hardest things he had ever done to turn his daughter away when she had come to his door, clutching her baby to her breast, her left eye blackened and her lower lip swollen to twice its normal size. She had begged him to give her and Jean-Paul shelter, but Antoine had known his duty. He had done exactly what a father should; he had sent her home to her husband. She had turned from him after that, coming to the house in Ste. Genevieve only when he was away. It was the last time Celene had come to him for anything, at least while Henri was alive.

"In the end Henri came to appreciate her skills," the Frenchman finally answered. "And she's teaching her son to read and write as well."

"That's most commendable." Cardwell bent forward again and neatly scooped up one of the corn cakes on the blade of his knife, offering it to his guest.

Antoine's stomach roiled. He'd had no use for food in these last days. "No, thank you," he muttered around the bile in his throat.

Burke made short work of the Shawnee cake and scooped up another.

Antoine looked away. "Let us speak frankly," he began. "You want to marry my Celene. Before I give my blessing, there are several things we must discuss."

The trapper finished chewing and set his knife aside. "Oh?"

"There is the matter of her bride price."

"Her bride price?" Cardwell couldn't quite hide his surprise. "Indians ask for a bride price; Frenchmen and Englishmen offer a dowry."

"Celene has no dowry, and I am in no position to give her one."

"Celene's a widow, after all. Is she even yours to sell?" It was clear Cardwell wanted his money's worth, and it was up to Antoine to make him see the wisdom of investing in his daughter.

"You want Celene's hand, and she doesn't want to marry you. It will be a difficult thing for me to convince her to accept your suit."

"And you want me to pay you for your trouble."

Peugeot inclined his head.

"It doesn't matter to you what my plans are for her? You don't care what happens to her and her son as long as she's no longer your responsibility?"

"I've not been a good father to her, nor a good *grand-père* to Jean-Paul," Antoine admitted in a heavy tone, "and I'm not likely to get any better at it so late in life. Once before I made the mistake of giving her to a man I did not know, a man who paid nothing for her and therefore did not value her. I know you, Cardwell. I know you treat your women well. And I also know that if you pay good money for her hand, you will see that she is properly taken care of. That's all I really want for her."

He could see the spark of anger in Cardwell's eyes, the outrage in his face. But there was dawning comprehension in it, too. If a man paid dearly for a prize, he treasured it above less costly things. When Antoine saw that the trapper understood that, he knew he'd won.

"How much do you want for her?" the younger man asked.

"I want two packs of beaver pelts."

"One."

"Celene cooks very well."

"One."

"She's healthy and strong as an ox."

"One."

"When handled properly she can be very accommodating."

"One."

Antoine sighed. Cardwell had gained the upper hand in

the bargaining the moment he'd agreed to pay a bride price, and both of them knew it.

"One," Peugeot agreed.

Burke rose immediately and went into the lean-to, returning with one of the packs on his shoulder. He dropped it to the ground beside the Frenchman. "I don't want Celene to know about this transaction. I will tell her in my own words, approach her in my own way."

"I will do exactly as you ask, *mon ami*. There is only one last thing that bothers me."

"And what is that?"

"I know you already have a wife *a la façon du pays*."

"It's a common enough practice for trappers, voyageurs, and *hivernants*."

What Cardwell said was true. Many men formed relationships with Indian women while they were in the wilderness. They were casual for the most part, as was the Indian fashion, and they often dissolved when the trapper moved on. But from having seen Cardwell with his country wife in years past, Antoine thought their bond a lasting one.

"What do you intend to do about your Indian wife when you marry Celene?"

Under Antoine's wily regard, Cardwell's expression seemed to solidify. "I wouldn't be the first trapper to have one wife in the country and another in town. Surely you yourself realize the advantages to that arrangement."

Antoine felt his face get hot. "*Oui*. I know a good deal of the practice, as you say."

"And your town wife seems to have tolerated the situation fairly well."

Antoine sighed. "Celene is not the same woman her mother was. Freja was captured by the Indians when she was a child and understood the reasons why a man might take a country wife."

"And Celene would not?"

Antoine sighed again, not wanting to say or do anything to change Cardwell's mind about marrying Celene. Yet for once in his life, he felt compelled to tell the truth. "I think if Celene knew you had another wife, she would be very angry. I know you can support my daughter, and I believe that once she accepts you as her husband she will do her best to make you happy. I do not have any doubts about the success of a marriage between you, except this one.''

Burke Cardwell nodded in understanding. For a long moment he sat utterly still, staring blankly ahead. ''Then rest assured there is no reason for concern,'' Cardwell finally offered. ''I no longer have a country wife. Morning Song died this winter.''

3

Celene sold five hams that day, each for at least three times the price they would have brought at home in Ste. Genevieve. The money would go a long way in providing for Jean-Paul and her, since the seventeen hams were Henri's only legacy. Perhaps it had been wise for her to come to the rendezvous with her father, after all—in spite of the long, difficult trip up the Mississippi; in spite of her reticence to leave her son; in spite of the dangers in the makeshift camp that even dressing as a boy could not completely alleviate; in spite of the strange, unsettling encounter with the trapper Cardwell.

Blinking the wood smoke out of her eyes, Celene added the last few ingredients to the pot of rabbit stew that was bubbling over the fire. As she worked, she kept watch over the trade goods spread on the table and blankets in front of the tent. It was common practice to have a few small items set out for the Indians to steal; it made for good relations when the trading began in earnest. But there was a limit to what could be taken in the friendly pilfering, and it was necessary to keep an eye on all the rest. That was much less difficult now than it had been at the shank of the day when the aisles between the tents had been crowded with Indians and trappers alike. Now that it was getting on toward suppertime, most of her customers had returned to their campsites.

As she looked up and down the makeshift street, Celene wondered where her father was. He had made it his custom to wander off in the late afternoon, leaving Celene to pack away the trade goods, eat a solitary meal, and crawl into her nest of skins and blankets with only her thoughts of home and Jean-Paul to comfort her.

Today Antoine's behavior ran true to form. It was his nature to cast aside responsibility wherever he could, and she knew it was a waste of time and energy to rail at her father for his many failings. You either loved Antoine for his vivacity and innate charm, or you hated him for his callousness and irresponsibility. Celene had made her choice years before.

With a sigh Celene bent to stir her pot of stew. When she glanced up a moment later, Burke Cardwell had materialized on the far side of the fire. She was surprised to find that such a hulking man could move so quickly and so quietly.

"Good day, Celene," Cardwell greeted her, doffing his wide-brimmed hat. "That stew you've concocted looks mighty good."

She stared at him across the fire, taking note of the marked difference in his appearance. He had bathed and changed his clothes since she'd last seen him, replacing the stiff, stained buckskins with dark woolen trousers and a blue calico shirt. There were wide woven garters of blue and green holding up the tops of his knee-high moccasins and narrower ones tied around his upper arms. The clothes were a distinct improvement—the clothes and the fact that he no longer smelled like weeks of accumulated sweat and beaver dope.

"My father isn't here," she told him inhospitably, an edge to her voice.

"It isn't your father I came to see."

Noting the smile that tugged at the corners of his mustache and the admiring gleam in his eyes, Celene backed away. "Now see here, Monsieur Cardwell, there's no reason to seek me out. I have no intention of marrying you."

Burke nodded as if unperturbed. "Well, whether you marry me or not, there's not a woman alive who doesn't welcome a bit of courting now and then." With a flourish totally incongruous with this afternoon's boorish behavior and his rugged looks, Cardwell produced a bouquet of wildflowers from where he'd had them hidden behind his back.

She stared at the flowers in his hand, bright bluets and common violets, yellow wood sorrel and lacy chickweed. The blossoms, delicate and bright, were dwarfed by the size of the man. Celene felt overpowered by him, too.

She stepped back a pace, refusing to take the bouquet. "Then you're a fool, Monsieur Cardwell," she finally said. "For if every woman alive welcomes 'a bit of courting now and then,' you're wasting your efforts on a dead one. I don't want to be courted by any man—and especially not by you!"

There was a moment of hesitation before a grin fought its way through Burke's luxuriant growth of whiskers. "Well, one thing's very sure, that stew smells far too good to waste on a corpse. Dead folks just don't properly appreciate tasty victuals and delicate seasonings. On the other hand, I certainly do. Do you mind if I join you for supper, since your father's not about?"

"*Mon Dieu!*" Celene huffed in refusal and disbelief.

"I'd be glad to pay you the price of the meal," Cardwell cajoled.

Her eyes narrowed as she glanced from the man to the pot and the pot to the man. She needed every sou if she and Jean-Paul were going to have any kind of a life together. "How much is supper worth to you?"

"How much are you asking for it?" Cardwell countered.

"I think one plus is fair."

"One plus! One beaver pelt for a dish of stew?"

Celene was suddenly reluctant to give him dinner even at so exorbitant a price. "I suppose you could have a new iron hatchet for that, six fire steels, or a twist of fine tobacco—"

Cardwell was undeterred by the price she'd asked but seemed determined to cut a bargain of his own. "I'll expect a second helping, if you please, and perhaps some biscuits or a cup of cider. And I expect I'll be paying for your company, too."

"You'll be paying for my company *at dinner*," Celene quickly clarified, though she could feel her cheeks get hot. She'd heard about women in New Orleans who sold a good deal more than their company at dinner, and she didn't intend to let Cardwell get any wild ideas.

His brows lifted and his eyes went all quizzical and warm. "Your company *at dinner*," he repeated. "If that's the way of it, how soon will we be eating?"

Celene turned her back, determined not to respond to the humor in his face. "I have our goods to put away and biscuits to make."

"Then let me help you."

With Burke Cardwell's assistance it took far less time than Celene had thought possible to haul the boxes of trade goods and the remaining hams into the tent. At the back of the enclosure the packs of peltries were already piling up. Perhaps, if things went well, by the end of the rendezvous, she and her father would be sleeping outside.

As she prepared the mixture for the simple biscuits and patted them into a pan, Burke packed and lit his pipe, then settled against one of the willow backrests. Through the waves of rising heat Celene watched him surreptitiously. He didn't look brutish, wildly impulsive, or mad as he sat there blowing smoke rings. Yet this morning, moments after she had pushed him into the mud and humiliated him, he had asked her father for her hand. What had possessed him to do something so utterly irrational? Why did he want her for his bride?

It didn't make sense. And it particularly didn't make sense for Celene to be more than civil to him. She fervently wished she had not agreed to feed him supper. If it hadn't been for the pelt he'd promised her . . .

Across the fire Cardwell gathered up the cluster of wild-flowers from where he had set them as he helped her stow her father's goods. "Is there something I can put these in?"

She glanced at the bouquet again. It was a ridiculous gift, the kind of gift a man brought when he was courting a girl. The very implication made her cheeks get hot. She should throw the flowers in the fire, cram them down his throat. Then she thought about the beaver pelt and took a calming breath. "There are some tin mugs sitting on a box inside."

Moving with a loose-limbed grace that seemed unusual in a man so tall, Cardwell ducked into the tent and returned to fill one of the mugs with water from the water keg. "Where do you intend to eat?"

Celene looked up from the stewpot, spoon in hand. "Under the tent flap, I suppose."

Setting the mug aside, Burke moved a small crate to the middle of the overhang, placed the flowers in the center, and went back inside the tent for a pair of mugs, some spoons, and two tin plates. There was something about watching Cardwell perform the simple domestic duties that sparked an unexpected resentment in Celene's chest. He did the chores so naturally, so unexpectedly. Yet his willingness to help did not change the kind of man he was; she had seen how he treated the Indian woman. His kindnesses meant nothing. Henri could be helpful or charming when it served his purposes. It had made him no better a man, and certainly no better a husband.

Celene finished the preparations for the meal in silence and ladled spicy stew onto both their plates. The biscuits, when she removed the covered skillet from the fire, were fluffy, soft, and golden brown. She poured cider for them both, then settled herself on a keg opposite Cardwell at the makeshift table.

"Do you and your son live in Ste. Genevieve, with your father?" the trapper asked after he had complimented Celene extravagantly on the evening's fare.

"Jean-Paul and I have just moved back from Kaskaskia to my father's house. Since I know far more about farming than I do about trade, it seemed a sensible choice. And our land in Ste. Genevieve has been lying fallow these last two years."

Burke looked up from the bite of biscuit he was about to take. "That doesn't surprise me. I can't quite imagine Antoine tilling the soil."

"No," Celene agreed. "My father will never be anything but what he is. Our arpents have not been properly tended since my mother died. I did the best I could with them before I married and moved across the river. While I was gone my father sometimes leased them out. But I have the land under cultivation now. We finished putting in a fine new crop just before I came here."

"And you hope for a bountiful harvest in the fall."

"If God smiles on us," she answered as she reached around to ladle another helping of stew onto Cardwell's plate. "In the meantime the profit from the sale of my hams will provide for us quite nicely, I think."

As he applied himself to the food, he introduced another subject. "Tell me about your son."

Celene looked up at him in surprise. "Why?"

"Because I want to know about him. Because when we marry he'll become my son, too."

"It is very generous of you to be so willing to accept Jean-Paul as your *beau-fils*," she answered with virulent sarcasm, "but since a marriage between us is impossible, it can hardly matter what you know of him."

Despite her declaration, Cardwell persisted. "Tell me about him anyway. Why isn't he here with you?"

Celene smiled in spite of herself. Leaving Jean-Paul had been the most difficult part of coming to the rendezvous, and it was pleasant, even in this company, to indulge her mother's pride. Perhaps talking about her son would ease the ache of loneliness for a little while.

"Jean-Paul just turned five, and I knew a rendezvous was hardly a place to bring a child as young as that. He is staying with my father's housekeeper, Pélagie. She's been with our family for years and years, since shortly after my mother died. She's the only person I'd trust with the care of my son."

She went silent for a moment, imagining the small, snug house at the river's edge. At this time of the day, Pélagie and Jean-Paul would be sitting down to supper, bowing their heads over the simple fare, offering up a prayer for her and Antoine's safe return. She and her mother and her brother had done that when Antoine was away, and she drew comfort from knowing Jean-Paul and Pélagie must be thinking of her now.

"Jean-Paul is a good boy," she went on and was appalled by the sudden quaver in her voice. "He minds me well and likes learning new things. I'm teaching him what I can about reading and writing. I hope to send him to school in Kaskaskia in a year or two. And after watching him in the fields this spring, I think he has a farmer's soul. He likes tending crops and is very good with animals. He's patient and kind, and they seem to trust him."

"What does he look like?" Burke asked, drawing her out.

"He's dark, tall for his age. It won't be long before he's taller that I am. He takes after my husband's family," she admitted with some reticence, "though he has my mother's smile and my father's eyes."

"He has his mother's eyes, you mean."

There was something in his voice that made Celene glance up at her dinner companion. Even across the table she could feel the pull of Cardwell's masculine magnetism.

"You have lovely eyes, Celene, and glorious hair. I long to see it hanging free and loose around your shoulders. I'd like to tangle my hands in it, feel its softness beneath my fingertips . . ."

Cardwell's sudden, deliberate charm rose like a separate presence between them, and Celene recoiled from it as she might a snake. She knew what masculine charm really was: empty flattery meant to salve hurt feelings, meaningless gestures in inadequate apology for a man's transgressions, a few glib words to smooth the way for favors to come.

Celene jumped up and snatched the half-empty plate from in front of Burke.

"Wait!" he protested. "I'm not—"

"Oh, yes! You're quite finished as far as I'm concerned."

Turning from him, she dumped the remainder of his dinner into the stewpot where the heat of tomorrow's fire could boil the taint of Burke Cardwell away. An instant later she heard the clap of his tin mug on the top of the crate, heard him come to his feet and move to stand behind her.

Depriving a man of his dinner was a grave offense, one a woman might well be punished for. Every muscle in Celene's body tensed. She could feel the heat of him against her back, could sense him looming barely a step away. She bit deep into her lower lip and waited. She had no idea what Cardwell might do. But curiously she was not afraid. Where once fear of a beating would have sung through her veins, there was now outrage, incipient anger. Her head came up. If he hit her, she would retaliate. For Celene, the willingness to stand up for herself against a man was a liberating experience.

But instead of the blow she had been expecting, Celene heard the trapper draw a long uneven breath. "You're going to need water to wash the dishes, aren't you?" he suddenly asked.

She heard him turn and snatch up the bucket standing beside the water keg, heard his footsteps swish through the grass. She looked over her shoulder just in time to see him disappearing between two tents in the general direction of the riverbank.

A tremor passed along her nerves. Whatever it was she had expected Burke Cardwell to do, he had not done. He had gone to fetch water for her instead. It was odd, she thought as she gathered up the rest of the dishes. His behavior was decidedly odd, and she didn't have the faintest notion what to make of it.

Even if he had nothing else to recommend him, Celene liked the smell of Burke Cardwell's pipe smoke. There was something mellow and fruity about it that tickled her nose, and though she wished he had gone anywhere else on the island to pack and light his pipe, his presence at her campsite was not altogether unpleasant.

After she had washed and put away the plates and cups, she turned to where Cardwell sat on one of the empty kegs. "*Pardonez moi*, Monsieur Cardwell. It is time for me to retire to my tent."

He looked up at her from the strands of fraying rope he had been splicing, then toward the streaks of golden sunlight still slanting through the trees. "But it's only just getting on toward dusk," he observed.

"My father warned me not to be abroad when darkness falls."

"Still, there's time for a turn around the island before you take yourself off to bed."

"Are you offering your protection as we stroll?"

Cardwell nodded. "If you like."

Being the only white woman within three hundred miles of the encampment had been a hardship for Celene. Before her father would even consider allowing her to accompany him, he had made her promise she would dress like a boy, do nothing to make herself conspicuous, and never, *ever* wander the camp alone once the evening meal was over. The *hivernants* and the Indians who had spent their afternoons consuming the profits from a year's worth of trapping in the form of watered whiskey would be drunk and unruly by sundown, and a menace to her welfare should they penetrate her disguise.

Yet as Celene had lain on her pallet these past few nights thinking of Jean-Paul and listening to the sounds around her, she had wished she could take a greater part in the rendezvous. Last night there had been shouting that had turned to cheers for the winner in one of the contests the trappers seemed to love. The previous evening the gay melody of a fiddler's reel had stolen through the camp, and later there had been the surprisingly pleasant blend of several drunken voices singing songs of sadness and lost love. The noises had not kept Celene awake; she had found them comforting, almost soothing. But they had also made her feel isolated and alone, curious about activities in which she could not participate. If she chose to accept it, Burke Cardwell's protection would allow her to be part of the festivities for at least a little while. It was a very tempting offer.

She was ready to accept, when a new thought struck her. "And how do I know I wouldn't be risking even more by walking out alone with you?"

"Well," Cardwell answered, hauling himself to his feet, "if I was of a mind to molest you, it would be a good deal easier if we stayed here."

Celene felt the heat come up in her cheeks. "I don't intend to give anyone the opportunity to molest me, Monsieur Cardwell. But I would welcome the chance to walk with you."

"Very well, Madame Bernard. I promise to behave myself."

Could she trust him to keep his promise? she wondered.

How good was his word? Still, curiosity about the camp and the evening's activities made her nod in curt acknowledgment.

Cardwell's eyes were twinkling as he stepped back to let her precede him into the narrow street. As she passed, the unexpected brush of his hand against her waist made her muscles jump and clench. She didn't know if the trapper had noticed her involuntary reaction, but Celene was instantly shamed by it. How long would it be before she could accept a simple touch without flinching away? How long would it take for the fears Henri had instilled to fade? The hand that rode at the small of her back seemed both casual and benign, and she began to like the protective arc of Cardwell's arm across her back.

As they moved through the uneven grid of streets toward the middle of the island, the waning sunlight raked across the campsite and caught in the drifting smoke that rose from scores of campfires. The sun's yellow-orange glow limned the planes and angles of the white canvas tents and cast long, dark shadows across the grass. It tinted the clouds that rode the crest of the hills and smudged the western rim of the sky with delicate pink and apricot.

As Celene and Burke approached the central area of the encampment where the traders from Michilimackinac and New Orleans had erected their standards and their tents, the crowd grew more dense. It was here where those in search of gaiety, liquor, or old friends gathered, here where the commerce of the rendezvous was carried on in its purest form. As Celene and Burke made their way through the crush, a wiry trapper pushed toward them.

"Goddamn, Burke Cardwell! Haven't seen you in a year and more," the man crowed, clapping Burke on the back. "Hear tell you been trapping up toward the Athabasca. Good beaver country from what they say. You going to race tonight?"

Burke hardly had time to shake his head before the man continued. "Damned Indian is beating all comers. Already won a full pack of Eisner's pelts. Taken skins from half a dozen others, too."

"That's too bad," Burke acknowledged and nudged Celene deeper into the crowd.

"Eisner's not near as fast as you. The way those long legs cover ground, I'd wager you could outrun any Indian alive."

"I'm not interested in running."

"Aw, Cardwell, don't be shy," the man persisted. "There's a score or more of us who would wager a full year's pelts on you."

Around them, others were becoming aware of Cardwell's presence so near the impromptu racecourse.

"You running, Cardwell?" someone shouted.

"Come on, Cardwell, show us your speed."

"We want to see this damn Indian beat."

Clamping a hand on Celene's shoulder, Burke steered her forward. But instead of the path he plotted taking them out of the crush, it took them deeper, until they came face to face with the man who had been defeating every trader or trapper willing to test his speed and endurance.

Cardwell stopped dead in his tracks when he saw the Indian, his expression freezing up faster than a beaver pond in a winter's gale.

"You," he muttered under his breath, then slashed a look at the woman at his side.

The brave's mouth curved in acknowledgment as the fires of challenge brightened the flecks of green in his hazel eyes.

Celene glanced from one man to the other, quickly taking her measure of the Indian who stood before them. He was almost as tall as Cardwell was, slender and long of muscle where the trapper was burly and broad. The brave's physique was as hard and brown as hand-hewn oak. The muscles of his naked torso and legs shone with a fine sheen of sweat, but it was the only evidence that he had run half a dozen races.

"Will you wager your furs against my speed?" the Indian challenged, pride and arrogance stamped indelibly on his face.

"I won't race against you, Darkening Sky."

The brave's nostrils flared, and he lifted his chin in a

gesture of contempt. ''Are you willing to admit that the white man has neither the speed nor endurance to win a race against an Indian?''

''I am not admitting anything. I'm just not willing to run.''

Cardwell tightened his hand on Celene's shoulder and urged her forward, but neither the men around them nor the Indian in their path would let them pass. The crowd had gone strangely silent, straining to hear what words passed between the trapper and the Indian. There was far more than the question of speed behind this confrontation, and Celene wondered what it was.

''You were willing to challenge me when I was hardly more than a boy,'' the Indian taunted. ''But you will not give me the satisfaction of beating you man to man.''

''What happened years ago has nothing at all to do with this.''

Darkening Sky's upper lip furled in a sneer. ''Except that you lack the courage to meet my challenge now.''

Word that the Indian had called Burke Cardwell a coward went through the crowd in a single breath. Anticipation of Cardwell's answer made the men strain even closer.

A flush came up in his face, making Celene aware of some subtle change in Burke. He had begun to radiate a primitive energy, as if the Indian's words had loosed something Cardwell had been fighting to keep in check.

''All right,'' he agreed in a voice as cold as a January dawn. ''Since you're so damn determined, I'll run against you.''

A cheer went up from the waiting throng, and the wagering began. Fortunes in furs were to be risked on a single footrace. That Burke himself refused to bet on the outcome sent another stir of speculation through the ranks of woodsmen. More wagers were made; more markers changed hands.

As Burke began to strip off his clothes, one of the bourgeois from Michilimackinac explained that the runners would circle the encampment twice, starting and finishing at the standard that held the Northwest Company's flag. It was the distance of nearly a league.

Burke flung his garters, shirt, and moccasins in Celene's direction. Unwilling to risk his wrath or the notoriety of refusing to see to his clothes, she gathered them to her chest and seeped into the edge of the crowd.

Cardwell seemed to forget her presence as he stretched his long limbs and drew deep breaths into his lungs. Though broad-shouldered and deep-chested, Burke was more slender than he appeared through his clothes. Celene found herself staring at the flex and slide of the muscles clearly delineated beneath the honey-gold warmth of his skin. They flowed in links across his shoulders and back, wrapped taut across his ribs and belly, undulated down his arms in pleasant masculine symmetry. His legs were long, his thighs tight, his calves bulging with muscles. As she studied him, Celene noticed the skin of Cardwell's left forearm was puckered in a scar. But it was the only flaw in his perfect physique.

A hollow seemed to form in Celene's chest as she looked at him, a hollow that made it difficult for her to get her breath. Clutching Cardwell's clothes even closer, she became aware of a faint piney fragrance that seemed to emanate from the cloth. The scent was spiced by the remnants of Cardwell's pipe smoke, the subtle musk of the man himself. As she watched the runners take their places, she was more aware of Burke Cardwell than she had ever been of any man: of the contours of his body, the scent of his skin, the strange suffocating sensation his nearness made her feel. And Burke, in his need to win the race against Darkening Sky, had forgotten she existed.

As the bourgeois raised his gun to start the race, the Indian's face was set with determination; Cardwell's body was coiled and utterly still. The setting sun seemed to touch the scene with copper and gold, the bright low rays catching in Cardwell's free-flowing hair, highlighting the men's bowed backs, glinting on the barrel of the starter's pistol.

As the single shot boomed into the silence, the two men exploded forward. The sound of a hundred voices roared through the encampment as Burke and Darkening Sky dashed toward the first turn. The Indian's movements were effortless and graceful, while Cardwell's seemed more labored and uneven. A sea of men closed behind them as the runners drove down the long, straight side of the oval-shaped course. From the cheers, Celene could tell when the racers made the turns on the far right and left. Though she knew it was useless, she pushed up on her toes to try to catch a glimpse of them.

The area near the starting line cleared as the two men came into sight around the near-left curve. The Indian was in the lead, his steps fluid and even. Cardwell trailed Darkening Sky by a few short yards, and he seemed to have settled into a rhythm of his own.

Shouts rose around her, a wall of impenetrable sound, and Celene momentarily glimpsed two pairs of long legs driving, bare feet pounding the earth, two torsos glinting with sweat. Then Burke and Darkening Sky were gone, lost again in the wake of trappers who flowed after them.

The second circuit of the camp seemed faster than the first. The hoots and shouts that went up as the two racers sped by marked their progress down the long left side. Celene peered toward the point where the men would come into view, her breath caught in her throat, her heart thumping wildly against her ribs. It surprised her how much she wanted Burke to win the race.

Hands waved in the crowd to herald the runners' approach, and a rippling roar began as they burst around the corner. Burke was hardly more than a step behind the other man as they sprinted toward the finish line. As she watched their thunderous approach, she could see Cardwell's stride lengthening as he pushed for greater speed. But the Indian was straining, too, leaning into the space ahead of him. Cardwell gained a half-step and a half-step more. They stretched toward the finish side by side, their feet falling in identical rhythm and time. But Cardwell's legs were longer, and they carried him past the standard a heartbeat ahead of the other man.

It was the kind of contest that would be talked about at rendezvous for years to come, over campfires in the wilds, over brandies in New Orleans and Montreal. It was of this that wilderness lore was made, of the Indian and the Englishman who flew like the wind in a race that made paupers of unlucky men and kings of those who had been wise enough to put their money on the winner.

Their momentum took the runners down the track, and the crowd surged into the street. Celene was whisked forward with the rest. It would have been futile to resist, and she had Cardwell's clothing to return to him. Between the bodies of other men she could see Burke grinning and delightedly accepting accolades. Somehow in the crush he saw her, too. He reached out, drawing her toward him through the mob.

She came, clutching his clothes against her chest. For an instant he stood before her, still breathing hard. His face was flushed with the exertion of his run, with a fierce exhilaration that lit dazzling lights in his turquoise eyes. His buckwheat-gold hair clung to his chest and shoulders as rivulets of sweat traced along the gleaming contours of his body. Celene's mouth went dry and the odd sensation of breathlessness assailed her again.

"I won," he said, an even broader grin hitching up the edges of his mustache.

Celene nodded, caught up in the glory of his success, his pride in his hard-won victory. Energy seemed to ripple off him, primitive, masculine, quivers of excitement that raised shudders of response in her. She could feel the vitality pounding in his veins, and her heartbeat quickened.

"You won," she repeated, her voice tinged with awe.

His grin grew wider still and his arm tightened around her shoulders, pulling her close. Even through her shirtsleeve, she could feel the damp heat of his skin. His muskiness surrounded her as he lowered his head to kiss her.

There was the scratchiness of his mustache and beard against her face, the pillowy softness of his lips against her mouth. The sweet-apple taste of him seeped into her before she could gather her wits to pull away. But when she finally began to push against his chest, he simply tightened his arm around her and lifted her off her feet.

Celene dangled there at the mercy of his whims as he took complete possession of her mouth. His lips wandered over hers, brushing gently, pressing deep, tasting her in a way Celene had never been tasted. The contact drew her into the aura of excitement that surrounded him, but it did not dispel the knowledge of the danger he was calling down on her head.

From around them rose a cacophony of hoots and cat-calls. Someone snatched her hat away, and the trappers and traders became suddenly, blatantly aware of a white woman's presence at the rendezvous. Ribald comments filled the air as Burke Cardwell set Celene back on her feet and raised his mouth from hers.

Furiously she glared up at him, incensed by what he'd done. Not only had he handled her in a way she swore she would never allow herself to be handled again, but he had made her conspicuous in a situation where it was impera-tive that no one notice she was a woman. Her loose-fitting boy's clothes and her diminutive size had gone a long way toward protecting Celene's identity, but Burke's impulsive actions had destroyed any advantage that guise might have given her. He had made everyone aware of her presence at the rendezvous, made them aware of it in a blatant, physical way that sent men's imaginations racing. And that meant trouble.

Angrily Celene twisted out of Cardwell's arms. "*Âne stupide*! Worthless fool! Do you have any idea what you've done?"

For an instant he stared at her, taken aback. Then she saw the realization, the dawning contrition in his eyes. "I'm sorry, Celene," he began. "*Je regret . . .*"

She was not willing to offer easy forgiveness for some-thing that might cost her dearly in the end. Instead she dumped Burke's clothes on the ground, kicked them twice for good measure, and wheeled toward her campsite. That the trappers gave no ground when she tried to push her way through the crowd was eloquent proof that her concerns for her safety were well grounded.

"Let her go!" Cardwell boomed from behind her, and like the waves of the Red Sea parting at Moses' command, a path opened before her.

Celene covered the distance to her father's camp with deliberate speed, but even with the tent flaps tied tightly behind her she did not feel safe. She wished fervently that there was a door to bar, stout shutters to fasten over the windows, her father to guard her as she slept. But she was alone, the only white woman in the camp of well over a hundred lonely men, separated from them by only the thin canvas walls of her tent.

She wanted nothing more than to take to her bed and forget what Burke Cardwell had done, forget how vulnerable he had made her. But Celene could not. Now that darkness was beginning to fall, it would be so easy for a man to creep into the campsite, slit the canvas by her bed, and have his way with her. The memory of being taken without her consent seared her brain. The feelings of impotence and fury knotted inside her. For eight endless years she had submitted to a husband she loathed, and she would never again allow herself to be used as Henri had used her. She would kill any man who tried.

Taking up her father's pistol, Celene measured the powder, rammed home the patch and ball, then primed the pan. With a snap she pressed the striker in place. Then, closing her fingers around the trigger, she lay down on her bed of boughs and blankets.

Inside the tent it was dim and close. The air was heavy and warm from the accumulated heat of the day, but Celene dared not undress. It would make her too accessible should anyone try to accost her as she slept. She had readily accepted the dangers she would face by coming to the rendezvous; God knows her father had warned her often enough what they were. But she had not expected to be made to feel so vulnerable, so exposed.

There was a press of fury at the back of her throat as she cursed Burke Cardwell and her own helplessness. Though she clenched her teeth and fought to hold them back, tears sprang to her eyes, burning like acid as they seeped between her lashes. After Henri died, she had sworn never to put herself in a position where she was so hopelessly out of control, never to let any man make her feel frightened, angry, or weak again. Yet Burke

Cardwell had done that almost without intending to.

"Damn you Burke Cardwell," she muttered as she nestled deeper into her blankets and tightened her fingers around the gun. "Damn your English soul to hell."

4

The sound of a pistol being cocked brought Celene instantly awake. Even before her eyes were open, her fingers had tightened around the stock of the gun that lay in her hand. The shape and weight of it nestled in her palm were reassuring as she peered around in the predawn gloom to discover who was accosting her. But the tent was empty save for the bales of furs and the boxes and kegs of trade goods. On the opposite side of the enclosure she could see that her father's bed had not been slept in, and she wondered where he was.

As if in answer to the question, his voice came to her from just beyond the canvas wall. "Please, Arnaud, can't we settle this in some more friendly manner?"

"You're a dead man, Peugeot," another man answered. "And it's going to be a pleasure to put an end to your worthless life."

The stranger's threat set off an ice-cold glow of fear in the center of Celene's chest. She scrambled to her feet, the pine boughs beneath her blankets creaking and snapping as she moved. The noise made her heart rebound off her breastbone and her hands go slick. Would her presence be discovered before she'd figured out what was happening and how to help her father?

From just outside the tent flaps a second man began to speak. "Do you deny, Peugeot, that last spring you gave us credit for three fewer bales of furs than we deserved? Can you prove that you didn't take our pelts back to Kaskaskia in your own name?"

"Surely there has only been some kind of bookkeeping error, Monsieur Rivard." Celene could imagine her father giving one of his dismissing shrugs. "If you will allow me to get my records from the tent, I'm sure we can—"

"You're not going anywhere, Peugeot. And I don't believe this is some damned bookkeeping mistake you've made, either. I think you cheated us deliberate like."

Celene crept toward the opening at the head of the lean-to and peeked between the flaps. Antoine squatted on his haunches before the fire, and one of the strangers standing over him had a pistol pointed at her father's chest. The second man sat beneath the lean-to's overhang less than an arm's length away, effectively blocking Celene's exit.

Whether her father had done what these men were accusing him of, Celene could not say, but she didn't intend to let them kill him for it.

"Perhaps you could take some additional goods to make up for the shortfall," she heard Antoine offer as she retreated to the rear of the tent.

"Additional goods," one of the men scoffed. "You mean you're willing to give us more of the watered whiskey you give the Indians, more of those damned dull axes, more of those worthless blankets."

"*Je vous promets*, the goods I handle for Monsieur LaVallier are every bit as good as the ones that come from New Orleans and Montreal. If you think you have been cheated in the past, let me make it up to you."

"There are some things that can't be easily ignored, Peugeot, and your chicanery is one of them."

As the men argued, Celene snatched up a knife and inserted the blade in the lean-to's low back wall. Once she was outside, there were friends of her father's she could go to for help, men at neighboring campsites who might come to their aid. But as she noiselessly slit the heavy cloth, Celene realized she didn't know her father's friends or where to find them. And after carousing till almost dawn, would anyone be willing and able to offer help? Her father's salvation was up to her.

Tightening her grip on the pistol, she snatched up her father's musket, as well, and pushed it through the opening.

The gun wasn't loaded, but the men threatening her father didn't know that. Nor was there the time to load it now. Celene scuttled out of the tent. She just prayed that the powder in the pistol had not been compromised by dampness the night before, and that it would ignite if she was forced to pull the trigger.

Coming silently to her feet, she laid the musket across her arm and hefted the pistol in her opposite hand. Stealthily Celene advanced down the side of the tent. As she approached the front, she could once again hear what the men were saying.

"Just do it, Arnaud. Go into the tent and see if the strongbox is where he says."

The trappers' threats of violent revenge seemed to have been tempered by the promise of immediate gain.

Arnaud moved toward the tent to do his partner's bidding just as Celene stepped around the corner. "Drop your weapons, messieurs, if you please," she told them as she leveled the pistol at her father's captors.

For an instant the two men stared at her in stunned surprise.

"*Mon Dieu!* It's a girl!" the one beneath the overhang exclaimed as he recovered himself. "Grab hold of her, Arnaud! I doubt she knows how to use that thing."

In answer Celene raked back the hammer on the pistol and centered her aim on Arnaud's chest. Twice he looked back and forth between the unwavering mouth of the gun barrel and the set of her jaw.

"I will not hesitate to kill you if I must," she promised him, extending the gun in his direction.

Abruptly Arnaud threw down his pistol. Rivard dropped his weapon a moment later.

"Now, you," she motioned to Rivard, "move over there with that *fou canard.*"

Rivard did as he was told.

"Celene! I did not think you were even awake," her father greeted her, coming to her side.

"Ah, yes, Papa. Luckily, I was. Now will you please conclude your business with these *gentilhommes* so that we need not awaken our neighbors with the sound of gunfire."

"I have told them that I did not cheat them out of any furs," her father huffed.

"But they don't seem to believe you, *mon père*. Isn't there something in the tent that would appease them, at least a little?"

"I did not cheat them, daughter. And it is Monsieur LaVallier's money you would encourage me to squander."

Not that you, mon cher Papa, hadn't been willing to buy them off with Monsieur LaVallier's money before I came to rescue you.

"Then send these two on their way with your apologies," she instructed. "But pay them for their weapons, since they've surrendered them to us."

Her father took some money from the fox head bag around his waist, grumbling to himself.

"We cannot deprive these men of their livelihood, Papa," she urged him, "not without giving them the means to replace their weapons."

"We will be sorry if we do," Peugeot prophesied as he handed over the payment.

The trappers accepted the money with markedly poor grace. "LaVallier hired us to hunt for him, and we expect to be treated fairly," Rivard protested.

"If there is more money due you, I will see that it is paid," Celene told him. "But in the meantime, take your leave of us."

"And consider your association with Monsieur LaVallier ended," her father added. "He prefers not to deal with swine like you."

Malice glittered in Rivard's black eyes. "Oh, no, Peugeot. Our association with LaVallier isn't ended and neither is this. We'll be back, Peugeot. Be assured that we'll be back."

Celene and her father watched as the two men moved off through the encampment, Rivard hulking and burly, the dominant personality of the two, and Arnaud as quick and jumpy as a small, gray squirrel.

As they disappeared among the tents, Celene shuddered with reaction, the guns sagging toward the earth. She was shaken by the confrontation, unbearably weary. She turned to her father, expecting his praise, needing it now, just as she had always had. Instead there was anger contorting his face.

"What right did you have to interfere in my affairs?" he demanded. "Why was it necessary for you to brandish guns at two of my associates?"

Unprepared for his reaction, Celene simply stared. "I thought—I thought you were in danger."

"Danger? Bah! From fools like those? *Sacrebleu*! I don't need a woman protecting me from men like that."

Feeling as if she'd been slapped, Celene set the pistol and the musket aside. Her hands were trembling and her throat went tight. For an instant she skimmed the edge of tears, but instead of slinking away to cry as she might have some months before, she turned on her father.

"Did you cheat them, Papa?" she demanded. "Did you steal their furs?"

"No, of course not!" he denied. "How could you think such a thing?"

Instead of answering, Celene snatched up branches from the woodpile and fed them into the smoldering fire.

"I have been on my own since I was barely fourteen," her father continued furiously. "I have paddled thousands of miles of rapids, hunted the most dangerous game, risked hostile Indians and worse. How could you think I would need your help in defending myself? How could you believe the charges those scoundrels made?"

He was pale with anger, white to the lips, and for Celene, it suddenly didn't seem worth the effort it took to argue with him.

All she had ever wanted from her father was recognition of her help, a bit of appreciation now and then. But he showed his appreciation only when he chose, on his own terms. There had been times when her father had hugged her against his side in mute praise for having learned to make a broom or milk a cow, when he'd left precious foil-wrapped candies from New Orleans on her pillow as thanks for mending his clothes, when he had patted her hip as she cleared the table in acknowledgment of her skill in preparing a particularly tasty meal. But his approval never seemed to come when Celene needed it most, nor was there ever quite enough to make her feel satisfied, really loved.

She had expected his thanks for coming to rescue him. Instead he had shouted at her, berated her. Why did he so resent her help?

In frustration Celene clanged the spoon around the rim of the iron pot in which she had begun to prepare porridge for their breakfast. The racket made her feel better somehow.

"Burke Cardwell was wrapped up in a blanket by our fire when I returned to the camp just before dawn," Antoine noted above the clatter.

"Was he?" Celene didn't even bother to look up. She had suspected as much when she smelled the fruity tang of Cardwell's pipe tobacco late last night, but she had been too angry to acknowledge his presence.

"He was watching over you as you slept."

"As well he might," she snapped, her resentment of Burke replacing her anger at her father. "He had no right to kiss me as he did. He had no right to make me so conspicuous."

Her father sighed. "He was a man celebrating a hard-won victory. He acted before he thought, I'll give you that. But he meant you no real harm."

Celene slammed the spoon around inside the pot harder than before, making her father wince. "No harm? *Mon Dieu*! No harm, Papa? He made every man at the rendez-vous aware that I am here, aware of me in a way that men are aware of women they hope to bed. I can no longer leave the campsite, day or night. Where I once passed safe and unobserved, I will be noticed and in constant danger."

"I warned you that a rendezvous was no place for a white woman. I told you I would sell your hams for you."

"But for how much, Papa? For how much? And how could I trust you to bring the money back to me? Last year you returned to Ste. Genevieve with hardly a sou in your pocket. How could I take the chance you would gamble my money away as you do your own? The income from the sale of those hams is all Jean-Paul and I have to live on until the harvest."

"All the goods and every pelt Monsieur LaVallier has entrusted to me over the years has been accounted for, hasn't it?" Antoine demanded, defending himself. "I know what the hams mean to you and *mon petit-fils*, and I would not betray you."

He turned to stare sightlessly into the fire. "You've always thought the worst of me, Celene. And since Henri died, you haven't been willing to put your trust in any man."

Were the reasons for her feelings really such a mystery to him? Didn't he know how many ways he'd wronged her over the years? And as for not trusting men—Antoine had taught her those first hard lessons at his knee, and Henri had completed her education.

She looked up at her father in the gray morning light, noticing how sharp and drawn his features seemed. He looked as discomfited and exhausted as she felt, and suddenly Celene was sorry for what she'd said, for being unable to trust him with the sale of the hams. But her concerns for her profits were real.

Because of that, she refused to apologize. She had spent her life holding her peace and trying to make things right. First she had swallowed her opinions because she was her father's child, then she had swallowed them because she was Henri's wife. But when Henri died two months ago and she'd become a woman on her own, Celene had promised herself that she would never smooth things over to keep the peace, never back down again.

"I need the money those hams will bring me, as well you know," she told him. "I came to the rendezvous because I had no choice. But I had every right to expect that by dressing as a boy and keeping to myself I would have a modicum of anonymity. Burke Cardwell has spoiled that now."

Her father snorted once and came to his feet. "Burke Cardwell is a good man at heart. I would never have agreed to his request for your hand if I had not been sure of that."

Celene clapped a lid on the pot of porridge and turned to glare at her father. "So you *did* give Cardwell permission to marry me in spite of how I feel!"

"I married you to someone I didn't know once before, and I wouldn't make that mistake again. Burke Cardwell will make you a good husband, *chérie*. And I want to see you settled."

"Settled? Bah! You told me Henri was a good man, too, and just look how he treated me."

Antoine sighed heavily and moved toward the doorway to the tent. "I know for a fact that Cardwell treated his first wife very well."

Celene swung around to where her father was untying the strings to the tent flaps. "His first wife?"

He pushed the canvas flaps wide. "*Oui.*"

"His first wife!"

"You'll have to ask Burke about her," her father suggested, "when next he comes by."

"But I want you to tell me, Papa," she demanded.

There was the sound of branches rustling as he settled onto his bed. "Hush, Celene," he ordered. "I need some sleep."

"I want to know about her now!"

But her father refused to answer, and very soon she could hear him snoring.

"Are you willing to accept my apology and a peace offering, or did my behavior last evening put me completely beyond the pale?"

Without even looking up, Celene knew it was Burke Cardwell who had come into the campsite. In spite of what he must have intended as soothing words, his stance, with his moccasined feet splayed and his hands on his hips, spoke little of apology and much of his determination to win her acquiescence.

Instead of acknowledging him, Celene focused on the sewing in her lap, jabbing the needle into the fabric and wishing it were his hide. She'd had a productive morning, selling three more hams and finally getting the trade goods arranged to her satisfaction, and she didn't intend to let Cardwell spoil her mood. After the kiss he'd pressed upon her the night before, after the crowd's reaction, after the conversation she'd had with her father just this morning, there was nothing Burke could say or do to change the aversion she felt for him.

And she didn't intend to be bought off for a few trinkets, either.

"I trust you slept well," he went on, still standing over her. "I had a rather restless night myself. The least little sound disturbed me."

As well it should, Celene thought uncharitably and continued to sew. If it weren't for his own damned foolishness, keeping watch over her wouldn't have been necessary.

"You did sleep well, didn't you?"

"Well enough, I suppose," she admitted grudgingly.

"I'm exceedingly glad of that."

She craned her neck to glare at him, cursing him for being so tall. "Papa isn't here, Monsieur Cardwell. I don't have any idea when he'll be back."

"It isn't your father I was coming to see."

"Certainly you and I don't have anything to discuss." She did her best to dismiss him, but Burke refused to be dismissed.

"I know you have every right to be angry with me, Celene," he began. "I'm honestly sorry about what happened after the race. Kissing you wasn't something I'd planned to do."

"Wasn't it?"

"I didn't think about how it would look, about how it would compromise your position here."

"Didn't you?"

"What I did was reckless, thoughtless, but I heartily apologize and bring these as a peace offering." As he spoke he hauled long, fluttering ribbons from where he'd hidden them inside his shirt. There were red ones, blue ones, and several that were a particularly vivid shade of green.

Her gaze shifted from the ribbons to his face. "Do you really think a few ribbons will make up for the fact that I dare not leave the campsite? Because of you I'm afraid to go to the river for water, to move unescorted through the camp, to sleep in my own bed. Your actions made every man at the rendezvous aware of my presence here."

"You seem to think you were invisible before."

"I *did* pass unnoticed among the crowd."

"I noticed you," he pointed out.

"You didn't notice me until I made myself conspicuous. And I'll warrant that the men who saw me push you down thought I was a boy."

Celene felt compelled to convince Burke that at a less than lingering glance, she could have passed for some bourgeois's young apprentice. It seemed imperative that he realize how his actions the night before had compromised her.

"I won't let anyone harm you," Cardwell offered by way of reassurance.

"Oh, won't you, now? And what an enviable choice I have to make: your company and my safety, or my solitude and being in danger."

She could see an angry flush come up in his face. He seemed to think that since he was taking responsibility for what he'd done, she should be endlessly grateful.

Cardwell slapped the ribbons onto the upturned crate beside her. "I don't know what the hell I'll do with these if you don't take them."

"And I'll warrant they cost you dearly, if you bought them here at the rendezvous."

Nettled, Cardwell turned away. "You're right, damn it. Those ribbons are worth a small fortune at back-country prices, and I intend to get my money's worth."

"Oh?" Celene was immediately wary.

"Your father said you brought a pair of scissors to the rendezvous, and I was hoping to trade the ribbons for your forgiveness and a haircut."

"You mean you're willing to let me near you with something sharp?"

Surprised humor flickered across his face before he masked it with a frown. "I've never had any problem defending myself," he assured her, "no matter how cunning the attack. I'll be forced to hack my hair off with a knife if you don't agree to cut it. Besides, your father said you wouldn't mind."

Damn you and my father both, Celene thought as she came to her feet and withdrew her long-bladed scissors from the neat brass holster dangling from her belt. With the barest of nods, she indicated that Burke should take her place on the wooden keg. It would serve him right if she scalped him, she told herself, or took a good-sized nip out of one of his ears.

It didn't seem to occur to Burke that a haircut might offer her several dire forms of revenge, and he calmly prepared to take his place before her. From the heavily beaded possibles bag that rode low on his hip he withdrew a comb and hard-backed brush for her to use, and before Celene could stop him, he had stripped off his white muslin shirt and cast it aside.

Seeing him bared to the waist brought on that strange, suffocating feeling Celene had experienced the night before. He was so big, so broad, so utterly overwhelming.

"Aren't—aren't you going to be cold like that?" she asked, turning her gaze from his muscular chest to the lowering sky. Since just after dawn the weather had been worsening; the wind was brisk and decidedly chill.

Cardwell shrugged and took his seat. "I'll be fine if you just get on with this."

Nodding she came closer, sliding her fingers through the honey-colored mass of his hair. She stood over him, separating tangles, stroking the heavy, slightly wavy strands. They were warm from the heat of his body, faintly damp from recent bathing. His hair was like a luxuriant pelt, silky and substantial between her fingers, unexpectedly soft. She raised the comb and drew it downward to where the strands tumbled across his back and arms, smoothing as she went. Furrows formed where the teeth of the comb glided through his hair, light gold at the crest where it had been brightened by the sun, and darker beneath, the color of caramel, of hazelnuts. The gentle abrasion of the tortoiseshell teeth left a faint, white pattern on his tanned skin, pale against the ruddy brown. She lifted the comb repeatedly, guiding it through the length and fullness of his hair, feathering the ends between her fingers.

As she worked, she entered Cardwell's aura, the hum of energy that surrounded him. The day was cool and gray, but Burke's body radiated a compelling glow that both warmed her and drew her nearer. His scent of soap and tobacco and resinous pine tantalized her. His sheer size made her feel slight and insignificant. Yet there was something about his quiescence beneath her fingertips that imparted a sense of power. She was aware of Burke down deep inside, as if something at the very core of her was quivering in answer to his nearness.

The way he held himself, alert, coiled tight, convinced Celene that he was every bit as aware of her. The color in his cheeks was high, and she could feel his muscles flex and knot at her lightest touch. To shut out her presence as best he could, Burke's eyes were resolutely closed, and she could see his heavy lashes drifting molasses-dark against his cheeks.

As she worked over him, he was completely open to her regard, the angular slope of his cheekbones, the glowing vitality of his sun-darkened skin, the vulnerable curve of his lower lip revealed between the arc of his mustache and the mass of brownish beard. Her gaze slid over the slope of his chest and shoulders, the wide bow of his collarbones, the faint trail of amber hair that defined the midline of his body. She studied the puckered, V-shaped scar that marred the inner surface of his left forearm, the thickness of his wrists, the size of his broad, long-fingered hands.

His legs were splayed so she could step between them as she worked, and she could see that the well-developed muscles in his thighs were wound tight beneath the dark-blue broadcloth trousers. As she stepped around his knee, she spotted a quite noticeable bulge along the inside of his left thigh. A blush seared up her neck. Her mouth went dry, and she was suddenly, painfully aware that there was more to what was happening here than the question of good grooming.

His reaction to her nearness made it clear that Burke Cardwell wanted just what every other man at the rendezvous wanted from her—her attentions as a woman. Only Cardwell was more adept than the others at sneaking under her guard, more willing than the others to pay dearly for her favors. He *said* he was even willing to marry her. But was he? The question rose in her mind again. What reason could he have for offering for her hand?

Unsettled by her awareness of Burke, by the evidence of his response to her, by the questions of his intent, she set the comb down with a resounding smack. "How short do you want this cut?" she asked.

Burke answered without opening his eyes. "Just long enough to tie back in a queue. They're still wearing queues in polite society, aren't they?"

"They're wearing them in Kaskaskia and Ste. Genevieve. Is that society polite enough to suit you?"

Without waiting for an answer, she began to snip. Bit by bit severed strands of golden brown began to slither down his shoulders and back, to dust the tops of his thighs and the earth at the base of the keg. They lay twined in matted grass, some of them fluttering a little in the rising wind.

As she worked over him, Cardwell opened his eyes and glanced up at her. "Celene, will you tell me something?"

"No, Monsieur Cardwell, probably not."

"Will you tell me why you attacked me yesterday? What made you push me in the mud?"

The regular rhythm of the scissors' snipping abruptly stopped, and it was several seconds before Celene was able to still the tremor in her hand and begin again.

"You were going to strike that Indian woman," she answered quietly, "and I couldn't let it happen."

"Indian woman?"

"You seemed to be arguing with her."

Cardwell's brow furrowed, then cleared. "Autumn Leaf."

"I saw you grab her wrist."

"I *did* grab her wrist," Cardwell conceded, glancing at Celene again.

"And you were going to hit her."

"No, Celene, I wasn't."

Celene paused and looked down into his face, knowing her own must be marked with patent disbelief. "You were," she accused.

"I wasn't going to hit her."

"Then why did you grab her as you did?"

Cardwell was silent for a moment as if mulling over

exactly what he was going to tell Celene about the other woman.

"Autumn Leaf wants me to marry her," he finally said. "I have lived on the periphery of her band of Chippewa for many years, and since this winter she has been determined to become my wife. Somehow she thinks I owe it to her."

"And why does she think that?"

Burke heaved a long, uneven sigh. "She just does. It's very complicated."

Under her persistent badgering, her father had told her that Cardwell's wife had died some months ago. Did that explain Autumn Leaf's demands? "Is that what you and she were arguing about yesterday?"

Celene could see the red come up beneath his skin. "Autumn Leaf has tried a lot of things to convince me to take her as my bride, but most of them have had to do with seducing me."

"And have you lain with her?"

Cardwell seemed startled by her forthrightness. The color in his cheeks intensified. "No," he answered.

Celene looked hard into those glistening turquoise eyes, trying to weigh and measure the veracity of his response. She could not tell if he was lying.

When Celene said nothing, Burke went on. "I didn't want her touching me. I didn't mean to hurt her; I don't think I really did. I just wanted to discourage her as quickly and as effectively as I could."

She lifted her scissors to finish trimming up his hair, but his fingers closed around her arm.

"Celene," he began, his touch and his voice surprisingly gentle, "why did that mean so much to you?"

"What?"

"That I might hit her. Why did it bother you so?"

It was a moment before she could think how to respond. "I don't believe women should be mistreated," she answered, jerking away. "Men seem to think it is their right to mistreat women, but I don't believe that's true."

Cardwell went silent, and Celene wondered if he was perceptive enough to guess what lay behind her views. All at once Celene could not stand to have Burke learn what kind of a marriage she'd endured. She was ashamed of the way Henri had treated her in those first years, ashamed that she had let him handle her as he had. She felt almost as if she were to blame for the pain and unhappiness. She could not bear to have Burke think that, too.

Burke shifted beneath her hands. "Celene," he said, breaking into her dark thoughts. "Celene, we've got to get the goods inside. It's starting to rain."

Celene noticed suddenly that there were indeed raindrops spattering through the leaves, and that slate-gray clouds were hunkering low over the tops of the river bluffs. Thunder mumbled ominously from somewhere beyond the swishing trees, and lightning pulsed against the sky.

"Pack as much as you can in the boxes," Burke ordered when Celene did not immediately respond to his words of warning, "and I'll carry everything inside."

Realizing the potential for losing most of what her father had brought to trade, Celene nodded and moved to obey. Except for the need for speed, it was not all that different from the way they had put away her father's goods the night before. Only now the wind yanked the blankets from her hands as she tried to fold them, only now there were raindrops splatting into her face and hair, only now there was breathless urgency in her movements. As quickly as Celene packed the boxes, Burke hauled them inside. He was tall enough to snatch the precious hams from where they swung from the churning branches overhead, strong enough to wrestle the barrels of rum and hogsheads of wine into the limited space of the lean-to's porchlike overhang.

As Celene scurried around battening things down to weather the storm, the rain began in earnest, turning from a bothersome drizzle to a soaking downpour. Wrapping an arm around her waist so she could not resist, Burke pulled her beneath the tent flap.

They stood mere inches apart beneath the snapping canvas roof, both of them breathing a little unsteadily.

"I think we got pretty much everything moved to safety," Cardwell observed as they looked out across the campsite.

"Except my ribbons."

They lay on one of the empty crates not far from his discarded shirt. Both were already limp and sodden.

"Your ribbons will dry," he consoled her.

"I suppose your shirt will, too."

The wind picked up around them, suddenly cold, knife-edged with damp. Involuntarily Cardwell shivered, making Celene aware, once more, of the state of his undress.

"Come inside," she offered, pushing open the tent flaps. "It will be warmer and drier there."

As they passed into the lean-to, the salt-sweet tang of cured meat filled their nostrils. It was close and dim inside, and Celene knelt to light the wick of a betty lamp. She hung it from a notch in one of the tent posts and turned to where Burke was settling himself on her bed of boughs and blankets. Alarm washed through her at the sight of him sitting where she had only lain alone, but in their haste to get everything inside, her father's bedroll had disappeared under baskets of bells and arm bands and mirrors, skeins of yarn, and bolts of colorful fabric.

Somewhere above them thunder ripped a hole in the quivering sky, and rain spilled through to lash the world below. It advanced like waves of footsteps across the lean-to's roof, and the run-off spattered noisily to the ground at the edges of the tent.

"I hope my father waterproofed this canvas well," Celene offered, glancing up in time to see the fabric above her flicker bright and dark.

"Antoine knows the value of a little linseed oil," Cardwell assured her. "We'll be warm and dry in here until the storm has passed."

"I wonder how long that will be?"

There must have been a note of uneasiness in her voice, because Burke's gaze seemed suddenly drawn to hers. "Do the thunder and lightning frighten you?"

She shook her head. "No, I rather like the wind and the rain."

"Then it must be me you're afraid of."

To avoid his knowing eyes, she glanced down at her lap where she was twisting her hands together. She flushed, and stilled the movement with an effort.

What she was experiencing was not exactly fear. It was a gradually growing awareness, of their complete isolation, of her vulnerability, of Burke himself. But no matter what she felt, she could hardly cast Cardwell out into the storm after what he'd done to help her get her father's goods inside.

"I'm not afraid of you at all," she assured him, moving to sit at the foot of the bed and crossing her legs before her as if she were erecting a barricade.

A wry smile flickered in the shade of his mustache. "Do you find me unpleasant to be near?"

"No."

He smiled again, but this time in a way that kindled a silvery glow in his azure eyes. "That's good," he told her, "exceedingly good."

"Why?" Her voice was breathy, much too soft.

"Because I very much like being close to you."

With a dizzying swoop, her awareness of him escalated: his husky baritone whispering words that flowed over her like molten honey, his woodsy scent enveloping her like veils of smoke, his strength enfolding and protecting her from a world where thunder detonated overhead and talons of white-hot lightning sizzled toward the earth.

"I like being close to you," he continued. "I like that the scent of lavender lingers in the air when you pass by. I could smell it on my clothes after you'd held them during the race. I can catch a hint of it now on your skin and in your hair."

As he spoke, he reached around and loosed the rawhide thong at the bottom of her long, thick braid, working slowly upward, spreading the plaited sections until his fingers were splayed against her nape.

"I like the way your cheeks get pink when you're flustered, the way you wring your hands when you're unsure. I like the shape of your mouth and the freckles on your nose. I like the way the lamplight fires the gold in your hair and reflects like spangles in your eyes."

Celene could hardly breathe for the bubbles of delight and panic rising in her chest. Burke's words described her in a way she had never expected any man to see her—certainly in a way she had never seen herself. They made her want to believe that what he was saying was true; that he found in her something surprising and wonderful, something that could be treasured and revered. Tears of hope and disbelief gathered beneath her downcast lashes. Celene felt as fragile and tremulous as dandelion down.

Burke must have sensed her uncertainty for he moved a little closer and let his fingertips feather from her nape to the curve of her throat.

"I've been wondering if your skin is as satiny as it looks, how you'd respond to my touch, whether you'd be afraid or eager when I finally had the chance to kiss you properly."

A covey of shivers awakened beneath his fingers and fluttered the length of her spine.

"This isn't wise," Celene warned him. There was a roaring in her ears and her head went light. "Oh, please, Burke. This isn't wise."

Though Burke smiled, he did not heed her words. The prickly graze of his mustache and beard against her skin were unexpected, undeniably pleasurable, a gentle preparation for the kiss to come. Still, she felt hopelessly compromised at the lush, heated mingling of their breath, felt seared to her soul by the first brush of his lips.

The kiss he pressed onto her mouth was both tentative and warm, sweet and undemanding. Yet there was unexpected power in the current that passed between them: something restless, compelling, relentless. Though neither moved, it drew them closer, stirred a rush of pure sensation. Celene felt Burke shudder with the effort it took to practice restraint, and she was awed by his tenderness and concern for her.

She raised a hand to touch his cheek, trailed fingers into his hair, and opened her lips beneath the press of his. Her own willingness to kiss him back amazed her, frightened her, enlightened her. Perhaps she was more willing than she'd ever suspected to venture into the realm of men and women, to explore a part of the world she had never allowed herself to contemplate.

As if sensing her thoughts, he hesitated for an instant before deepening the kiss. But when he did, he slanted his mouth across her own, drinking slow and deep of her.

When the kiss was over, Burke withdrew, waiting, calm and patient, for her response. It came like a storm that swelled through her veins, sluiced along her limbs, and tingled all the way to her toes. She felt breathless, weightless, wonderful.

From a mere handspan away, Celene could see the bright, persistent glow in Burke's turquoise eyes, and for the first time in her life she was flattered by the desire she had been able to awaken in a man. She liked knowing that Burke's breathing was a little unsteady because of her, liked seeing the flush she had brought to his face. Instead of dreading the effect her femininity would have on a man, Celene was proud of it, intrigued by it.

Yet in spite of what he seemed to want, Burke was giving her the choice of accepting or rejecting a second kiss. He was offering her control over what intimacies they would share. That challenged Celene's perceptions of how a man and woman dealt together, made her wonder what it would be like to learn to know a man on her own terms.

But before she could do more than recognize what he'd done, what he'd offered, what she wanted, Burke took the decision away from her.

"Perhaps you're right," he said, shifting beside her on the bed. "Perhaps being here together isn't wise."

Celene was stunned by his withdrawal, disappointed, confused. It was as if something new and wonderful had been ripped from her hands, as if something she was struggling to understand was inexplicably lost.

As attuned to her feelings as he'd seemed only moments before, Burke was oblivious to them now.

"I think the storm has let up enough so I can return to my campsite," he went on. "I have my animals to tend and my own goods to look after."

He clambered to his feet and stood beneath the drooping roof of the tent looking down at her. "Thank you for cutting my hair."

She nodded once, but before she could force so much as

a word around the knot of confusion and regret that clogged her throat, Burke Cardwell was gone. Celene could do nothing but stare after him, wondering what she'd done wrong. In spite of his words of praise, had she fallen short of his expectations?

Her knees were inexplicably wobbly as she rose from the bed. She felt dazed, confused. She stared blankly for several moments before she began to rebraid her hair. When she stepped outside, she found the rain had abated, though a persistent drizzle cast a hazy, gray pall over the landscape. It was the kind of dismal day that would fade into a dismal night, and the only thing to do was to hole up somewhere warm and dry.

That probably meant that most of the trappers and voyageurs had taken refuge in the big tents near the center of the camp, tents where they could guzzle the traders' whiskey, swap stories, and play hand after hand of cards. If that was so, her father would not be back for hours yet. Perhaps that's where Burke had gone, to spend his time in more lively pursuits than wooing a woman who wouldn't be wooed.

Sighing, Celene stepped beyond the overhang to where the wet, bedraggled ribbons he'd brought her clung to the edge of a packing crate. Burke's shirt, of course, was gone, snatched up from where it had lain as he left the campsite. But as she turned to gather up the trailing ribbons, she noticed that something else was missing, too.

Because the rain had come up so suddenly, they had left Burke's fresh-cut hair scattered on the ground at the base of the keg. Now every strand was gone. It seemed unlikely that the ferocity of the storm had swept the campsite clean, not when the ribbons that had lain less than a yard away were undisturbed.

It was odd, she thought as she returned to the tent, decidedly odd. Yet Celene could think of no other explanation.

"Damn Celene Bernard! Damn her!" Burke muttered as he stomped through the rain in the direction of his own campsite. Damn her wide green eyes and her vulnerable mouth. Damn her soft, lush body and that half-inviting, half-terrified way she had of looking at a man. Damn him for wanting her to be something he'd begun to suspect she was not. Damn her for turning into something he didn't want her to be.

He'd been plotting his return to England for most of the winter, spurred on by the letter from some fancy London solicitor that he'd received at last year's rendezvous. It had asked for information about a man reportedly trapping in the Northwest, a man who called himself Burke Cardwell. At the time Burke had received it, he had tucked the letter away. Content with his life, he'd had no need for contact with the outside world. But in the dark months after Morning Song died, he'd taken the letter out again.

And with it came all the anger, all the bitterness he'd carried with him to Michilimackinac. In the solitude of his empty days and sleepless nights, questions plagued him: questions that had lain fallow and festering for eleven long years, questions he had never before had the need or the courage to answer. When his grandfather sent him away, had he also planned Burke's exile to the wilderness? Had he gone so far as to plot his grandson's death?

Each question brought with it confusion and pain, hours of searching his mind for answers, days and weeks of calling up memories that Burke had long ago banished. Alone in the lodge on the Athabasca, Burke conjured up days spent at Longmeadow, his family home; weeks of traveling at his grandfather's side. What had he done to earn such enmity from the man who'd led Burke to believe that if he was not his grandfather's heir, he was at least his favored grandchild? How could he have so misjudged the older man? Or was it someone else who'd plotted Burke's downfall and demise?

In the long, lonely hours he'd spent tending traps and scraping pelts, Burke began to plan a return to England, a confrontation with his grandfather. After his years in the wilderness, he was a moderately wealthy man. Returning to England would be a damn-sight less strenuous and dangerous than continuing to live in the wilds. He could repine to the bosom of his family, impress them with what he'd made of himself, find his answers, and extract a suitable and extremely satisfactory revenge.

In the end the decision about returning to England had not been difficult to make. There was nothing to keep him in America.

From the inception of his plan, he had wanted a woman at his side when he reached his family's home. He'd wanted someone to point up the disparity of what he'd been and what he'd become, someone who would understand his need for vengeance and help him accomplish it. When Celene had pushed him in the mud two days ago, he thought he'd found the woman he'd been looking for. The more he learned of her, the surer he was of his choice. He liked that she had forced her father to bring her to the rendezvous; that she had traveled four hundred leagues in an open boat; that, if the tales were true, she had faced down two of the Northwest's meanest trappers with a single-shot pistol and an empty musket. Being Antoine Peugeot's daughter seemed to virtually guarantee that Celene would be bright and shrewd, single-minded and practical, a woman with no illusions.

But today, curled beside him on her blankets, Celene had changed from that virago into a compelling, vulnerable stranger. She had looked at him with wonder in her eyes and trembled at his kiss. Where he had expected a married woman's experience, he had encountered inexplicable innocence. Where he'd expected a certain toughness, he had seen quaking vulnerability. He'd played the gentleman through it all, but Celene's responses made no sense in light of what he'd come to expect of her. And things that didn't make sense always made Cardwell's hackles rise.

Reaching his own lean-to, Burke paused to check on the welfare of his animals. Tethered beneath the canvas he had strung between two trees, his dun horse, Plato, stood stalwart, too sensible to let the fury of even so impressive a thunderstorm upset him. Flora, one of his pack mules, had followed Plato's example and stood munching the clover Burke had cut. But Fauna and Jane, his other mules, had been spooked by the weather and needed to have their ears scratched and their necks stroked before he went inside.

As the tent flaps dropped in place behind him, a figure rose up from behind his bundles of pelts. With instincts honed sharp by years of surviving unexpected dangers, Burke's hand snapped to the knife at his waist.

He had drawn his weapon, fully prepared to defend himself, before he recognized his visitor. "My God, Autumn Leaf, you could get yourself killed sneaking up on a man like that!" he said, speaking to her in the Chippewa tongue.

The Indian woman oozed toward him, her hips swaying suggestively. "I came to pass the storm with you. Where is it you have been?"

"I've been doing my best to stay out of the rain."

"Have you, now?" she asked, adopting a skeptical pout. Burke could feel her gaze slide over him, noting the moisture pearled on his chest and shoulders, the sopping shirt clutched in his hand. "It doesn't look like you succeeded."

"It doesn't look like you did, either."

Autumn Leaf must have been out in the worst of the storm. Her hair was hanging in dripping strings, and her calico shirt and rawhide skirt were molded to her body, delineating every curve.

Burke swallowed hard and glanced away. Damn Celene Bernard for getting him all riled up. Her ingenuous responses had sparked a fire in his blood, and if he didn't watch himself, what Celene had kindled, Autumn Leaf might very well end up extinguishing.

"I think you've been with Peugeot's slut of a daughter," the Indian woman accused. "I think you spent the afternoon naked in her tent, mating like rabbits."

It was so far from the truth, Burke almost laughed. "It's none of your business where I've been."

Even through the gloom he could see the woman's face contort with anger, with the possessiveness he'd been fighting since the day Morning Song had died.

"I know you were in Peugeot's camp. I saw your shirt left out in the rain."

How many other people had noticed it, Burke wondered, and had drawn their own conclusions? And how would that effect Celene's reputation and safety while she was here at the rendezvous?

"All I was doing was keeping dry," he contended stubbornly.

"All you were doing was fucking that French whore."

Burke could feel his face get hot. "What Celene and I did or didn't do is no concern of yours."

"Isn't it? I think it's my concern since you are my dead sister's husband. I think you've forgotten the loyalty you owe to her. It is hardly six months since Morning Song died, and already you are taking up with someone else." Before Burke could draw breath to defend himself, Autumn Leaf continued. "I have not forgotten my loyalty to Morning Song as you have. She was your wife, and she should live in your heart as no other woman ever will. But you have forgotten. You have found someone else you fancy and put my sister out of your mind."

With the virulence of Autumn Leaf's reproach, the breathless pain of loss ripped through Cardwell's chest once more. It froze the air in his lungs and staggered the beat of his heart. He didn't need to be reminded of what Morning Song had meant to him. Every day seemed bleak without her presence; every night was long and dark. She had provided the only joy, the only real happiness he had ever known. He had shared his thoughts, his hopes, his life with her. How could anyone doubt his feelings? How could anyone doubt his loyalty or his love for his dead wife?

The soft stir of desire he had felt this afternoon with Celene Bernard was nothing compared to the passion Morning Song could rouse in him. He'd wanted to make love to her half a dozen times a day. How often had he kissed her awake, taken her to bed in the middle of the day, and made love beneath the starlit sky? He could not imagine needing or wanting a woman as much as he had needed or wanted his wife.

But perhaps Autumn Leaf was right. Perhaps he was being disloyal to Morning Song's memory by feeling anything at all. Was marrying Celene Bernard, even for expediency, a betrayal of all Morning Song had meant to him?

"You have forgotten how your wife loved you," Autumn Leaf accused, "forgotten that since Morning Song is dead you owe your loyalty to her sister. It is the custom, as you well know. Morning Song would hate that you have taken up with another woman. She would hate that you have asked this French whore to be your bride when you owe your allegiance to me.''

A wave of anger rolled through Burke as he realized Autumn Leaf meant to stir up his feelings of guilt and doubt so that she could win her way.

"I have forgotten nothing, owe you nothing!" he answered. "I don't want you as my wife, and nothing in Chippewa law decrees that I must marry you."

She moved toward him unexpectedly and caught his hand. Before he could jerk it away, she had raised it to her breast. He felt the fullness of her flesh beneath his palm, the upthrust of her nipple. He could smell the malice in her, smell her obsessive need for possession. Sick loathing swept through him.

"Perhaps there is nothing in Chippewa law, but our customs say that I am yours. If you want to take a woman, come to me. Peugeot's daughter is pale and ugly, too small to bear you fine strong sons. I will love you as you deserve to be loved, and give you many living children."

Another jolt of pain shot through Cardwell's chest as he pulled away. "Damn it!" he shouted. "I don't want you! Get away from me! I mean it, Autumn Leaf! You have no place in my life! You never will!"

She brushed close against his body as she moved toward the doorway. "You may not want me now, Eyes Like the Sky," she told him, "but there are ways to make you mine. Since you refuse to do the right and honorable thing, you leave me no other choice."

The words were ominous in the dark and damp, but before Burke could ask her what she meant, Autumn Leaf had swept aside the tent flaps and disappeared into the hissing downpour.

5

It was the murmur of men's voices that woke Celene just before dawn, the sound of her father and Burke Cardwell exchanging pleasantries. Their conversation gave evidence that once again Burke had spent the night by her campfire, and Celene had to admit she did feel safer knowing he had been watching over her. Still, for all Cardwell's cordiality, Antoine was taking advantage of his goodwill. While her father was spending his nights drinking and carousing, throwing himself into the rendezvous festivities, he was letting Burke provide protection that by rights should be up to Antoine.

Nor was that the only responsibility he was shirking. By leaving Celene to oversee the acceptance of the pelts he had bargained for, Antoine was not living up to his responsibilities to Monsieur LaVallier, either. Then again, Celene thought as she rubbed the sleep from her eyes, perhaps this was how her father comported himself at every rendezvous. Certainly such behavior would not have been out of character.

With a sigh, Celene dismissed her irritation and rolled out of bed. Since it was doubtful that trappers and traders who had spent the night in drunken revelry would be abroad at such an early hour, it seemed a good time for her to go down to the river for a bath. Perhaps she could even convince her father to keep watch while she bathed. Though she quickly gathered up what she would need, when she drew aside the tent flaps, neither Burke nor her father was outside.

Suspecting that Antoine had gone to refill the water keg, Celene turned in the direction of the river. As she ambled through the shimmering, dew-soaked landscape, the low, droning melody of a liturgical chant reached her ears. One of the priests attending the rendezvous was saying morning mass, and as she passed the grove where the faithful had gathered, the tinkling of the consecration bells brought Celene respectfully to her knees. The priest had pressed the flat, rounded bottom of an inverted canoe into service as an altar. In its center, on a heavily embroidered cloth, stood his golden chalice and paten. With a murmur of Latin, the priest raised the host, and Celene joined the worshipers in whispering the response. The chalice glinted in the rising sun as the priest lifted that toward the heavens, too. *"Mea culpa, mea culpa, mea maxima culpa,"* she replied with all the others, gently striking her breast. When the priest placed the chalice on the altar, Celene rose and moved away, the tang of incense drifting heavily on the damp, cool air, lingering in the mist that stalked the hollows along the riverbank.

Just as she was skirting one of the small coves at the river's edge, she caught sight of her father. He was deep in conversation with an Indian. She recognized the brave instantly. He was the one Burke had raced several nights before, the one named Darkening Sky. That Antoine barely reached the brave's shoulder did not deter Peugeot from poking a finger into the other man's chest as he argued his point. Curious to hear what the two were discussing so heatedly, Celene slipped behind a screen of willow trees and crept closer.

" . . . absolutely no interest in seeing Indian lands protected," she heard her father assure his companion as she moved to within earshot of the two men. "None at all."

"This is too important an issue for you to ignore," the Indian insisted, no less adamant in his assertion than her father had been. "I know there are men who would listen to your concerns if you chose to voice them."

Growing even more agitated, Antoine shook his head. "What you don't seem to understand is that years ago the land you want set aside for the Chippewa was promised to the whites. The old chiefs agreed—''

"Damn their agreements," the younger man cut in. "They didn't know what they were signing, what they were giving up."

"That's none of my affair."

"None of your affair!" Darkening Sky's face flushed with ire. "How can you say it's none of your affair when you were one of the men who helped explain to the old chiefs what those documents meant? How can you believe it's none of your affair when you were one of the men the Chippewa trusted?"

"I did what my employers told me to do. I had no choice, and now it is no longer my concern." As he spoke, Antoine bent to hoist the refilled water keg onto his shoulder and turned away.

"If you refuse to help us now," the brave went on, "when we most have need of you, you will be denying the only legacy your son and grandchildren will ever have."

Darkening Sky's words confused Celene. Did her father have a son in the Chippewa band? Did she have a half brother she had never even known about? Her muscles tightened, and her heart beat faster.

As the Indian went on, Celene noticed the sparks intensify in the brave's silver and green eyes. His eyes were exactly the same color as her father's, exactly the same shape, with the same dark wing of eyebrow sketched above them. For an instant Celene could not get her breath.

"Are you so callous," the brave continued, "that you will refuse us a chance to regain our lands, that you will deny your offspring the only opportunity we have for making a secure future? If you ignore my plea, if you hold your peace, that is exactly what you will be doing."

She saw her father's eyes spark with pain, and the tripping of her heart intensified.

"Please, monsieur," the Indian continued his impassioned plea, "speak now while the fate of the lands is still being decided. Do what you can to secure a real future for your children's children and the whole of the Chippewa nation. Do this now and I will never ask anything of you again."

As the two men stood facing her, the meaning of their words and the similarities between them erased any doubts Celene might have had about the Indian's lineage. Darkening Sky was Antoine's son. She caught her breath, quivering with confusion, aching with the need to deny the truth. But who was Darkening Sky's mother? When and where had he been born? Why hadn't Antoine seen fit to mention him once in all these years? Betrayal burned through her insides. It was so like her father to keep this from her.

Her father's face crumpled with defeat. "I will do the things you ask, *mon fils*," Antoine finally conceded, "but I warn you, it will do no good."

Having Antoine call Darkening Sky "my son" was the ultimate confirmation. Disillusionment and anger racked Celene. Why hadn't her father told her about Darkening Sky? Didn't he think she would want to know? How many other people were aware of the connection between the two of them? Had Burke known the other night when she and her half brother had come face to face for the very first time? And if he had, why hadn't he told her who the Indian was?

With his face set in lines of pain, Antoine stalked away. Both his children watched him go, and to Celene he was suddenly not as bold and invincible as she had always imagined him to be. He seemed tarnished and weary, weary in a way that cut through spirit and bone.

When Antoine was far enough away, Darkening Sky turned directly to where Celene was hiding. "You may come out, *ma soeur*. I have waited a very long time to greet you properly."

Horrified and fascinated by what she had just discovered, by her half brother's greeting, Celene rose from her crouch and scrambled down the slope at the edge of the muddy beach. She stopped a mere foot from the brother she had never known, drinking him in, compelled to seek similarities between them.

His eyes were exactly the color of hers, with the same thatch of lashes, the same angled brows. But that was where the resemblance began and ended. Celene took after her fair-haired German mother with her pale skin and broad features, just as Darkening Sky must have taken after Antoine's Indian wife. It must be from her that he had inherited his height, his graceful proportions and long limbs, his high forehead and narrow lips.

"I saw that you were hidden in the trees listening to our father and me," he told Celene, anticipating her question.

"The night you raced Burke Cardwell, did you know I was your half sister?"

"I should have known, but I did not—not until I asked what fool had brought a white woman to a rendezvous."

Celene fought to suppress a smile. "I didn't give Papa any choice about bringing me, and now I'm doubly glad I came."

Though his expression didn't change, she could see new warmth in the Indian's eyes.

"I didn't even know I had a brother until just now," she told him.

"I have known about you all your life."

"But why would Father tell you about me when he said nothing to me about you?"

"He did not have to tell me. I have known about you from the day you were born. I knew about my white brother, too—when he was born and when he died."

Emotion closed her throat and tears pooled in Celene's eyes. "You knew about Emile?"

Darkening Sky nodded again. "What happened to him?"

"He was drowned," Celene told him, fighting for breath around the ache at the base of her throat. Emile had been young and vital and carefree, infinitely dear to everyone who knew him. Both she and her father had been staggered by his loss. "The canoe he and father were paddling ran into a snag in the river and capsized. Father tried to save him, but the current was too swift. We never found his body. And since that day I have never been able to look at the river without seeing an overturned canoe, without being afraid."

Her half brother reached across to clasp her arm, to convey his sympathy for the loss of a boy he had never known. His palm was callused and broad, his fingers firm and reassuring even through the rough fabric of her sleeve. But with the touch, something warm and nourishing flowed between them. It was a strong, tingling current, a connection of spirit that suddenly and irrevocably bound them both. Celene looked up into her half brother's eyes, felt the noose of tears draw close at the base of her throat, sensed an answering emotion rising in him. And she knew that if they never saw each other after today, they would never be strangers again.

It took a moment for each of them to recover themselves. Finally Celene spoke. "Do I have other brothers and sisters I don't know about?"

The Indian shook his head. "Our father was with my mother for only four years. Less than a year after he met and married his white wife, he gave my mother up. He found a trapper who was a kind man and offered him a dowry of many pelts so that we would be treated properly."

The consideration her father had shown this Indian woman revealed a side of him Celene did not know. Had Antoine really given up the convenience of having a country wife so he could remain faithful to her mother? Antoine must have loved her mother very much to go to such lengths to honor his vows. It seemed so out of character for him, and yet she was pleased that her father was capable of such loyalty and concern.

"But you had come down to the water to have a bath," Darkening Sky said, interrupting Celene's thoughts.

"How did you . . ."

With a nod of his head, he indicated the objects in her arms.

"Oh, of course."

"And you were hoping that our father would keep watch while you bathed."

"But he's returned to the campsite now and must be wondering where I am."

Darkening Sky paused almost imperceptibly, cocking his head to one side. "No, he has stopped to talk to an old friend. There will be time. If you want, I will keep watch for you."

Celene instinctively and implicitly trusted Darkening

Sky. "If you're sure that you don't mind . . ."

"There's a shallow spot just beyond those trees."

"I know the place."

He settled himself on a rock not far from the fringe of whispering willows. "It would not be wise to take too long," he called after her.

Within minutes Celene had bathed, washed her hair, and returned to the place where her Indian brother was waiting. His warning about needing to hurry had been a valid one, for already there were men making their way down the bank. Some had come to fill water kegs as her father had, others were checking on their canoes, a few had come to wash.

One man stood at the river's edge making his stream, and when Darkening Sky saw what he was doing, he snorted in disgust. "Whites like him will foul the water with their filth, rape the forests, and ravage the land. In the end that will kill them all, but they will not realize what they've done until it is far too late to save themselves."

Celene didn't know how to respond to her brother's dire prophecy. There was something in his face as he spoke the words that made her believe they were true. Yet how could he, how could anyone, know or predict the future?

She had no time to ponder what Darkening Sky had said, because a moment later she came face to face with Pierre Rivard on the narrow path to the top of the rise.

Recognition was instantaneous. Both of them jerked to a halt. Celene's eyes widened with surprise and dread; Rivard's narrowed with cunning and malice.

"*Bonjour*, Mademoiselle Peugeot," Rivard greeted her with a sneer.

"Madame Bernard," she corrected him.

"Oh, pardon me, madame," he apologized with a nod of his head. "We've not been properly introduced."

"Only because there was nothing proper or friendly about our meeting."

"Then perhaps you'll agree to walk with me so we can rectify the situation?"

Instead of answering, Celene tried to brush past him on the narrow trail.

Rivard reached out and caught her arm. "I think I really would like to talk to you, *ma belle*. Perhaps I could show you some things in my camp, some things I think you might enjoy."

Celene set her heels and tried to wrench away.

Rivard's grip on her elbow tightened. Tingles of pain ran up her arm. "I'll show you a few things in my tent, and then we'll talk about the money your father owes—"

From somewhere behind her Darkening Sky appeared, looming over her like a protective spirit.

Rivard took a half-step back.

"If you harm her," the Indian offered quietly, "you will die. If you touch her after today, the birds will pick your bones."

Her half brother's words were unexpectedly harsh and seemed more a statement than a threat. In spite of Rivard's punishing grip, Celene turned to look at the Indian.

Darkening Sky's mouth was drawn with determination, but his eyes had gone blank, flat, and as impenetrable as silver mirrors. "The birds will pick your bones," he repeated in a soft, slow voice. "I will see to it myself that they have the chance."

Rivard's hand abruptly dropped away, and at a nudge from Darkening Sky, Celene scrambled up the slope.

"This isn't over," Rivard called after her. "Tell your father it won't be over until he pays us what he owes."

Turning back, the Indian caught the front of Rivard's shirt, jerking the Frenchman off the ground. "Hurt her and you die. You have been warned."

Then, dropping Rivard as a crow might a bit of carrion, Darkening Sky followed his newfound sister up the path.

After nearly six months of jerky, pemmican, and dried fish, the dinner of roast duckling with a maple sugar and whiskey sauce, wild rice, baked squash, and biscuits must have seemed to Burke Cardwell a meal fit for a king. He said as much when Celene set the plates before her father and him, but Antoine Peugeot waited until the meal was over, until the bottle of tart red wine had been consumed before he reached across and patted his daughter's hand.

"A fine dinner, *ma cher*," he commended her.

Celene flushed with pleasure at his praise, though she noticed as she cleared the plates away that he had eaten very little. Still, she was glad Antoine had decided to join them for the evening meal. She had seen very little of him in the last few days and was torn between exasperation at his frequent absences and loneliness when he was gone. Had they taken their evening meal *en famille*, she might well have told her father about meeting Darkening Sky and garnered his response. But having Cardwell as a dinner guest prevented that, and she chafed at the constraint the trapper's company forced upon her.

Still, it had been a very good day. Not only had she met Darkening Sky, but she had sold six hams at prices that would enable Jean-Paul and her to live quite comfortably until the harvest. And, under the protection of both men, Celene was going to venture as far as the central campfire to sample a bit of the evening's entertainment.

As Celene washed up the dishes, her father and Burke Cardwell settled themselves by the fire and lit their pipes. Sitting there together, they seemed opposites in every way: the small, grizzled trader, wrinkled and world-weary, his shoulders curled inward so that he seemed huddled around the warmth of his pipe bowl, and the strapping young trapper, broad, clear-faced, sitting with knees and elbows wide, ready to take on the world. They were the father she loved in spite of herself, and the man who, for reasons of his own, wanted to take her as his bride.

Across the clearing Celene studied Burke. He had arrived for supper with an ornate birch-bark mocock filled with maple sugar candy, but it was not the gift he'd brought that had taken Celene so much by surprise. It was that Cardwell was bathed and freshly shaved, revealing the strong chin and angular jaw that had been hidden beneath his unruly snarl of chin whiskers. The mustache that had obscured his upper lip was gone as well, and Celene could not help but notice that Burke's mouth was mobile and expressive. It seemed a mouth that was likely to narrow with anger, curl with disdain, soften with tenderness or the hint of a smile. Bare-faced, with his freshly cut hair bound back in a queue,

Burke had miraculously changed from an unkempt, intimidating man to a heart-stoppingly handsome one.

Without his beard Cardwell seemed younger, more accessible, more compelling. Just looking at him brought a curious tightness to Celene's throat and a wash of hot blood to her cheeks. It stirred memories of how his beard and mustache had rasped against her skin, of how he'd pressed those full, faintly smiling lips to hers. She remembered the strange fluttering that had swelled and risen in her chest, her unexpected willingness to kiss Burke back. She had been confused by the sensations he had roused, unsettled by how much she had enjoyed the simple intimacy, disappointed when he had withdrawn from her. The memory of what had happened the previous afternoon, the knowledge that from across the clearing Burke was scrutinizing her every move, set her cheeks to burning more brightly and turned her clumsy even at these oft-repeated tasks.

At length, when the dishes were finished and put away, the three of them made their way through the last blue wash of daylight toward the center of the encampment. Some of the traders from New Orleans and Montreal were still selling their wares by lantern light. But most of the concessions were already closed, and the trappers had begun to gather in the glow of the central campfire.

As fresh wood was heaped over the fierce, red heart of the blaze, sparks erupted toward the purpling sky. Firelight bronzed the faces of those who had been drawn into the circle by the need for companionship or by the strains of a familiar song. A man with a violin joined the Frenchman who had been squeezing tunes from an ancient concertina, and he caught up with the lilting melody at the refrain. One by one other musicians joined the band. They came playing mouth organs, Indian flutes, ocarinas, and bright tin whistles. Without moving from where the three of them had settled themselves in the shadows, Antoine pulled out his own harmonica and began to play along. The instruments blended surprisingly well, providing a pleasant accompaniment for the transition from twilight to dark.

As the music swelled, the men around the fire began to sing. They burst forth with the rousing melodies the voy-

ageurs used to pass the toil and miles of the yearly trips
from Montreal, raised their voices in bawdy ballads with
words that scorched Celene's uninitiated ears, turned mel-
ancholy with soft, sweet songs of unrequited love. Both
Burke and her father joined in the singing. They knew all
the melodies, all the words, and seated between them, listening to their voices blending with half a hundred others,
she was caught up in the bittersweet mood of the rendezvous. Suddenly Celene understood that each year's gathering was a celebration edged with sadness, a gathering that
could never dispel each trapper's loneliness, an inexorable
measure of both the moments and the months, the joys and
sorrows of each man's life.

After a time a more skillful fiddler joined the band,
and the music turned to jigs and reels. Some of the men
began to dance, alone or in groups of two or three. It
wasn't long before several of them came to haul Antoine
to his feet, and in spite of his protests, he soon joined
them in their frolic. Circling the campfire in time to the
music, each of the dancers tried to outdo the others.
Gracefully they leaped and whirled, performing intricate
steps, calling out insults or encouragement, driven to ever
more complicated steps by the competition and by the
fiery cascade of notes and rills. As they spun and swirled
through the smoke and firelight, the long, braided sashes
and their knee and elbow garters flared around them. Orange and gold reflections winked from the polished-silver
medallions sewn to the voyageurs' knitted caps. The men
spun around the fire in a blur, the pattern of their steps
becoming ever more frenzied and complex as the music
swept toward its crescendo. And when it ended, the men
threw their arms around each other, hooting and laughing
breathlessly as they made their way toward where drinks
could be procured.

As her father moved off with his cronies, Celene became
uncomfortably aware that Burke was still beside her. Even
seated, he was a full head taller than she: big, broad, overwhelming, and unpredictable. She sat up straighter, shifted
away. Still, the heat of him seeped through her clothes. His
nearness sent ripples of awareness chasing along her

nerves. She fought to ignore the power of his masculinity, struggled to concentrate on the music, on the trappers who continued to dance. In spite of her determination to ignore the man beside her, she failed miserably at the task.

She stole looks at Cardwell from beneath her downcast lashes, and with each one, her gaze skimmed the smoothness of his cheek, dropped to the sharp turn of his jaw, dipped lower to the muscular column of his neck. As she studied him, she could not help but wonder what it would be like to press her cheek to his, to trace the angle of his jaw with her lips, to lave the half-moon hollow newly revealed at the base of his throat. They were new thoughts, frightening, unexpected thoughts, but she was intrigued by the possibilities in spite of herself.

Beside her Burke stirred uncomfortably, almost as if he were able to discern what she was thinking. His face, in the reflected firelight, looked every bit as flushed as hers.

Abruptly he came to his feet. "Someone somewhere's making apple fritters," he announced a trifle too loudly, offering her his hand, "and there's nothing I like any better."

They followed the sweet-tart smell of apples through the compound and found that a man from New Orleans was selling mounds of the confections to an eager crowd. Buying an order of fritters, steaming hot and dusted with real white sugar from the Santo Domingo, Burke and Celene continued their ambling tour of the camp. All sorts of activities were underway, each keeping time with the music that drifted through the encampment.

Contests of strength and skill went on wherever the men gathered. Gambling brought the trappers and traders to their knees with an eagerness any priest might envy.

As she and Cardwell stood watching the gaming, Celene became aware of an Indian woman eyeing them from behind one of the nearby tents. Though her face was cloaked in shadow, Celene thought she was the woman she'd seen with Burke, the one called Autumn Leaf. Even in the darkness Celene could sense the longing and frustration in her eyes. There was something malevolent in the way the woman stared at Burke, something dire and dark about her presence. It set a chill of premonition blossoming between Celene's shoulder blades, a flicker of apprehension skittering down her spine. She reached out to touch Burke's arm, to draw his attention to the woman, to express her concern. But as if sensing Celene's intent, the squaw abruptly turned away. Shaken, Celene stared after her.

Unaware of what had transpired, Burke took her elbow and steered Celene between two tents. The paths that wound through the encampment were crowded and it seemed that the entire population of Prairie du Chien was on parade.

"Is it usually as busy as this?" she asked as they brushed past an Indian girl selling handsome birch-bark boxes, decorated with porcupine quill designs.

Burke shook his head. "Not every night. The trappers who have been here since the beginning of the rendezvous will be heading upriver tomorrow. Tonight is their last chance to enjoy themselves. Some will be back in the fall, but most will be too far upcountry to return until spring."

"And the biggest rendezvous is in the spring?"

Burke nodded. "It's when a trapper has the best fur to trade. An animal's coat thickens in the winter, and pelts taken then are of the highest quality."

"But winters this far north are very cold."

"It's not easy running traps in the winter or wading hip-deep in icy streams to retrieve them," he agreed, "but there are fortunes to be made."

"Is that why you are here? To make your fortune?"

"Money's only important to a man if he has something he wants to spend it on," Cardwell observed.

Celene sent him a sidelong glance, but before she could pursue Burke's motives further, he steered her toward where nearly a score of men were huddled around a campfire. "Gabriel Belanger is telling stories," Burke whispered in explanation as they took places at the edge of the crowd. Heads nodded cordially in Burke's direction, but no one spoke. And in a moment it was evident why.

Belanger sat at the far side of the circle, a short, rotund man with a round, dark-skinned face that was accented by a pointy white beard and eyebrows that flared up like birds on the wing. Beneath his brows his eyes shimmered green as bottle glass, and from his cherublike mouth issued forth a voice that was as mellow and rich as honeyed wine. In an instant it was clear that Belanger was a true raconteur, a weaver of spells, a teller of tales, a revealer of truths. He knew what was buried deep in his listeners' hearts and understood how to tap their most deeply held emotions. With nothing more than his compelling voice and the graceful movement of his hands, he was able to leave his listeners touched and fascinated, entertained and enthralled.

As they settled themselves on the ground, Celene could not help wishing that Jean-Paul was here with her. He loved stories of any kind, from the old French lore passed down through the generations to the tales of her father's adventures as a voyageur. The boy would have been mesmerized by Gabriel's drama and skill. He would have sat for hours, just as the men around the circle seemed prepared to do.

Belanger was in the midst of telling the Indian legend of Old Crooked Nose and how he had earned his name in an encounter with the Great Spirit. In less than a moment they were caught up in the story, watching breathlessly as Belanger, in the guise of the Great Spirit, motioned the immovable mountains nearer. It was just what Old Crooked Nose had done some moments before, but to no advantage. They listened to the Great Spirit's deep-voiced command that the mountain do *his* bidding. Caught up in the story, Celene could almost hear the ground rumble as the mountain slid closer, could almost feel the mashing of the Indian's nose as he turned his head against the solid rock wall that had sprung up beside him. Celene and Burke applauded when the tale was done and were as eager as the others to hear more.

"Tell the story about the Ice Queen and the prince," someone called out.

"Or the one about the how the rabbit got his long ears."

"Tell the one about the foolish *manger du lard* and his first trip to Fort Mackinac."

Belanger's bright green gaze swept around the circle. His eyes narrowed and his eyebrows rose in what might have been recognition or surprise as they came to rest on Burke.

A smile snagged the corners of the storyteller's mouth and twisted them upward, both mischief and malice in his expression. "Is that really the story you want to hear?"

Beside her Burke shifted on his haunches.

"*Oui*, tell us about the pork eater," a man in a blue knitted cap called out. "I've not heard that tale in many years."

Belanger swept around the circle again as if to gauge his listeners' interest in the tale, his eyes burning brighter, lit with emerald sparks. "Very well," he said.

"It was not long after the treaty with England was signed," the raconteur began, casting another glance at Burke, "that we reported one morning to our bourgeois in Montreal. He was an ambitious man, one who cared not what he did to make his pay. As we prepared to load our *canot*, we found a tall, fair-faced Englishman lying drunk in the bottom of the boat. We tried to rouse him, and when we could not, we asked the bourgeois what to do. He told us to let him sleep, and so we loaded the *canot* around him. We loaded the boat, waved *au revoir* to our wives and families, and set off down the St. Lawrence without the young fellow ever waking up. We paddled for a distance, and, as is the custom, we stopped at the end of the island to make an offering at St. Anne's church to insure our safety on the voyage.

"I thought that surely such a callow fellow, so obviously unused to the wilds and off to such a shaky start, would be in need of God's help and blessing, so I shook the man awake and led him in the direction of the chapel. As you also know, when they reach the church each voyageur is to put a mite in the poor box and pray for his soul. But this *manger du lard* had not a sou to his name and lost his dinner on the steps to the chapel instead."

She heard Burke draw a hissing breath and turned to glance at him. His shoulders had tightened, his back had gone stiff. But before she could account for the change in his demeanor, Belanger's fluid voice drew her attention.

"The Englishman's offense against God was an omen of things to come. That night, clambering out of the canoe, he put his foot through the bottom and nearly sank it—and himself—in the river. The next day he lost his paddle and later dropped the packs he was portaging into the rapids below. We came to call him 'Trouble,' for it accompanied him wherever he went.

"Trouble was not suited to the life of a voyageur. He was like a grasshopper with legs too long to fit in a canoe, like a woman with arms too weak for the hours of constant paddling. Our pipe smoke made him cough. The pea soup and salt pork he was given to eat did not fill him up. And it seems he was unable to sleep on the cold, hard ground.

"One night not far from Lake Nipissing, he made his bed in the tall, soft grass. But very late, when the moon was down, he was awakened by a strange buzzing sound. He sat up and looked around just as a rattlesnake slithered out from between his legs. It had come out of its hole only to share the warmth of his blanket, but Trouble was a most inhospitable host. He killed the snake with his bare hands. In his search for a comfortable bed, Trouble had lain down just above the rattlesnake's nest. How he survived that adventure, none of us will ever know. But he did, and he plagued us with his presence day after miserable day."

As his voice rang through the clearing, Belanger glanced at Burke again, his gaze focused narrowly on his face.

"It seems that Trouble was a rich man's son," Belanger went on, "come from England to Montreal for a visit. He maintained that he was carried off into the wilds by some mistake, but the *commis*, the clerk of our battalion of canoes, said that someone had paid our bourgeois well to take the young man away and see that he never returned. He had been trouble to his family, just as he was trouble to us.

"Trouble knew nothing of life in the wilds, and to keep him, and ourselves, from further disasters, we gave him the job of starting the campfire while we unloaded the goods for the night. He performed the duty satisfactorily until one evening when the wind was blowing hard. That night he chose to make the fire inside his fine beaver hat. But try as he might, he could not get the char to catch. To remedy this, he added a bit of black powder to the mix. And when the char still refused to flame, he added a little more. And a little more. And more. And more."

Around the circle Belanger's listeners were chuckling, edging forward, anticipating what would surely happen next. Celene was drawn like all the rest, but beside her, Burke seemed able to resist Belanger's mesmerizing spell.

"We saw the flare of light when the tinder finally caught," Gabriel continued, "like a ball of fire it was, billowing toward the sky. It was orange and yellow and blue, and we stopped what we were doing to watch it rise into the treetops. But before any of us could guess what Trouble had done, he came pelting toward where we were standing on the beach, his shirtsleeve all aflame. He was in the water faster than a weasel skitters off a bank, and while he doused his clothes, we built our fire around his hat."

A laugh of delight rose from the men who had gathered to hear the story, their faces wreathed in grins for the greenhorn's foolishness and misfortune. Cardwell mumbled something under his breath, his fists balled in his lap, his glare leveled at the man who was telling 'Trouble's' tale. Celene sent Burke a quelling glance.

"Trouble became no more proficient a woodsman or voyageur as we continued toward Fort Mackinac. After the portage at *le Grand Ricolet*, the canoe that he was tending was sucked away from the bank and under the falls. We lost the canoe and a quarter of its goods. Trouble nearly drown. Then he stumbled off the trail at *la Grande Chaudière*. It was a most unfortunate trip for all concerned, and it is a wonder we did not bury Trouble on the way."

"What happened to him in the end?" someone called out.

"The story has a sad ending, I'm afraid. For all the difficulties that Trouble caused us, he was a winning lad. And before we reached Fort Mackinac, we had grown quite fond of him. But we reached the fort in June of 1763, just before the Chippewa made fools of the British and captured the fort. The Indians waged their battle with guile and cunning, and afterward killed many of English blood. We French were best served by blockading ourselves inside the houses within the fort's walls and letting the Indians do their worst. Trouble must have died with the many English who were slain because, until this day, he has never been seen or heard from again.''

As he spoke the very last words of 'Trouble's' tale, Belanger's voice went low and deep, hovering and echoing around the campfire like the final notes of a requiem. Around Celene the storyteller's listeners gave Trouble the moment of silence his untimely death deserved.

Then suddenly Burke was on his feet, glaring across at Belanger with glowing, ice-cold eyes. As Celene turned to stare up at him, she saw that Cardwell's face had lost its definition, that it seemed flat and unyielding as weathered stone. His mouth was narrowed, his lips white and pinched together.

Belanger met Cardwell's stare across the circle, a challenge in the Frenchman's face.

She could feel Burke's defiance mounting, emanating from him in waves. She could see how tightly his muscles were wound along his limbs, sense how sternly his breathing was repressed. She felt buffeted by the wash of the forces inside him, felt inexplicable sympathy, undeniable awe.

"Well, *mon ami*, have you something to add to the tale of our *manger du lard*?'' Belanger baited, aware that the trappers who had gathered to hear his stories were avidly watching the confrontation.

Burke drew a hissing breath, as if straining to suppress both his feelings and his words.

"I have met the man you know as Trouble,'' Cardwell finally announced. "He was taken at Fort Mackinac by a Chippewa brave and lived among the Indians for many years. He learned the Indian ways and took a wife, trapping and trading to support her. He moved farther and farther west. He trapped the Athabasca River, became an Athabasca man.''

With the slightest of nods, Cardwell acknowledged the murmurs of awe from the men around him. Becoming an Athabasca man and prospering in the very depths of the wilderness was something only the bravest and most skillful trappers aspired to.

"He proved himself.'' Burke's voice sounded as if it was

being dragged from his throat. "No matter what Trouble once was, no matter what you remember of him. He proved himself as a trapper, as a trader—and as a man."

The others were utterly silent as Cardwell spoke, watching the wily raconteur and the defiant free trapper, feeling the animosity, the battle of wills being waged between them.

"And is he in the wilderness still?" Belanger asked quietly.

"No, he's not. During his years in the wilds Trouble took many rich pelts and became a very wealthy man. He returned to England then, to the bosom of his family. It was something he had to do, a way to regain his self-respect. He made it his business to learn who it was that sold him to the bourgeois in Montreal, who it was that wanted him dead. And he had his revenge—a very satisfying revenge. Or so I'm told. He lives now in a fine manor house in England, happy with his life and rich as any king."

Cardwell's words might have been a clap of thunder for the way the last syllables reverberated in the silence.

Slowly Belanger smiled, a smile that set his round cheeks bobbing but did not reach his eyes. "I think you take licence with the tale, *mon ami*, but if you swear what you've said is true, I will change my story accordingly."

Burke nodded, his mouth set. "Then change your story, Belanger. What I've told you is the truth, and Trouble's story deserves a better ending than the one you've always given it."

The old man nodded and dropped his gaze. "As you say, Cardwell. Trouble deserves a better ending, and I am glad he has become a man we can all admire."

Damn fool! Goddamn fool! Burke cursed himself as he spun away from the group of people gathered around the fire, away from their curious stares, away from the craven certainty that had sparked to life in the storyteller's eyes. Here, where no one need acknowledge his past, where every man was accepted for who or what he claimed to be, it was madness to speak out. Yet Cardwell had felt compelled to set 'Trouble's' story straight, to bring it to what he hoped would be its logical conclusion. It was just as well that he would be leaving the wilderness when the rendezvous was over. For here, where he'd lived without notoriety for eleven long years, he would never be anonymous again.

"Burke! Burke?" From some way behind, Celene's voice reached him. She sounded concerned, uncertain, breathless.

He slowed his steps. He had no idea where he was going, no desire for her company. Yet when she lay a hand upon his arm, he turned to her.

"Burke, are you all right?"

In the light of one of the lanterns, he could see her face: a determined face, broad at the cheekbones and jaw; a full, inviting mouth, with questions poised on her half-open lips; wide silver-green eyes, alight with concern and curiosity.

Damn her, he thought in frustration and caught her against his chest. Damn her, and damn him, too.

To silence what she was preparing to ask, he slanted his lips across her mouth and bound her more tightly to him. When she made no real effort to escape his embrace, Burke deliberately deepened the kiss, enveloping her mouth with his. He sought the seam of her lips, teased it with the tip of her tongue. After a moment's hesitation, she opened to him. Her sweetness flowed into his mouth, the subtle spice of apples and cinnamon, the potent tang of curiosity and incipient surrender. The lush swell of her breasts and hips contouring to his long-limbed frame set Burke's responses flaring up like tinder in the wind. He gave himself over to the luxury of her delicious femininity, becoming more aware of the woman in his arms than of the questions and suspicions he was trying to quell, becoming more conscious of his need for intimate contact than of the world around them.

"Celene," he breathed into her mouth. "Oh, God, Celene!"

Yet his raw, impassioned words seemed to break, rather than intensify, the sensual bond between them. Celene pushed away and looked up into his face. As she did, he could see the rosy hue of her freshly kissed mouth, the intensity of the color in her cheeks. But sparks of curiosity were still bright in her eyes, undimmed by the passion he had tried to rouse in her.

Gently but firmly she withdrew from him, and Cardwell let her go with unfeigned reluctance. "I want you to tell me the rest of the story," she said when she was beyond the sphere of his embrace.

"What story?"

"You know very well what story. Belanger's story. Trouble's story."

Cardwell shook his head gravely, as if what she was asking were impossible.

"Your story."

He looked away from her upturned face, looked beyond her, toward where the flames from the central campfire licked toward the ebony sky. There was no one he could blame for this, Burke thought wearily. No one had forced him to admit what he had; he had betrayed himself. This curiosity was the price he must pay for speaking out. Celene was only the first of many who would want to know the truth.

"Burke, I saw the scar," she reminded him gently, "the burn on your forearm. You got it trying to start a fire with gunpowder, didn't you?"

There was a heaviness in his chest. "No."

"The story Belanger was telling was how you came to the Northwest."

"No, it's not."

"It doesn't matter that you were green and inexperienced."

"It's not my story. I'm not Trouble."

"Not anymore. But you were once, and I want to know how you came to be the man you are."

He could sense the wearing persistence in her, the absolute determination to learn the truth. Her doggedness was awe-inspiring.

Burke didn't want to admit to being Trouble. Trouble had been an arrogant, careless bastard, a braggart and a fool. On the trip west he had nearly cost several of the voyageurs their lives. He was ashamed of how Trouble had behaved, appalled at how Trouble had treated the other men. And now for reasons he could not comprehend, Burke as much as admitted his secret to the world.

"Please, Burke," Celene continued. "You've offered for my hand. You've said you want me for your wife. Don't you think I deserve to have my questions answered where your past is concerned?"

Cardwell didn't have an argument for that. It made him furious all over again. Muttering the most vile imprecations he knew, he caught Celene's elbow and swung her around.

"Where are we going?" she demanded, setting her heels. They left two long furrows in the earth as he pulled her along.

"We're going to my tent. If you're determined to hear the whole of this, you'll hear it there or not at all."

He could see the skepticism in her face, the mutinous set of her jaw. It was pure curiosity that made her give in. Once inside the lean-to, Burke struck fire with flint and steel—without benefit of gunpowder—and lit a betty lamp.

"Sit down," he ordered and indicated his bed of skins and blankets.

After glancing around for some less intimate alternative, Celene sat. Burke eased himself down beside her.

She took off her hat, set it between them, and moistened her lips. The latter gesture made Burke think of at least ten things he would rather do than try to explain his past to her.

"Well?" she prodded, none too gently. "I'm here and you've promised me the whole story."

He sighed, settled back on one elbow, and stretched his long legs before him.

"I was just eighteen when my grandfather decided I was in need of a trip to Montreal," he began. "I thought of it as exile of sorts. I'd been giving the old man fits since I was old enough to toddle, and that term I hadn't exactly been the most diligent student Cambridge had ever seen. I was more caught up in playing pranks than reading books, more intent on guzzling wine than quaffing knowledge. I kept more regular company with the women of the town than I did with the dons. But what really set him off was that I dueled with the son of one of his friends over the attentions of a whore and jabbed a good-size hole in him. That I'd face off with someone I'd known most of my life made Grandfather furious, so he sent me away.

"My family had holdings in Montreal: land, an interest in one of the fur-trading firms, ownership of a good many ships that plied their trade between Quebec and Bristol. I wasn't sorry to put my studies aside for a spot of adventure, and when I arrived, I found nearly as many saloons and pretty girls on this side of the Atlantic as on the other.

"We had been in Montreal nearly three weeks when my grandfather's solicitor, who had never seemed particularly fond of me, suggested a night on the town. I got drunk, of course. I don't know that I had so much to drink that he could load me into a canoe without my being aware of it, but I suppose it's possible. Maybe he drugged me; I don't know. All I remember is that one minute my hand was up some barmaid's skirt, and the next Belanger had his fists tangled in my shirtfront and was hauling me out of the bottom of a canoe."

"Did you really throw up on the steps of St. Anne's?" There was laughter in Celene's voice.

Burke nodded, letting himself smile in answer. It was as ignoble a moment as a man could have, but time had allowed him to see the humor in it.

"And did you really try to start a fire with gunpowder?"

Burke rubbed the spot where the scar was hidden beneath his sleeve. "Yes."

"Then everything Belanger said was true?"

"I'm afraid it was, as far as he knew."

"But how did you escape the Chippewa's attack on Fort Mackinac? Why did Belanger think you'd died?"

"Surely you've heard the story of what happened at the fort: how the Indians drew practically all the soldiers out of the compound by playing and betting heavily on a particularly spirited game of lacrosse, how they finally sent the ball flying through the fort's front gates, how they chased it inside and returned fully armed with guns and knives. They killed or imprisoned virtually every Englishman on the field."

"How did you escape?"

Burke shrugged, his face gone dark. "Through no cleverness of my own, I assure you. I had been watching them play lacrosse. It was a game I had never seen before, and I was fascinated by the Indians' skill and speed. And of course, I had placed a bet or two. I was at the far end of the field when the Indians came out of the fort with their weapons, so I had some small advantage. Though I gave them a run for their money, several of the braves caught up to me just at the edge of the woods. Two of them held me down while a third prepared to cleave my skull in two. But as I fought to break free, my left sleeve ripped away. The third man froze with the war club in midswing, falling back as if I were some apparition. The other two seemed every bit as terrified. After a few moments the brave who had been about to strike me down caught my arm and brushed aside the cloth. He stared at the burn for a very long time. It was just healing then. It was red and raw. Once he'd had his fill of looking, he extended his left forearm for me to see. He had a birthmark in the very same place. It was exactly identical in size and shape."

With her seated so close beside him, Cardwell could see an eerie shiver shake Celene.

"The Indian said the scar and the birthmark made us brothers of the same skin," Burke continued. "He said that he'd seen our reunion in a vision. He also assured me that no matter what happened to the others, I would not die. Lone Wolf kept his word. While other Englishmen at the fort were being tortured and killed, he took me away and adopted me into his family to keep me safe."

Though Burke's voice faded into silence, the memories of those dangerous days and the knowledge of all he owed Lone Wolf were as vivid as ever. His throat closed with guilt at being one of the few Englishmen to survive the capture of Fort Mackinac, with sorrow that circumstances had changed his relationship to Lone Wolf, with regret that the man who had saved his life and become his most trusted friend would soon be part of his past.

Celene must have sensed his mood. Though there was no way for her to guess what prompted Burke's feelings of anger, self-loathing, and grief, she reached out to him, slipping free the elk horn button at his left wrist and pushing back his sleeve.

"And this is what saved your life?" she asked.

Cardwell nodded.

Celene's fingertips skimmed the inner surface of his forearm, tracing the scar. "It's almost the shape of a bird in flight. You can see its body, the breadth of its wings."

Her touch was provocative, soft and tickly, like being stroked with feathers, with milkweed down. Waves of shivers broke across Burke's shoulders and trickled along his ribs.

"Celene . . ."

He knew what she was offering was comfort, comfort for the confused and frightened youth he'd been. Yet, when she touched him with such exquisite tenderness, with such ingenuous provocation, he could not prevent himself from responding as the man he had become.

"Celene."

His voice was deep with a warning he hoped she would not heed. He wanted to feel her hands drift over him, stroking his forearms and his wrists, his calloused palms and the pads of his fingers. He wanted her to touch him in places he dared not even think about.

"Celene?"

His skin began to throb in time to the beating of his heart. He couldn't seem to get his breath. Did she know what she was doing to him?

"Celene!"

She looked into his eyes. Hers were bright and mysterious, shimmering like moonglow. Dazzled by their brightness, Burke felt compromised, mesmerized, lost.

She shifted beside him, her fingers furrowing through the dusting of hair on the back of his forearm as her thumb played soothingly over the pale, puckered scar. Then abruptly her hold tightened; she pulled him closer. She leaned across to brush his lips with hers. Softly. Experimentally.

Heat melted through him. It seared the skin of his face

and throat, sluiced through his veins, rose in him turgid, hard, and hot.

"Celene." His hands came to tighten around her shoulders. Nudging her hat aside, he tumbled her down beside him on the bed of blankets and furs. The small calico pomander bag she wore on a ribbon around her neck slipped out of her shirt. The air was filled with the scent of spicy, sweet lavender.

As they lay there side by side, their lips still fused, she murmured something that sounded warm and intimate. It was a seductive sound, throaty, rich, and welcoming.

Burke rolled above her and deepened the kiss, his lips encompassing hers, nibbling, drawing her in. His tongue explored the widening seam between her lips, slid along her teeth, dipped into the honeyed cavern beyond. She shuddered in his embrace, quivered as if with pleasure, and met the tip of his tongue with hers. With lips brushing and bodies tangled close, they played the age-old game of chase and challenge, engaged in a flirtation so intimate and provocative that it seemed to presage something more.

Burke was swept up in the promise of pleasures to come. His blood thundered in his ears; his breath shuddered in harsh, uneven gasps. His body throbbed, responding potently to the womanly press of hers. He went dizzy and hot, his world narrowing, melting to encompass the woman in his arms and the excitement she was capable of stirring in him. It had been so long . . .

As he plied her with a spate of deepening kisses, Burke was grateful that Celene was no green girl, no virgin to be patiently courted and pampered. In spite of her reticence the previous afternoon, he knew she was a woman of experience, a woman with years of marriage behind her. He would court her pleasure as he would his own, but he need not linger on endless seduction.

Rolling over her, Burke pinned her hips with the breadth of his thigh, cupped a hand around the mound of her breast. She was voluptuous and womanly, and he moaned his appreciation of her.

She writhed against him as he sought her nipple with his thumb, and the haze of his passion deepened. His thoughts became filmy and diffused as his hunger grew. More than drawing another breath, he wanted to make love to her.

Desperate to ensure that Celene was as ready for their joining as he, Burke dragged his mouth from hers and nibbled across her cheek, proceeding toward her ear. He worried the lobe with the tip of his tongue, whispered breathless endearments and tasted the salty tang of tears.

The taste of her distress and the incongruity of tears with moments of such desire dispelled a bit of the sensual haze. She stirred beneath him again, and it suddenly came clear that there was more in her movements of panic than of passion, more in his actions of subjugation than of seduction. The desire-drugged part of him fought the conclusion, but even as he tried to deny his perceptions, he knew they were indisputably accurate.

When he finally raised his head he could see the tears streaming from the corners of Celene's silver-green eyes. She was sobbing with terrified desperation, without making a sound.

Shocked and confused by her response, Burke snatched his hand from her breast and shifted away.

"Celene! For God's sake, what's the matter?"

Her throat worked as she fought to drag breath into her lungs around her convulsive, silent sobs. "He used to hold me down and force me," she finally managed to gasp. "He'd force me to submit to him."

The passion fogging Cardwell's brain made it work more slowly than usual. "Force you? Who forced you?" he demanded. "Your husband? Henri?"

A fresh wave of tears rolled down her cheeks in wordless acknowledgment.

Some fierce, primitive emotion poured through Burke. He was appalled by what Henri Bernard had done, angrier at Celene's dead husband than he could ever remember being in his life. Perhaps there had been a time when he would have seen nothing wrong with a husband forcing his wife to submit to him, but if he'd ever truly believed that, it had been long ago. "That swine!" he breathed. "That goddamned bastard!"

Burke had never forced himself on a woman in his life.

He'd never had to, and he couldn't comprehend what had driven Henri Bernard to use Celene in such a disgraceful and demeaning way. Cardwell was incensed and suddenly wildly protective of the small, soft woman huddled beside him.

Burke leaned nearer, though he was reluctant to so much as lay a hand on her arm. "Celene, I'm sorry," he whispered. "I'm sorry for what your husband did, and I'm sorry if my touching you brings all his cruelty back. I didn't mean to hurt or frighten you."

She nodded once while tears scored new trails down her face.

Frustration burned in Burke. He ached with his thwarted need for her. But even more, he wanted to take Celene in his arms and comfort her. Yet he was not sure if the natural expression of his concern would please or terrify her. "Celene, I don't know how to help. I want to hold you, but I'm afraid that will make things worse."

She heaved a shuddering sigh. "No, it's all right."

Glad that she would trust him that far, he slid an arm around her and guided her head into the crook of his shoulder. She rested against him gingerly at first, then gave another racking sigh and settled in.

She seemed so small and delicate curled trembling in his arms, so painfully vulnerable. What could have possessed her husband to hurt and victimize her as he had? What kind of monster had Henri been? But Burke knew. Henri had been a husband, determined to have a husband's rights— even if it meant raping his own wife. The question was why Antoine had allowed such treatment of his daughter? And if he knew what she'd been through, why hadn't Antoine told Burke what brutality Celene had suffered?

But Cardwell knew. Antoine was a trader through and through, and only a fool devalued something he hoped to sell for gain. Fury burned inside Burke at Antoine's callousness, but Cardwell understood it. Many Frenchmen, and Englishmen as well, considered women little more than property. They believed that men could do with women what they liked. If ever he had shared that belief, living with Morning Song had changed it irrevocably.

He held Celene for a very long time, until bit by bit her breathing steadied and her crying ceased. Once she'd quieted, he gathered her closer than before and leaned his cheek against her hair. She smelled of lavender and wood smoke, spicy, sweet, and warm. To his surprise he found the way she smelled and looked and felt nestled beside him pleased him. It pleased him in a way he had not expected, pleased him in a way that, knowing how her husband had treated her, Cardwell could never act upon. He was beginning to understand far more about himself and the complex woman he had asked to be his bride than he'd ever wanted to.

Sadness clogged his throat as he stared sightlessly into the semidarkness. What a sorry pair they were, Burke found himself thinking as his fingers trailed absently along the curve of Celene's shoulder—a lonely, bitter Englishman bent on revenge and a fragile, frightened widow who needed and deserved far more from their alliance than he could give.

It was ironic that everything he'd believed about Celene had proved untrue. She was not the fiery virago he had seen the day she'd pushed him in the mud. She was not a single-minded opportunist who could help him with his plans and walk away, substantially richer and unscathed. Celene could never serve his purposes, nor he hers. After what had transpired here tonight, there was nothing to do but break off the arrangement he and Antoine had made. Besides, unless Cardwell missed his guess, Peugeot would have need of his daughter at home before the year was through.

Having made the decision to give Celene up, Burke let his thoughts drift to happier days, to days when Morning Song had been alive. For long months he had denied himself the luxury of thinking of her, of how much he had lost, of how devastating her death had been. But today, with another woman in his arms, he was able to abandon himself to the memories. They came like wraiths across a moonlit moor: memories of Morning Song at seventeen, frolicking through a meadow lush with wildflowers, her face alight with the joy of spring; memories of the day he'd taken her as his bride, so beautiful, so ethereal, so filled with love;

memories of surprising Song one evening at her bath, the way she had turned to him, naked, taunting, and unafraid.

Unlike Celene, Morning Song had welcomed his advances, met his passion with her own. As she'd touched him and welcomed his body into the depths of hers, she had assured Burke of her love for him with tempting touches and words so sweet and eloquent that they had filled him with unutterable joy. She had taught Burke all he knew of love, of concern for others, of sharing and of real and enduring passion. He'd had so very many lessons to learn, and Morning Song had had the patience and kindness to teach him all he needed to know. She had been his life, his reason for awakening day after day.

Now she was gone from him forever. The loss was shattering and soul deep. So deep that there would always be a void in him. And all he had to take her place was his grief and a growing need for vengeance.

As the memories of Morning Song swept through him, Burke's hands had worked absently, kneading the fabric of Celene Bernard's shirt, smoothing along her back, drawing her closer in a mindless agony that had nothing to do with desire. He crushed his face into her hair, let his body curl around her seeking comfort, solace.

While she had not been able to offer a passion to answer his, Celene could give Burke comfort, wordless consolation, basic kindness, some semblance of peace. Without realizing what he'd done, Burke nestled closer and accepted what she was able to give. Lost within his loss, he closed his eyes and clung to her.

6

Celene Peugeot Bernard had never slept with a man before. She had lain with her husband, been crushed beneath him as he'd had his way with her, huddled at the edge of the mattress trembling with revulsion once he was done. She had stared into the dark on many a night, devastated by the knowledge that she had no alternative to her life with Henri.

Never had she been lulled to sleep by the rhythm of a man's breathing; never had she felt his warmth envelope her. She had never known the security of a strong, broad body arced against her back, nor drifted dreamlessly in the curl of a man's embrace. Not until last night. Not until she'd slept with Burke.

And she hadn't liked it. Not one bit.

As she picked her way through the tattered wisps of fog, making her way from Cardwell's tent to her father's, a cold lump of resentment burned in her chest. She hated that she had spent the night in Burke Cardwell's arms. She hated that he had been able to coerce her into staying with him. Though he had asked her to be his bride, Celene had done her best to eschew any form of intimacy between them. She was appalled to think that by sleeping in his bed, she might somehow have lead him to believe she was ready to accept his suit.

Celene Peugeot Bernard was her own woman now that Henri was dead, and she had sworn to remain so. As a widow, she had rights she never had as Henri's wife, and she wasn't eager to give them up.

Hoping for anything that even vaguely resembled caring or concern from a man was a mistake, she reminded herself, one that was bound to leave a woman aching with disillusionment. It was also certain to leave her dependent and vulnerable—things Celene never intended to be again. She had devoted these last months to proving her independence, to developing her ability to provide for herself and her son. She had come very near to convincing the world she didn't need a man to look after her. And she certainly didn't need Burke Cardwell making her feel warm, secure, protected—and confused.

By accepting his offer of marriage, Celene knew she could have had the security she had been working so hard to achieve. According to her father, Burke had amassed a tidy fortune over the years. And after what had transpired in his tent, she was certain Burke would never mistreat her as Henri had. Yet Cardwell was a danger to her in a way that Henri had never been. Henri had been a brute; he had hurt her again and again. But Burke had the potential to abuse her in a far more insidious way. He could appeal to her emotions. His looks, now that he was shaved and bathed, were the kind that would send most women into a swoon. There was a genuine warmth in him, and by merely draping an arm around her shoulders, by showing up at her father's campsite with a brilliant smile and mocock of maple sugar candy, he could make her feel clever, revered, wonderful.

And Celene hated him for it.

After what had happened the previous evening, she wasn't about to let Cardwell near her. She was going to stop feeding him meals, stop listening to his marriage proposals, chase him away from their campsite—at gunpoint if necessary. She was angry with herself for being susceptible to his charms. She was furious with Burke for exploiting her weaknesses. She had to prove that she could make her own way in the world, prove it to her father, to Jean-Paul. And to herself.

Lost in her thoughts, Celene was oblivious to her surroundings, so that when a man loomed up before her, he seemed to come from nowhere. She recognized him instantly, though. It was Jacques Arnaud.

Fear sluiced through her as she spun away. Rivard was directly behind her as she turned. Celene ducked to the left, drawing breath to scream. Rivard's hand clamped over her mouth before she could. He hauled her back against his chest, clamped his opposite arm around her ribs. Frantic, she twisted against him and bit down hard. The tang of his blood was on her tongue as he jerked his hand away.

Celene broke his hold and wheeled to run. Arnaud was on her almost instantly. He caught her by the arms and swung her around. Rivard's fist came down in a vicious arc. White-hot pain exploded through her head, then burned away to nothingness.

It wasn't the morning that should have followed the night before. Burke should have awakened frustrated, angry, aching with the same emptiness that had afflicted him since Morning Song had died. Instead he felt rejuvenated, cleansed.

Celene was gone, of course. He hadn't expected to find her still nestled in his arms when he awoke, but he'd never felt her stir, never heard her leave. He'd slept deeply, dreamlessly, for the first time in months.

Leading his animals from their makeshift stable to the riverbank, Burke let them drink their fill as he watched the activity on the uneven beach at the western edge of the island. Trappers were gathered in unruly clumps, some loading their canoes, some saying goodbye to friends, all making their final preparations for the trek into the wilderness. Many were already on the river, their canoes heavily loaded with coffee, sugar, tobacco, and trade goods that would see the men through another long, cold winter in the wilds.

As he'd told Celene the night before, today marked the rendezvous's first great exodus. From now on, the size of the encampment would dwindle day by day. Burke intended to stay until the end, sell his animals to another trapper, and hitch a ride on one of the pirogues bound for New Orleans. Once he reached the city, it would be easy enough to find a ship bound for Bermuda or maybe even one that would take him directly to England.

Or he might, Burke thought with the slightest of smiles, go as far as Kaskaskia with Antoine and Celene. He could collect the money Monsieur LaVallier owed him in person, rather than waiting for a draft to be transferred to New Orleans. Either way, he needed to see and talk to both Celene and her father.

In the light of day the decision to withdraw his marriage proposal seemed the only sensible course. Celene didn't want a husband, much less a husband who had intended to use her to further his own ends. It had been a damned foolish notion to take a bride out of spite in any case, and thrusting a woman with Celene's sensibilities into the midst of family intrigues and his plots for revenge was unconscionable.

Squatting at the river's edge, Cardwell stripped off his shirt and began to wash.

There really were several things he needed to talk to Antoine about: that Burke intended to withdraw his suit, the final amount Antoine was willing to offer for the furs Cardwell had brought to the rendezvous, the possibility of garnering transportation to Kaskaskia. But he would speak to Celene first. Both he and her father had ignored her in settling the betrothal, and he saw no reason to ride roughshod over her feelings again. He also sensed that after last night Celene would not welcome his presence in her camp. She needed time to come to terms with the intimacies they had and hadn't shared. Suppertime would be soon enough to happen by, and perhaps, Cardwell thought with real enthusiasm, Celene would ask him to stay to eat with them again.

Burke dried himself and stood for a few minutes more watching the trappers depart. The men on the water pulled hard against the current, their shoulders straining beneath their calico shirts, their voices raised in good-humored jests and final farewells. A knot of regret swelled in Burke's throat. He'd loved the trapper's life, the grandeur of the land, the solitude and the occasional camaraderie, the constant lure of adventure, the utter freedom of the wilderness. Was it a mistake to leave all this behind? Was he a fool to give up the only happiness he'd ever known? But then, Morning Song had been at the core of that contentment, and Morning Song was gone forever.

He stood on the riverbank for a very long time watching his former comrades embark. But gradually an uncomfortable, icy awareness came to settle between his shoulder blades. It was like a warning hand across his back, like some primitive, irrational part of him was stirring slowly to life. Oddly shaken by the sensation, Cardwell turned.

Barely a dozen feet up the bank Autumn Leaf stood watching him. Her eyes were shaded, her heavy lids all but obscuring the intensity of her gaze. Still, Burke felt it vibrate through him. He seemed frozen where he stood, staring back, taking in the complexity of the embroidery on her dark-blue blouse, the way the buckskin skirt clung to the flare of her hips. He waited for her to speak, but her only response was to reach up and touch the tiny buckskin bag hanging between her breasts.

As her fingers tightened around it, Burke felt a matching constriction in his chest, felt his heartbeat accelerate. He drew a shaky breath and tried to break the sudden, inexplicable contact between them. Somehow he could not drag his gaze from hers, could not turn away. Awareness crackled between them, making the hairs stir along his arms, sending a wave of gooseflesh down his legs.

As if patently aware of his reaction to her, Autumn Leaf smiled a haunting, mysterious smile. She took a step toward him, and the sensations rippling through him intensified. Then abruptly she lowered her hands to her sides, and the contact between them was broken.

Burke sucked in another breath. He felt drained, lightheaded. His body was slick with sweat in spite of the cool wind off the water.

A knowing light flared in Autumn Leaf's eyes. She walked directly toward where Burke stood, passed so close beside him that he could feel the warmth of her body, feel the flare of her skirt brush his legs. But as close as she passed, she said not a word, and as she moved gracefully up the beach, Burke could do nothing but turn and watch her go.

* * *

"Celene. Celene, are you here?"

The bustle of the rendezvous camp was quieting at the end of a busy day. The sun was setting the sky to the west ablaze, and by rights there should have been good things to eat cooking over the fire in Antoine Peugeot's encampment. There should have been biscuits baking in the camp oven, pots trailing delicious-smelling steam, something popping and sizzling on the spit. But when Burke arrived with two fat grouse already cleaned and prepared for roasting, no meal was under way. Nor was there any sign that either Celene or her father had recently been about.

Touched with confusion, Burke called out again. "Celene, where are you?"

There was no answer.

"Celene?"

Ducking beneath the canvas overhang, Burke reached for tent flaps just as Antoine slapped the fabric aside and emerged from the lean-to. His hair and clothes were mussed, his eyes red-rimmed, and his skin a particularly pasty shade of gray. It was patently obvious he had just awakened and was in no mood for entertaining visitors.

Burke looked into the tent and, finding it empty, turned to where Antoine was hunkered beside the fire. As Cardwell watched, the Frenchman picked up the coffeepot, gave it a disgruntled shake, then hauled several logs from the woodpile and pitched them onto what was left of the campfire. Ash flared up in a cloud of white, and Antoine cursed volubly, swiping at his eyes.

"Is there anything I can do to help you, Antoine?" Burke offered solicitously, though he had to bite his lip to keep from smiling.

"Not unless you have some secret for enjoying a full night of revelry without paying the price."

Burke chuckled and shook his head. "No."

"God has cursed me with a head three times its usual size, a stomach churning with bile, and now"—Peugeot moaned, sitting splay-legged by the fire and bracing his head in his hands as if it needed additional support—"and now, *bon Dieu*, he has sent you by to disturb my rest."

"I won't be of any more bother," Burke offered with as much sympathy as he could muster, "if you'll just tell me where Celene is hiding."

"That's one of the few mercies God has seen fit to show me today. The girl hasn't been here to bedevil me."

Something cold and unpleasant moved through Burke. "What do you mean she hasn't been here?"

"Just that. She hasn't been here." Antoine raised his head from his clutching hands. "You mean she hasn't been with you?"

Cardwell dropped the two birds by the fire. "I've been hunting."

He'd crossed the river at midmorning and spent a most productive afternoon tracking game and tracing the river bluffs southward as far as the mouth of the Wisconsin River. During the early afternoon he'd bagged the grouse and continued along the bluffs to a point of land that looked out across the two merging river valleys. An eagle had been scribing lazy circles above the half-submerged islands in the middle of the stream, and Burke had wished that Celene was by his side to share the moment, the innate sense of peace, the utter—

"Then where is she if she has not been with you?" Antoine demanded.

"We spent the night together." Burke could feel warmth creep up his neck. It felt as if he were admitting to far more than had actually passed between Celene and him. "But when I awoke this morning, Celene was gone."

"And why didn't you come here to be certain she had made it back to our encampment in safety?" Antoine accused.

"I don't know. Did you stop here last night to be certain she was safe?" Cardwell shot back. "Or did you simply assume that I would take care of her?"

There were bright red splotches on Antoine's pale cheeks. "*Sacrebleu*! You are her betrothed. Isn't her care your responsibility?"

"You're her father. Isn't it yours?"

The two men glared at each other across the fire before Antoine looked away.

"*Merde!*" he muttered. "Where can she be?"

Both men knew what her absence meant.

"We need to search the encampment," Burke began, "check every tent if we have to. She's got to be here somewhere. You don't suppose she'd wander off alone?"

Peugeot came to his feet. "I'll take everything to the east of the central campfire, and you take everything to the west."

"Talk to everyone you know. Someone must have seen or heard something. If someone's hurt her . . ." Burke didn't finish the thought.

"I tried to tell her how dangerous it was going to be if she came to the rendezvous with me," Antoine mumbled, half to himself. "I tried to tell her, but she wouldn't listen. It was those hams, those damn hams and not trusting me . . ."

Antoine headed off toward the narrow swampy inlet that divided St. Feriole Island from the eastern bank of the Mississippi, while Burke began his search of the camps closest to the river's main channel. He peered into the tents he passed, talked to the trappers and traders who were gathered around their fires preparing their evening meal. He searched the occasional wooded thickets and the bank of the river, chilled to the marrow by the thought of finding her hurt or dead. Most of the traders and trappers were honorable men who would not have hurt Celene intentionally, but nearly every man in camp had been drunk last night and might not have been responsible for his actions. Burke gave particular attention to the area between his lean-to and Antoine's, but if there had been any clues tramped into those intersecting paths, they had been obscured by hundreds of other footsteps in the course of the day.

Slightly more than an hour later, Cardwell returned to Antoine's camp to find the Frenchman throwing his belongings into a pack. His bedroll was already tied up tight, and his long gun in its waterproof sheath stood nearby.

"Where are you going? What have you learned?"

"I'm going after Arnaud and Rivard. They left the encampment just after daybreak."

Something seemed to freeze up inside of Burke at the

mention of the two trappers' names. "Are you sure they took Celene?"

"Sure? Not sure, but it makes sense. They are gone and so is she. They were furious that she spoiled their fun the other morning. She made them a laughingstock by running them off. And they have been making threats. Though they didn't say what they planned to do, they did tell several trappers they were going to get back the money I owed them."

"And you think they intend to hold Celene until you pay them."

Antoine nodded. "If only I had been able to convince them I had not cheated them. But if giving them the money will keep Celene safe . . ." There was pain in the older man's voice, lines of strain beneath his eyes and around his mouth.

Burke looked at Antoine long and hard. Peugeot was in no condition to undertake what might prove to be a long and arduous journey. He had neither the strength nor the stamina for such an undertaking. And what would happen to Celene if Antoine wasn't able to rescue her?

Celene's vulnerability the night before had shamed Burke, had moved him. It had left concern for her nestled deep in his chest, a need to protect and nurture her. To the very last of his days, Burke would never forget the tears glistening on her cheeks, the silent misery in her eyes as he'd tried to make love to her. He had been as tender as he knew how to be and had stopped the instant he had become aware of her distress, but she had been so fragile, so desperately afraid. The thought of what Arnaud and Rivard might do to her terrified him. If they raped her, he'd grind their bones to dust.

"Let me go after her, Peugeot," Cardwell offered.

The Frenchman looked up from his pack.

"Let me go in your place."

Antoine shook his head and resumed his packing. "This is not your fight, Cardwell. Rivard and Arnaud took Celene because of a debt I refused to pay. They took her because of me, and I am the one who must go after her."

Cardwell looked down at the older man, at his bent

shoulders, at his gnarled hands. He could see the excruciating mortality that surrounded him.

"I'm Celene's fiancé. You gave your daughter's hand to me. Let me go after her."

"And I have been her father for all these years."

"Antoine, please."

"I haven't been a very good father, I freely confess. But perhaps now I can make that up to her."

"Can you?" Cardwell asked.

The Frenchman stopped what he was doing and looked up at Burke again, weighing his words, his meaning. "I'd like to think I can."

"There will be other ways you can make up for your parental lapses once Celene is safe. But she needs more than your best efforts when it comes to finding and rescuing her. It has been years since you have tracked someone into the woods, years since you have plied the rivers. I know where Rivard and Arnaud make their camp, what route they are liable to take. Let me go after her. I swear to you I'll bring her back."

Peugeot hesitated, his head bowed and hands lying motionless on his thighs. "I want to prove I am still man enough to rescue her," he whispered.

Sympathy and confirmation of something Cardwell had only guessed made pain twist through his insides. He understood now what had driven Antoine so relentlessly these past few days, understood his underlying anger, his subtle desperation. "Is it more important that you prove yourself everything you were once or that you ensure Celene's safety?"

"*Mon Dieu*, Cardwell!" Peugeot's voice was as brittle as autumn leaves. "Show an old man some mercy."

"Are Arnaud and Rivard liable to show you any?" Burke went on relentlessly. "Will they show mercy to Celene? Antoine, I wouldn't say these things to you except that your daughter's life may be at stake."

There was a long silence that seemed to echo inside Burke's chest. Antoine seemed to feel it, too.

"*Oui, mon ami*," Peugeot finally answered. "*Oui*. I see that it is best to let you go after them."

Defeat radiated from every cell of Antoine's body, and Cardwell fought down the need to recant all he had said. He felt responsible for the other man's pain, for his acceptance of the inevitable restrictions age and infirmity put on a man.

"I'll be on the river at first light," Burke pressed on, in spite of his regrets, "but there are things I will need you to do for me."

They spoke about a dozen practical matters, but even as they did, their thoughts were only on Celene.

The stranger arrived at Antoine Peugeot's campsite just after midday. He was tall, swarthy as a Spaniard, with the sly, superior air of a man who knew very well what it was life had in store for him.

Antoine hated him on sight.

"Are you Antoine Peugeot?" the stranger asked.

His voice was as cold and inscrutable as his midnight-blue eyes. English, he was by the sound of it, upper class, superior, and contemptuous of any but others of his ilk.

"Who are you to inquire after him?" Antoine asked.

"Bayard Forrester."

"Forrester," Antoine said, rolling the name around on his tongue like thick, rich ale. "Forrester."

The man's long, sharply angled face registered dawning annoyance. His thin, aristocratic nose seemed to grow an inch in length; his lips began to furl, ruffling slightly at the edges with impatience and distaste.

"Are you Peugeot or not?"

Antoine bowed his head in faint acknowledgment. "At your service, monsieur. What is it I can do for you?"

Forrester picked up a string of bright red trade beads. They were made of shoddy material and looked soft and crude in this stranger's elegant hand.

"They told me you might have word of a man I'm seeking," the stranger said.

"Oh?"

"A man who appears to have been known in these parts by the name of Monsieur Burke Cardwell."

Antoine took the measure of his guest, letting his gaze

rove from the wide-brimmed hat nestled over crisp, dark hair; the impeccably tailored clothes that hugged the man's slim but well-muscled form; the polished boots buckled in gold across the insteps. To Antoine he seemed like an apparition here, incongruous with his surroundings, suspicious and malevolent.

"What is it you want with this Burke Cardwell, should you find him?" Antoine asked, every instinct crying out that he not reveal too much.

Forrester's slate-cold eyes fixed Antoine with a measuring gaze. "I don't want anything from the man himself. What I want is proof that he is dead."

7

The panic flowed out of the darkness. It clawed inside her chest, swirled through her with all the destructive intensity of a maelstrom. Celene was confused, too terrified to move, to voice her fear. She lay rigid, utterly still, opening her eyes to more blackness as hot, silent tears coursed down her face. She hurt all over, her back, her arms and legs. Her head throbbed, the deepest ache settling in her cheek, along her jaw. There was some rough, prickly fabric muffling her that stuck to the skin beside her mouth, and she could taste the dust and fiber, stale and acrid on her tongue.

Slowly her mind began to clear, pushing past her discomfort, fighting through the fear. There was the rushing sound of water beneath the keel of a boat, the faint regular forward thrust of paddles pulling against the current. She could hear the rhythmic spatter of the oarsman's strokes, could feel the press of canoe ribs against her spine. She was bound hand and foot, bundled in a canoe moving swiftly upstream.

Rivard and Arnaud—the thought burst through her consciousness. Memories flared behind her eyes, of meeting the men as she'd picked her way through the silent dawn on her way between Burke Cardwell's campsite and her father's, of struggling, of being subdued. Rivard and Arnaud—the blinding terror came again. She was caught, helpless, at the mercy of two of the most vile, unscrupulous men she'd ever met. She was alone on the river with them. Fear went through her like a high-pitched whine. Her throat worked to suppress the sobs that spasmed in her chest, her body trembled with the effort at maintaining some semblance of control.

In spite of her best efforts, she must have done something to draw the attention of her captors. She felt the canoe lag against the current, and an instant later rough hands jerked her upright and dragged the woolen blanket from her face.

"Awake are you, *chérie*?" Arnaud asked, kneeling beside her amid the packs and kegs of trade goods jammed into the canoe.

She made a quick inventory of their surroundings. The river channel was narrow, hemmed on both side by a dense growth of forest. "Where are you taking me?" she demanded.

"And just why is it you're so eager to know? Don't you fancy our company?"

"Shut up, Arnaud," Rivard ordered from the stern of the canoe. "She'll see where we're taking her once we get there. We want to put as many miles as we can between us and Prairie du Chien before night falls."

"As you see, *chérie*, there is no time to waste in idle chatter. We will have a better chance to get acquainted once we make camp," Arnaud promised. He scrambled over several packs to his position in the bow of the canoe and took up his paddle again.

"I want to know where it is you're taking me. I want to know what it is you hope to gain." Celene's voice quivered as she made her demands, and she silently cursed the evidence of her weakness and vulnerability.

Though she asked her questions again and again, it was clear the men meant to ignore her. They took up the regular rhythm of seasoned oarsmen, guiding the canoe upstream with the single-minded diligence she had seen in all the best voyageurs.

She sucked in a ragged breath and tried to calm herself. There were no other canoes nearby, no one she could turn to for help. If she was going to escape whatever the trappers had planned for her, she would have to do it by herself.

By taking her hostage, Rivard and Arnaud clearly felt they had gained some advantage in their argument with her father. Clearly they intend to sell her back to Antoine for what they thought he owed them. Would her father come after her, as Rivard and Arnaud thought? And if he didn't come to bargain what would happen then?

Panic clutched her. Arnaud and Rivard might keep her as their woman or sell her to the Indians to recoup their loss. Her mother had been an Indian captive when she was a girl; it was a part of her life she had never been willing or able to talk about. Would Celene share her mother's fate?

Visions of her home, of Ste. Genevieve, and Jean-Paul filled her mind. Her son had clung to her the morning they had left for the rendezvous and begged her not to go. She had dried his tears and reassured him that they would only be parted for a little while, that Pélagie would see to him while she was gone. Now that Rivard and Arnaud had taken her as their captive, would she ever hold her son in her arms again, ever run her fingers through the unruly waves of his dark hair, ever kiss him good night and tuck him into bed?

Tears rose in her eyes and spilled helplessly down her cheeks. With her hands tied behind her back, she could not even wipe the tears away. They trickled off her chin, ran down her neck and into the fabric of her shirt.

She and Jean-Paul had planted their fields with such hope and determination in the weeks before she left. Was there any chance that she would be in Ste. Genevieve when the harvest was brought in?

Celene drew a shuddering breath and swallowed hard. Surely her father would come to rescue her. His pride would never allow Rivard and Arnaud to get the best of him. If for no other reason than to make them pay for this affront, Antoine would come. She could not let herself believe otherwise.

But what would Rivard and Arnaud do before he arrived? They had struck her, beaten her, and bound her already, and their treatment of her would not be likely to improve. She had suffered brutality at Henri's hands, and she knew she could bear rough handling better than many women. But Arnaud had hinted that they would want vile things of her. Once they made camp, would the two men force themselves on her? When her husband died, Celene had sworn that she would never again allow a man to take her against her will. But here, alone in the wilderness, without anyone to turn to for help, what could she do?

Men were vile, savage creatures, Celene reflected bitterly, feeling her indignation rise. They took whatever they wanted, spoiled what little harmony there was in the world, overpowered the gentle and the meek. They thought only of what they needed, what they wanted, without once considering the needs and wants of others. Why hadn't God given women the strength to protect themselves from such as these, to prevent themselves from being victims?

Anger and terror proved to be incompatible bedfellows, and as Celene's fury grew, her terror fled. She would have to find a way to protect herself. She would have to count on her own cleverness and determination to keep her safe until—*please, God*—her father came.

The afternoon passed in a blur. Rivard tied her hands before her so that she could eat and drink when they stopped for water and a sparse meal of parched corn and jerky. But that was the only concession they made to her comfort. They paddled on through twilight, journeyed into full dark. The moon came out, casting shimmers on the rippling surface of the river, cloaking the shallows and the riverbank in velvet blackness. When at last the moon sank into the trees, they pulled up onto a narrow beach. Celene spent the night huddling just beyond the glow of firelight, waiting for one or both of the men to accost her. They never did.

Instead they thrust her back into the canoe at daybreak and resumed their journey. The day passed as the previous one had. Celene dozed and woke a dozen times, starting as she opened her eyes, trying to remember where she was and why she ached from head to toe. She was too numb to be terrified by her captors, too exhausted to muster the anger that had sustained her the day before. The journey seemed endless, and with each mile they covered, her hope of rescue faded.

Just at sunset they rounded a curve in the river and saw

two voyageurs' canoes drawn up on a sandy beach. Arnaud called out a greeting from his place in the bow, and when the answering shout came from men he recognized, Rivard steered toward where the other boats were beached. Four trappers came down to the water's edge to help them unload, and they seemed surprised when they discovered Celene trussed up among the cargo.

"That Peugeot's daughter there?" one of them asked.

"*Oui*," Rivard answered. "She's insurance on a debt the old man owes. He'll pay us that and more before we give her back to him."

"Peugeot is not a man to be trifled with," another of the trappers warned, "and he won't take kindly to what you've done. You'll be bargaining with the devil for a comfortable place in hell when Antoine catches up to you."

The trappers laughed and said no more, but Celene was surprised that the other men considered her father someone to be feared. To her he had never seemed a force to be reckoned with in quite this way.

Celene was allowed a few moments of privacy to see to her own needs as the men finished making camp. With her face washed and her hair returned to a semblance of order, she felt somewhat renewed and turned her thoughts to how best to prepare herself for the evening ahead. Now that they were returned to dry land, there might be a chance to escape. She had no idea where they were, and no idea how she could return to Prairie du Chien except by following the river. Perhaps once the men were asleep, she could steal a canoe. She had lived on the Mississippi all her life and was an accomplished steersman, but she wasn't sure she could launch one of the heavy canoes without assistance.

Or she could set out on foot, Celene thought without enthusiasm. She well knew the hazards of wilderness travel. Even if she stole weapons to defend herself, she might wander endlessly through the woods without ever finding the way to Prairie du Chien. She had reached no point of resolve when Arnaud came shambling down the bank in search of her.

"Not thinking of taking your leave of us, are you, *chérie*? It's dark out there in the woods. All kinds of critters are stirring that would make a meal on such as you."

As he came closer she could smell the whiskey on his breath. The men must have broken open a pin of spirits to make the evening merry. Drunkenness boded ill for her continued well-being, and Celene resolved to get her hands on a weapon in the hope of being able to defend herself.

"I've no desire to go wandering in the woods alone," she assured him, determined not to make the man suspicious. "I think I'll stay on instead to watch what my father does to you when he arrives."

"Brave words for the daughter of a worthless wretch. Still, unless Peugeot shows up, we won't get what's coming to us."

It seemed ill advised to express the hope that he and Rivard would get exactly what was coming to them, so Celene headed toward the campfire glowing bright in the gathering darkness.

As she brushed past Arnaud, he grabbed her arm, his fingers digging deep into the flesh above her elbow. "Before your father comes to pay your ransom, I intend to taste your charms. So don't get all high and mighty, thinking you'll escape me."

Sudden nausea clawed at the back of Celene's throat. Panic jolted through her. With a muttered imprecation, she kicked him in the shins and spun away.

" . . . make camp just this side of St. Anthony Falls and wait for Peugeot to come to us," she heard Rivard confide to one of the other men as she neared the fire.

So that was what they intended, Celene thought. If only she could find a way to fend off Arnaud's advances until her father arrived, until she found a way to escape. If only she could find a way to get her hands on a weapon of some—

"Would you like me to cook the meal for you?" she asked, standing over where one of the men was cutting strips of rabbit to thread on sticks for roasting over the fire. "I fix a passible meal if I've a little something to work with."

The five men looked up at her as if she'd materialized out of thin air.

"An awfully agreeable captive, to my way of thinking," one of them observed.

"Want to get your hands on my knife, little girl? Want to hide it in your clothes and skewer us as we sleep?"

The men laughed and Celene felt her cheeks go hot. She would have to be more subtle in securing a weapon. "I will cook your meal in return for the promise that I sleep alone tonight," she bargained.

Rivard snorted once, an indication of what such a promise would be worth from men like these.

Still, Celene persisted. "If you have some flour, I will make up a batch of pan biscuits. I'm noted for my biscuits back home. They're light and fluffy as down and eating them will give you far more pleasure than you're likely to find in forcing yourselves on me."

They were bold words, bolder and more frank than any Celene had spoken in her life. They made the men laugh again.

"She drives a hard bargain, doesn't she?"

"She's her father's daughter in that," another man agreed.

"We'll taste the biscuits before we agree to all the rest," the first man said.

The answer was not quite what Celene had hoped, but it was better than nothing. "It may be a fool's bargain, but I'll cook for you."

With that Celene set about her work. As she finished spearing the strips of meat and began mixing the biscuit dough, she caught sight of a small ax that had been left stuck into a piece of wood after the logs for the fire had been split. It would be harder to steal than a knife and harder to conceal once she had taken it, but it would offer her a way to fend off the men if the need arose. Common sense told her she could not possibly save herself if six men took it into their heads to rape her, but she would not submit to them willingly. She would do what damage she could before they overpowered her.

It did nothing to ease her misgivings that the men continued to fill their dipper cups with whiskey from the keg one of them had tapped. Still, drunk men were easier to

elude than sober ones, she supposed, and she continued
with preparations for the meal. When it was ready, she set
the food out on plates. After taking one for herself and
palming the ax, she slipped into the shadows at the edge
of the clearing. Arnaud made as if to join her, but the other
men dragged him down to sit with them by the fire and
filled his dipper with whiskey again. She slid the ax into
the shadow beneath her leg, and began to eat, watching
nervously as the men's talk and laughter grew more slurred
and raucous.

She gathered up the dishes when they were done and
went down to the water to wash them, taking some small
comfort in the reassuring weight of the ax she'd managed
to slip into the waist of her pants. With it hidden beneath
the flare of her capote, Celene felt more secure than she
had since the morning Rivard and Arnaud had abducted
her. She scoured the dishes with sand and rinsed them in
the river. Then, knowing she was just far enough over the
rise in the bank to be unobserved, she heaved her weight
against one of the boats. If she could launch it by herself,
her chances of escaping multiplied. She could hear the sand
grind beneath the skin of the canoe, but no matter how she
tried, it would not move.

"Madame Bernard." Rivard was standing at the top of
the rise. "You wouldn't be thinking about stealing one of
those canoes, now would you?"

"Of course not." It was a barefaced lie, and both of them
knew it.

"And here we were beginning to think you'd grown fond
of our company."

Celene gathered up the pile of plates. "I wouldn't go so
far as to say that," she demurred.

Rivard's mouth curled at the corners in the semblance of
a smile. "Got spunk, don't you, woman? But you're as
conniving as your father, and that's no lie."

"I'll tell him what you said when he comes to get me.
I doubt he'll take kindly to such an insult."

She swept toward the man, jammed the pile of tin plates
into his midsection, and resumed her place at the edge of
the clearing. In the cover of the shadows she slipped the

ax free and spent the rest of the evening watching the men drain the pin of spirits.

Exhaustion assailed her as she sat listening to their lurid stories of life in the wilderness and their crude jokes. She must have slipped into a doze, for it was the shadow that fell across her face that brought her suddenly awake. Arnaud was standing over her, weaving like a man buffeted by a gale. In an instant she realized he was fumbling at the buttons on his pants. Her hand closed around the handle of the ax as she scuttled backward.

"Tol' you I'd come t' you t'night. You gonna like 'is. You gonna like 'is a lot."

Beyond Arnaud, Celene could see that the men seated around the fire were watching with glassy, avid eyes.

"No," she breathed, her heart hammering in her throat. "No, I won't let you do this. Leave me alone!"

"C'mon. C'mon. Be ni—nice."

Her breath seemed trapped in her lungs. Her mouth went dry. Her fingers tightened on the ax. She'd have to wait until he was nearly on top of her for a blow to have any effect. She tensed, waiting, her hands gone cold. If Arnaud forced himself upon her, would she really be able to do anything but scream?

He had freed his organ from his pants and seemed ready to throw himself on her when a shot rang out.

Celene saw the orange and yellow burst of flame from the impenetrable darkness on the far side of the fire. Arnaud wavered above her, dropped to his knees, his open, staring eyes fixed on her. She scuttled back as he crashed to the ground. His limp, dead weight pinioned her.

Muffling a scream, she fought her way free. On the far side of the clearing a tall figure was emerging from the trees. He was leveling a pistol at the five remaining men, holding a smoking musket in his opposite hand. He seemed to move in a blur, the fringe on his clothes writhing around him. His hair glinted gold in the firelight. The cheeks he'd shaved were three days old in beard.

"Burke," she breathed in disbelief. "Burke!"

But five trappers could not be subdued by a single man. Skirting the fire, they moved like an army mobilizing for attack, flanking Burke, arming themselves. He retreated a single step and then another. Even if he shot one of them with the pistol, there were four others to take him down. Tightening her fingers around the ax, Celene launched herself across the clearing. She slammed it into Rivard's arm, severing flesh and bone. He yowled in agony and wheeled on her.

The unexpectedness of her attack threw the other men into confusion. Burke fired and one of the trappers dropped like a stone. Swinging his musket like a club, Cardwell stopped another in his tracks. The other two lunged at him with weapons drawn. They went down in a tangle of arms and legs.

There would be no further help from Burke, and Rivard was silently stalking her. Even with his left arm hanging useless at his side, the Frenchman was a formidable enemy. Fury burned bright in his eyes. His lips were drawn back in a snarl. Celene retreated, terrified. He would show no mercy to her.

With panic rushing through her veins, she swung the ax at the level of his chest. He leaped away, the well-honed blade passing within a hairsbreadth of his body. Overbalanced by the stroke, Celene hesitated. Rivard thrust his body against her, driving hard. He slammed her to the ground. The air left her lungs in a *whoosh*. She gasped, fighting for breath, flailing and twisting beneath him. He flattened her to the earth, stilling her legs with the weight of his thigh. Arching her back, she tried to jab upward with her knee. She swung the ax, but his good hand jarred into her wrist. His grip tightened, and her bones ground together with a sickening rasp. Her hand went numb, but she refused to release her hold on her only weapon.

Abruptly Rivard lowered his head, smacking her forehead with his. Lights flared before her eyes. Pain tightened in a band around her skull. The world went out of focus. When it righted itself, the ax was gone, and Rivard's hand had closed on her throat.

"Bitch," he rasped as his hold constricted her windpipe. Her lungs spasmed in her chest. She twisted beneath him, gasping. It did no good. His thumb tightened, digging deeper. Sounds dimmed. The scene around her swirled with red.

Then all at once Rivard's crushing weight was gone. She could suck air into her burning lungs. Though she struggled to make some sense of what was happening, she was aware of nothing but the effort it took to breathe. Her throat ached; her limbs seemed shackled to the earth.

Finally the world began to reassert itself, and she became aware that there was someone standing over her, someone tall. His legs were splayed, and the ax she'd used to defend herself hung in his hand. The fire at his back cast his face in shadows, but there were feathers angled in his hair.

With a moan Celene levered herself into a sitting position. An Indian was looking down at her, and there were more than a dozen others in the clearing. One guarded two of the trappers; one was binding Rivard. Two more were struggling to subdue Burke. As she watched, a third struck him a glancing blow with his war club. Cardwell sagged to his knees, and before his senses could clear, they tied his hands behind his back.

The Indian standing over her muttered something in a language she did not understand. When she did not respond, he jerked Celene to her feet and hustled her across the clearing to where the other prisoners sat. Her captor bound her hands and shoved her down beside where Burke was beginning to come around.

"Are you all right?" Celene whispered when the Indians turned their attentions to looting the camp.

"I've been better," Cardwell answered.

There was blood on his face, trickling from the wound above his ear. There was also a rent in his blue capote, which was edged with glistening red. One of the trappers must have knifed him in the scuffle, but neither of the wounds seemed serious.

"How about you?"

Celene shrugged. "I was glad to see you."

"Were you, now?"

"I didn't expect it would be you who'd rescue me."

Cardwell gave a derisive snort. "Some rescue it's turned out to be."

She scanned the camp. The braves were dividing up the spoils. "Why are the Indians here?"

"I haven't got it all figured out. They're Chippewa, and it seems they've have some trouble with the trappers Rivard and Arnaud threw in with."

"Then they're going to let us go."

One corner of Burke's mouth quirked upward. "I wouldn't count on that if I were you. They haven't sorted us out yet, but I don't hold much hope of the Indians being willing or able to discriminate between us and them. Besides, whatever happens, it's a damned good thing that they came by."

"What do you mean?"

"I mean I'd figured on something a little more subtle than charging into the camp like a platoon of infantry. Something more like sneaking into camp after the fellows there had drunk themselves insensible and simply taking you back to Prairie du Chien. But then, I doubted you'd be any more willing to share your favors with Arnaud than you were with me."

The fact remained that Burke had come for her, and Celene was grateful.

"I did the best I could," he continued, "but if the Indians hadn't happened by, neither you or I would be having this conversation."

Celene didn't want to dwell on what had happened. The ache in her throat was reminder enough of how close Rivard had come to choking her. Might Burke have been killed instead of subduing the other men?

"What will happen now?"

"The tall one over there said something about their band being pleased with the supplies they've captured. My guess is that we'll be taken, along with the supplies, to join a larger band of Chippewa somewhere north of here."

"Then you'll explain what's happened, and they'll let us go," she offered hopefully.

"I only hope it will be as simple as that."

"But you lived with the Chippewa," Celene insisted. "You said they adopted you."

Burke's face took on a gravity and concern Celene had

never seen in it before. It frightened her.

"Lone Wolf took me as his brother. That doesn't guarantee I'll have any influence in another band. It will depend on who the leaders are. In any case, Celene," he warned, "we've got a few hard days ahead of us."

She searched the depths of his turquoise eyes for some glimmer of hope and found not so much as a spark. A ball of emotion swelled in her chest. Would she ever see Jean-Paul again? Would she ever get back to Ste. Genevieve? She bit her lip to stifle a sob, but tears she could not seem to control tracked silver patterns down her face.

Burke moved closer, pressed his arm against her sleeve. She knew he meant to comfort her, and for reasons she could not comprehend, that made the tears fall faster than before.

8

The forced march took three days. They traveled north and west, moving parallel to the river through heavy forest and then into more open country until they arrived, just at dusk, at a well-established Chippewa camp. It was one of several in the area, and though Burke had never visited it, he had some knowledge of the chief. Two of the braves had raced ahead to alert the village that the band was returning with prisoners, and a crowd had gathered to cheer the warriors and taunt the captives.

Though living on the Athabasca with Morning Song had taken him out of contact with most of the Chippewa bands, Cardwell hoped he would be able to use his influence to get Celene and him released. As the prisoners stood clustered in the center of the encampment awaiting their disposition, Cardwell glanced across at her.

She stood silently beside the brave who had captured her, her hands bound before her and a rope encircling her neck. Pale purple circles ringed her eyes, and there were scratches on her face and arms from the constant scrape of vines and branches. Her clothes were ripped; she was dirty, sweaty, and clearly exhausted. But in spite of her weariness and discomfort, Celene's head was high, and a spark of determination lit her eyes. Her spirit had not been broken by their ordeal, and Burke knew her bravery would be respected by the Chippewa.

Straining against his bonds, against the rope that encircled his own neck, Cardwell turned his attention to the camp set up in the lee of a grove of trees. Elm bark wig-

121

wams were arrayed outward from the central area where the Midewiwin lodge stood, and beyond them to the south were small, well-tended fields where crops of corn and squash were already flourishing. Burke still had no clue as to why the Chippewa had attacked the party of trappers and made them prisoners, but he suspected that their transgression would be made clear in the next few minutes.

As they waited, the women and children moved in to inspect the newcomers, to pinch or poke at them. One woman jerked Celene's trailing white-gold braid, but instead of crying out, Celene looped the plait across her shoulder and turned away with stone-faced dignity. Older men soon joined the throng, nudging the captives with their elbows, enjoying the easy sport. One of them prodded the knife slash Burke had received in the fight four nights before, and he bit down hard to muffle a grunt of pain. The excited yapping of the village dogs added to the general noise and confusion. Burke had no doubt that Celene was frightened, though she hid her emotions well.

At length the chief emerged from his wigwam, and silence descended over the crowd.

The leader of the band who had made them prisoners immediately stepped forward, speaking to his chief in the Chippewa language. "We have brought you captives, Running Dog. These are the men who stole our pelts on the way to the rendezvous. The goods they received in trade are rightfully ours, and we have taken them back. We have brought the thieves to you so they can be punished for their treachery."

"You and your men are a credit to the tribe," the chief responded. "I accept your gift, with many thanks."

With a jerk of his head, Running Dog motioned one of the trappers forward. His captor flung the man to his knees.

"Did you steal peltries from these men on the way to the rendezvous?" the chief asked in heavily accented French.

"We didn't steal no pelts," the trapper barked. "If that Indian says we did, he lies."

Running Dog seemed to consider the white man's words. "Cut out this man's tongue," he finally said.

The crowd seethed and cheered as the order was carried out, pleased by Running Dog's well-drawn sense of justice.

Across the way Celene had gone white to the lips and stood trembling like an aspen in the wind. Burke wished there was something he could do to spare her this, but for the moment it seemed wiser to hold his peace.

As the trapper was dragged back to his place, Running Dog turned to the brave again. "Did you lose any warriors in the attack?" When the brave answered that he had not, Running Dog inclined his head. "Then the prisoners belong to the men who took them."

"We thank you for your generosity, Running Dog. To-morrow we will let the council decide their fate," the leader of the raiding party answered. "It is the right and proper thing to do."

A current of fear crept through Burke's insides. To be sent before the council boded ill for all of them. But that would be the time to reveal his connections to other Chippewa bands and plead their case. It would be useless to do it tonight when both the crowd and the chief were in a vengeful mood. At least he would have the chance to explain their situation to Celene before they faced the council.

Just as they were about to be hauled away, a voice boomed across the clearing.

"The woman has had no part in this."

With the words all movement around them stilled as a tall Indian in full regalia of the Grand Medicine Society stepped from the doorway of the Mide lodge. The crowd turned avid and curious as he strode across the clearing to stand before Running Dog.

Celene's eyes widened in stunned surprise as she recognized her half brother. Burke was every bit as shaken by Darkening Sky's unexpected appearance as she was. But he was of the Midewiwin and travelled freely from band to band. It was pure good luck he'd turned up here. The power of his position among the Chippewa might well keep Celene safe, though Burke had no illusions that Darkening Sky would speak on his behalf.

"This woman is my father's daughter," Darkening Sky continued addressing Running Dog, "and came to the rendezvous with the trader Peugeot. She could not have had a part in the theft of the furs.''

With a raise of his hand Running Dog motioned Celene and her captor forward. ''Are you truly the daughter of the trader Peugeot?'' he asked in French.

She glanced once in Burke's direction. ''*Oui*,'' she answered.

''Are you half sister to this man here?''

''You can see we both have the color of our father's eyes,'' Sky put in.

The chief nodded. ''I see that there is some resemblance,'' he acknowledged in his own tongue. ''But what is she doing with men like these?''

''Why are you with these men, Celene?'' Darkening Sky asked in French.

''I was taken from the rendezvous encampment by Rivard and Arnaud to force our father to settle a matter between them.''

''Do you know anything about furs stolen from the Chippewa by these other men?''

''Furs? *Non*. We only shared their camp.''

Running Dog nodded again. It was clear that he could not challenge Darkening Sky's claim to the woman, nor was it wise for any man, even a chief, to displease a member of the Midewiwin.

''What would you have me do with her?'' he asked Darkening Sky.

''I would have her released from her bonds and placed under my protection. I will pay her captor well if he agrees.''

''And what of these other men?'' the chief asked.

''You may do whatever you will with them.''

It was evident that Celene was able to follow at least a bit of what was being said, though she did not understand the words.

''Burke had nothing to do with stealing the furs,'' she told her brother. Though Darkening Sky slashed her a scathing glance, she did not heed it. ''You must see to his release, as well.''

The expression in Darkening Sky's gray-green eyes was

implacable. "I will do nothing to help the trapper Cardwell."

"But you must help him. He had nothing—"

"Celene," Sky warned.

"But he—"

"Are you sure you want to look after one as argumentative as this?" Running Dog asked with a slight twist of his lips.

"She does not understand the ways of our people. I will take responsibility for her. Release her now."

With another nod from Running Dog, one of the men slipped the rope from Celene's neck and cut her bonds.

Though his own future was uncertain, Cardwell felt a swell of relief that Celene was safe.

Now seemed the time for Burke to speak up in his own defense. "It is true that I had nothing to do with stealing the furs. I followed the trappers on Peugeot's behalf to see that the woman was returned to him. I have long been a friend to the Chippewa and—"

"Did this one have a part in stealing the furs?" the chief demanded of the raiding party's leader.

The brave shrugged. "All whites steal from us," he answered noncommittally. "It is their way."

Running Dog was silent for a long moment while he considered the other Indian's words. "Face of the Moon is wise," he finally said. "We will decide the fate of this man and the others tomorrow."

Again, fear of the council's ruling spiraled through Burke. He knew what their judgment was liable to be. As he and the other men were prodded roughly through the encampment, Darkening Sky took Celene by the wrist and led her in the opposite direction. Burke looked back through the gathering dusk, knowing this might well be the last glimpse he would ever have of her. Still, he had kept at least the spirit of his promise to Antoine Peugeot. No matter what fate the new day brought the rest of them, Celene would not be hurt. There was nothing for him to do but trust that Darkening Sky would see his sister safely home.

* * *

Sleep had settled over Celene like a heavy, dark cloak the night before, partly because of her exhaustion and partly because of the potion Darkening Sky had given her. But now, many hours later, sounds and smells began to penetrate her consciousness. She could hear dogs barking, the hum of garbled voices, the rhythm of a drum. There was the tang of unfamiliar herbs prickling her nostrils, carried on a drift of wood smoke. There was sunshine on her face, warm and soothing as a balm. She stirred sluggishly and discovered that every muscle ached. Her skin stung as if she'd been flayed; her neck and wrists were rubbed raw. With an effort she opened her eyes and forced herself into a sitting position.

Around her were arrayed the scant contents of the wigwam. On the low platform that hugged the walls, two beds had been made up with skins and blankets. There was a pot of cooked meal and several birch-bark containers sitting along the edge of the unlit fire pit in the center of the lodge. Gourd bottles were stoppered and hanging near the door, and at the head of the bed opposite hers hung a blanket coat and bear-paw medicine bag.

The night before, Darkening Sky had brought her here, given her food, something soothing to drink, and put her to bed. Though she had tried to ask him where Burke and the others were being taken and what would happen to them, her half brother had evaded her questions. But now that she was rested, Celene meant to seek out the answers for herself.

Pouring water from one of the gourd bottles into a mocock, she completed her ablutions and tidied her hair as best she could. She blinked as she emerged from the dimness of the wigwam into the bright sunlight and saw that several of the women seated on the ground nearby paused in their sewing to stare at her. When they made no move to prevent her from leaving the shelter, Celene turned toward the center of the encampment, drawn by the swelling beat of a drum, the droning chant of voices. As she approached it, the crowd began to thicken, as did a malevolent air of expectancy. Coming to the central area from just left of the Mide lodge, Celene saw the reason, and her heart constricted inside her chest.

Across the clearing Burke Cardwell and two of the trappers were hanging, tied hand and foot, to a torture rack. They were shoeless and shirtless, and the skin of their torsos was marked by long, bloody stripes that wrapped around their bodies like livid, writhing snakes. Celene skirted the edge of the crowd, covering the distance between her and the trappers without once taking her eyes from Burke. With a knot of tears lodged tight in her throat, Celene looked up into his averted face. It was flushed, sweat-slicked, and contorted with pain. Through the drape of his straggling hair, she could see that his eyes were closed, that there was a bruise purpling his temple and another swelling beneath his eye. A trickle of blood had clotted at the corner of his mouth as if he'd bitten through his lower lip. His chest heaved with the effort it took to breathe. His muscles knotted and bunched as if he were trying to ease the drag of his weight on the joints of his arms. The skin on his back and shoulders was raw, and Celene realized that while she had been sleeping peacefully, he had been beaten or flayed. The other trappers were in no better condition, but they moaned and cried out instead of making a show of their stoicism.

"Burke," Celene whispered as she crept nearer. "Burke?"

Cardwell seemed either too focused on maintaining his silence or was too far gone in misery to hear her.

When she moved as if to scale the ladder that led to the platform where the men were hung, one of the Indian men hauled her roughly away. His face was contorted with anger and disapproval.

"No, no," she panted as she fought his hold. "I must help him. Please, let me . . ."

As she struggled with the man, trying to twist away, Celene became aware that there was a new commotion in camp. She looked up, searching the crowd for Darkening Sky. Surely her brother could have Burke cut down. Surely he could arrange for Burke to get the care he needed. Even if Sky had refused to help Cardwell the night before, he had to help him now. Without Sky's help, Burke would die. Celene could not let that happen.

But instead of Darkening Sky, she saw that another party of Indians was moving into the camp. There were about two dozen men, eight or nine women, a few boys in their early teens, and a flock of children. By the weight and number of packs they carried, it was evident they were returning from the rendezvous. Because these Chippewa were not greeted as the returning warriors had been the night before, Celene suspected this band was simply passing through. Nonetheless, their footsteps lagged as they saw the three men tied to the poles, the newcomers' faces becoming avid, curious.

While their leader inquired either about the men on the rack or about their welcome in Running Dog's encampment, she saw one of the women lower her pack and step out of the ranks. Celene recognized her instantly; it was Autumn Leaf. The Indian woman's eyes narrowed as she recognized Burke, her lips taking on a self-satisfied leer.

Gripped by some emotion she could not name, Celene watched the other woman move closer to where Cardwell was hanging on the rack. Wanting to rush forward and drag Autumn Leaf away, wanting to wipe the gloating expression from her dusky face, Celene stood helpless, still held tight in the grip of one of the braves. As the Indian woman slunk nearer still, her hand closed around an embroidered bag that hung on a thong between her breasts.

As if in response, Burke began to stir.

At the slight movement Autumn Leaf's mouth twisted, and her fingers clutched convulsively.

Cardwell raised his head and opened his eyes. They were red rimmed, cloudy with pain. Autumn Leaf caught his gaze and held it with her own. Even from where Celene stood a dozen yards away, she could feel the contact slice through the air between Burke and Autumn Leaf. It was like the flash of sunlight in a mirror, like a sizzle of summer lightning.

Autumn Leaf's grip tightened around the medicine bag and for an instant Burke's eyes cleared. He hung suspended, as if hovering in space, mesmerized by some mysterious power emanating from the woman. Celene fought desperately to break her captor's hold, terrified by the malignant force emanating from the Indian squaw; horrified that it was directed at Burke when he was in no condition to defend himself. Cardwell maintained the contact for a few seconds more, then his eyes rolled back. He sagged against the pole almost as if the bond with Autumn Leaf had drained away the last of his strength.

There was malice in the Indian woman, something frightening and dark. Celene could sense it, taste her own fear of Autumn Leaf's power on the back of her tongue. Shaken by what she'd observed, by what she felt, by her own inability to change what was happening, Celene jerked free of the Indian's hold and slipped away. With Burke on the torture rack, with Autumn Leaf's arrival in camp, with the strange power the Indian woman seemed to wield, Darkening Sky was the only one who might be able to intervene. It was up to Celene to convince her half brother that he had to put aside the past, that he had to save Burke Cardwell's life. She had no other choice. If she could not convince him, Burke would die.

There was blood on his hands, blood spattered on his chest and legs. A feral light flickered bright in his silvergreen eyes, and beside him in the grass was what looked like a swatch of thick, dark hair.

Celene drew a ragged breath and stared in horror at where her half brother knelt on the bank of the stream. Because he had left no orders governing her movements, no one had tried to prevent Celene from prowling through the camp or ranging through the woods around it. Though she had been searching for Darkening Sky, she had come upon him quite by chance. He must have stopped at the stream to wash away the evidence of what he'd done before he returned to the wigwam and to her.

Though she was sure she had made no sound, when he raised his head, Sky looked directly at where she stood.

"Celene!" he said, coming to his feet in a single fluid movement. "I didn't expect to find you here."

In an instant he was across the stream on a path of scattered stones, and as he approached, she could smell the blood and sweat on him. Revulsion seethed through her, and she stumbled backward.

"Celene," Sky said, seeing how repelled she was. "Celene, listen to me. I bought Rivard from Runs Like the Wind because it was destined that I do this. It was destined that I kill the man who took you prisoner."

Fighting back nausea, Celene could do no more than stare at him.

"I saw it in a vision that morning at the rendezvous. I told him what would happen. Rivard could have changed his fate, if he had heeded my warning. But he did not. After what he and Arnaud did, I had no choice but to seek revenge. Surely you understand."

A biting sense of betrayal made her turn away. How could he expect her to understand something as gruesome and grizzly as this? Darkening Sky had killed Rivard; he even seemed proud of what he'd done. Though she could not bring herself to mourn the trapper's passing, there was something appalling about her brother's deliberate, cold-blooded brutality. And had he scalped the trapper, too? Was it Rivard's scalp she had seen lying in the grass?

Darkening Sky's behavior was totally alien to everything she knew of him. He had been so kind in his dealings with her, so reasonable, so filled with concern. It had never occurred to her that Darkening Sky was capable of killing a man so callously.

"I thought you were different," she finally breathed. "I didn't think you were a savage."

She heard her half brother suck in his breath, and he jerked her around. "And why did you think that? Because the blood of a white man flows in my veins? Because it is the same blood that flows in yours? White men kill—sometimes with far less provocation than I had today. I do not regret what I have done."

Staring up into her half brother's face, Celene could feel the bond between them. It was a bond of blood and of emotion, a bond that would connect them all their days. But now it was tempered with his anger and defiance, her fear and shock.

"I thought you would help them," she said in a small choked voice. "I thought that you would help me."

"I have helped you. I have claimed you as my sister. I have killed a man for you."

She glared up at him. "That isn't something you did for me. You did that for yourself—for yourself and for your honor."

Darkening Sky's expression froze, his eyes gone gray and stormy.

Celene met his gaze, wondering as she did, if he had any inkling how this side of him terrified her. Could he see the fear in her eyes, smell it on her skin? Yet deep in her heart she was glad Rivard was dead. Did that make her a savage, too?

"Then, what *is it* you want of me?" Darkening Sky finally demanded.

Celene considered carefully what she should say. Her most desperate wish was to go home, back to Ste. Genevieve and Jean-Paul. But before she asked for freedom, there were others she must consider. "Burke Cardwell is tied to the rack back in camp. He's been beaten, tortured. And they're going to kill him."

Darkening Sky frowned and looked away.

"He doesn't deserve to die," she continued, anger and entreaty mingled in her tone. "He had no part in stealing the furs. He risked his life to rescue me when our father would not. He's done his best to keep me safe. And your people are going to kill him if you don't go and cut him down."

"He and the other prisoners were made to run the gauntlet early this morning. Only three of them survived, and those three will hang where they are until they are dead. There is nothing I can do."

Shaking her head, she glared at him. "There must be something," she insisted. "Some way—"

"This a less painful way to die than many he could face," he answered. "Cardwell knows that. He is brave. He will die well, I promise you."

Horror clotted at the base of her throat. After coming to

her aid, Celene could not allow herself to be the cause of Burke Cardwell's death.

"Please, Darkening Sky, I beg of you. You are a powerful man, a leader of this tribe. You are one of the Mide. They would listen to you. You can find a way to save him."

"I can do nothing. I was one of the council who voted for his death."

"But he is innocent," she argued. "He did not steal the furs. He was a good husband to his Chippewa wife, a friend to the tribe. Doesn't that count for anything?"

"He is a white man. All white men steal from the Chippewa." His tone was dismissive. Without another word he recrossed the stream and resumed his washing.

Celene stared after him, appalled by how easily he could dismiss the death of another man. Was life so cheap to him and his Chippewa brethren that they accepted death without counting the cost? Was the warmth and concern she had sensed in her half brother a lie, a facade he had showed her to hide the savage within? Or was Darkening Sky a man caught between two worlds, condemned to endless and unlikely compromises?

Either way, there was no question about what Celene must do. Back in the encampment Burke's life was seeping away. The marks the lash had cut deep in his skin were draining his strength. The lines of pain that etched his face and his shallow, labored breathing gave evidence of how close he was to giving up. She could not let him die; she would do what she had to to save him.

Whirling, she raced back toward the camp, but before she had run a dozen yards, Darkening Sky caught up to her. "What is it you intend?" he demanded, closing his hand on her shoulder and hauling her to a stop.

"Since you will not help me, I'm going to cut Burke down and help him get away."

"You can't do that!"

"Why? Will your people stop me? Will they kill me, too?"

"Celene, listen—"

"Don't you understand? Except for Burke I might be dead," she shouted, her voice gone frayed and shrill.

"When our father lacked the honor and concern to rescue me from Rivard and Arnaud, Burke came in his place. He accepted their challenge in our father's name. If you've killed Rivard to avenge your honor, you must save Burke to pay the debt our father owes. It is something that must be done. Either you will do it for me, or I will do it myself."

Sky shook her roughly, and it was only then that Celene realized tears were spilling down her cheeks.

"Burke did the best he could," she insisted brokenly. "I owe him my life, and I cannot stand idle and watch him die. Save him because I am your sister, because I am pleading for his life. Save him for any reason that you like, but please, Darkening Sky, don't let him die."

Pain and confusion sparked and flared in her half brother's eyes. Though this was a battle of wills she dared not lose, she suddenly understood the price Darkening Sky would pay if he granted what she'd asked. He was caught between his concern for her and the love he bore for his Chippewa brothers, caught between the two compelling forces that warred in his blood. How could he make such a terrible choice? How could she ask him to?

Yet she had. She had asked him because she couldn't help herself, because she had no choice, either. She would save Burke's life or she would die at his side. There was nothing else for her to do.

With his mouth set and his eyes gone hard, Darkening Sky wheeled back toward the Indian camp.

To Burke, the pain was like a separate entity dwelling inside his skin. The ache that ran the full length of his body was a tuneless drone, ceaseless and monotonous. The lashes he'd received running the gauntlet early this morning were stinging, throbbing tentacles wrapped tightly around his back and chest. The muscles in his shoulders and arms burned with the constant strain, and his joints seemed ready to pull apart. He tried to drift above the misery, but its constancy wore him down.

He was going to die. That was inevitable, and though he was not yet ready to consign himself to eternal nothingness, he knew a time would come when he would welcome the escape. Already one of the other trappers had succumbed, and now there were only two of them to provide sport for this village of Chippewa. He moistened his lips and blinked the sweat out of his eyes, trying to catch sight of Celene somewhere in the crowd. He had seen nothing of her since the night before, and he knew he had no choice about trusting her safety to Darkening Sky. Still, he longed for one last glimpse of her.

Instead of finding Celene, his gaze was drawn once more to Autumn Leaf. What hold she had gained over him, he did not know. He seemed suddenly obsessed with her: with the blue-black lights in her long, straight hair; with the ripe voluptuousness of her body; with the lush femininity he yearned to explore. If he had been free, he would have sought her out and mated with her in a primitive rutting that would have had nothing to do with the love he had felt for her sister or his tenderness for Celene. His attraction for Autumn Leaf was an impulse foreign to all his perceptions of himself, incompatible with everything he knew of her. Yet he felt incapable of resisting her strange allure. As he watched, she raised one hand to the embroidered deerskin bag that hung on a cord around her neck. His heartbeat quickened as she closed her fingers around it. He felt his breathing accelerate. His gaze held Autumn Leaf's, and he was snared by the fearsome, self-satisfied glow that burned in her night-dark eyes.

It was Darkening Sky's voice that broke the spell. Cardwell did not catch the meaning of the words, but he saw two braves draw their knives as they came toward him. It seemed he no longer had a choice about when he would die. Darkening Sky had denied him even that last prerogative.

His heart slammed against his breastbone. Weakness sluiced down his arms and legs. Sweat oozed from his pores. Could the Indians smell the fear in him? Terrified by the knowledge of the torture and the pain to come, Burke wondered if he would die screaming like a coward, or silent like a man.

He searched the crowd again, desperate for one last look

at Celene's sweet face. She was there, a yard or two behind where her half brother stood. Her eyes were wide and wet with tears. Her face was the color of chalk, and the fear that slashed across her features was for him, not for herself.

There was something about seeing such terror in her that steeled his resolve. He flexed his muscles as the Indians jumped up beside him. He bit down on his lip as they raised their knives. He was determined not to cry out, no matter how they tortured him. Instead they hacked through the thongs that bound his ankles and wrists. When the rawhide gave, he crumpled to the floor of the wooden platform.

Burke sucked air into his burning lungs as he tried to make some sense of what was happening. But he was conscious only of the pain that quivered through every cell, of his pulse thrumming in his ears, of the utter exhaustion that made thinking or moving impossible.

As Burke fought his dizziness and confusion, someone threw a war club down in front of him. The implication of the act was clear, and Cardwell forced his aching muscles to respond. Though his body screamed in protest, he reached for the war club and closed his fingers around the handle. With an enormous effort he hauled himself to his feet and staggered to the edge of the platform. A wave of noise burst over him, raised from half a hundred throats.

"You see he is willing to defend himself," he heard Darkening Sky shout above the roar. "He is willing to fight me to the death."

"Oh, God!" Cardwell whispered, hoping he'd somehow misunderstood. He was in no condition to do battle with Darkening Sky. Swaying, he sliced a glance in Celene's direction. Her face was marked with outrage, fear, and disbelief.

"Fight me, Cardwell," Darkening Sky taunted, shifting his own war club from hand to hand. "Surely you're able to muster some sort of defense."

Cardwell shuffled his feet and flexed his arms. It was like trying to animate unyielding stone. His joints creaked as he fought to find his balance and heft his weapon. The war ax hung like lead in his hands.

The ground seemed miles below the platform on which

he stood. He teetered at the edge before stepping into thin air. The earth rushed up to meet him, the contact jarring up his legs and back before he fell to his knees in the dirt. With his head reeling, he staggered to his feet. He took one step backward to regain his balance, then quickly retreated another step.

Darkening Sky pressed his advantage. He took a swipe with his war club that whistled within inches of Cardwell's ribs.

Burke bowed his body to escape the arc of the hatchet's lethal blade. Pain rippled along his muscles in a sleek, bright wave. He drew a hissing breath and stepped clumsily to his right.

"I am not as easy a quarry as I was once, am I, Cardwell? It is not so simple to disgrace me now as it was when we fought for Morning Song."

Burke set his feet and swung the war club.

Sky easily defended himself. The weapons clashed together. The contact rattled through Burke's wrists and up his arms. The vibration shuddered at the base of his skull and ricocheted down his spine. He gritted his teeth and swung again.

The Indian leaped out of the way.

Air raked down Cardwell's throat as he fought for breath. His ears rang with the sound of shouting. The sting of sweat was in his eyes. With a groan he raised his club again. If this was a fight to the death, he might as well get on with it.

Darkening Sky stepped backward, drawing Burke on. Cardwell came at him with another stroke. The ripple of his muscles as he moved turned the skin on his back to a sheet of flame. Again Sky stepped aside.

With his full weight behind the blow, Burke stumbled and went down. He landed hard, the concussion shuddering through his bones. A moan worked its way between his teeth.

Sky reacted with a swift, backhanded blow that sent pain erupting through Burke's shoulder. It tingled down his arm; his hand went numb. With a triumphant smile the Indian turned and danced away.

Burke hurt everywhere. He could hardly force his quivering muscles to respond. His head was fuzzy, and his vision fogged. Darkening Sky wavered before him as three separate entities, each of them strutting, laughing, goading him. Moving slowly, he fought his way to his feet.

Before Burke was ready to defend an attack, Darkening Sky jabbed the handle of the war club up beneath the apex of Cardwell's ribs. He went down like a felled tree, slamming into the earth. Pain rippled along his nerves and detonated at the base of his skull. The jolt of landing jarred the handle of the war club loose. It went skittering, spinning across the earth. When Burke felt it slip from his grasp, he began to count the rest of his life in seconds.

Around him the cries of the crowd were coming in waves. They buffeted his ears, undulated through his head. As hard as he tried, he could not get his breath. The world dipped and swayed around him. And looming over him, like a vision from a nightmare, was Darkening Sky. His teeth were bared and the light of victory was bright in his eyes.

The Indian's muscles flexed as he raised the war club for the final stroke. From where he lay, Burke's gaze followed the twisted line of the Indian's body: up the extended leg, across the rippled expanse of his chest, along the tensile curve of his upraised arm to where the war club's polished wood and stone gleamed high above him. There was a primitive beauty about his executioner, and Burke accepted with shattering resignation that he was about to die.

A hiss of anticipation moved through the crowd. Darkening Sky coiled back, like a striking snake. Time seemed poised on the edge of the lethal blade.

As the club began its downward stroke, the Indian's war cry split the air.

"No!" A woman's scream slashed through the barrier of the Indian's cry, and Celene's soft, protective weight came heavy across Burke's chest. Through the screen of her tumbled hair, he saw Darkening Sky fight to stay the blow. The ax swerved to the right, thudding to the ground a handsbreadth from where they lay.

Celene's small, strong fingers clenched tight on his

shoulders had jerked Burke back from the edge of the abyss. She had spared his life, at least for a little while. He went trembly and weak from the shock of it.

Her gaze skimmed over him before she turned on her half brother like one gone mad. "You will not hurt him any more!" she screeched at him. "I have agreed to be his wife, and I will not let you kill the man I've chosen as my husband!"

"Celene, don't," Burke warned in a whisper, but Celene continued as if she had not heard.

"Before I was taken from the rendezvous, I spent the night with Burke. I gave my promise that I would marry him, and I will not let you hurt him any more."

"What is this?" Darkening Sky demanded, his eyebrows lifting in perfect arcs above those telltale gray-green eyes.

"Our father gave me to this man," she declared, rising up before her brother, "and I have agreed to marry him."

"Is this true, Cardwell?"

What Celene was attempting was either incredibly foolhardy or unbelievably courageous. Her failure or success would determine which.

"I have offered for your sister," Cardwell conceded, struggling to stand. He knew he was swaying, but couldn't seem to help himself.

"And have you paid a bride-price to her father as is the Chippewa custom?"

It was as if Darkening Sky somehow knew about Burke's agreement with Antoine, as if Celene's brother was privy to the concessions Peugeot had wrung from him. The thought was dizzying, impossible. "I have paid a bride-price," he declared.

"How much was that?"

"A pack of peltries. He wanted two."

Darkening Sky drew a long, slow breath and turned to Running Dog. "Though it was my intention to kill my life-long enemy, I find he has been accepted as a member of my family. I would spare him for my sister's sake, but you and the council have voted for his death."

Running Dog looked from Darkening Sky to Burke Cardwell as if he thought their declarations were a trick.

But the stark fear on Celene's tear-streaked face must have convinced him of their sincerity.

As the silence lengthened, Celene came forward as if to plead Burke's case, but her brother caught her wrist.

Running Dog turned to the leader of the party who had captured the trappers. "I ask again, is this one of the trappers who originally stole the pelts?"

"No," the brave answered.

The chief was silent for a long moment as he studied the question before him. "If we grant this man his life, he must agree to work for the tribe and be married to your sister by nightfall."

"It will be done," Darkening Sky assured him.

So Celene was going to marry him after all, Cardwell thought, trade her promise for his life. There was selflessness in what she'd done, especially when Cardwell knew how desperately afraid she was of all that marriage meant. It was a sacrifice he would not let her regret, he told himself, a sacrifice he would never do anything to betray.

He turned to where Celene stood beside him, wanting to take her hand, wanting to thank her for what she'd done. But before he could act, he became aware that Autumn Leaf was standing on the periphery of the crowd, a dozen feet beyond Celene. And at the sight of her, with her hand clasped tight around the embroidered bag, his heart began to pound.

9

Her wedding dress was made of fawn-colored doeskin, shimmering with disks of trade silver and thick with fringe. Two Indian women arrived at Darkening Sky's wigwam during the late afternoon with the dress, the leggings, and the appropriate accessories in hand, come to prepare Celene for the ceremony that would take place at sunset.

Despite her determination never to marry again, Celene felt unexpectedly accepting of her forthcoming wedding. Perhaps the prospect of this marriage did not frighten her because she could not consider the ceremony binding. There would be no mass to bless her union with Burke, no priests to pray for their happiness and fecundity. As Darkening Sky explained it, there would only be a few questions asked and answered, a few words spoken over the couple by one of the Chippewa shamans. Then she and Burke would return to Darkening Sky's wigwam to start their life together.

Or perhaps the reason for her calm acceptance of her marriage, Celene reasoned as she fingered the buttery-soft doeskin of the wedding dress, was the certainty that Burke no longer wanted her for his wife. The night they had spent together at Prairie du Chien had convinced her of that. She had been unwilling to grant him her favor, and Burke had been gentleman enough not to force himself on her. She was sure he would not want a wife who refused to perform her marital duties, and she suspected that if Rivard and Arnaud had not abducted her, Burke would have broken whatever marriage contract he and Antoine had made. What would occur this evening was a marriage of convenience, one that was taking place only to save Burke Cardwell's life.

She would not allow herself to think about what would happen after this. Darkening Sky had maneuvered an impossible situation to their advantage, and for the moment it was enough to know that once were wed, Burke would be safe.

Before she would allow the Indian women to prepare her for the ceremony, Celene managed to convey her wish to bathe. Though she was not eager for their company or their help, the two women took her to the stream and waded in beside her to scrub away the grime of the forced march and wash her hair. Back in the wigwam, they brushed it dry, commenting to each other, it seemed, on the unusual sunshine color. Once her body had been scented with flower blossoms crushed and rubbed over every inch of her skin, a process that brought the hot blood of modesty to Celene's pale cheeks, the women began to clothe her. The soft leather dress was gathered up and dropped over her head. The doeskin skimming along her body had the same sensuous feel as silk. It was drawn tight at the waist with a belt that was accented with bright, flower-patterned beadwork that exactly matched the one on the dress's leather straps. There was a waist-length jacket with long, fringed sleeves, leggings tied below the knees with woven garters and matching moccasins to complete the ensemble. The women exclaimed over her as they worked, decking her with necklaces of trade beads, with her own calico pomander bag, plaiting and wrapping her long, thick hair with deer-hide thongs. When at last the two women seemed satisfied, they led her outside where Darkening Sky was waiting.

He nodded once at the women before turning to Celene. "You look very beautiful," he commented as he took her hand.

"I want to thank you," she told him as he led her toward the center of the camp. "I want you to know how much I appreciate what you've done for Burke and me."

"I did what I did for honor, nothing else," he answered, not meeting the look she flashed at him.

Though he might deny his reasons for saving Burke, Celene knew what they were. She knew they were based in love for a sister he barely knew, in respect for a father who had refused to acknowledge him. Darkening Sky was a special man, and Celene would never forget what he'd risked to save her and Burke.

But now that the moment of the wedding was upon her, Celene was not quite as sanguine as she had expected to be. Her hand, curled inside her half brother's warm one, was cold as winter rain. At the doorway of the Mide lodge, one of the band's shamans was waiting. Beside him Burke stood, dressed in full Chippewa regalia: a matchcoat trimmed with gaily colored ribbons, a deer-hide breechclout and leggings, beaded garters and moccasins. An otter fur headband hung with polished disks had been woven through his hair, and there were a silver gorget and several loops of trade beads strung around his neck.

When Burke saw her, his face brightened, and though she tried not to notice the cuts and bruises that marked him, she could not ignore the flash of pain and exhaustion that shone briefly in his eyes. Still, he stood tall and straight beside the shaman, allowing nothing of what he was feeling to be revealed in his expression.

As they approached the Mide lodge, Darkening Sky maneuvered Celene into place, so that he stood like a guardian between her and Burke. They remained standing silent for several unsettling minutes before the shaman began to speak. First he addressed himself to Burke as if he were questioning Cardwell's intent. Then he turned to Darkening Sky. Without understanding the words, Celene could sense that her half brother was being asked if he would give her to the other man. As Sky listened to the questions, she could see the color come up in his face, sense his reluctance in trusting her future to Burke. The animosity between the two men glowed as fierce and bright as the sun setting fire to the western rim of the sky, but somehow Darkening Sky managed to muster the appropriate assurances. Finally he passed Celene's cold fingers from his firm, encompassing hand to Burke's strong and even larger one.

"You look lovely," Burke murmured under his breath. "The Indian garb suits you."

Celene lowered her eyes and drew a shaky breath. How could he issue mundane compliments when his future and hers would be decided in the next few moments?

Burke's thumb stroked the back of her hand. "I appreciate what you're doing to save my life. I know how hard this is for you."

She raised her gaze to his and stared into those clear, compelling eyes. They were brilliant turquoise, a perfect mingling of blue and green, as bright as a mountain lake reflecting the summer sky. They were filled with warmth, pride, and an appreciation of her courage that made her turn away.

"I promise you'll never regret for a moment what you're doing for my sake."

Celene's heart beat unsteadily inside her chest. She did not know how to accept his admiration, did not know if she was worthy of the respect he seemed to feel for her. As unaccustomed as she was to warmth and gratitude, they were emotions she could not seem to assimilate. And as frightened as she was of marriage, agreeing to be Burke's bride seemed suddenly a very small sacrifice to make.

The slowing of the shaman's unintelligible words and the focus of his unwavering gaze made Celene realize that something was expected of her.

"He wants to know if you accept me as your husband, giving me dominion over your goods, your behavior . . ." The grim hint of a smile tugged at the corner of Cardwell's upper lip. "And your body."

"Do I have to promise that?"

"If you want to get us out of this." When Celene hesitated, Burke urged her on. "Damn it, Celene, promise it for the moment at least. We can negotiate the fine points later!"

Her heart thudded hard against her breastbone. Her mouth went dry. "What must I say?"

"*Uh* means yes. It means that you agree."

She inclined her head. "*Uh*."

The shaman nodded in return and began to speak to the small group gathered around them. It was not all that different from the way a priest would have prayed over them during a wedding mass.

"This man and this woman are now joined together," Burke translated in an undertone. "They have each agreed to live in peace and unity. The bride's family has accepted the marriage in exchange for the payment of a bride-price. The husband has given his word to care for and honor his bride. The wife has given her word to care for and obey her husband. Together they will become an asset to the band. The strength and stamina this man has proved today will make him a formidable hunter and warrior. The courage and determination this woman has showed . . ."

"It sounds as if they expect us to live here with them," Celene breathed, distress bringing gravity to her face.

Breaking off his translation, Burke spoke even more softly. "That's exactly what they expect."

"But aren't we going to leave—"

"Hush."

"But I thought—"

The expression he slashed at her from under his angled brows was more eloquent than any words he could have spoken.

Celene subsided, shaken by what she had discovered. It had never occurred to her that once she had taken Burke as her husband they would be expected to stay on with this band of Chippewa. Certainly Darkening Sky had never hinted that accepting her status as a captive of the tribe would be the price she'd have to pay for saving Burke's life. She turned to look at her half brother, but he would not meet her gaze.

But I want to go home! something inside Celene cried. *I want to hold my son in my arms, sleep in my own bed, tend my fields. I don't want to end my days as an Indian squaw.*

As if he'd heard her silent plea, Burke's hand tightened reassuringly. She looked up to see if she could read the promise of home in his eyes, but they were cloudy with pain, dark with fatigue. And suddenly all she wanted was for the ceremony to be over.

The shaman's voice rose in a discordant, droning chant. When it came to an end, he shook his turtle-shell rattle to the north and south, the east and west. And she and Burke were man and wife.

It was the sun burning orange against his closed eyelids, the bright rays peeking between his lashes that awakened Burke to the brand-new day. He shifted on the narrow bed, fighting to avoid the light, fighting the dawning consciousness. But as he did, he realized that the movement did not elicit the stretching, tearing pain it had a fortnight ago. He was recovered from the ordeal of Indian torture and restless to leave the encampment behind.

Slowly Burke sat up at the edge of his bench opposite the wigwam's doorway. The hide covering had been pushed aside to admit the brilliant dawn. The way the sun streamed through the opening reminded him of England, of light blazing through arched cathedral windows, of the sun twinkling in the thousand mullioned panes of the drawing room at Longmeadow. Though the revenge he plotted had been far from his mind in these last days, memories of his family home had begun to pull at him in a way he never thought they could. But Longmeadow was thousands of miles away, and for the moment his life and future were here in the Chippewa camp.

Turning from the brightness, Burke noticed that Darkening Sky's bed was empty and his Mide bag was gone, giving evidence that there was sickness somewhere in the camp. Almost reluctantly Burke let his gaze drift to the opposite side of the firepit where Celene still lay nestled deep in her blankets. From where he sat, he could see the shape of her legs, the crest of her hip, the swooping vale of her waist, and the bare hummock of one pale shoulder where the covers had fallen away.

In spite of his best resolves, Burke rose and moved to stand over her, looking down into her face. Her cheek was pillowed on one crooked arm, and her hair tossed about her in cascading disarray. Her mouth was ever-so-slightly bowed, her skin awash with pink, her spiky lashes dark against it. There was a clutch of tenderness in his chest, a swirl of desire that moved relentlessly through his blood.

Celene had become his wife in the Chippewa ceremony, and though it was his right, he had not touched her. That last night at the rendezvous, she had made it clear that she could never reciprocate the desire he felt for her. Nor would he ever force her to come to him. Still, the tenderness remained. It was a tenderness roused by Celene's vulnerability, by her determination to survive in spite of all she had suffered. It was a tenderness based in the concern she had showed for him and in her limitless courage.

She looked so fragile lying there, so sweet and innocent, so incredibly helpless. Yet he was beginning to understand that she was a woman of strength and heart, whose contradictions and inconsistencies he was only beginning to know. He had seen so many women in Celene: the hoyden fierce with anger who had pushed him down, the single-minded termagant who might have been capable of helping him carry out the plans he'd made for his return to England, the skilled trader bartering pelts for hams. And just when he was sure he knew what to expect of her, Celene had turned into the trembling shattered widow, weeping silently in his arms. It was impossible to reconcile that fragile, timid woman with the one who had withstood abduction by Arnaud and Rivard and capture by the Indians. How could that bitter, frightened woman, who had been terrified by all that marriage meant, have claimed him as her husband and saved his life?

The essence of Celene Peugeot Bernard was as elusive as quicksilver. It was as bright and multifaceted as a glittering gem. It made her impossible to understand or qualify. Yet he felt boundless respect for who she was, a compelling curiosity about who she might next become.

She was as different from Morning Song as midnight was from noon, he found himself thinking. But she intrigued him in a way his wife never had. Morning Song was as simple and as constant as daylight following dark. Celene was complex and contradictory.

What would happen to them once they found a way to leave the Chippewa band, Burke could only guess. They would need to get on their way in the next few days, before he was pressed into the service of the tribe as all Indian captives eventually were. The one thing he knew for certain was that he wanted Celene by his side when he made good his escape. He wanted to see how she fared on the long voyage to Ste. Genevieve, wanted to watch the reunion between her and her son, wanted to be more than her friend. That seemed impossible, and yet . . .

Irritated with himself for dwelling on things he had no business thinking about, Burke turned away. He donned the leggings and shirt Darkening Sky had given him, then hastily left the wigwam. It grated on him to have been protected by Darkening Sky, to be dependent on a man who had long been an enemy. He sensed that the Indian was no more fond of the arrangement than he was.

At any rate, he was well enough now to begin to hunt for himself and Celene. He need not ask her brother for food, at least. And if Darkening Sky was tending to the sick, there would be no one to provide their evening meal, anyway. It was unlikely that Burke would be allowed to wander freely in search of game, and more unlikely still that he would be allowed a weapon of any kind. But that didn't mean he could not fish for his supper, and he slunk back into the wigwam for a net bag and a fishing spear.

As he wandered through the sleeping camp in the direction of the stream, he savored the first taste of freedom he'd had in many days. That freedom was an illusion, Burke well knew, but it fed the determination that he and Celene must get away.

His feet whispered along the well-worn path as he followed the stream, stopping only when it joined a somewhat wider channel. With fishing spear in hand, he hunkered down on a broad, flat rock and waited for his supper to swim by. As the sun burned its way across the sky, the number of fish in the basswood-fiber bag multiplied. When he was sure he had caught enough for several meals, Burke shucked his shirt and stretched out on the rock to enjoy the solitude. The wind stroked across his skin; the water gurgled by. The heat and quiet lulled him. He fell into a dreamless sleep.

Sunset was painting the sky when he awoke. Scrambling

around, he gathered up his belongings. His return to the Indian camp was swift and direct. But as he reached the break of trees that sheltered the camp, chills blossomed between his shoulder blades. His steps lagged. His mouth went dry. He tightened his grip on the fishing spear.

Autumn Leaf emerged from the opposite side of the grove. Burke's feet seemed to root themselves in the earth as he watched her approach. For reasons he could not rationally understand, he was mesmerized by the sway of her vermillion skirt, unwillingly enticed by the press of her full breasts against the fabric of her embroidered blouse. The golden sheen from the setting sun caught and reflected in her blue-black hair. She stopped before him, and the knowledge of what he was feeling gleamed in the depths of her eyes.

"Where have you been?" she asked. "Darkening Sky and the others have been looking for you."

The words came to Burke as if through a haze, blurred, muted, almost unintelligible. "I went to catch some fish for our supper," he answered slowly, gesturing with the bag he held in one hand.

She reached to take it from him, and even that brief contact sent tingles up his arm.

"No, I . . ." Burke stammered, jerking back. "That— that isn't meant for you."

"Of course it is," she insisted.

"No—"

He saw her raise her hand to touch the embroidered bag that hung on a thong around her neck, and a buzzing started in his head. It was like distant music, a Siren's song. She swayed closer and the hum intensified.

"Whatever you've given other women is now for me. You understand that, don't you?" As she spoke she lay her hand in the center of his chest. His heart leaped against his breastbone as if she had the power to draw it into her palm.

With her standing so close in front of him, Burke couldn't breathe. He couldn't move. He couldn't think. He was responding to Autumn Leaf's nearness as he never thought he would. Heat raked through him. Desire rampaged through his blood.

Looking up into his face, Autumn Leaf smiled, and there was smugness in her eyes. "You want me," she told him.

"No."

"You want me."

It was the truth, but Burke tried to deny it with the shake of his head.

The fingers of her free hand tightened on the doeskin bag. "You want me," she insisted.

Every time she whispered the words, a bit of his will seemed to trickle away. He had never trusted Autumn Leaf. He had never wanted her, but he had no strength to voice the denial. His head went fuzzy, and he was aflame, consumed with a need for her he could not explain.

"Yes," he conceded. "I want you."

"Then kiss me."

The fishing spear and mesh bag thudded softly into the grass. Autumn Leaf stepped closer, nestling her breasts to the front of his shirt. The doeskin bag and its contents, something small and hard, pressed against the arch of his ribs. It seared as if he had been branded with red-hot steel.

Of their own volition his arms coiled around her back, pulling her closer until the whole of her was contoured to his body. Her musky scent was in his nostrils. Her breath pooled against his skin.

No, no some faint voice inside him insisted as he lowered his mouth to hers, but he was incapable of heeding the warning.

Her lips were wet, her taste cloying. She thrust her tongue into his mouth. He experienced a swell of distaste, but could not seem to stop kissing her.

It was as if he were floating outside himself, both participant and observer in what was happening. He tightened his hold, binding Autumn Leaf to him, deepening the kiss and drawing on her tongue. In some faraway corner of his mind he knew he did not want this woman, that no good could come of taking her. Yet he had no strength to pull away.

Her hands were ranging over him, one abrading his nipple through the fabric of his shirt, one snaking beneath the fold of his breechclout to fondle the base of his spine. Desire consumed him, and he consigned himself to the flames, lost to whatever alchemy Autumn Leaf had used to entrap him.

"Mon dieu! Burke!"

The words swam around in his brain for several moments before he grasped their meaning. The realization came slowly. As it did, he fought to raise his head.

Celene was here. Oh, God! Celene!

Autumn Leaf must have been aware of Celene's presence, too, for she severed the kiss Burke could not seem to break. The Indian woman both turned and nestled closer in his arms, and though he wanted to, he seemed incapable of pushing her away.

Across the clearing, he recognized the disbelief, the anger, and the betrayal mingling in Celene's bright eyes. There was a clutch of panic and regret inside his chest. He hurt for her and for himself.

"Go away, French whore," Autumn Leaf taunted. "Can't you see this man no longer wants you?"

But Celene's unwavering gaze never strayed from Burke's face. "Is that so, Monsieur Cardwell? Would you rather have this woman as your wife instead of me?"

Before Burke could gather his wits to speak, Autumn Leaf turned to him. "You know how easy it is to end a marriage here. No one would blame you for leaving a woman as pale and ugly as she."

As she spoke, Autumn Leaf leaned even closer to his chest, and Burke could feel the jab of the object in the doeskin bag she wore around her neck. Suddenly he was more befuddled than before, aching, frightened of her power, and hopelessly confused. He wanted to explain to Celene what had happened here in the trees, wanted to beg her forgiveness. But what could he say? He didn't understand what hold the Indian woman had on him.

"Tell her you want me for your wife instead of her," the Indian woman prompted.

A wave of dizziness nearly brought Burke to his knees as he fought the need to repeat the words. He fought the urge with every ounce of will he still possessed. His breathing went stark with the effort. His skin went cold.

"No, I—I don't . . ."

Autumn Leaf slid her hand between their bodies to touch the embroidered bag again, but before she could close her fingers around it, Celene sprang across the clearing to where the two of them stood. With a curse she caught the Indian woman's arm and yanked her out of Burke's embrace. He let her go, but Autumn Leaf's nails raked across his back and down his arms as Celene determinedly hauled her away.

Burke reeled backward, staggering into a tree. Lights swirled and winked before his eyes. When Celene had pulled Autumn Leaf away, it was as if she had ripped a hole in his chest, as if she'd deprived him of something he needed to survive. Yet he was glad to be free, glad to be out of the sphere of the Indian woman's inexplicable power. He clung to the pine tree's nubby bark, clung and prayed for his head to clear.

From somewhere beyond the lights he heard his name. It wavered in his ears, demanding, compelling. From what seemed like a million miles away, he saw Autumn Leaf reach for the doeskin bag again.

But Celene was too fast for her. She ripped the bag from the thong around the Indian woman's neck. Holding her prize aloft, she whirled and danced away.

The instant Celene's fingers curled around the doeskin bag, she knew there was something evil inside. Even through the thickness of the hide she could feel it cold against her palm, an ungodly chill that penetrated deep into her flesh. Autumn Leaf had brought something dark and powerful to bear against Burke, and Celene knew that for his sake it must be destroyed.

"Give me the bag," Autumn Leaf cajoled as they maneuvered around the clearing. "This is nothing that need concern you."

Celene tightened her grip on her prize. "It feels as if there's a carving inside. But what carving could possibly be worth the store you seem to put in it?"

"Stop your prattle and give me the bag."

Celene shook her head and backed away. As she did,

Autumn Leaf lunged for her, her yelp of fury echoing through the trees. Celene skipped nimbly aside, knowing her only advantage over the taller, stronger woman was in her agility and speed.

As the Indian woman struggled to regain her balance, Celene spared a glance for Burke. Pale as whey, he clung to a tree as if it was his only anchor in a treacherous, unsteady world. What had Autumn Leaf discovered that gave her such power over him?

There was no time to question what that power was. Autumn Leaf was leaping forward, clutching at the bag, her fingers curled like claws. Again Celene managed to swirl away. With all her weight behind the movement, Autumn Leaf sprawled facedown in the dirt. But as she scrambled to her feet, she drew a knife from somewhere in her clothes.

Celene focused on the glinting blade. In the last rays of the fading sun, its edge gleamed like a strip of fire. She carried no weapon of her own. It never occurred to her that she might be called upon to defend herself, or Burke, in quite this way. She sucked in a ragged breath and stood her ground, steeling herself for battle.

Autumn Leaf stepped closer, slashing her blade from side to side.

From the edge of the trees Burke staggered toward them, his hand extended to deflect Autumn Leaf's attack. He intercepted the sweep of steel instead. The knife blade slashed across his palm.

The three of them stood frozen as dark blood welled up from the open wound: Celene angry and appalled, Burke stunned and wavering on his feet. Autumn Leaf's eyes were huge with disbelief, as if she had not meant to harm Cardwell in quite this way.

A new flare of cold burned through the hide, numbing Celene's fingers and sending a bone-deep ache spiraling up her arm. The evil inside the bag had to be destroyed, and Celene spun back toward the Indian camp. Darkening Sky would know how to break the spell, how to save Burke from whatever sinister magic Autumn Leaf had loosed.

The Indian woman pounded down the path behind Celene, leaving Burke swaying and staring after them. They

raced between the wigwams, dodging around children playing in the dirt. Driven by fury and desperation, Autumn
Leaf was gaining ground. Celene hurdled a woodpile and
sidestepped one of the village dogs. It cost her a step or
two, the few precious seconds it took for Autumn Leaf to
snag her arm. They skidded to a stop at the edge of one of
the communal campfires.

Autumn Leaf was trembling, breathing hard, and before
the other woman could recover herself, Celene meant to see
what evil lurked inside the bag. Jerking free of the Indian
woman's hold and working open the bag's drawstring
mouth, Celene dumped the contents into her palm. Without
the protection of the leather container, the thing seared into
her skin, ice that burned as hot as flame.

Sparing a glance at Autumn Leaf, Celene looked down
at the object in her hand. It was a pair of carvings not much
larger than two of her fingers side by side. One of them
was clearly male and cut from pine, the other female and
of some smoother, darker wood. The two pieces fit together
perfectly, bound tight with a long, thick strand of honey-
colored hair.

"What is this?" Celene demanded, though she hardly
had to ask.

"It's a charm."

"A love charm? You meant to win Burke's love with
heathen magic?"

As if in answer, the two entwined figures seemed to
glow. The ache of cold radiated through her flesh, unfurled
frigid tendrils up her arm. Such magic was the devil's work.
She had seen proof of its power in Burke today. With a
muttered prayer for deliverance on her lips, Celene cast the
charm into the fire flaring bright beside her.

"No. No!" Autumn Leaf cried and went to her knees
beside the blaze. Dropping her knife, she reached toward
where the two small figures lay.

Celene sank to the ground beside Autumn Leaf and
caught the Indian woman's wrists. The heat of the blaze
was too intense for her to recover the charm, though she
fought Celene's shackling hold. Then, as the two women
watched, the strands of hair that bound the figures together

burned away. The tiny man and woman fell apart, and Autumn Leaf began to sob.

Drawn by the noise of the argument, by the sound of the Indian woman's keening, a crowd began to gather. When Celene looked up she could see that the Indians' faces were marked with uncertainty, anger, hostility. She had done some grievous hurt to one of their own, and she could feel their animosity rising around her. She clambered to her feet and turned to go. Surely someone among them would see to Autumn Leaf.

Knowing Burke was out in the darkness somewhere, hurt, bleeding, and confused, Celene hurriedly retraced her steps. The fishing spear and the bag of fish still lay in the grass at the edge of the grove, but Burke had vanished. It made sense that he would return to Darkening Sky's lodge, and the dark traces of blood she could just barely see on the ground seemed to indicate he'd gone in that direction.

When she reached the wigwam, Cardwell was there, sitting on his cot with a makeshift bandage around his palm. His head came up with a jerk as she approached. "Are you all right?" he asked, struggling to stand.

She pressed him back down on the edge of the bed. "I'm fine, not hurt at all."

"Good," he said with a shaky smile. "And Autumn Leaf . . ."

"She wasn't hurt, either," Celene assured him. "But she won't be bothering us again."

Burke nodded and let out a long, slow breath. "I—I don't know what came over me this afternoon, why I was there with her. I didn't want to be, especially after what you risked to claim me as your husband. I didn't want to kiss her. I just couldn't seem to help myself."

Celene nodded and knelt beside him, loosening the bandage around his hand. "She had a charm," she told him.

"A charm?"

"A love charm. Two carved figures tied together with a strand of your hair."

"My hair?" Burke seemed utterly confused. "But how did she get that?"

"She must have picked it up when I cut your hair at the

rendezvous. After the storm, I noticed the clippings had disappeared, but I didn't realize the significance—not until now.''

Burke nodded slowly. "I found Autumn Leaf in my tent that day. She was soaked to the skin and full of threats."

They were silent for a moment, both busy with their own thoughts. Celene's centered on the gash in Burke's right palm. It was deep and in need of stitching. She rose and gathered up the things she required to do the job: a steel needle, thread, water, and a length of cotton cloth. She wished she had a bit of whiskey to pour into the wound. It would sting like fire, but her father swore it made a cut heal clean. But then, she thought with the hint of a smile, her father was quicker to extol the virtues of strong drink than any man she'd ever met. There was no whiskey to be had in the wigwam, though. Darkening Sky was of the Mide, and the Mide never touched the white man's spirits.

Just as she was settling at Burke's feet to begin her task, she saw a shudder rack his frame. She looked up into his face, becoming suddenly aware of the spots of red at the crest of his cheeks and the haziness in his eyes.

"Burke, are you all right?" she asked as she reached across to touch his cheek.

"I don't know. I feel so odd, all achy and hot."

The heat in him might well have set tinder ablaze.

"Darkening Sky said there was a fever in camp. I think you have a touch of it."

Leaving the things she had gathered on the floor, Celene stripped him out of his shirt and leggings. Within moments of settling on the cot, Burke dropped into a restless sleep. While he slept, she tended his gash in his palm, cleaning, stitching, and binding it.

Even before she had finished, the fever staked its claim on him. He was lost in it, consumed by it. His eyes, when he opened them, were dark and glazed. He began to shiver convulsively.

Celene had tended fevers scores of times before and went efficiently about her task, soothing him, bathing him, trickling water into his mouth. Yet the fire in his blood raged higher, filling his head with fancies and Celene with dread.

He opened his eyes to stare at her. "Morning Song?" he asked.

"No, I'm Celene," she told him, renewing the cold compress on his brow.

"Celene," he mumbled. "Yes, Celene. I remember now."

A few minutes later he asked again.

"Was Morning Song your wife?" she questioned him in a semilucid moment.

"My wife," he murmured in confirmation.

"And you loved her desperately, didn't you?"

Burke did not answer. She had not expected that he would. From what little her father had told her, she knew he had. A twinge of envy tweaked her. Perhaps one day, if God was kind, she would have a man to love her as Burke loved Morning Song.

Thrusting the thought aside, she continued to work over him, bathing his burning body, swaddling him in blankets, moistening his lips. Nothing she did brought any ease. As night deepened through the camp, Burke slipped further and further away from her.

He had lain quiet for a very long time, when he suddenly cried out his first wife's name. There was something different in the way he spoke the words, something of joyous greeting, something of poignant welcome.

Celene's hands went still against his scorching skin. When she looked down into his face, his eyes were wide and strangely bright. Half-turning, she followed his gaze to where moonlight poured in the open door. It was as pale and unsubstantial as drifting smoke.

"Morning Song, why are you here? Why do you want me to go with you?"

Celene's heart thudded thick and hard inside her chest. The hairs on the back of her neck began to stir.

Was there something there in the filmy light? Something Burke could see and she could not?

A shiver tingled the length of her spine, like the stroke of an unseen hand. Her mouth went dry. Her head went light. Gooseflesh rose along her arms and legs. Hastily she crossed herself.

He was delirious, she insisted stubbornly, turning back to her task. His mind was playing tricks on him.

Yet whatever Burke saw in the wavering light was unquestionably benign. It calmed him, comforted him. He watched it with unwavering intent until pure exhaustion closed his eyes.

Fear steeled Celene's resolve. She bathed him, and crooned to him, mumbled litanies of prayers over him. But in the hours of darkness, Burke's breathing became shallow and labored. His eyes went hollow. His skin was papery and hot, and the flesh of his face seemed to be shrinking against his bones. There was the thick, flat scent of fever about him, of death, of defeat, of hopelessness.

It was not the first time Celene had fought to save Burke Cardwell's life, but this battle seemed harder, more demanding than the ones before, infinitely more important. It went on unabated until almost dawn.

The wash of light was still spilling through the door when Darkening Sky returned. He halted abruptly in its path, his brow furrowing, his eyes narrowing. As he prowled across the lodge to kneel beside Burke's bed, he moved as if his every sense was fully alert, as if he was brittlely aware of whatever presence Burke had sensed.

"I think Burke is going to die," Celene told her half brother, "and there's nothing more I can do for him. If I'd had any idea of where you were, I would have sent for you."

"I have been with Autumn Leaf."

"Autumn Leaf?"

"She died of a fever I could not cure."

His words sank in slowly, tempered with shock and disbelief. How could Autumn Leaf be dead? Celene had fought with a strong and healthy woman mere hours ago. It seemed impossible, and yet . . .

"Can you help Burke?" Celene asked, returning to more pressing concerns. "Are there herbs that you can give him to make him well?"

Darkening Sky let his assessing hands drift over the man on the cot and shook his head. "His illness is the same as

Autumn Leaf's. A curse of some kind, like a fire consuming them.''

Darkening Sky's words buffeted Celene, faint hollow sounds that echoed in her ears.

A curse of some kind, like a fire consuming them.

The significance slowly penetrated her haze of confusion and grief. Her head spun with images: of Burke's responses to the charm, of the two small figures surrounded by flames, of Autumn Leaf's confidence and fury turning to inconsolable grief. Celene caught her breath. By throwing the charm in the fire, she had thought to destroy its power. But she had not. Its malevolence was here, dwelling in Burke's burning body, stalking Darkening Sky's lodge. She suddenly realized that there was only one thing that had been keeping Burke alive, only one thing that might save him still.

In a single, up-thrust movement, she came to her feet. "Stay with him," she ordered. "Don't let him die!"

Without waiting for Darkening Sky to respond, she ran from the wigwam, out into the half-light of the pearl-gray dawn. She knew exactly where she must go, exactly what she must do to call Burke back.

With desperate haste she raced through the sleeping camp toward where she and Autumn Leaf had fought, toward the fire where she had thrown the charm. Most of the logs had burned to ashes during the night. But deep in the fire's heart, red-orange coals still glowed to seed the fire for the coming day.

Sliding to her knees, Celene poked through the smoking ash. She had seen the strand of hair holding the figures together burn away, had seen them tumble apart. The carving of the woman had fallen toward the center of the blaze, and since Autumn Leaf was dead, it must have been consumed. But Burke was still alive. That meant the figure of the man must be intact, lost in the fire somewhere.

The heat singed her knuckles as she groped closer and closer to the glowing coals; sparks hidden in the ashes bit into her palms and fingertips. Tears of pain and frustration rose in her eyes. The carving was so small, so fragile. How could she hope it had survived the night? How could she hope to find it?

"Please, God, please!" she whispered, wondering if she was asking God to help her do the devil's work. Could she expect an answer to such a heathen plea? Or perhaps what she was asking was that good would triumph over evil, that life would triumph over death. Perhaps that was a plea that God could grant.

Then, in a bed of ash mere inches from the central glow, she found the tiny wooden shape. It rose knobby and hard beneath her fingers, buried in the ash. Without feeling the pain, Celene snatched the carving from the bed of living coals. Holding it gently, almost reverently, in the center of her stinging palm, she blew the ash away. She had not noticed the details before, the queue tied back at the nape of the neck, the faint outline of a white man's shirt and breeches, the undeniable proof of the gender the carving was meant to represent. It was singed, slightly charred along one side, but still intact. It was miraculous that this bit of wood had survived all through the night. As she looked back at where it had lain, she could see it had been shielded by the broad, dark butt of an unburned log. There was no sign of the woman made to be its mate. The small wooden carving was gone, consumed by fire and by the evil it embodied, just as Autumn Leaf had been.

Celene clambered to her feet and crossed the encampment toward her half brother's lodge. Her heart thumped hard against her breastbone as she entered. The light of moon glow was gone. Was Burke gone, too? Had her understanding of the magic come too late?

Darkening Sky looked up from where he knelt beside Burke's bed, curiosity and concern alive in his gray-green eyes.

She swallowed hard and met his gaze. "Is Burke dead?" she asked.

"No, he's better," her brother answered. "The fever broke a few minutes ago."

Relief welled through her, calming and sweet. Exhaustion trickled down her arms and legs. She swiped away tears with the back of her hand. She had been right. The carving was the key to saving his life.

It took almost more effort than she could muster to cross the lodge to where Burke lay. A faint flush had replaced his ashen pallor. His chest rose and fell with even breathing, and beads of moisture were clustered on his brow and gathering in the hollows below his eyes. He was going to get well. As she tightened her fingers around the small, wooden carving, Celene understood that in some strange, irrevocable way, Burke Cardwell now belonged to her.

10

It was time. Burke Cardwell looked up from where he sat in the shade of Darkening Sky's lodge and watched a hawk sweep slow, lazy circles across the turquoise sky. The heat of full summer was upon them, clinging close in the dawn, sending shimmers skyward at noon, muffling the world like a blanket, even in the dark. As he watched, Celene trudged toward him up the slope, a gourd water bottle in either hand. He came to his feet and went to help her. As he approached, he could see the hopelessness in her face and knew why it was there. Lying awake in the night, he had heard her call out Jean-Paul's name in her sleep. He had seen the tears she'd shed as she watched the Indian mothers with their children. And that convinced him more than his own need to get away, more than his own need for freedom, that it was time to make their escape.

"Let me get those," he offered, taking the heavy bottles from her. "I would have been glad to fetch water for you."

"It's all right. I didn't mind the walk."

"I'm quite recovered from my illness, you know."

She nodded, her eyes on the rising ground in front of her.

"Celene, what happened wasn't your fault."

She nodded again and made her way toward the wigwam across trampled, sun-blasted grass.

"It was Autumn Leaf who called up the magic, not you," he insisted. "You didn't know what she had done. You had no idea what forces she'd tampered with."

He followed her into the dimness of the lodge, slung the

161

ropes on the gourds over the pegs at the side of the door, and turned to her. "You can't go on blaming yourself for this."

"And who else is there to blame? I wanted her power broken. I threw the charm into the fire. I wanted her gone. Now Autumn Leaf is dead. It's as if I wished it, and it came true."

He heard the guilt and vulnerability in her words and reached across to stroke her cheek. There was pain and unhappiness in her silver-green eyes. Tenderness flared up like a bonfire in the center of his chest. He moved closer to take her in his arms. It was testament to how badly she needed comfort that she did not pull away. She seemed so small standing there, so delicate, so utterly demoralized. This was another side of Celene he had not seen. He lowered his head, bowed his body around her protectively. In the heavy air the spice and sweetness of lavender rose from the pomander bag she wore around her neck. The scent and her nearness stirred other things inside him—things he had no business feeling.

He drew her closer in spite of it, and with her nestled safely in his arms, Burke began to plan. In three days' time Darkening Sky would be leaving to meet with Mide from other bands. While he was gone, they would have a chance to get away. The rendezvous was long since over, and Burke knew it was to Ste. Genevieve, more than four hundred leagues to the south, that they must go. During the next days he would gather what they needed for the long trek home. He was used to living off the land, but Celene would require more than the land could provide. He would make a cache in a tiny cave he had found near where he went to fish. And when the time was right, they would melt away into the darkness.

At dawn on the third day, Darkening Sky prepared to take his leave. Standing by the lodge with two other Mide at his side, Sky gently brushed his hand along the side of his half sister's face. "Be well, Celene," he said in a voice that seemed somehow both comforting and sad. "Know that I am always with you."

Celene answered with a nod. Burke had not told her what

he'd planned, that this would be the last time she would
see her half brother. Still, she seemed to sense the poign-
ancy of the parting. "Have care as you travel, Darkening
Sky. Thank you for everything you've done for us."

Sky's hand dropped away from his sister's cheek, and he
turned his bright gaze to where Burke stood. "Take care
of my sister while I am gone. You are her husband now,
and it is up to you to keep her safe."

"I'll do that," Burke answered, and for an instant Cardwell had the eerie feeling that the Indian knew exactly what
he meant to do. Yet the Indian had said nothing, had set
no guards to keep them in the Chippewa camp.

Turning with his two companions, Darkening Sky
headed off into the rising sun.

The day passed slowly, as did the next. Burke bided his
time fishing at his favorite place, and each time he set out,
he took a few more things they would need on their journey. The cache grew slowly until it held two knives, a
basswood-fiber bag, a hatchet, several bags of parched corn,
another of jerky, two twists of pemmican, a blouse for Celene and a shirt for him, sinew for setting snares, a fire steel
and flint, a bow and a quiver of arrows. They would take
a blanket with them when they left, and as Cardwell headed
back for the camp at sunset, he knew everything was in
readiness for their escape.

Well past midnight Burke awakened Celene. "We're
leaving," he told her in a whisper. "We're going home."

She nodded once and hurried to dress. As she did, Burke
made a blanket into a sling and looped it around one shoulder. When she was ready, they stole out of the lodge, moving through the sleeping camp like wraiths, like creatures
of the night. Burke had made note of where the Indians
posted their guards, and they slipped past them without
rousing an alarm. Pausing to gather up the things he'd put
by, they followed the course of the broadening stream south
and east. It was dangerous to stay so close to the water,
Burke well knew, but until full daylight came he dared not
leave it and take the chance of losing his way in the woods.

At sunrise they forded the stream to the opposite bank,
hoping that if they were followed, the tactic might confuse

their trackers. They continued on under the cover of the stream's heavy growth, since the country to the south was too open to cross in daylight. They hurried on, pausing to rest only when they had no choice, putting as many leagues as possible between them and the Chippewa camp.

The sun was well past its zenith when Burke caught a flash of color and movement in the trees. A party of braves were on their trail, barely a league away and moving fast. Cursing under his breath, he grabbed Celene's arm and hauled her down the far side of the slope where the stream bank fell away. He knew what the Chippewa did to captives who had tried to escape, and with Darkening Sky gone from the camp, there would be no one to save them this time.

As they pounded down the narrow path at the water's edge, Burke tried to plan. The underbrush along the trail was too sparse to conceal them. He's seen no caves in the high shale walls that hemmed the stream. They could not travel fast enough through the woods to outdistance their pursuers. Though leaving the shelter of the forest felt like a mistake, Burke had run out of other options.

With desperation driving him, he scrambled up the steep, mossy bank, climbing the crumbling rock face with the help of roots and vines. Celene struggled up behind him. At the top, a wide grassy meadow stretched for what seemed like miles.

Once they left the trees for the open country beyond, they would be as visible as crumbs on a tabletop. But they had no choice. They could travel faster here than they could over the broken ground of the streambed below. Clasping hands, they burst from cover at a run.

From somewhere behind them came the whoop of a single voice. It blossomed into a cacophony of shouts and trills. The Indians has spotted them.

There was no shelter in the yellow expanse of field, and they could expect no quarter from the pursuers at their back. Burke pressed for greater speed, and somehow Celene kept up the brutal pace. Though she was clearly terrified, determination shone in her face. This was, Burke suddenly understood, how Celene managed to survive the things she had.

They forged ahead, the thick summer growth hissing and crackling underfoot. The afternoon sun beat down on them, in dazzling, merciless rays. The air hung heavy and hot. It rasped in their throats, burned in their lungs as they fought for breath. Though the open field made running easier, the drag of the hip-deep grass gradually wore them down. They staggered onward, panting and spent, the angle of the ground deceptively steep. Half a league ahead Burke could see the crest of a rise. Beyond it lay recapture or escape, safety or death.

Glancing back, he could see that the party of braves had breached the line of trees. They, too, would move faster over the grassy expanse. Trembling with fatigue, he and Celene fought their way to the top of the hill. What Burke saw when he reached it made his blood run cold.

Gasping, they stood on a point of land at the edge of a cliff. More than a hundred feet below was a blue expanse of river. There was no way forward and no way back.

Celene stared up at him with terror in her eyes.

With every second that passed he could hear the shouts of the Indian braves grow louder, nearer. He looked down at the water, up at the sky.

He looked at the woman beside him. "Can you swim?" he asked.

Her eyes widened even more. She gave a jerky nod.

Burke clamped his fingers tight around her arm. Running the three long steps to the edge of the cliff, he leaped out into clear, thin air, pulling Celene behind him.

The drop seemed to take forever. Celene's heart stopped beating as they fell. Visions of Jean-Paul flashed before her eyes, visions of her father, of her mother, of Emile and Pélagie. Unconfessed, unshriven, with Autumn Leaf's death on her conscience, Celene was going to die. She was going straight to hell, and it was all Burke Cardwell's fault.

At the edge of her vision, she could see the buff-colored rockface hurtling by. Below her the water shone like a silver-blue mirror in the sun; a bright, impenetrable barrier impossible to avoid. The surface of the river shattered like handblown glass. The icy water slapped her hard and closed like doom above her head.

Opening her eyes with an effort, Celene watched the world recede. She went down, down in a stream of sparkling bubbles, down in a tunnel so cold that her skin tingled and her fingers burned. The light turned murky green. Sounds swelled and blurred around her. Her heels slammed into the muddy river bottom, her knees absorbing the shock. One moccasin came off, weighted with sticky river mud.

She hung motionless among the shifting shadows, a band of pressure tightening around her skull. She fought the urge to breathe, aware of the danger and the cold. The sunlit surface above her seemed impossibly far away.

The river current dragged at her, and visions exploded through her brain. They were memories too vivid to bear, understandings she'd never thought to have, pain too sharp to endure. Terror swamped her, engulfed her, consumed her. Her heart thudded against her eardrums. Her lungs spasmed with a need for air. Panic raked up the back of her throat.

When something constricted around her arm, Celene fought to twist away. But Burke was at her side, shaking her, calling her back, driving the memories away. He was clinging to her arm as if his fingers were part of her flesh. She let him draw her toward him, toward the light so far above. It wavered and came closer. It seemed within her grasp.

They burst through the shimmering barrier with what seemed to her a resounding crash. She sucked air into her lungs. It tasted of clean, fresh mint and marzipan. Triumph surged through her blood. She gave a breathless laugh and grinned at Burke.

High above them, the Indians hung over the edge of the cliff. They were watching to see if she and Burke had survived the fall. When they spotted the two of them in the water below, they raised their muskets to their shoulders, fit arrows into their bows.

Burke traded the hold on her arm for one at the scruff of her neck. "Swim to the island," he gasped and towed her farther from the bank.

Arrows swished into the water where they had been mere moments before. Guns cracked on the cliff above them. Shots spattered into the river just to their right. As some of the Indians paused to reload, several braves began scrambling down the face of the cliff.

"Swim!" Burke implored and kicked away. Drawing a hasty breath, Celene dived and swam after him.

The island was half-submerged in the middle of the stream. There was a floating mesh of dead trees and tangled branches, remnants of this spring's high water, clustered at the nearest end. Living trees sunk trunk-deep in river slough stood beyond them, leading to a sandy rise of solid land, roughly the shape of a turtle's shell.

To Celene their refuge seemed impossibly far away. Just staying afloat took most of her strength, and her legs kept getting tangled in the flare of her skirt. But the Indians weren't far behind, and that knowledge kept her paddling.

Three of them were already in the water at the base of the cliff. The rest were clambering down the bluff.

Burke headed for the far side of the island, so that they could leave the water unobserved. But once he had rounded the pile of debris at the northern end, he tucked in close beside it.

"What are you doing?" Celene hissed, mindful of how voices carried across the surface of the river.

"We're going to hide underwater, in the floating island of debris."

Celene knew better than to question him. In spite of her doubts about the wisdom of what he proposed, she followed where he led. As they neared the backside of the clutter of trees and branches, she could see how dense the tangle was. Was there room for them to penetrate the web? Could they somehow hide themselves inside? Motioning her to tread water where she was, Burke drew a breath and silently disappeared beneath the floating miasma of scum and weeds. She could hear the Indians calling to each other from the island's west side. She wished she understood their words.

After waiting what seemed like forever, a fear far more potent than her fear of recapture began to take root in her. What would she do if Cardwell didn't surface? Exhaustion weighted her limbs. The water's chill bit deep into her flesh. Her mind was fuzzy, too tired and confused to make plans of her own for eluding the Indians. If Burke was dead, if he left her alone out here in the wilds, how would she survive?

Suddenly something swished against her legs. She bit down hard to stifle the scream that rose in her chest as Burke broke the surface at her side. Bits of bark and weeds clung to his face and hair. He looked like some monster from the depths until he nodded victoriously and grinned at her.

She glared back, utterly terrified. Burke almost seemed to be enjoying himself.

Placing his hands firmly on both her shoulders, he pushed her beneath the water and followed her down. It was dark beneath the surface, swirling with weeds, with eddies of mud and sand. He guided her a dozen feet ahead, straight into the tangled mass. Tree roots snatched at her. A jagged branch scraped along her arm. It was close and sinister here; panic returned and grew in her. Then she saw a break in the murk overhead, a triangular patch of clear water framed by a gnarled, hump-backed branch and the crotch of a fallen tree. Burke eased her toward it, and they broke the surface side by side in a space nearly four feet wide, overhung with twigs, some still clinging to their shriveled leaves.

From near at hand they heard the ring of the Indians' voices and saw two of them emerge from the trees on the island's back. Through the filigree of branches, she watched them move down the sandy slope toward the slough and the floating mass of debris. She held her breath as their gazes scanned over the very spot where she and Burke were hidden. Only when the Indian's scrutiny had passed did she let it out again.

Three more Chippewa came out of the trees, and eventually another pair joined them. They stood conversing not thirty feet away, gesturing, speculating, arguing about where the man and woman they were seeking might have gone.

"They're going to search the eastern bank for some sign

of us,'' Burke breathed against her ear as the party of braves moved around the edge of the island and out of sight.

''Does that mean we're safe?'' she asked softly.

''I don't think they're going to give up on us so easily,'' he answered. ''They'll look for us along the opposite bank, then check the island again.''

''What are we going to do?''

''We're safe here for the time being. We shouldn't leave our hiding place until we're sure they're gone. Can you hang on a little longer?''

She was battered and exhausted and the water was unbearably cold. ''Yes,'' she said. ''I'm fine.''

There was a flicker of what might have been respect in the clear depths of Burke's blue eyes. One arm came around her shoulders as he took her weight against him. ''Lean on me,'' he told her. ''Try to rest.''

The warmth of him seeped into her as she let herself sag along the length of his body. There was something infinitely comforting about letting him look after her. She closed her eyes and let herself drift, riding the flow of the water, depending on Burke.

She didn't know how much time had passed when she felt Cardwell stiffen beside her. The Indians were searching the island again. Their investigation was much more thorough and organized than before. One of the Indians even slogged through the muck in the slough and clambered over the floating debris. Celene and Burke clung together, afraid to move, afraid to breathe. But the shadows had lengthened, and he passed within an arm's length of where they were huddled without seeing them. The leader of the band seemed angry with the futility of the search. But the Indians finally gave up, wading into the river and swimming toward the western bank.

Not until Burke had accounted for all seven of the braves at the top of the bluffs did he allow them to leave the floating island. With shivers raking her and limbs gone numb, Celene was too weak and exhausted to fight her way back through the branches and debris. Burke towed her instead, then carried her up the sandy slope toward the thicket perched on the island's sandy back. She clung to him as if he were life, letting him absorb the shudders of cold and fear racing down her limbs. She wished Burke could build a fire to warm her and knew he dared not. She wanted to give way to helpless tears and knew she would never stop crying if she did.

Whispering reassurances, Cardwell began to strip off her sodden clothes. She mewed a protest as he pulled her blouse away, as he dropped her skirt to the ground. The wind on her bare skin was warmer than her clothes had been. Still, murmuring soothing words, Burke threw his clothes down beside hers on the wind-whipped grass.

Once he had settled her on the sand under the protective arc of a low-hanging tree, he joined her, wrapping his arms and legs around her as if he meant to draw her into himself. Nestled beside him she could feel that his skin was cold, but he possessed some primitive internal heat that drew her to him. She turned in his embrace and pressed her nose against his chest. She caught the deep rumble of a chuckle as his hands moved over her icy flesh, chaffing her, warming her, fitting her body more closely to his. He was solid, steady, and most of all, warm. Lying with a man had never felt so good. With an almost incoherent murmur of thanks, exhaustion overtook her. She fell asleep in the shelter of Burke Cardwell's arms.

Safe. Wrapped in the filmy, intransigent world between wakefulness and dreaming, Celene felt safe. Swaddled in warmth. Suffused with languor. Culled by contentment. And safe, safer than she could ever remember feeling.

She stirred, shifted, and opened her eyes. And in a heartbeat the illusion of safety evaporated. In her immediate line of sight was a hairy arm, a short stretch of sand, and a snarl of broken branches. She sat up so quickly that she smacked into the broad, hard shoulder to which that arm was attached. With a muttered imprecation, she thrust it aside. Its owner grumbled gruffly in complaint. She turned to him, to his wide, even-hairier chest; his strong, beard-shrouded jaw; and his long-lashed turquoise eyes, blinking in confusion.

Burke.

The first shock of seeing him lying naked beside her snatched her breath. The second shock of finding herself every bit as naked as he was made her gasp. Scanning the immediate area around them, she spotted the spattered pools of their discarded clothes and made a dive for the closest one. The cloth of her skirt was cold and damp beneath her hand. She snatched it up and clamped the fabric across her chest, pulling it down so it covered as much of her as possible.

"Morning," Burke said, standing up to stretch, utterly naked and blatantly male.

She hastily averted her eyes.

"Sleep well?"

The appalling thing was that she had. Sprawled in the sand on this speck of an island, without so much as a stitch to cover them, with who-knew-how-many Chippewa searching for them, she had slept as well as she had in her life.

Burke didn't wait for her answer. Gathering up their clothes, he dropped hers beside her and slithered into his leggings, breechclout, and shirt. While she pulled on her clammy blouse and skirt, while she searched for and found the calico pomander with the small wooden carving tucked inside, he continued gathering up their things. Some of Burke's hoard of supplies was gone, one of the knives, the bow and arrows, his extra shirt, the moccasin she'd lost in the muck at the bottom of the channel. But most of what they needed for the trek downriver was still there: the parched corn, somewhat worse for its soaking but edible, the flint and fire steels, their single blanket. He gave her a handful of soggy corn and a strip of jerky on a redbud-leaf plate, eating his own ration without bothering with such niceties.

When he disappeared into the trees, Celene stumbled the scant dozen yards to the water's edge to wash. It was shortly past dawn and the sun was just cresting the trees on the limestone bluffs to the east. She cast a long, dark shadow on the shimmering gold and gray water. Far beyond, she could see the line of bluffs to the west, the cliff where they had risked their lives in that perilous jump. She shivered with the memory. But though she scanned the full crest of the ridge, there was no sign of Indians, no sign of anything moving at all.

She became suddenly aware of a longer shadow sliding across the water beside her own and jerked around.

"They won't be back," Burke assured her, "at least not here. If they're really interested in what happened to us, they'll search downstream in the hope of finding our bodies."

"How can you be so sure?"

Burke shrugged. "That's what I'd do. Still, it doesn't seem wise to tarry here in case I'm wrong."

"Just what exactly do you have in mind?"

"We need to get across to the east bank as quickly as we can. Unless I'm mistaken about where we are, the bluffs recede a league or two south of here, and the land along the river flattens out. That will make walking a little easier."

"And how will we get over there?"

"We'll have to swim. That channel isn't quite as broad as the west one is."

In the last few hours Celene had had enough swimming to last a lifetime and said as much. Being on the river always brought the memories back.

Burke shrugged again and turned away. "Then I guess when I get to Ste. Genevieve, I'll have to tell your father I left you here."

Ste. Genevieve. Jean-Paul. *Home.* The words set off images in her head that beckoned irresistibly. Burke might well have promised her a kingdom and mounds of gold for how eagerly she followed after him.

Before they set out across the eastern branch of the river, Burke tied their scant belongings into the blanket and fastened the bundle to a log. He floated it ahead of him as he waded in.

"You coming?" he asked without a backward glance.

She splashed up behind him. "Of course I am."

They crossed without incident and made packs for each of them to carry as they walked. But before they started out, Burke produced an odd-shaped piece of birch bark and several lengths of sinew.

"A slipper for my lady's dainty foot?" he offered. "You can't troop through several hundred leagues of forest without being properly shod."

"You make me sound like one of your horses," she accused, smiling, caught up in his unexpectedly playful mood.

He waved her to a seat on a fallen log. "Now, don't complain. I've gone out of my way to make sure this is what all the most fashionable ladies in Paris are wearing."

"Is there such a place as Paris?" Celene asked almost wistfully as Burke began lacing the bark around her foot.

"Of course there is."

"Have you been there?"

"Oh yes," he answered, "to Paris, Vienna, and Amsterdam."

"And to London? London is in England, isn't it?"

Burke nodded without looking up. "I've been to London dozens of times."

"Will you tell me what they're like, all those places so far away?"

"Of course I will. I'll tell you while we walk. It will make the time pass more quickly." He drew the ties tight across her instep. "Why are you so curious?"

Celene could feel warmth rise in her cheeks. "Monsieur LaVallier once lent me a geography book. There was a map of the world inside. I liked looking at it and reading about all the places I would never see."

There was a softness in Burke's eyes when he glanced at her. "And where have you been to, Celene?"

"To Ste. Genevieve and Kaskaskia. I've never even been to St. Louis, and that's a good deal closer than Paris or London."

"We'll pass St. Louis on our way to Ste. Genevieve. Would you like to pay a visit while you have the chance?"

Burke's offer made the heat in her cheeks intensify, and she averted her eyes. The idea of going somewhere she had heard about and never been made her chest go tight. "Oh, no. No. I wouldn't want to trouble you."

Burke gave her a long look before he rose and helped

her to stand. "Is that comfortable?" he asked. "Does it seem to rub anywhere? The birch bark doesn't bend very well without a bit of steam to make it more flexible."

Celene looked down at the shoe he'd made. He'd cut a flap that was laced on both sides from toe to instep and tied with a thong around her ankle. "It seems just fine," she assured him.

"Then let's be off."

They walked all morning and most of the afternoon. He had been right about the land flattening out at the base of the bluffs, and as they walked, Burke talked about the places he'd been, the things he'd seen, the people he'd met. They were impersonal reminiscences for the most part, and there was no constraint in his voice as long as she kept her questions to a minimum. But when she asked about when he'd gone or who he'd been with, his answers became guarded or abrupt. There was much Burke Cardwell did not want her to know, and she found herself resenting that he had learned so much about her life and refused to share more than a bit of his with her. Still, she liked his stories about places she would never go and things she'd never see.

It was midafternoon when Burke stopped abruptly at a point in the trail where it widened at the edge of a swampy beach. Thankful for the chance to rest, Celene dropped down on a thick clump of prairie grass. Burke put his pack beside her and stomped off into the trees. He returned a few moments later with a shoulder-high stick and proceeded to wade out onto the tiny mud flat. As she watched, he began to poke the point of the stick into the swampy ground to a depth of several feet, pull it out, move one or two steps to the side and repeat the process.

When he had done it half a dozen times, her curiosity got the best of her. "What are you doing?"

"I'm looking for a boat."

"There? In the mud?"

"Canoes are precious things because they're hard to carve. The Indians and the trappers like to keep a canoe for several years. But the canoes will crack and warp in the cold weather if they store them in their camps. What they sometimes do is bury them in the mud at the edge of a river to protect them. This looks to be a likely place: the river is near, the mud is soft . . ."

Celene nodded and watched him, noting his concentration, his diligence. He had moved about halfway across the little beach when the stick thudded as he poked it into the mud. It took a few more pokes and a little excavation to make sure of what he'd found. Celene rose from the grass to have a better view of what he was doing.

"Have you found a boat?"

"It looks that way."

"Do you want me to come and help you get it out?"

Burke straightened and looked back at the bluffs rising behind them. "There's a flat place in the hill about a third of the way up, just to the right of that broken tree. Do you think you could climb up there and see if it's a decent place to camp? This job is going to take more daylight than we have left, and I'd rather get settled before we begin."

Celene did as Burke had bid her, clambering up the slope on her hands and knees until she discovered a path. They were not the first travelers to take advantage of the protection of the underside of the cliff; she could see the ashes of other fires in a circle of broken stones.

When she reported back to Burke about what she'd found, he nodded and squinted his eyes toward the west. "I'll help you carry things up there and you can make camp. Spread the blanket in the grass and see if you can get it dry, and I think we can chance a little fire."

"I'll do that myself. There isn't that much for me to carry, and it looks as if you've already started digging here."

Burke nodded and turned back to where he'd left the shovel he had fashioned from a piece of heavy bark.

From the rise above, Celene could see Burke hard at work and went about making camp. She scrambled along the face of the cliff gathering dried grass and twigs to start a fire. She found an abandoned mouse's nest in one of the hollows in the rock and knew that she could use it in the place of char. It took only a moment with the oval-shaped fire steel and flint to get the nest and grass to catch, and she hovered over the tiny flames, feeding them twigs, then thumb-size branches. She had made very sure the wood was dry so it would not smoke, and when the fire was crackling softly, she went about setting up the rest of the camp. She stored their scanty goods in one of the natural hollows in the face of the cliff, then cut fluffy pine boughs for their bed. Celene had vowed not to sleep with Burke again, knowing it might invite liberties she didn't want him to take. But there was only one blanket between them, and she couldn't think how she could avoid sharing it.

Before she had quite reconciled herself to what the night might bring, Burke appeared at the crest of the rise carrying a good-size fish. "Supper," he announced and dropped it beside the fire. He took a moment to scan the tiny camp and nodded in approval. "You certainly do know how to make things comfortable, Madame Bernard," he told her. "There are places I've slept that haven't been half as nice as this."

Celene bit her bottom lip to hide a smile, absurdly pleased with his compliment. "How are you coming with the canoe?" she asked.

"I was hoping you could help me."

Celene followed him down the path. He had completed the preliminary excavations and the boat lay sunk in a yard-deep hole.

"I want you to help me lift it out."

Getting purchase in the squishy mud was difficult and lifting even the tiny log boat was almost impossible. It took a fair amount of grunting, a bit of cursing, and a good deal of cooperation to get the boat out of the hole, but somehow they managed. Once they had, they sat in the muck beside their prize grinning as if they'd just unearthed some pirate's priceless treasure.

"I've seen pigs in a wallow cleaner than you," Celene offered, once she'd caught her breath. Burke had slid into the hole as they'd struggled to right the boat and was glazed with mud down the length of his side.

"And I'm particularly fond of that wide brown stripe you've taken to wearing in your hair," he countered.

"Your eyebrows are all spiky and caked."

"You've got a big wet patch in a place no gentleman would mention."

Celene laughed and struggled to her feet. "I think we need a bath."

"I thought you'd had your fill of swimming."

"There's a difference between swimming and getting clean."

"It's a fairly fine distinction when you're bathing in a river," Cardwell pointed out. "Let's haul the canoe under the cover of those trees before we debate the difference."

It was dark when they returned to the clearing, clean but wet again. The tiny fire set sparks dancing invitingly into the night, but neither of them felt compelled to sit beside it and watch them flutter toward the sky. Once the fish was cooked and eaten, they stripped off their still-damp clothes and fell exhausted onto the makeshift bed, wrapping the single blanket around them.

As Celene nestled in, she was aware of Burke's body like a bulwark at her back, his woodsy scent and his warmth enfolding her. His arm came around her shoulder to draw her close, his broad, capable hand curling around her forearm, his calloused fingers moving against her wrist in a raspy caress. As she drifted at the edge of sleep, Celene felt safe. Even hundreds of leagues from home, knowing the Indians might still be looking for them, knowing that untold dangers might be lurking in the dark, Celene was utterly secure. Burke Cardwell was here and that was all the reassurance she needed. Feeling the soft even fall of his breath against the side of her neck, Celene smiled and closed her eyes.

Celene Peugeot Bernard was not a woman to be trifled with. But then, Burke had known that the moment she'd barreled into him at the rendezvous. Now more than a fortnight after they had escaped from the Chippewa band, he was becoming intensely aware of it again. And he was more puzzled than ever by her moods and inconsistencies.

Ahead of him in the bow of the canoe, he could see her shoulders bow and flex as she paddled, see the precise sway of the thick yellow braid that coincided with her even movements. It had taken them two days of hard work to ready the boat for the voyage south, days spent patching its hull, boiling pitch to seal the seams, and carving paddles. Celene had not shirked even the most arduous and unpleasant tasks. Nor had she complained about the hours of paddling once they'd gotten underway, though it was clear she didn't like being on the water. That struck him as odd, considering where she'd grown up, but it was no odder than the constraint that had been growing between them.

When they'd started out, there had been a sense of camaraderie, shared jokes and stories, spontaneous bursts of song. But in the last few days Celene seemed to have withdrawn from him, stopped talking of her life in Ste. Genevieve, stopped asking questions. Perhaps it was her woman's time, Cardwell reasoned, thinking how much less complicated that natural occurrence had been with Morning Song. She had simply disappeared into her hut in the woods until her monthly courses stopped. Still, Burke could not quite shake the feeling that Celene's silence was somehow his doing, his fault.

Celene still prepared their evening meal, the fish he caught or the rabbits he managed to snare. She found things in the woods to add to their simple fare, a bit of wild asparagus that had not yet gone to seed, some edible mushrooms, some berries she had picked. He was grateful for her resourcefulness and her stoicism. But her sudden constraint bothered him.

Or maybe the thing that unsettled him so was the disparity between the cool, competent woman who traveled at his side and the one who curled against him in the night. That woman with her soft, lush body and her spicy lavender scent taunted him with her nearness and made him ache.

Of necessity they slept in varying stages of undress, depending on whether the single suit of clothes they each wore had gotten wet as they beached the canoe. Lying beside a half-naked woman would tax any man's restraint, and having Celene curl trustingly in his arms night after night was slowly driving him mad. As she slept he found himself nestling nearer; breathing her sweet, elusive scent; pressing his lips to the curve of her shoulder; and imagining all the wondrous, erotic things he'd like to do to her. With his arm around her, his hand lay mere inches from her breast, and his fingers itched with the need to cup the fullness of her bosom in his hand, to bring her nipple erect with the gentle, persistent stroke of his thumb. He wanted to turn her in his arms and awaken her with his kiss, wanted to fondle her and stroke her until she moaned. He wanted her to feel the desire for him that he had come to feel for her. But he was afraid.

The memory of her silent tears, of the pain and resignation he had seen burning in her eyes that night at the rendezvous was etched indelibly in his mind, and he knew he couldn't do anything to abuse the trust she'd finally put in him. So he would lie awake, with the need for her clawing deep in his belly, with streamers of desire flickering down his limbs, with his body gone hard and hot. And he would do nothing, nothing to let her know how much he wanted her; nothing to make her feel as though here, alone with him in the wilds, she was in any way compromised. But doing nothing cost him. It cost him dearly.

With a sigh, he turned his thoughts from Celene to the river lying in shadows before him. The land to the west had flattened out, and the sun was sliding toward the horizon. High above them the sky was streaked with mauve that melted into orchid and powder blue. Tomorrow was going to be another pleasant day, but for the moment he must turn his thoughts to where they were going to spend the night. Scanning along the eastern bank, he looked toward the line of low bluffs turned orange by the setting sun. He preferred to camp with the hills at his back, and there seemed to be a likely landing just ahead. Changing the angle of his paddle, he steered them toward the spot. Celene sat back, balancing her paddle across the bow, letting him propel them the last hundred yards to shore.

As they reached the shallows, she leaped out of the canoe like a seasoned voyageur and guided them up onto the narrow beach. Burke vaulted out and waded toward shore.

"There's a stream that enters the river just ahead. That seems as good a place to camp as any we'll find."

Celene nodded in agreement, then set about trying to

loosen her tired muscles in an arching stretch. It drew her soaking blouse tight against her breasts, contoured the fabric of the skirt across her hips. Burke bit down hard on his lower lip and turned away. There was nothing provocative in her movement, but it was becoming more and more difficult to pretend she didn't stir him.

Snatching their belongings from the bottom of the boat, Burke began to wrestle the canoe in the direction of the overhanging trees. Celene pitched in to help, and in a few moments they had the boat stowed safely away.

It was dim in among the trees as they made their way toward the stream, and at the base of the bluffs they found a sheltered clearing. High above, the stream spilled from the lip of the cliff, the steady trickle of water shining like gold where the raking sunlight pierced the trees.

Beside him, Burke heard Celene's sigh of appreciation. It was a lovely place, unspoiled by any sign that travelers had camped here before. The trees rustled softly overhead, nearly muffling the spattering sound of the tiny waterfall. There was the clean, woodsy scent of the forest around them.

Burke cut pine branches for their bed while Celene lay and lit the fire. He cleaned the fish that he had caught earlier in the afternoon. Celene returned from her foraging with her skirt full of berries and began to cook their meal. They fell into the routine they had been performing daily since their escape, each silent, each busy with the tasks at hand.

The silence held until they had cooked and eaten their meal, until they were sitting contentedly by the tiny fire.

"We should make St. Louis in less than a week," Burke noted as he poked at the coals with the end of a stick.

"As soon as that?" Celene asked, glancing up at him.

"The current's helping us. We're moving fast. Haven't you noticed that there's more traffic on the river now?" They had passed several bateaux late this afternoon, a canoe of Indians, and a pirogue with two white men pulling upstream. They had avoided them for safety's sake, weighing the possibility of securing supplies against the danger of approaching strangers without having weapons to defend themselves. Burke had made the decision only for Celene's sake.

"And how much longer before we make Ste. Genevieve?"

"A day or two after that I should think."

She nodded once, and then the silence between them seemed to change. It went brittle and taut. Burke felt the difference in the buzz that started in his belly, in the chill that brushed between his shoulder blades.

"Then I think it's time we talked about Morning Song." Celene did not look up as she said the words, but Cardwell sensed how focused and intent she had suddenly become.

For himself, the quiet words thudded into his chest with all the force of a cannonball. His lips went numb as he fought to catch his breath. Speaking about Morning Song seemed very nigh impossible. He had nothing to say, no desire to awaken the memories slumbering at the back of his mind. When the air came back into his lungs, it was with an audible rasp. "Morning Song?"

Celene raised her head, and her eyes glittered silver and gold in the firelight. "Morning Song. Your wife."

Burke wanted to scramble backward, escape from her questions, disappear into the dark. "How did you . . . ? But I never . . . Did Antoine . . . ?"

Her gaze was level but strangely warm. "You talked about her when you were ill."

The night he'd had the fever was like a void, a hole in his life. He felt as if the hours he'd been lost in delirium had happened to someone else. "Morning Song," he mumbled again.

"Yes."

She wasn't going to be put off; he could tell by the singular way she was watching him. Still, he felt compelled to try. "Morning Song is dead. There is nothing to talk about."

"You asked my father for my hand. You married me in the Chippewa camp. Don't you think I deserve to have my questions about your first wife answered?"

"I won't hold you to the Chippewa marriage," Burke bargained, desperation gnawing in his gut. "And I was going to break off our betrothal anyway.''

''Were you? Without consulting me?''

Confusion momentarily muddled his thinking. He couldn't believe that she would object after the night they had spent at the rendezvous. And yet . . .

''Tell me about Morning Song.''

There was more to what he'd said while he was ill than she was letting on. He could see it in her eyes, read it in the tension that hunched her shoulders. But he didn't want to know what he had mumbled in delirium, didn't want to know why Celene was so perversely interested in something that was none of her concern.

Burke knew he had two choices: He could stay here and answer her, or he could storm off into the dark. But leaving would accomplish nothing. She had ten days, more or less, to wear him down, and he knew how determined she could be. He would have to stay. He would have to tell her everything now or have her extract it drop by drop.

It was just that the pain of losing the wife he'd loved was still so fresh and sharp. He was not sure he could talk to anyone, much less Celene, about what Morning Song had meant to him.

He thrust the stick into the fire and waited until he saw the flames wrap around it, consigning it to oblivion.

''I've told you about how I came to be in the Northwest, about how Lone Wolf saved my life during the slaughter at Michilimackinac. To keep me safe, he took me away to live with his band of Chippewa. And Morning Song was there. She was the most beautiful woman I'd ever seen. Her hair was as dark and glossy as a raven's feather. Her skin was a delicious warm and golden hue. And her eyes . . . There was such depth to her eyes, such concern and compassion in them when she looked at me. When I was with her I felt as if I had come home, as if being with her was the only thing that should ever matter. God knows why, but she felt the same.

''But she had another suitor, Darkening Sky. He was everything I was not, wise, solicitous of her feelings. As one of the Midewiwin, he was a young man with an important future in his tribe. I had nothing to offer her, but

Morning Song chose me. And I fought your half brother to claim her. He was younger then, not quite fully grown. I might have killed him in the fight if Morning Song had not intervened. I won her, though, and we were married less than six months after Lone Wolf saved my life. After that we moved away, deeper into the forest so I could hunt and trap for our livelihood.

"And it was as if I'd never had another life. Morning Song taught me what I needed to know about living in the wilderness, about trapping, about the Indian customs and the language. But more important, she taught me how to care for her, how to accept her love, how to love her in return."

Burke realized suddenly that he was breathing hard, the air fighting for room against the constriction that bound his chest. He ached down to his toes, ached with anger, ached with loss. He didn't want to tell this Frenchwoman any more, expose any more of his anguish, any more of himself.

With the heel of his hand, he swiped at the moisture gathering at the corners of his eyes. His head hurt and his throat was tight, but there was more he felt compelled to say to her. Once the words had begun to flow there seemed no way to cut them off.

"Morning Song taught me how to be a man, how to be a husband. She taught me I could turn away from what I'd been, from how I'd lived for the first eighteen years of my miserable life. And I wanted to change because I loved her, because I liked the man I was becoming, because she deserved the best man I could be.

"There was so much joy in the years we had together. The only thing that could have made our life better, more complete, was the birth of a child. But Morning Song never conceived. It was her secret sorrow, I think. The only thing she wanted that I could not seem to give her. And then last winter a fever came and took her away. We were so far up the Athabasca, there was no one living near. There was no one with medicines to save her, no one to grieve with me, no one to help me bury her."

He closed his mouth against the furious, self-indulgent words of grief that pressed hard at the back of his throat.

Celene had wanted to know about how his wife had lived, about what Morning Song had meant to him, not about how much her husband mourned her passing.

And suddenly, sitting beside this woman whom he had lusted after, whom he had briefly thought could take Morning Song's place, he felt unfaithful and unclean. He had loved his Indian wife more than life, yet he had carried on without her. He had turned his back on the place where he'd laid her to rest, decided to return to England, planned his revenge. He had even asked for Celene's hand in marriage. How could he have done that when he still loved Morning Song? He was behaving as if Morning Song had never been, as if his world had not ended with her death, as if he was no longer the man she had taught him to be. What he'd done felt like a betrayal.

With a jerk, he came to his feet and turned away. The darkness around them was thick and welcoming. He sought it as if it could offer oblivion from his pain, a balm for his grief, an anodyne for his terrible guilt. He heard Celene call out to him, but he did not stop his headlong flight. He needed the solace of the river's lapping water, the anonymity of the moonless night surrounding him.

He reached the overhanging trees where they had hidden the canoe and sat down beside it, bracing his back against the side. The water whispered by. The breath of the river brushed his cheek. He could taste the freshness all around him. The quiet and the solitude cleared his head, but did not cleanse him of his grief. It was a heavy, hot stone glowing in his chest. It was an emptiness that echoed from every cell. It was an excruciating presence that he feared would never go away. He lowered his head to his hands, raked his fingers through his unkempt hair. He closed his eyes against the sting of tears. He needed to think about his past, his future. But most of all he needed to think about Morning Song.

While he did that, no other woman could intrude. Celene could sleep alone tonight.

11

Celene paused in her paddling to look toward the pale, towering bluffs that rose up to the east of the river's channel. Here, a scant two miles south of where the Illinois River spilled its waters into the Mississippi, the country had changed. Now it was to the west that the wild, green islands lay, while on the east, the rolling riverbank had given way to spires of buff-colored rock. They thrust upward into the azure sky like probing fingers of stone, like the turrets of some ancient castle. Shaped and scored by centuries of wind and rain, they gave testament to nature's strength and endurance. Celene let her gaze stray to the undulations in the rockface, to the piers of limestone jutting out from the cliff, to the narrow canyons that disappeared into the hillside behind them. There were trees on the top of the bluffs, growing well back from the edge, and more clumps of linden and cedar that assaulted the base of the precipice. They seemed to claw for a place to set down roots, but the stone was inhospitable, unyielding, and the trees seemed stunted, their foliage ragged and thin.

"Look at the eagles," Burke called out softly from the stern of the canoe.

Celene turned her head to where the three huge birds were circling high above, effortlessly riding the currents of air that rose off the face of the cliff. Their creamy white heads and tail-feathers gleamed bright against the sky, while their bronzed bodies and the breadth of their wings were dark in the blaze of the sun. They had seen eagles that nested in the trees on the islands several times before, but they had never seemed so majestic, so magnificent.

Celene nodded and flashed Burke an appreciative smile.

In spite of his seeming cordiality, things had been different between them this last week, since the night they had discussed Morning Song. Celene had expected things to change after she'd asked Burke about his wife, but they had changed in ways she hadn't quite anticipated. To his credit, Cardwell showed every bit as much concern for her as he had before. He made her lot easier when he could and took care to see that she was safe and comfortable. But he had also subtly withdrawn from her. He avoided her company when he could, tending to some real or imagined problem with the boat or disappearing to set snares in the woods rather than sitting by the campfire in the evening. And that bothered Celene far more than she cared to admit.

But most of all, Celene was aware of the constraint between them when they lay beneath their single woolen blanket. She had grown used to sleeping in Burke's arms, and she had liked the security she felt enfolded in his woodsy scent and welcome warmth. But now he slept as far from her as the width of the blanket would allow, and that simple alteration in their accommodations held the sting of rejection.

Celene had not realized the subtle currents flowing between them until Burke had dammed them up. They had been currents of a faint, elusive tenderness; of masculine protectiveness; of his awareness of her as a woman. Until he turned away, she had not realized how unsettling it must have been for him to sleep so intimately entwined or how gallant he had been in his restraint in such compromising circumstances. She should have felt grateful for the sacrifice he'd made in withdrawing from her, from any temptations she might have posed. But she missed the closeness, the companionship. And she had the sense that by demanding that Burke tell her about his wife, Celene had allowed Morning Song's memory to insinuate itself between them.

But then, she reminded herself, they would reach Ste. Genevieve in a very few days, and once Burke had returned her to her father, he would leave forever. He had made it clear that he no longer wanted her as his wife, and that made their parting inevitable. It was something she must accept, but she found herself wishing that things could be different between them.

It was midafternoon when the houses began to appear on the western bank, rising up like apparitions from a fluttering field of prairie grass. Celene raised one hand to shade her eyes so she could get a better look.

"That's St. Louis over there," Burke told her as he continued to drive the canoe through the water with long, powerful strokes.

"It hardly looks bigger than Ste. Genevieve."

"It hasn't been settled as long, but I think you'll see some differences in the town itself."

"You mean we're going to stop?"

"I thought it would do us both some good."

Celene swung around to look at him. "What do you mean?"

"We could do with a good meal and a change of clothes. I'd hate to turn you over to your father dressed in rags, and the things you're wearing now are really little more than that. Besides, I have some people I'd like to see. And surely you wouldn't mind spending the night in a bed."

Though his reasoning made some sense, Celene was eager to be home and said as much.

"We'll only spend one evening. We can leave tomorrow at first light." When Celene said nothing, Burke continued. "I know you're eager to be with your son, and if you really object to stopping, we can press on."

Celene thought it over. She was desperate to see Jean-Paul, to hold him in her arms again. Until she did she could not let herself believe that she was really safe, that her life was returning to some semblance of normalcy. Thoughts of her son were with her constantly, concerns about his welfare, worries that he was forgetting her. She knew that Pélagie and, by now, Antoine himself were watching over Jean-Paul. And in the end, what was one day more or less? She glanced once more at the town and back at Burke.

"I suppose we can stop if it is what you want."

Whether he heard the reluctance in her voice, Celene did not know. Perhaps he was too busy altering their course toward the muddy landing for her reticence to register on him. But she had to admit that by the time they beached their canoe beside two or three dozen other boats, her curiosity had begun to get the better of her.

As they moved up the rise and across the square in the center of the town, past the Spanish flag snapping briskly on the flagpole, Celene found herself intrigued by her surroundings. Many of the houses here were similar to the ones in Ste. Genevieve. They were small, built of vertical logs with daubing in between, their roofs hipped in the West Indies style and shingled with wood. There was an overhanging porch on nearly every one, a small fenced yard in front, and a palisaded garden in the rear. There was a whitewashed church with a graveyard beside it, and close to the center of town were three or four larger houses made of rough-cut stone. Burke led her toward one of them.

After mounting the steps to the porch and banging loudly on the half-open door, he turned to her. "Fabrice Rouseau is a friend from years ago. You'll like him, I think. He reminds me of your father."

Celene had no time to consider what she might think of Burke's old friend before the man himself was standing before them. He was hardly taller than she, ruddy complected and quite rotund.

"Cardwell! You worthless dog!" he barked, enveloping most of Burke in a chest-high embrace. "*Comment ça va?*"

"*Très bien*," Burke answered, clapping his friend on the back.

"How long has it been since I have seen you? Five years, at least. Come in. What has brought you to *St. Louie*?" Looking past Burke, Rouseau noticed Celene for the very first time. "And who is this enchanting creature? Surely she has no business being with you."

Entering the good-size chamber to the left of the hall, Burke completed the introductions and explained a little of what had transpired in the last six or seven weeks.

"Then that explains your *déshabillé*," Rouseau said, eyeing them. "I thought perhaps you and your companion hoped to start a vogue for Indian dress here in *St. Louie*."

Without waiting for either of them to answer, their host

stepped into the doorway and called out a woman's name. In a moment she bustled toward him from the opposite end of the house.

"Anna, this is Madame Celene Bernard and Monsieur Burke Cardwell."

The woman's gray eyes lit with speculation as she looked at Burke. "I have heard a great deal about your prowess as a trapper, Monsieur Cardwell."

"But then, Madame, surely you know how your husband lies."

The curiosity in Madame Rouseau's face disappeared behind a teasing smile. "Only when it's to his own advantage, I assure you."

"And you, Madame Bernard, has this man been dragging you through the wilderness?"

Celene was taken aback by the strange woman's frankness, the tartness of her tongue. "Something like that," she answered.

"Then perhaps if you will come with me, I can offer you a comfortable chair to sit in and a cup of strong tea. Surely those things have been in short supply if you've been keeping company with such a man."

Without waiting for an answer, Anna Rouseau ushered Celene toward the kitchen at the opposite end of the house and put the kettle on to boil. It was a comfortable room with a wide stone fireplace along one wall. A trestle table sat beneath a wrought-iron chandelier, and Anna motioned Celene past the backless benches to the single rush-seated chair at the head of it. There were bright rag rugs on the floor, shiny copper kettles hanging from a movable rack in the rafters, and a tall sideboard where real china dishes were on display. The furnishings, though simple, were an indication that whatever Monsieur Rouseau did for a living, he did very well indeed.

There was a baby sleeping in a cradle near the hearth, and the child's presence brought thoughts of Jean-Paul to Celene once more. How clearly she remembered him sleeping in a cradle much like this one. He had been so tiny then, so helpless and dependent. His birth had been the only good thing to come of her marriage to Henri.

As Madame Rouseau bustled about preparing tea, Celene let her head sag against the high-backed chair, wondering for what might have been the thousandth time how Jean-Paul had accepted her long absence. Had he missed her as much as she missed him? Had he begun to believe that she would never return? Only her death would have prevented that. But would a five-year-old understand that his mother would never willingly abandon him? Without warning, tears swam across her vision, and she lowered her head so the other woman wouldn't see the signs of weakness in her.

But an instant later Anna was offering her a cup filled with bracing tea and settling herself on the end of the bench. Frowning a little, Anna studied her.

"You're worn out, aren't you?" she observed. "Why hasn't that Cardwell man been taking proper care of you?"

"He's done the best he could," Celene answered, instinctively defending Burke. "We've come four hundred leagues in a canoe with little more than the clothes on our backs."

"Then I suppose you're right. He did his best," Anna Rouseau conceded. "Well, you drink up your tea, and then you can lie down for a little rest. There's a party at one of our neighbor's tonight, and you'll want to—"

"A party? Surely you don't expect us to attend."

"But of course you'll go."

"I don't know anyone in St. Louis," Celene argued.

"We're not a town that stands on ceremony."

"I haven't got a thing to wear."

"You're only a little smaller than I am. Surely I have something that will fit."

As she spoke, Anna Rouseau carefully moved the cradle to the opposite side of the hearth, pulled out and lowered the seat of the wooden bench that stood beneath the window, and unrolled a feather palate to form a makeshift bed.

"We have lots of unexpected visitors," Anna explained.

Until now Celene had not realized how exhausted she was, how tired of paddling, how tired of scrabbling for every bite of food. Even the bracing tea did nothing to assuage her bone-deep weariness, and the moment she felt the crush of the down palate beneath her, Celene was asleep.

It was nearly sunset when Anna awakened Celene and urged her toward the large wooden tub that was set before the hearth. The water inside was hot, and the fine-milled soap that Anna gave her to use must have come all the way from France. Heedless of the other woman's presence or that her hostess was acting as her maid, Celene stripped off her clothes and settled down to bathe. The warmth of the water teased the ache of the wilderness from her bones, and when Celene had finished bathing, Anna stood beside the tub and offered her soft linen towels to dry herself. There was lavender-scented powder in a enameled tin for Celene to use, and she shamelessly indulged herself in the unexpected luxury. Then, snuggled in a cotton wrapper, Celene let Anna comb out the length of her fresh-washed hair.

"Your hair is such a pretty color," the woman observed as she fanned out a section so that it would dry more quickly. "It's silver and gold all at once, the color of cornstalks in November."

Anna's hair was properly hidden by a fashionable lace coif, but ringlets of mahogany red peeped out along the hairline.

"No prettier than yours, I'm sure," Celene offered, enjoying the sensation of someone brushing her hair for her. It was something she rarely experienced since her mother died more than a dozen years before.

"You've had a hard time of it, haven't you?" Anna offered as she brushed. "Burke told us a little about what you'd been through."

Celene gave the slightest of shrugs, wondering what Burke had said. "It's never easy for a woman alone," she answered.

"But now you have Burke to care for you."

Celene allowed herself to think how it might be if that were true. Burke was a man capable of the deep, abiding love a woman craved; he had proved his constancy and devotion to Morning Song. But for all that he had once asked Celene to be his bride, Burke did not feel that kind of love or devotion for her. And in that unguarded moment the realization made her sad.

"My life is in Ste. Genevieve with my father and my son," she answered softly. "Burke's future lies far across the sea. And I have grown used to fending for myself."

At Celene's quiet words, Anna's brushing slowed. "A woman makes choices every day of her life. Just be certain the ones you make are the ones that will bring you happiness."

Celene look up at the other woman, but Anna had turned away to gather up a batiste chemise. After slipping off the wrapper, Celene pulled the undergarment over her head and fastened the back flap at the front of her waist. Once the lavender pomander bag was settled between her breasts, and the lace-trimmed neckline was adjusted and tied to Celene's satisfaction, Anna handed her a pair of pockets embroidered in blue, a padded roll to tie around her hips to enhance her natural curves and a soft bleached-muslin petticoat. The second petticoat Anna passed her was of a blue and white striped chintz. When the tapes of the petticoats were securely tied, Celene donned a sleeveless bodice of heavy, deep blue fustian. Anna laced it at the back, and gave her guest cotton stockings and embroidered garters to tie at her knee, a soft white apron, and a coif. Once her hair was wound in a knot at her nape and the coif adjusted to suit them both, Anna stepped back and ran an assessing eye over her guest. "Lovely. Simply lovely. Burke will be so proud of you."

Celene was not so sure of that, but once she had stepped into Anna's extra pair of wooden *sabots*, there was nothing to do but go and find the gentlemen.

They were on the porch at the side of the house, smoking their pipes by lantern light. Burke straightened as the women approached, his bright eyes sparkling as they came to rest on Celene.

"I thought I'd like the way you looked when I finally saw you in women's clothes, but you've quite exceeded my expectations."

Did that mean he thought she was pretty or not? Celene wondered, letting her gaze drift over him. While she had been sleeping, he had bathed and shaved and managed to find a change of costume for himself. One of Monsieur Rouseau's bleached muslin shirts would have been cut full enough and long enough to accommodate Burke's larger proportions, but where he had found breeches to fit him among the Frenchmen here in St. Louis, Celene could only guess. The sleeveless russet vest had apparently been appropriated from a somewhat smaller man, for it refused to meet across the front and brushed Burke's thighs several inches higher than was fashionable. Still, with his honey-colored hair tied back in a queue, with his blue eyes shining, with a smile on his lips meant only for her, Celene thought him one of the most attractive men she'd ever met.

Celene smiled shyly in reply to Burke's compliment, and his eyes went suddenly smoky and dark. He came toward her across the porch, one hand extended as if he meant to clasp her fingers in his own. She lifted her hand to accommodate his movement, and as their two hands met, the faint abrasion of her fingertips gliding across his calloused palm sent spangles tingling up her arm. Burke must have been aware of the sensation, too, for after a moment's hesitation, his grip tightened possessively.

"Well, then," Anna offered, sounding smug, "let's get on to the party, shall we?"

Celene had no time to demur. The party was three doors away, and though the music had yet to start, the house was packed to the rafters with what seemed like every man, woman, and child in St. Louis. In the crush near the front door they met their host and hostess, Monsieur LaClede and Madame Chouteau. Burke seemed to know LaClede and most of the rest of the men who crammed into the house and filled the overhanging porch.

"Most of them trade in furs," Burke answered when Celene asked about his acquaintance with them. "Your father would be every bit as much at home here as I am."

"My father makes himself at home wherever he goes," Celene answered almost bitterly.

"Your father is well-known and well-liked for his cordiality and generosity," Burke pointed out.

"He is liked because he sings louder, dances longer, and

drinks more than any man should.''

"He is liked because he knows how to be a friend.''

Celene stopped in the doorway at the back of the house and glared up a Burke. How could he know what kind of a man her father really was? she thought with a stir of resentment. He hadn't suffered through her father's long absences, hadn't done without because Antoine had gambled his money away, hadn't been lied to again and again.

"Antoine may be a wonderful friend, but he leaves a good deal to be desired as a father,'' Celene told him as she spun away.

Heedless that Burke was calling her name, Celene clattered across the porch and out into the yard. Here beneath strings of bobbing lanterns, women were laying out tables of food. Celene moved past them into the dark.

Tomorrow, or the day after, she would be forced to face her father again. Her father—the man who had refused to come when Rivard and Arnaud had taken her, the man who had sold her into marriage when she was barely fifteen, the man who had sent her back to a husband who beat her when she had gone to him for help. That had hardened her heart against him as nothing else could, and now there was one more transgression to be laid at Antoine's door. Her reunion with Jean-Paul would be something wonderful, something tender, something filled with love. But when she saw her father, Celene would be hard-pressed to contain her anger and disillusionment. He had been right about the rendezvous being no place for a woman, but that did not excuse him for shirking his responsibility where she was concerned.

The music had begun when Burke finally found her. "Celene,'' he began, stepping into the shadows at the back of the yard where she had taken refuge. "Celene, are you all right?''

"I'm fine,'' she answered shortly.

"Is something bothering you?''

"No,'' she lied.

Burke must have heard the antipathy in her voice. "Are you angry with your father? Or is it something I've done that's upset you?''

"It's nothing. Only a woman's foolishness."

He caught her arm as she brushed past him, moving in the direction of the house. "You aren't a foolish woman, and I won't dismiss you on that account. I want to know what's wrong."

Words of anger leaped to her lips before she could bite them back. "Why was it you who came after me when Rivard and Arnaud took me from the rendezvous?"

"Instead of your father, you mean?"

"They took me because of a debt they thought he owed. It was his responsibility to make things right."

Burke hesitated, a frown drawing the corners of his mouth, a line appearing between his angled brows. "He wanted to go after you."

"Did he?" Sarcasm thickened her tone.

"Yes, but I convinced him it should be me."

"And how difficult was that?"

"More difficult than you seem to think." Burke paused again, his frown deepening. "I told him that if I was going to be your husband, you were my responsibility. I told him it made more sense for him to complete my business and his own while I went after you. Neither of us suspected then how complicated rescuing you was going to be."

There was something about what Burke said that did not quite ring true, but Celene suddenly did not want to question her father's motives further. It was enough, for the moment, that Antoine had argued with Burke, that he had wanted to go after her.

"Celene, your father cares for you more than you know," he went on unexpectedly. "He knows he has not been all a father should be where you're concerned, and it pains him."

Celene gave a snort of disbelief.

"Talk to him when we reach Ste. Genevieve. There are things that need to be resolved between you." When she made no reply, Burke continued. "Celene, talk to him. That's all I ask."

Celene shook her head and looked away. Why was Burke being so adamant about all this? There was no reason for

him to plead her father's case, no reason for her to be
swayed by his arguments.

"Celene, please. I want you to promise me you'll talk
to him."

There was something in Burke's voice Celene had never
heard, a note of command and unflinching determination,
a note of sadness and compassion. Strangely affected, she
gave a slight inclination of her head. She would talk to
Antoine, though she couldn't imagine what good it would
do.

She heard Burke shift beside her, stepping closer, bending near. The warmth of his palm came against her back.
"Antoine is sorry about so many things, Celene. You'll
never have anything to regret if you settle things between
you while you can."

Then, as if he feared he'd said too much, encroached on
matters that were none of his concern, Burke stepped back
a little and offered his hand. "It is too nice an evening to
waste standing here. There is music and dancing, food
aplenty, and pleasant company to enjoy. Come with me.
Let's join the party. I want a turn with you on the dance
floor."

Celene pushed her anger at her father away and let Cardwell lead her toward the house. There were three fiddlers,
a man with a concertina, and one with a guitar in the largest
of LaClede's three rooms. The sets were forming up for
the contradanse, and she and Burke joined the nearest one.

Once the music began to play, thoughts of Antoine
drifted away, and Celene began to enjoy herself. Cardwell
danced with remarkable grace for one so tall, and Celene
found herself moving in tandem with her partner as if they
had danced together a thousand times. His eyes lit with
appreciation as the figures of the dance brought them together again and again, and Celene began to allow herself
to enter into and enjoy the flirtatious nature of the dance.
It was a pleasant enough diversion, and Burke was by far
the most handsome man at the gathering. His hair shone
gold in the light of the candles; his smile was intimate and
warm. She felt her awareness of the man with whom she
had traveled escalate, liking the flare of possession in his

turquoise eyes, liking the warmth of his hand at her waist, liking the knowledge that for the moment at least, they were merely two people each happy with the company of the other.

They danced for quite some time before Burke ushered her toward where the tables of food and beverages offered a diversion from the music and the gaiety inside the house. They filled pewter plates, procured mugs of cider, then found a quiet place to sit and eat at one end of the porch.

"I liked it better when your hair was not all coiled up beneath your coif," he observed, slicing the ham on her plate with the hunting knife he took from his waist.

" 'A virtuous woman covers her head in reverence to God,' " Celene quoted both her mother and her priest, " 'and her elbows in deference to a Frenchman's lust.' "

Burke laughed outright at the platitude. "Since I'm an Englishman, I'm afraid it's other parts of your anatomy that inspire my lust."

Just what those parts were, Burke did not say, but Celene found that she was curious. Was he enticed by her ankles, plainly visible beneath the hem of her borrowed skirt, the swell of her breasts peeping out above the gathers of her chemise? Celene felt her face get hot and turned her attention to her food. Surely she didn't want to inspire lust in Burke Cardwell, did she?

They finished their meal and took a few more turns on the dance floor, but the long days of travel and the need to be underway at first light began to take their toll on Celene. Burke seemed to weary of the noise and dancing, too, and when he suggested returning to the Rouseaus' house, Celene readily agreed.

The sound of the voices and the music followed them down the street. It was a warm, still night, the air hanging close as they entered the house. Burke left her at the kitchen door.

"I think I'll have a pipe before I retire," he told her.

"I'm glad we stopped in *St. Louie*," she conceded, not quite meeting his gaze. "I admit I have enjoyed myself."

"I'm glad," Burke answered as he turned away. "I'll see you in the morning."

When he was gone, she removed her coif and apron and let down her hair. She kicked out of the *sabots* and stripped off her garters and stockings. It was only when she reached for the ties at the back of her bodice that she realized she needed help undoing them. Padding barefooted through the house, she searched for Burke. He was sitting on the porch railing, just where she and Anna had found the two men earlier in the evening.

He turned at her approach, though she was sure she'd made no sound to alert him to her presence.

"Is something wrong?" he asked.

"Only that I can't seem to loose the laces on my bodice," she answered. "Can you help me?"

As she came to stand before him, he set his pipe aside. "They're tangled by the look of things," he offered, bending over her. "It will take a bit of doing to get them loose."

Burke took one elbow and adjusted her closer, moving her to stand between his knees. As she drew her hair over one shoulder, she felt the flicker of his breath across her back. She was aware of the brush of his thighs against her hips, could feel him fumbling with the ties at her waist.

"Men's hands aren't made for tasks like this," he said quietly, a hint of exasperation in his tone.

She thought about his hands working the ties at her back, broad, capable hands, scuffed and roughened by the life he lived. She thought about his strong brown fingers, plucking at the knot, the delicate silken ribbons snagging on his calloused fingertips. She thought about the faint quirk of irritation that must by now have gathered between his brows, the intensity in his eyes as he worked to unravel the tangled web of ties, the slight pursing of his mouth, the way that expression squared his chin.

She bit her lip to keep from smiling. As she stood there motionless, his warmth enfolded her. His woodsy scent was crisp and clean. There was the drift of pipe smoke across her senses; the slow, sweet sound of distant music in her ears; the rhythm of his breathing in subtle counterpoint to the violin's plaintive song.

There was an intimacy in asking Burke to perform this simple task. It was so personal a request, imbued with trust and familiarity. It was the kind of request a wife might make, the kind of favor a husband might grant. And when the ties were loose, the wife might turn to her husband and touch his cheek by way of thanks, might stroke his hair by way of subtle provocation. Perhaps that husband would smile and draw her close as his wife offered up her lips for her husband's kiss. She might open her mouth to the press of his, savor the sweetness of his flesh, the taste of cider and tobacco that clung to him. As they kissed, her body might mold to the contours of his, her hips nestling to the juncture of his splayed thighs, her breasts crushed to the muscles of his chest. His tongue might dip into her mouth, and she might answer that thrust with a questing of her own. The kisses might flow from one to another, separated only by the need for breath.

"Celene?" Burke's voice intruded on her thoughts. "Celene, are you all right? You seemed to be trembling a little."

Heat rose beneath her skin. She was sure the roots of her hair were sizzling. She was shaky, light-headed, strangely disoriented.

What was the matter with her? Burke was helping with the knots in her laces, nothing more. She had spent weeks with this man, seen him at his best and at his worst. She had helped him, hurt him, and slept naked in his arms. There had been none of this strange awareness then, no prickles rising across her scalp, no sensation of feathers dancing on her skin. She wanted to jerk out of his hands and run away. She wanted to bury her face against his chest and chance whatever came.

"I'm fine," she managed to answer, though her voice sounded strained and breathy in her ears. "Have you gotten the laces loose?"

His hands were splayed against her waist, his thumbs at the back and his fingers near to spanning the breadth of her. "Yes," he answered, but his voice sounded a little unsteady, too.

If she turned to him now, would she see the same awareness in him that she was feeling? If she turned to him now, would he take her in his arms and kiss her? And if those kisses led to something more, could she abandon herself to Burke and allow him to make love to her? How much courage did she have when it came to this?

Not enough, she decided all at once. Not enough to chance that panic might overtake her as they lay together, not enough to chance looking into Burke's bright eyes and finding that she could not measure up to his memories of Morning Song.

Holding the loosened bodice against her chest, she stepped away, pausing to look back at Burke only when she had reached relative safety at the corner of the house. The lantern at his back cast his face in shadows. Still, she sensed that he was waiting, tensed, watchful, ominously quiet.

"Thank you for your help," she said.

"Think nothing of it. I've always enjoyed undressing you."

At his offhand comment, her heart slammed against her ribs and her mouth went dry. For the briefest instant, she considered going back, letting him steal away her clothes, letting him press her to his naked flesh, letting him make his body part of her. But it was too frightening and reckless a thing to contemplate for long. Without a word she spun away. Burke's voice followed her into the dark.

"Sweet dreams, Celene," was all he said.

12

With each league they traversed southward from St. Louis, Celene's paddle dipped a little deeper. With each landmark she recognized, the tempo of her strokes came a little faster. They moved swiftly downstream, through water pinked by dawn, past low banks thick with trees, past herons wading in the shallows. Birds wheeled in the brightening sky and massive gray-gold cliffs rose far to their left, set well back from the river across meadows lush with wildflowers. Burke drank in the beauty around them, but Celene was like one struck blind. She paddled with furious energy, focused only on the river before them, intent only on their destination. As Burke matched her stroke for stroke, he let the single-minded exertion quell his inexplicable need to savor the infinite peace and solitude of their last morning on the river.

In due time Ste. Genevieve came into view, a strip of whitewashed houses with broad hipped roofs strung out for nearly a mile along the rim of the western riverbank. The landing was at the foot of the town, and he could sense Celene straining to cover the last scant hundred yards as quickly as possible.

The moment her wooden shoes touched the riverbank, Celene was clambering up the rise. Leaving their few belongings in the canoe, Burke scrambled after her, and even he, with his far longer legs, had trouble keeping up. As they strode along, Cardwell took stock of his surroundings. Though he had visited in Kaskaskia, slightly downstream and across the river, he had never been to Ste. Genevieve.

It was a town in the Old French style, with the houses clustered close, and the fields stretching out behind them toward the shallow, knobby hills that marked the western horizon. It was clear that much of the river's bottomland was under cultivation, given over to flickering chest-high walls of cornstalks, broad patches of yellowing wheat, and squat tobacco plants growing in well-tended rows. Though architecturally the town resembled St. Louis in many ways, it was older, the buildings smaller, the focus more on agriculture than on trade.

As they made their way along *la Grande Rue*, the only street important enough to have earned a name, people turned to stare at Celene and him. It was clear they had heard of her abduction and were startled to see her among them now. Though many called out greetings, Celene never paused until she reached one particular gate in the tall, palisaded fence that hemmed the street. Lifting the latch, she pushed the gate aside and moved toward the porch where a boy of five or six was playing with a wooden top.

"Jean-Paul," she called out softly as if she thought her sudden appearance might frighten him. "Jean-Paul, *c'est moi*."

The boy looked up from his game, his eyes widening. "*Maman*! Where have you been?"

In an instant he was on his feet and across the porch, throwing himself against his mother's body. Celene's arms closed around him as she sank to her knees, hugging him close, burying her face in his thick, dark hair. Her shoulders shook with silent sobs. She clung to her child, balling the fullness of his shirt and vest into her fist. The fingers of her opposite hand made furrows in his shaggy hair. She bowed her body around him as if to take him into herself.

Burke stood just inside the gate, seeing how Jean-Paul's hands knotted behind Celene's neck, seeing how he nuzzled the side of his mother's throat. It was as if Celene and Jean-Paul were joined in some intimate way no grown man could understand. There was such joy in them, such trust, such closure. It was as if there was no one in the world except the two of them. It was as if neither of them would ever forge a bond so complete as the one that bound them now.

Such love between parent and child was well beyond Burke's knowledge or experience, though he was pleased that what he'd done had made this reunion possible. As he watched them, some bittersweet emotion curled beneath his ribs, a poignant tinge of what might well have been loss, or even jealousy.

But it was gone as quickly as it had come, and Burke's attention was diverted from Celene and her child by the man and woman who had come to stand at the edge of the porch. Antoine was even thinner than he had been at the rendezvous. Though the breadth of his shoulders and the fire in his eyes belied the truth, Burke had seen the signs of this wasting illness in men before. Would Celene be perceptive enough to see the change in him? Burke wondered. Would she understand the need for Antoine and her to make their peace?

Beside Antoine stood a woman who could only be their taciturn housekeeper Pélagie. She was as tall and rangy as a man, hatchet faced, and utterly intimidating. Burke liked her on sight and immediately understood why Celene had been able to entrust Jean-Paul's care to her.

As Jean-Paul wriggled free of his mother's arms, the three adults converged on the mother and son. Celene was not quite willing to let Jean-Paul free and tugged the sides of his vest into closer alignment. She used her fingers to comb his tumbled hair, hiding her need to touch him in a flurry of motherly admonitions and good grooming.

Burke bit his lip to hide a smile and turned his attention to Jean-Paul. Cardwell recognized the Peugeot stamp in the color of his eyes, and in spite of the darker hair and complexion, there was a good deal of his mother in the boy. Burke could see it in the wide, bowed mouth and the set of his chin; the breadth of his cheekbones; in the energy and determination that seemed to sit so well on him. He would grow taller and broader than a Peugeot had ever been, and there were other things about his features and his stature that Burke did not immediately recognize. But he was a handsome lad, and Cardwell understood why Celene was so proud of him.

'' . . . killed a crow with my slingshot,'' Jean-Paul was

saying. "And *Grandpère* took me to Monsieur Vallé to collect the bounty. And when Phillipe Beauvais heard what I'd done, he tried to punch me in the eye. So I pushed him in a mud puddle . . ."

Must run in the family, Burke found himself thinking and fought a smile again.

Celene must have intercepted his thought somehow, for she rose and gazed down at her small son. "I do know how much bigger Philippe is than you. It must have made you feel both very brave and very much afraid to push him down. I know that is how I would have felt."

The child nodded once in something that was not quite acknowledgment, then twined his arms around his mother's waist.

Burke watched silently as she greeted Pélagie and Antoine. He could see Celene look past the signs of her father's illness. Instead of expressing concern for his health, she kissed him quickly on either cheek and jerked away, oblivious to his hands lingering on her hair, to the way his eyes drank in the sight of her. How could she greet her son with such joy, such thankfulness and such love, and not feel those same emotions in her father's touch? For herself, Pélagie took the younger woman in her arms and thumped her soundly on the back. It must have been some incomprehensible ritual between the two of them, for Celene nodded in answer to something Pélagie whispered in her ear and did the same.

Once the family greetings had been said, once Celene had disentangled her son from the blue-striped folds of her skirt, she turned to Burke.

"Jean-Paul," she began. "There is someone I would like you to meet. This is Monsieur Burke Cardwell."

The child looked up at Burke, his eyes narrowed and speculative. "Are you the one who's been with her all this time?"

Burke didn't know quite how to answer, what the boy wanted to know. "Why, yes, I have," he acknowledged carefully.

At his words, the child lowered his head and charged, ramming his outstretched hands against Burke's thighs.

Startled and confused, Cardwell gave ground.

"Get out! Get out! We don't want you here!" the boy cried, continuing his assault, pushing until Burke had backed the few scant yards into the street.

"Jean-Paul!" Celene cried, finding her voice. "What are you doing?"

Before answering his mother, Jean-Paul swung the tall gate closed and lowered the latch. "I won't let him take you away with him again. I won't. I won't!"

Celene came after her son, caught him under the arms, and settled him on her hip. He was more than half as big as she was, but he clung to her like a monkey to a tree, his face buried in the curve of her neck. "Monsieur Cardwell did not take me away," she told her son softly as she stroked his back. "He brought me home. He rescued me from two of your grandfather's enemies and a whole band of Chippewa Indians. We should welcome him for that, not bar the gate against him. Now that you know the truth about Monsieur Cardwell, may I offer him our hospitality?"

Without showing his face, Jean-Paul gave a grudging nod.

"I'm sorry, Burke," Celene said as she lifted the latch. "I had no idea . . ."

Burke answered with a nod of his own, strangely unsettled by the child's actions. He understood Jean-Paul's fear, his need to protect his mother, but the barb of his childish distrust went deep.

Silently he let Celene and her son precede him up the walk and onto the wide gallery that surrounded the house. It was then that Pélagie took charge, steering Celene toward the back. Burke would have followed, except that Antoine caught his arm.

"Sit here and have a pipe with me. The women will have much to discuss, and I would have a word with you."

Burke settled on one of the two backless puncheon benches in the shade of the roof. Antoine made himself comfortable on the other. He produced a twist of tobacco and offered it to Burke before packing and lighting his own clay pipe.

As Burke waited, he let his gaze drift over his surroundings. Peugeot's was one of the older houses in the compound, built of the heavy, squared-off vertical logs so common in French colonial construction. Yet in spite of the fact that the house was shabby and in need of repairs, there was a solidity to it that was welcoming and comfortable. At his back a wisteria climbed a trellis onto the roof casting the two benches in deep shade, its faded blossoms fluttering softly in the intermittent breeze.

"I want to thank you, *mon ami*," Peugeot finally said, "for doing what I could not. Since it has taken you so long to return, I assume you encountered some trouble along the way."

Briefly Burke recounted the weeks since he'd left the rendezvous.

Antoine listened in silence, then drew a long unsteady breath. "Then I owe you far more than I realized," he said softly, shaking his head.

"You owe me nothing. I did what I did to help Celene."

"For Celene," Peugeot repeated, peering at Burke from beneath his brows. "But not because you wish her to be your bride."

Burke took a moment to weigh his words. He still lusted after Celene. In spite of what had happened at the rendezvous, in spite of his memories of Morning Song, in spite of her fears of marriage, Celene still haunted his fantasies. But he could not take her as his wife.

"No," Burke answered almost grudgingly. "I did not rescue her because of that. I would not have forced my suit upon her if I had known what she'd been through with Henri Bernard. Why didn't you tell me?"

Peugeot looked down at his hands. "That he beat her, you mean?"

"That he beat her and used her in most despicable ways. That she is afraid of everything marriage means."

Antoine shrugged. "When you offered for her, all I could think about was the chance to see her settled before I die. I did not want to leave her alone, unprotected."

Peugeot's acknowledgment of his mortality, of his impending death, brought a knot of sorrow to Cardwell's throat. For whatever else this man had been, he had always been a friend.

"You must tell Celene that you are ill," Burke urged him softly.

Antoine shook his head. "She has enough to think about. It's not something she needs to know."

Burke leaned closer, his eyes intent on Antoine's face. "I think you're wrong. Celene needs time to accept what is going to happen. She needs time to make her peace with you. And you deserve your goodbyes."

"That's why I went to the rendezvous," Antoine admitted reluctantly. "I needed to say *au revoir* to life-long friends. I'll never see those men again, never drink to their health, never tell the stories from the time when all of us were young, never share their laughter. I'll never dance around the fire, never sing those songs, never . . ."

Antoine took a shaky breath, fighting for control. "I wanted to leave something for Celene, some memories perhaps, my share of the furs. And when you asked for her hand, I thought I would be leaving her with a husband who would care for her and make her happy."

Touched by his old friend's words, Cardwell fought a brief difficult battle with himself. In spite of everything that had passed between them, he supposed he could marry Celene and stay on in Ste. Genevieve, make a life for himself as a trader as Antoine had. But with his plans to return to England, with the scores he had to settle there, it was impossible to do what Antoine wanted. It would be wrong to let regret or Antoine's wishes change his mind. Wrong for Celene, wrong for Burke himself.

"You must tell her," Cardwell repeated. "Celene deserves to know."

"I will not tell her," Antoine insisted, meeting Burke's gaze. "And I want your word that you will not tell her, either. It will only hurt her if she knows."

"Celene's far more resourceful than you seem to think."

"I know what she is. She's brave and single-minded, like her mother was. But she's also alone and vulnerable."

"And you were willing to entrust her care to me?" Antoine's faith gave Cardwell pause.

"Haven't you proved that you are worthy?"

Burke wondered if he had. Would he have had the tenderness, the patience, and the insight to wed Celene? Could he have cared for her enough to win her trust? Could he have met the challenge of being a father to her son? Burke had never told Antoine why he'd offered for Celene's hand. Would her father have been willing to entrust Celene to Cardwell's care if he'd known the truth?

"Then if you wish it so," Peugeot went on, disappointment marking his face, "the marriage agreement is dissolved. I will see that the bride-price is credited to your account. But I am sorry it has come to this."

On more levels than Antoine would ever realize, Burke was sorry, too. He was sorry he would never again awaken with Celene in his arms; sorry he would never see desire flare in her bright eyes; sorry that after today, he could never share her sorrows and her joys. He was sorry he could never claim this strong, fierce woman as his own or call her child his son. But the decision was made, and he was sure it was the right one.

"Then there is something else we must discuss." Antoine's tone went even more quiet and grave.

Burke looked up from where he had been toying with his pipe, an odd, cold sense of premonition seeping through him.

"The morning after you left the rendezvous, a man came in search of you."

"Who was it?" Cardwell wanted to know.

"He said his name was Bayard Forrester—and that he was seeking proof of your death."

Cardwell straightened at the older man's words. "Where was he from? Who sent him to seek me out?"

"He was an English mercenary, by the look of him. Arrogant, sure of himself, and dangerous. I think he might have found some reason to kill you himself if he'd had the chance."

"And what did you tell him?"

"I told him you were very much alive. That you had left several days before with some traders bound for Michilimackinac."

"And he believed you?"

"You know how well I lie," Peugeot answered around a conspiratorial chuckle. "He was in his canoe and under way before the paddles had stopped dripping."

"My family must have sent him," Burke murmured, half to himself. "There was a letter at last year's rendezvous summoning me home. If they were desperate enough to send someone looking for me there must be money involved, a great deal of money. Perhaps it is just as well that I am bound for England as soon as my business here is settled."

"And just what is it you intend to do when you reach England and your home?"

Burke smiled as he answered Antoine. "I intend to prove that I am very much alive, then make every last one of my relatives wish that I were dead."

It was good to be home. It was good to have her son well within her reach after all the weeks of missing him, good to smell gumbo bubbling in the pot, good to have Pélagie's stolid, bullying presence at her elbow. Celene smiled to herself and accepted the wooden mug of cider the older woman thumped onto the table before her. Jean-Paul had brought the jug from down the well, and the cider was sharp and cool against her tongue. As she drank, she let her gaze slide over the familiar surroundings, the narrow fireplace with its rows of hanging utensils; the freestanding sideboard with its stacks of pewter dishes; the scarred wooden table with its two long, backless benches; the deep-set windows where the late afternoon sun streamed in. It seemed necessary to make a thorough inventory of all she'd left behind, as if seeking reassurance that nothing had really changed.

Stepping from the kitchen onto the back gallery of the house, Celene surveyed her small domain. The apples on the trees to the left of the porch were fully formed and ripening. The grapevines trailing over a makeshift fence were hung with grapes, and the hops at the back of the yard were tied up and flourishing. Smoke trailed from the smokehouse chimney. Cackles came from the chicken coop, and the pigs were fattening in their sty. The stable stood with open doors, ready to house the cow that had been taken to the commons to graze.

Pélagie had been busy in her absence, and it was only the kitchen garden at the back of the house and the clusters of herbs that were in need of Celene's attention. Weeds had begun to encroach, and the task of pulling them must be high on her list of priorities. Then, too, there were the pressing repairs to the house, this season's coat of whitewash to be applied, and the broken board in the back steps to be fixed before someone tripped and hurt himself. Tomorrow she would go into *le Grand Champ*, the Big Field, to see how their crops were doing. Pélagie said the weather had been mild, and that there had been adequate rain. What Celene found here in Ste. Genevieve was infinitely reassuring. It was almost as if she had never been gone, almost as if the trials and dangers of these last weeks had happened to someone else.

Then, from around the corner of the house, came the ring of masculine voices, the drift of sharp-scented pipe smoke. And that illusion abruptly shattered. Burke was here, sitting with her father beneath the drape of the wisteria, and his presence in her world unsettled her. It made her wonder what he saw when he looked at her home, her family. She wondered how it fit with what he knew of her.

The way Jean-Paul had reacted to Burke had embarrassed her, but in a way she understood it. He was not a boy who liked most men. Since they had moved back to Ste. Genevieve, a bond had been growing between her father and her son. But Henri had resented the child. The love she gave her son, time she spent with him, made Henri's domination less complete. He had wanted Celene to himself, and Jean-Paul had sensed his father's feelings.

Her son must see Cardwell as an encroachment, too. Jean-Paul must be threatened by his arrival, perhaps even jealous of the time this strange man had spent with her. Still, she wished he had not reacted as he had. She had wanted Burke to like Jean-Paul, to see what a winning child he was, and that seemed unlikely now.

Sighing, Celene turned back into the house, knowing she

must find Cardwell a place to sleep. Pélagie had an alcove in the kitchen. Antoine and Jean-Paul shared the tiny bed-chamber at the front of the house with its curtained tester and trundle bed. Her own palate in the attic was hemmed by sacks of flour and barrels of salt, ready to be sent to New Orleans when the prices were right. That left only the sparsely furnished front room that served as her father's office and, in winter, the family's gathering place. There must be a feather tick tucked away somewhere, and there were sheets in the chest in her father's room. She would make up Burke's bed in the parlor.

As she glanced toward the door propped open at the front of the house, she saw that Burke Cardwell was making his way down the walk and through the gate.

"Is he leaving?" she asked as she joined her father at the top of the steps.

"He's only gone for the things you left in the canoe. He'll be back in time for supper. Would you be sorry if he was gone?"

"I only thought that if he was leaving for good, he would say goodbye."

"He's broken off the marriage agreement," Antoine offered.

"Has he?" She could feel her father's gaze on her, probing, unsettling somehow. She made an effort not to squirm.

"Are you sorry?"

Celene shrugged. "Burke's still in love with Morning Song."

"Two women can hold a place in one man's heart."

"And you should certainly know the truth of that," she shot at him before turning away.

Her father followed her down the hall. "Cardwell told me Darkening Sky helped you while you were with the Chippewa."

"Your Indian son claimed me as his sister," she acknowledged. "He saved Burke's life."

Antoine caught her arm and pulled her around. "He saved Burke's life by giving him permission to marry you."

She could see the questions in his eyes. He wanted to

know what had happened between her and Cardwell, wanted to know how she felt about Burke going away. But even if she'd known how to answer him, she was not inclined to share her thoughts and feelings with her father. Antoine had kept secrets from her all her life; he had not even told her about Darkening Sky. It was one more thing Celene could not forgive.

"You know as well as I do that Indian marriages are not binding," she snapped. "You never even acknowledged yours."

"Your mother knew. That was all that mattered. It was something between the two of us."

"And how did *Maman* feel about being second choice?" Celene demanded. "How did she feel about knowing you had a child by another woman?"

A dark red flush moved up her father's neck. "How do you think Burke would feel about Jean-Paul if he was going to marry you? Would he think poorly of your son because you'd had him by another man? Would he be threatened by Henri?"

His eyes were narrowed and knowing, his pale lips pursed.

The need to deny his implications came strong in her. "It's not the same at all," Celene declared. "And I'm not threatened by Burke's memories of Morning Song. I don't want to be his wife."

She spun away, hurrying through the kitchen and into the yard. She took out her anger at Antoine on the weeds that had sprung up among the tangled vines of winter squash, ripping them from the earth, cursing the questions her father had raised. For all that she spent what was left of the afternoon pulling weeds in the garden, Celene found no satisfaction, reached no real conclusions about her relationship to Burke.

As she sat across the dinner table from the man whose proposals she had repeatedly eschewed, the questions her father had raised returned to haunt her. She should be happy that Burke had broken off things between them, she told herself, delighted that she was no longer expected to be his wife. But somehow Burke's decision to end their betrothal cast Cardwell in a strange new light. Or perhaps a woman looked at a man differently once she'd given him away.

For as intimately as she had known him, as much time as she and Burke had spent together, it had never really registered what a breathtakingly handsome man he was. As she sat poking at the food on her plate, she felt mesmerized by the candle glow reflected in his turquoise eyes, by the way it caught and shimmered in his honey hair, by the shadows it cast across his angular features. Burke's masculine power assaulted her: the breadth of his shoulders and his height dwarfing the tiny kitchen, the scent of pine and pipe smoke prickling her nostrils, the resonance of his deep voice vibrating inside her chest. His laughter seemed to tickle through her and made her feel like laughing, too. It was as if her skin was creeping with new awareness of Burke, warm across the bare flesh beneath her collarbone, fluttering up from her toes and fingertips.

With an effort, she turned her eyes away, staring at the flowered fiancé candlesticks brought out for the celebration of their return. Their elegance was at odds with the plain pewter plates and wooden tankards, with the crumbs scattered across the tabletop. Yet her gaze was repeatedly drawn to Burke, to the sweep of his freshly shaven cheek; to the soft, wry humor that tweaked the corners of his lips; to the lambent flicker in his turquoise eyes. His gaze touched hers and flitted away, as if he knew what she was thinking, as if he knew how aware of him she had suddenly become. It made her chest go tight, made drawing every breath something she had to think about.

When the meal was over, she rose and began to gather up their plates, placing them in the washtub. As she did, she could feel Burke's gaze follow her, feel it brush from the nape of her neck to the base of her spine. Warmth swelled across her skin, pinking her cheeks, sending caressing tendrils down her arms.

"Pélagie has made gooseberry tart!" Jean-Paul announced as the older woman settled the pan on the table at Antoine's side.

"I think I have eaten my fill," he said. "Shall I cut a piece for you, Jean-Paul? Would anyone else like a slice?"

While Celene poured hot water from the kettle into the tub, she could hear her son's exclamations of delight and Burke's quiet compliments. Pélagie's skills as a baker were known far and wide, but Celene refused a piece of pie and continued with her washing.

Gradually the gathering at the table dispersed, Jean-Paul restless and eager to leave, her father moving slowly outside to enjoy his pipe, Pélagie excusing herself to get some mending done. Burke lingered longest at his place, watching her in an intent, unsettling way that glued her tongue to the roof of her mouth. Her silence finally drove him away. Mumbling something about wanting a breath of air, he took his leave.

At a leisurely pace Celene dried the last of the dishes, stacked them away, and went in to put her son to bed.

"Will you be here tomorrow when I wake up?" Jean-Paul asked as she sat beside him on the narrow trundle bed. His face was shiny and damp from recent washing, and he had already said his prayers.

"I missed you too much ever to go away again," she answered, stroking his hair.

"Do you promise?" His voice croaked a little on the words. Uncertainty lingered at the back of his eyes.

Her chest felt weighted, heavy and hot. She knew exactly what she'd done to make him so afraid. "I promise, Jean-Paul. I give my word. I'll never leave you alone again."

Tears burned in the back of her throat, and she bent to kiss his cheek so he would not see the suspicious shimmer in her eyes. "*Je t'aime, Jean-Paul,*" she whispered against his ear.

"*Je t'aime, aussi, Maman.*"

Holding his hand in hers, she stayed beside him until his breathing went heavy and soft. "Sleep well, *mon coeur,*" she whispered as she pinched out the candle and rose to go.

Needing a few moments to herself, Celene slipped down the hall to the back of the house. Until just now, she had not realized what their separation had cost Jean-Paul. No child should live with that kind of loss, that kind of fear for his mother's return. No mother should be separated from a child she loved. If it wasn't for Cardwell, she might never have reached Ste. Genevieve, might never have come back to be with her son. Lifting her hand, she lay it over the pomander bag that hung between her breasts. She had so very much to thank Burke for.

As she stepped out onto the porch, the thick summer night rose up to greet her. She breathed the heavy fecund smell of the earth, listened to the peepers, looked up at the distant stars, and savored the sense of home. From the front of the house, she heard the others saying their good-nights and shuffling off to bed. She was tired, too, aching and bone-weary. The next day would start early, and there was much to be done.

Deciding to make a final circuit of the house before she barred the doors, she turned the corner and came upon Burke, still seated beneath the drape of wisteria.

"Nice night," he said.

Celene moved toward him, nodding her head. "A lovely night." He was a soft black shape, silhouetted against a sky of midnight blue. "I thought you'd gone to bed."

"It's far too pleasant to go indoors."

"The mosquitoes will eat you alive if you don't."

He chuckled, a compelling, intimate sound that drew her nearer. "As if they haven't been feasting on both of us."

He was right, of course. She had more bites and itches than she cared to count.

"Celene." Something about the tone of voice made her look down into his upturned face. It was all hollows and shadows in the dimness.

"Yes."

"Your father told you that we dissolved the marriage agreement, didn't he?"

"Yes."

"Is that all right with you?"

"Yes." What did he expect her to say? That she wanted to marry him? That she would miss him when he was gone?

The odd part was, she would. She would miss his laughter and his anger, his vulnerability and his strength. She would miss the faint hum of physical communion she had only recently begun to acknowledge.

It struck her then that he was really going away. That when he left for England, she would never see him again. That knowledge filled her with regret. She'd grown so used to his presence in her life. He'd become a part of her days, part of her security, part of herself. How would she bear it, she wondered, when he was gone?

And suddenly she wanted to kiss him one last time, savor his essence on her own terms. Before she could think better of it, she bent above him and sought his mouth. As she brushed his lips with her own, she could feel his surprise, his unthinking withdrawal. Then his mouth went pliant beneath the press of hers, eager and sweet. His lips were moist, deliciously warm, unexpectedly soft. The taste of him washed through her. There was the tang of tobacco, the bite of the ale he'd drunk at supper, the tartness that was uniquely Burke. It drew her in, deepened the kiss. She moved her mouth against his, the contact slow and lingering.

She heard him take a ragged breath, but he sat unmoving, his hands curled around the edge of the bench. Emboldened by his quiescence, she traced the opening of his mouth with the tip of her tongue. She explored the texture of his lips, the faint roughness giving way to the silky smoothness inside. She nibbled gently, letting a bit of herself flow into him, her appreciation and her regret, her curiosity and her reticence. She touched his face, let her fingers skim over his hair, let her thumbs trail the length of his throat.

She retreated, letting the pressure on his mouth go soft and light. Without seeming to move, Burke strained toward her. She felt his muscles knot beneath her hands, felt him trembling. A thrill of power tingled along her nerves. For once in her life she was able to control what passed between herself and a man.

Tightening her palms around his collarbone and letting her tongue dip into his mouth, she renewed the kiss. At the deeper contact she heard a rumble deep in his throat. At the sound, emotion spilled through her, response and elation, need and constraint, power and responsibility. Her head went light and her heart had began to thud erratically against her ribs. There was a tightness in her throat that trickled down the midline of her body toward the most intimate, secret part of her. The feeling shocked her, pleased her, challenged her, but she also realized her response might be either a prelude to something wonderful or a threat to everything she was struggling to become.

Fearing that in an instant she would be lost and beguiled, she fought her own needs and desires. She wanted the feel of Burke's hands on her skin, the press of his body against hers and the strength of his arms around her, but she also needed to know that she could turn away. She needed to know that Burke would let her go, that she was strong enough to practice such restraint. Still, she had never suspected that refusing a man could be so difficult.

Her palms flexed against his shoulders. She stepped back one pace and then another. Her head felt fuzzy and the blood sang in her veins. Deep inside herself there was a tug of disappointment, a compelling physical ache that made her want to kiss him again.

She stood beside him in the dark, her full skirt rippling against his knees, her hands caught in a knot at her waist. She waited for him to speak, searched her mind for something lighthearted or inane to say. In the end, the most obvious thing seemed best.

"Well, good night, Burke. When you come to bed, will you shut the doors?"

His voice seemed unusually deep, breathless, and frayed. "Indeed I will. Good night, Celene."

With a swish of skirts she turned to go, moving silently down the hall, climbing the angled ladder to the loft. She undressed in total darkness, pulled aside the drape of netting that surrounded her bed, and lay down on it quivering.

Oh, Burke, she thought as she closed her fingers around the calico pomander that hung on a ribbon around her neck, touching the tiny wooden carving still hidden inside. "Oh, Burke," she whispered into the darkness. "Oh Burke, what have I done?"

"Celene Bernard needs a husband."

Cardwell took the letter of credit from the top of Charles LaVallier's desk and glanced across at the older man. His fingers were steepled beneath his chin, and his piercing black eyes were fixed on Burke.

Cardwell shook his head. "You might better talk to Antoine about that."

"I want to discuss it with you," the Frenchman insisted.

"It's no concern of mine."

"But it was."

Yes, it was, Burke thought wearily. But not anymore.

"I don't know what you've heard," Burke answered, "or what Antoine's told you, but asking for Celene's hand was a mistake. She turned out to be a very different woman from the kind that I was seeking, and I'm not a man who could make her happy."

"Yet you rescued her from Rivard and Arnaud; you married her in the Chippewa camp."

"You seem to be remarkably well-informed."

LaVallier shrugged his burly shoulders. "It's my business to be well-informed. Besides, you know how people talk."

Burke raised his eyebrows in acknowledgment. Indeed, he supposed that Ste. Genevieve and Kaskaskia had been abuzz with gossip and speculation in the fortnight since he and Celene had returned from the wilds. As it turned out, he'd stayed with the Peugeots a good deal longer than he had intended. It was just that it had taken so much time to settle his accounts with LaVallier, and there had been so much to do once Celene arrived at home.

In spite of his need to leave, he had spent several days helping her meet her responsibilities in the upkeep of the fence that hemmed the Big Field where the community's crops were grown. If it had not been for his willingness to work on her behalf, she would have had to hire a *journalier*, a day laborer, to do the job Antoine could not. Then there had been the repairs to the house to claim Burke's time and energies. He had fixed the broken step, reshingled one portion of the roof, and helped Celene mix the *bouzillage*, the straw and clay used to repair the mortar between the posts. He had come home from *le Grand Champ* one day to find the house gleaming with a fresh coat of whitewash, and Celene, Pélagie, and Jean-Paul sitting on the back steps, all thoroughly spattered with the lime and water mixture. It had not been an unpleasant time, but his future was in England. He had accounts to settle with his grandfather, and the longer Burke stayed in Ste. Genevieve, the more difficult it was going to be to take his leave.

"I don't care how people talk," he said at last. "I did Antoine a favor in bringing her home. That's as far as it goes. I'm leaving for New Orleans and England as soon as I can."

"You should marry Celene and take her with you," LaVallier insisted.

Burke shook his head again. It had been a mistake to try to involve Celene in his intrigues. In retrospect, he was appalled that he'd even considered it.

"There isn't a place for her where I'm going, and Antoine needs her here."

"Antoine will die in either case."

Burke let out his breath in a heavy sigh. "Yes, I know. I tried to get Antoine to tell her that he's ill."

"He'll never do it," LaVallier said. "It's not his way. He's never told Celene he loves her, and he's not likely to tell her this.

"But it's Celene I'm thinking about, in any case," the Frenchman went on. "She's an exceptional woman, and she's faced far too many difficulties for one so young."

"Being married to Henri Bernard, you mean."

"It's more than that. Antoine is one of the best traders I've ever seen, but he leaves a good deal to be desired as a father. Her mother died when she was only nine, and until Antoine hired Pélagie ten years ago, Celene ran her father's house. Things were better for Celene after Pélagie came. She knew some happy times. But then her brother drowned in the river."

LaVallier's words confirmed what Burke had observed as they were traveling, that Celene was afraid of the water, that the river held some special terror for her.

"She's never spoken about her brother to me."

LaVallier nodded sagely, as if that made sense. "It was a very bad time for all of them when Emile died. Though he was only four years younger, Celene had raised her brother. She treated him as if he were her own child. When Emile died, it was as if all the love, all the stability Celene had known was ripped away. She was only fourteen, little more than a child herself. She couldn't understand why her brother had died. She didn't know how to accept the loss. She was angry, devastated.''

''Couldn't Antoine help her?''

''Antoine blamed himself. He was with Emile when the accident happened. And you know how Peugeot is. He couldn't answer her questions, couldn't share either his grief or his guilt with her. One day when I came to the house, I found Celene crying as if her heart was breaking. I held her and talked to her about Emile, but I never knew if anything I said helped.''

LaVallier paused to light his pipe, his hands shaking a little as he held a flaming splint to the bowl. ''It was soon after that Antoine agreed to Henri Bernard's suit. I don't know that Celene ever really understood, but Antoine couldn't accept responsibility for anyone just then. Not even for himself. Peugeot thought he was doing what was best for her. He thought he was providing Celene a secure future when he gave her to Bernard. He was a tradesman, a butcher. She should have had an easy life.''

The hair along Burke's arms stirred with sudden insight. Now, at another crisis in his life, Antoine was trying to give his daughter away again.

''For the first few years Celene tried to make the best of her marriage,'' LaVallier continued. ''With her living here in Kaskaskia, I made an effort to keep an eye on her. I was the one who taught her to read and write. She came to me and asked, thinking it would please her husband if she could keep his business records. Jean-Paul was a baby then, and I think she wanted to learn for his sake, too.''

''Was her husband pleased?''

''He beat her to within an inch of her life.''

Burke could feel his face get hot. ''That bastard,'' he muttered under his breath.

''The beating Henri gave her, and learning to read, changed Celene. Though she remained a proper and subservient wife in every way, she grew stronger somehow.

She began to see her life differently, began to want more for herself and for her son. It was a long, slow process, but when Henri died, it gave her a chance to taste the independence she'd been working for, a chance to become the woman she truly wants to be.''

LaVallier's words explained so much, Celene's strained relations with her father, her desperate love for Jean-Paul, her need to make her own way in the world. It even cast her refusal of Burke's suit in another light.

"Ah, but, Cardwell," the Frenchman said, "I think you have a *tendre* for our Celene. I see it in your eyes when we speak of her. I hear it in your voice. You would be good to her, and she needs someone just now. Marry her and make her happy.''

"It's not that simple.''

"Celene Bernard is a strong and independent woman, but she had fought her battles alone for far too long. She needs a husband, a good man who will care for her and her son, a man who could give her the love she needs and deserves, a man who can accept the woman she has become. You could be all that to her. And as I understand it, you have need of a wife.''

Burke shook his head in refusal and resignation, then rose to go. If he had a modicum of sense, he'd take his letter of credit and head downriver at first light.

LaVallier slapped Burke on the back as he walked Cardwell to the office door. "Just think about it. That's all I ask. And be happy, Cardwell, wherever you go.''

Burke thanked him and turned away, heading toward where he had beached his battered canoe. The afternoon had been strangely unsettling. Receiving the letter of credit at long last and being victim to LaVallier's well-intentioned meddling left Burke feeling more than a little compromised.

His emotions were all tangled up where Celene was concerned. There was no question that he wanted her, and the kiss she had given him that first night on the porch had left him aching. The promise in that kiss was part of what had kept him in Ste. Genevieve all this time. But Celene had never approached him again, never given a hint that she would offer him more. Frustration was not a new emotion where Celene was concerned, but Burke was growing weary of waiting for something more, something that might never happen.

When he thought about it, what did he really need with a woman like her? Her innocent sensuality stirred his senses. Her presence made his heart beat fast, but she was afraid—and with good reason—of everything marriage meant. What could he possibly gain by marrying her? He wanted children of his own, and he was not even sure he could convince Celene to make love with him if he chose to wed her.

He launched his canoe and propelled it into the channel with long, angry strokes. Aside from his lust and his feelings of inexplicable tenderness, what did the woman have to recommend her as a wife? She had a son who had hated Burke on sight, a father who was dying by inches, a broken-down house at the edge of the wilderness. Why would any man with brains in his head consider taking all that on? He was furious with LaVallier for raising the question again, furious with himself for giving the idea more than a passing thought.

The letter of credit the trader had given him today made him an extremely wealthy man. He should take the money and go away, far from the Mississippi Valley, far from his memories of Morning Song, far from the multitude of questions Celene could rouse in him. He should turn his back on the life he'd lived here in North America. If he had any sense at all, he would.

After he beached his canoe, he climbed the bank and slammed his way into the house. Burke was glad there was no one about. He was in no mood to be cordial. Celene and Pélagie must be out in the fields. Antoine was probably on François Vallé's porch, sitting with the other men, smoking their pipes and discussing the weather, politics, or the town's latest scandal. Burke was glad to be alone.

Yet because he was used to the bustle of activity in the house, the unusual quiet made his skin crawl. He prowled into the parlor and began to gather up his things, jamming them haphazardly into his packs. He had half a mind to simply leave, to start down the river without saying goodbye. It would be easier that way, easier for everyone.

It was the sound of someone in the yard that interrupted his task. He moved quietly through the house and glanced out the open kitchen door. Jean-Paul was at the woodpile with ax in hand, trying to split wood for the cooking fire. Celene, Burke suspected, would be far from pleased by what her son was doing. Since there was no one else around, he should probably step outside and keep an eye on the boy.

Pausing to dipper water from the keg, Burke wandered onto the back gallery of the house and settled himself on the top of the steps. Jean-Paul was really too young to be wielding the sharp, short-handled ax, but he seemed so determined to split the log before him that Burke decided to let him try. He was here, after all, to make certain the child didn't hurt himself.

His thin wrists wavering with the weight of the ax, Jean-Paul went ahead with his task as if Cardwell was not there. He drew it back again and again. His chin jutted out farther with every stroke, and Burke realized that Celene had passed on far more to her son than the color of her eyes. As the minutes passed, Cardwell could sense the child's frustration growing.

"You might try hitting closer to the edge," he offered, then bit down hard on his tongue. He hadn't meant to do more than watch.

The child pretended he had not heard and swung the ax in another stroke. It landed directly in the center of the log. Wood chips flew, but not much else. Under Burke's watchful gaze, Jean-Paul worked the blade out and tried again.

"It's easier to split if you hit it near the side," Burke repeated in spite of himself.

The child slashed him a scathing look and swung again.

"It's a trick everyone has to learn."

"I don't need your help," the boy finally spoke up, pausing to wipe the sweat from his brow. "We don't need you here. I can take care of *Maman* myself."

Burke's grip tightened on the mug he held clutched between his hands. "I'm glad you can, because soon I'm going away. I care about your mother, and it's good to know there's someone here who cares about her, too.''

Jean-Paul worried his lower lip between his teeth. ''Where are you going?'' he finally asked.

''Back to England, where I grew up.''

''Is that far away?''

''A thousand leagues across the sea.''

The boy nodded. ''Are you coming back?''

Burke drew a long, uneven breath. ''I don't think so.''

''Will you miss *Maman*?'' the child wanted to know.

Sharp pain curled beneath Cardwell's ribs. ''Yes, I will.''

''I'll take care of her when you're gone.''

It was odd to be comforted by a child, odder still to feel reassured. ''I know you will, probably better than I could myself.''

Jean-Paul resumed his chopping, placing this stroke at the edge of the log. A splinter broke down the length of one side. He pulled back the ax and swung again. Another piece fell away. ''What you were telling me works,'' the boy acknowledged.

Cardwell smiled. ''You might want to try holding the handle farther back.''

The boy's accuracy suffered a bit with the change in grip, but it didn't take long for Jean-Paul to get used to it. Burke set aside his mug and moved into the yard to stack the wood the boy had split.

As he worked at Jean-Paul's side, Burke had the fleeting sense that this was where he belonged, here with Celene and her son, here where the land was wide and free, here where he could be content with all he'd become. He could imagine himself stacking wood for many a long winter at the side of this house, settling down in the kitchen night after night to the delicious meals Celene had cooked, sitting on the gallery with his wife while their children played in the yard, reaching out in bed and knowing infinite satisfaction when she turned to him in love.

But those were foolish fancies, dreams that could never be. He couldn't make them happen by himself, and Celene was striving for something else. That this was beginning to feel like home was reason enough for him to leave.

And there was unfinished business to attend to in England. He needed to face his grandfather with his accusations, needed to flaunt his newfound wealth, needed to wreak revenge on whoever had exiled him to the wilderness and eagerly awaited news of his death. The letter he'd received from England and the mercenary who'd been sent to find him were realities he could not ignore. After eleven long years, he had to go back. If he was honest with himself, there was really nothing in Ste. Genevieve to keep him here.

13

The full, muggy heat of August flowed across the Mississippi Valley like soup. But even at midday Celene was bustling about the kitchen, preparing the evening meal. Burke Cardwell was leaving for New Orleans at first light, and Celene intended his last evening in Ste. Genevieve to be something he could remember them by. Pélagie had wrung one of the chicken's necks, and it was stewing slowly over the fire. With it Celene planned to serve beans fresh from the garden, apples baked with cinnamon, and the buttermilk biscuits Burke seemed to love. She had even bartered one of Pélagie's pies for a bottle of Monsieur Vallé's imported wine to make the meal more festive.

"I hope there's nothing I'm forgetting," she mumbled, hovering over the stewpot with spoon in hand.

Pélagie slid her a sidelong glance from where she sat with the butter churn clamped between her knees.

"Oh, I know I'm being silly, but after everything Burke's done for us, giving him one last good meal seems the least we can do."

The churn thumped a little louder, declaring the housekeeper's opinion that preparing the meal had nothing to do with thanking Burke.

"It's been nice to have him here," Celene went on almost grudgingly. "He's been an enormous help. And I've liked having someone who will listen to my plans."

Determined to avoid responding to the speculative lift of Pélagie's unruly eyebrows, Celene bent to stir the pot again.

"I'm glad that Burke and Jean-Paul have managed to

make their peace," she added in spite of herself. "And I wish he was staying on for Jean-Paul's sake."

But it was not only for Jean-Paul she wished Burke would stay. What Celene could deny to Pélagie, she could not deny to herself. She didn't want Burke to go. Since he'd announced his plans two days before, she had been jumpy as a cat. She had snapped at her father when he'd asked her to fetch him a fresh twist of tobacco, dropped three eggs on the way in from the chicken coop, and been short-tempered with Jean-Paul. When she'd burned her hand on a pot the night before, she'd burst into tears. And Pélagie's meddling today wasn't making things any easier.

"All right, damn it! I will miss him when he's gone," she finally admitted, trying not to notice the smugness in the older woman's eyes. "But Burke has his life to live, and there's nothing I can do to keep him here."

The churn thumped louder than before, and the memory of the kiss she'd given Burke that night on the porch leaped into Celene's mind. It was crystal clear, resonant with the pine-fresh scent of his skin, the velvet brush of his lips beneath hers. Nor had her awareness of him gone away, not in all the days he'd been with them. She listened for the sound of him stirring in the dawn, had begun to anticipate his comings and his goings. She liked the tingle that raced across her skin when Burke came into a room, the warm rumble of his laughter in the background of her life, and the realization that while she was watching him, he was watching her. But for all that they had talked and laughed and worked together, they had not touched since that first night. They had not shared a knowing glance. They had not spoken of their feelings.

And what could she say to him, after all? She could only say that she did not want him to go. A man like Burke would not stay for less than declarations, for less than promises. A man like Burke would not stay for words alone.

Celene checked the stew once more and moved toward the front of the house. "I told Jean-Paul to be back at noon. If I go out to look for him, will you make certain our dinner doesn't burn?"

Neither expecting a reply nor getting one, Celene plopped her wide straw hat on her head and jerked the strings tight beneath her chin. Even with the heat rising in shimmers from the dusty street, it was cooler there than in the house. She clipped along at her usual pace, her wooden shoes slapping against her heels. A crowd of children had taken refuge in the shade of one of the trees, and she headed toward them, thinking Jean-Paul must be there, too.

"He went fishing with the Englishman in his canoe," one of the older children answered when she asked about her son. "They've been gone for quite a while."

Celene's heart seized up inside her chest. "Fishing in a canoe? Are you sure that's where they went?"

Before the boy could answer, Celene wheeled around, running toward the riverbank. She never allowed Jean-Paul to go out on the river in a canoe. Except for trips back and forth to Kaskaskia, she'd never taken him out herself. She didn't want him on the river, and Jean-Paul knew it.

Without volition, her mind slipped back in time to another child, another man, and the ill-fated fishing trip that had cost her brother his life. As she raced toward the river, the single word that came to her lips was her brother's name. "Emile," she whispered. "Oh, Emile."

She was trembling when she reached the edge of the water and had to dash the tears from her eyes before she could bring the scene before her into focus. She scoured the rippling blue river for Jean-Paul and Burke. Shading her eyes with her hand, she willed herself to find them bobbing in the current. She looked as far as she could to the north, then turned her eyes to the south.

Sensing her agitation, the children had scampered after her. "Do you see them?" she asked frantically. "Can you see any sign of a canoe?"

They had to be out there somewhere, she tried to reassure herself. If Jean-Paul was with Burke, he would be all right. Burke wouldn't let anything happen to her son.

A long silence descended as the children looked. "There!" one of them finally shouted. "Over there."

Ice sliced through her breast when she spotted the boat. The upturned shell of a canoe drifted just beneath the surface, bobbing half on its side, rolling in the current. It was her nightmare image come to life.

Panic burst like a fuse burning through her blood. The world swirled around in a whir of blue and green. A moan worked its way up her throat.

The same. Oh, God, it's the same.

It had been hot like this the day Emile had died, the sky blazing its brightness on the surface of the water. Her father and Emile had gone out to fish, and Antoine had come back alone.

Fighting for air, Celene turned to the children. "Bring my father," she managed to gasp. "Bring Pélagie here to me."

Without waiting to see if they did her bidding, Celene ranged along the river's edge, calling her son's name. "Jean-Paul! Jean-Paul!"

Her heart pounded in her ears. The trees on the opposite bank moved in a blur; the water rippled by. She searched the surface of the river for Burke and her son. But there was nothing, no sign of them at all.

"Jean-Paul!" she cried out, frantic with anger, frantic with fear. "Jean-Paul, where are you? Answer me!"

The silence around her was suffocating.

"Jean-Paul! Jean-Paul!" she shouted, withering inside. "Jean-Paul! Burke Cardwell! Will one of you please answer me!"

This couldn't be happening, couldn't be happening. She was sobbing, shuddering, shaking so hard she could barely stand.

Then she spotted something well out in the water, off to her left. A hat, perhaps? A clump of leaves? A child flailing against the current? With hope wavering in her chest, she raced along the bank and waded in. The river rose cold around her calves, swirled around her thighs. Her skirts dragged against the current, heavy and binding. She floundered forward, fighting the river's insistent flow.

"Oh, Holy Mother, please," she prayed, her lips moving in a breathless litany as she forged ahead. "Please, Blessed Virgin, keep them safe."

There was splashing somewhere behind her. Intent on

reaching the object in the water, Celene was hardly aware of it until strong hands closed around her shoulders. She fought as someone pulled her back, lashed out as one of the men from the town swept an arm beneath her knees and lifted her against his chest.

"No, no!" she shrieked, flailing, struggling, pushing hard against him. "It might be one of them. Let me go!"

Against her will, he carried her back to the bank. As he set her on her feet, she saw there were people there—her neighbors gathering at the top of the rise.

She turned from them, scanning the river again. Whatever she had seen in the water was gone, swept away to oblivion as Emile had been.

"Jean-Paul!" she screamed, keening to the cloudless sky. "Burke Cardwell, will you answer me!"

From somewhere her father appeared at her side, grabbing her, holding her. He had come to her once before on the riverbank; he had come to tell her Emile was dead. She fought to push him away.

In spite of her struggles, Antoine held her fast, his finger's digging deep into her flesh.

"This isn't like the other time," she sobbed. "Please tell me it isn't like the other time. Jean-Paul can't be dead."

Desperate for reassurance, she looked into her father's face. It was like pale, crinkled parchment. There were tears in his eyes. His emotion penetrated her own fear and grief. She had never seen her father cry. He had never even wept when Emile had drowned.

"He should have been safe with Burke," Antoine told her fiercely, tightening his hold on her arms. "He should have been safe!"

Something inside her died as he spoke the words. Antoine must know exactly what she was feeling today; he had lost his son to the river, too. Had Antoine felt as shattered and as devastated, as frightened and as empty when Emile had died? He had not allowed her to see his emotions all those years ago, but she could see them in him now. She could see the ugly, painful scars he bore, the grief and despair at losing Emile, the horror of losing Jean-Paul in the very same way.

Celene gave a breathless gasp and sagged against her father's shoulder. He smelled musty and old, not nearly as tough and hard as he'd always seemed. Yet she needed his understanding, his succor, and his strength. She needed all the comfort and consolation he could give. With tender, fragile hands, Antoine tried his best to soothe her. They clung together, helpless, lost.

Then, from somewhere far away, she heard a cry.

"Maman! Maman!"

She raised her head. It came again.

"Maman! Maman!"

Celene jerked out of her father's embrace and glanced around just as a child skidded to a stop at the top of the rise. His clothes were wet and caked with mud. His hat and shoes were gone.

"Jean-Paul?" Her voice rasped as she spoke his name. "Jean-Paul, is it really you?"

Quivering like glass about to shatter, Celene moved toward him. Her son raced down the slope, closing the distance between them. She snatched him hard against her chest, sank breathless to her knees. Sobs racked her as she clutched him close.

"I'm sorry, *Maman*." His arms tightened around her neck, his body shaking, his voice frightened and shrill. "I'm sorry. I'm sorry."

Burying her face in his soft, wet hair, she absorbed her son's vitality and warmth. She breathed deep of his familiar, boy-child scent. Tightening her arms around him, she wished she could take him back into her body where for nine long months she had kept him safe.

Jean-Paul began to cry. "I'm sorry I worried you, *Maman*. But I'm all right. Burke took care of me."

Celene nodded against his cheek, unable to speak.

"Burke let me paddle the boat, and we caught nine fish! When the canoe began to leak, Burke helped me swim ashore. But we lost all the fish." His small hands patted her shoulders and stroked her back: soft, tender pats of reassurance, tamping down her panic; gentle, rhythmic strokes that calmed and soothed. It seemed odd to be held and comforted by her own child, strange to find their usual roles turned inside out.

The dread began to recede, but Celene couldn't seem to release her hold on her son. Her hands curled into his sopping clothes. She nuzzled against his neck. She didn't know whether to spank Jean-Paul for disobedience or hug him closer still. With fresh tears on her cheeks, she chose the latter course.

"I'm sorry, *Maman*," Jean-Paul kept whispering. Slowly relief began to nullify the fear, elation and exhaustion taking possession of her senses.

At length, she sat back on her haunches in the mud. She dried her son's tears with the corner of her apron. She raised it to her face and blotted her own wet cheeks.

"I told you not to go out on the river," she admonished him. "I told you how dangerous it was. I told you—"

"But Burke said it would be all right."

Burke.

He was waiting at the top of the rise, his eyes dark with understanding. To Jean-Paul and him this had been an afternoon's adventure; to Celene it had been a mother's most heinous nightmare.

Fury went up her spine like red-hot steel.

"Jean-Paul, are you sure you're all right?" she asked in a voice that had turned from scolding to seething.

"*Oui, Maman*."

"Very well, then," she said, rising to her feet, lifting Jean-Paul in her arms. "Your *grandpère* needs to hug you, too."

She shifted Jean-Paul to her father's arms and turned on Burke.

Cardwell must have known what was coming, but he stood his ground. It took her only a moment to cover the distance between them. Too furious for words, she rammed her fist into the hollow beneath his ribs. Burke emitted a satisfying grunt and bowed his body to absorb the blow.

"How dare you!" she shouted up at him, her voice quivering. "How dare you take my son onto the river! How dare you put him in such danger?"

Burke said nothing in his own defense.

"Jean-Paul could have drowned because of you! He could have been killed! What in God's name were you thinking about? You risked his life for an afternoon of fishing! For an afternoon of *fishing*!"

"Celene," her father put in, coming up behind her, still carrying Jean-Paul.

She refused to be deterred. "Damn it, Burke! How could you do such an irresponsible thing? You know full well—"

"Celene," Antoine interrupted again. "He did bring the boy home safe."

As thankful as she was for Jean-Paul's return, it didn't change what Burke had done. "You didn't even ask me if you could take him out! You didn't ask my permission! I'm his mother, and I—"

"I gave him permission," Antoine broke in.

Celene whirled on her father, filled with fresh anger and disbelief. "You what?"

Pélagie was, as always, hovering in the background, and Antoine took a moment to shift Jean-Paul into her bony, capable arms.

He caught Celene's elbow and dragged her away. "I asked Burke to take him out."

She sucked in a long, uneven breath. "For God's sake, why?"

"All the other boys go out fishing with their fathers," Antoine tried to explain.

"I don't care what the other boys do."

"He's been wanting to go."

Far too shaken to be reasonable, Celene stormed at him. "It doesn't matter what he wants. He's only a child."

Antoine went on, implacable. "I preferred not to take him myself, so I asked Burke to do it in my place."

She turned on Burke. "And you agreed?"

Cardwell nodded. "When I heard his reasons."

The two men stood arrayed against her, completely in league.

"You know how I feel about the river!" she shouted at both of them.

"I know how you feel," her father acknowledged. "I know why you feel as you do. But it's time for Jean-Paul to learn how to handle himself on the water.''

"No, it's not! He's far too young." The panic came again, her fear of the river, her fear that as hard as she tried to protect him, she could not keep Jean-Paul safe.

"Jean-Paul will need to make his living on the river," Antoine said. "He needs to learn the skills."

"He's going to be a farmer," Celene insisted, her voice shaky and thin.

"Would you rather he took a boat out by himself?" her father went on. "He would have, you know. Neither your admonitions nor your threats would have stopped him."

She glared at the men, feeling helpless, feeling betrayed. What her father said was true. Every child embraced things forbidden to him, and Jean-Paul was no different from the rest. In time he would have gone out on his own, in spite of her. Her only child was growing up, and there was nothing she could do to change what was inevitable.

Cursing both Burke and her father, she spun away, running toward *le Grand Champ* as if all the furies of hell were at her heels. She needed to be alone to think this through. She needed time to accept that her son was safe, that the babe she had nurtured was growing up. The furrows of plowed fields were crumbly and dry beneath her feet. Her skirts slapped heavy and damp around her knees. She stumbled once and righted herself.

By the time she reached the small stone block that marked the boundary of her holdings, fresh tears had pressed up the back of her throat. She deliberately lost herself in the maze of cornstalks, sank down on the ground between two tall, green rows and began to sob. She cried not only from grief but from gratitude, wept not only with sorrow but with relief. She was hurt, disillusioned, and furious with her father and Burke. She hated being a woman in a world of domineering men. She hated that Jean-Paul was growing up. She hated being helpless.

She had no idea how long she'd huddled weeping in the dust and the heat. It took a series of quivering breaths, a few long gulps of air, and the odd inelegant sniff, but eventually her crying ceased. She took out the handkerchief she had not realized she had and wiped her face. She blew her nose twice and tucked the scrap of linen cloth away.

It was then she became aware that Burke was calling to her. "Celene. Damn it, Celene! I want to talk to you! You can either tell me where you are or we can play hide-and-seek among the crops until daylight turns to dark. I don't care if you're mad at me. I don't care if you call down curses on my head. I'm not going away."

She came to her feet and shouted his name. As he rounded the end of the row, she noticed things she had been too angry to see before. He was wet to the skin and caked with mud. A bloody graze marred one bronzed cheek, and his honey-gold hair had come loose from his queue.

She had been sick with fear at losing Jean-Paul, mad with terror, wild with grief. Those minutes on the riverbank had been her worst nightmare come to life. She had faced the knowledge that without her son her world would have been empty, hollow, devoid of any happiness, any joy. There at the water's edge she had come to terms with what losing Jean-Paul would have meant.

Standing here in the cornfield, she suddenly realized what her world would have been if she'd lost Burke. It would have been every bit as joyless, every bit as bleak, every bit as lonely and black. A part of her would have died with him. It would have been far worse than having him go off to England, worse than knowing she'd never see him again. She would have had to accept that the only man who had ever acknowledged her abilities, ever encouraged her, ever stirred tenderness and hope in her heart had gone forever beyond her grasp. A lump wedged at the base of her throat. Tremors racked along her nerves. She started to cry again.

Burke stopped three paces away and stared into her shimmering eyes. His expression was stark, solemn. He looked as if he'd rather face a firing squad than her.

"Oh, Celene, please don't cry," he began in a voice that was deep and rich with sincerity. "I'm sorry. I'm so sorry. I should have let you know what Antoine asked me to do. I should have known better than to take Jean-Paul out on the river without asking your consent. I should have—"

She closed the distance between them and wrapped her

arms around his waist. He stiffened a little in wary surprise.

"Thank you," she breathed into the center of his chest.

"Why in God's name are you thanking me?"

"I'm thanking you for making sure Jean-Paul was safe, for bringing him back alive. And I thank you for coming back yourself."

"Oh, Celene," he muttered in answer, crushing her close. He sounded exhausted, relieved, confused.

They stood leaning into each other for a very long time, as if each was holding the other erect. The silence they shared in the midst of the cornfield was like the quiet after the storm. It was a closeness that seemed necessary to both of them after the anger and recriminations that had passed between them.

After a time Celene tipped her head back to look into Burke's face. She could see the goodness in him, dependability in the angle of his jaw, tenderness in the turn of his lips, strength and compassion that radiated from every line of his body.

She knew it would be easier to let him go without telling him how she felt. She could let him leave Ste. Genevieve without acknowledging the feelings she was only just coming to understand. But it seemed wrong to hold her peace, dishonest somehow. Still, the words came hard to a woman like her, a woman who had seldom heard tenderness expressed, a woman who had learned not to speak her deepest feelings.

It took courage to force the declaration past the knot in her throat, but she took her courage in her hands and told him.

"I love you," she said softly.

Burke went very quiet, very still. She wasn't sure he was even breathing.

"I love you, Burke," she repeated in a raspy voice.

When he said nothing, she stepped away. She hadn't expected him to answer in kind. That would have demanded concessions he could not make, presumed far too much. But she was not sorry she had spoken. That he had earned her love was something he deserved to know.

But after she had said the words, there was nothing left

to do but walk away. She brushed past him, moving back down the row of cornstalks, back to the life she'd always known. Nothing had really changed, yet she felt stronger than before—calmer, more sure of herself, whole. In a way she had never expected, loving Burke had set her free.

Burke stared after her, stark, breathless confusion twisting his insides. He had come here to apologize for what he'd done, to offer Celene what consolation he could. God knows, she had every right to be furious with him. If the current had been faster, if the boat had been farther from shore, the fishing trip might well have ended in disaster. And it would have been his fault. But instead of ripping into him again, Celene had thanked him for saving Jean-Paul—then told him she loved him.

How could she tell him that after he'd put her son in danger? *How could she tell him she loved him and then just walk away?*

With hope and fear and disillusionment singing in his veins, Cardwell started after her.

"Celene," he demanded when he had pulled her to a stop near the end of the row of cornstalks. "I want to know why you said what you did."

"That I love you, you mean?" She was staring at the ground like a naughty child.

"Were you telling the truth?"

He wanted to hear her admission again, needed to hear it.

"I always tell the truth."

"Then you do love me?"

"Yes, I love you." She said the words as if she were ashamed of them—or desperately afraid of the consequences.

That did crazy things to his insides. "Why?"

Celene simply shrugged. "Who can say why one person comes to love another."

"Why did you choose to tell me you loved me today?"

The brim of her hat veiled her face completely. He wanted to rip the dammed thing off. He needed to see the expression in her eyes.

"What happened on the river made me realize what you've come to mean to me."

"Celene, for God's sake! I endangered your son." Anguish colored his tone. "He could have drowned because of me!"

Her gaze rose to his, steady and calm. He wasn't prepared for what he saw in her eyes, exoneration and unexpected tenderness.

"You didn't endanger him by your carelessness. What happened was an accident. And in the end, you brought Jean-Paul home to me. If someone had to take him out on the river, I'm glad it was you. I trust Jean-Paul with you above all men. Even more than I trust him with my father."

"I don't know that I'm worthy of your trust."

She stepped closer, looking up at him. The sun through her straw hat cast a pattern across her face, gray shadows and gold highlights falling on her cheeks, her forehead, and her lips. "I don't give my trust easily, as you well know. You've earned it a dozen times over. I trust you with my son. I trust you with my love . . ."

She paused.

Burke's stomach took a long, slow drop.

"And I trust you with myself." Her voice was breathy and low, but there was no hesitancy in her eyes.

She trusted him with herself? What exactly was she saying?

As if in answer, she raised her hand to the graze on his cheek, tangled her fingers in his still-damp hair. She stretched up along his length, the laces of her bodice grazing his stomach, the fullness of her breasts pressing softly into his ribs. She offered him her mouth, delicate, blossoming, half open in an invitation so potent that he ached.

Was this really what she meant? That she was willing to give herself to him? Burke wondered, breathless with hope and panic. How could this be happening now? Now when he had finally decided to leave? Now when he finally felt ready to face his family?

Still, he couldn't refuse what Celene was offering. How could any man?

He bent above her, touching his lips to hers. The kiss

was questioning, reticent. With gentle insistence she drew him in, nibbling, stroking, kissing him with a sweet, deliberate languor that went to his head like the bubbles in champagne. He closed his eyes and savored her, letting her incipient sensuality lead him on. The texture of her lips intensified the pleasure of the lightest caress. The warmth of her breath against his mouth offered subtle provocation. The press of her body fired a reckless need in him. He melted toward her, against her, into her. He splayed his hands across her back.

Clinging together, they kissed: soft, dizzying kisses imbued with infinite care and tenderness; long, sultry kisses, lazy with teasing and anticipation. He'd never thought Celene could kiss like this, with such eagerness and desire, with such beguiling and deliberate abandon. He ached for her from the top of his head to the soles of his feet. His body burned hard and hot, filled with the need to make her his. But he had to make certain that it was more than raw emotion driving her, more than gratitude, more than fear. He wanted to be sure that this was what she wanted, too.

Valiantly he tried to raise his head. "Celene," he whispered against her mouth. "Celene."

Her lips clung to his, her tongue feathering against them. Delicious sensations swelled through him in a soft, slow wave. He sank helplessly into her kisses, until there was only the feel of her, the taste of her and the fierce, bright alchemy that bound them both.

With a moan hovering in his throat, he raised his hand to caress her breast. It was yielding and soft beneath his fingers, ripe and full in the curve of his palm. Need rolled over him, but even as it did, he sensed that Celene was pulling away.

"It's all right," he whispered, struggling with his own desires, taking back his hand. "If this isn't what you want, all you have to do is say so."

"It is what I want. I have been longing for you to touch me in just this way."

"God knows it's what I've wanted, too."

"Then touch me, show me. I'm tired of being afraid."

In the name of self-preservation, Burke put some small

space between them. He knew what she'd been through with Henri Bernard. Burke knew how much he wanted her. If she was willing to offer herself to him at last, he was going to take his time, going to make sure she had no reason to be afraid. She needed to be courted, deserved to be wooed. She should be treated like a princess, pampered and revered.

He smiled softly and reached across to take her hand. Tracing the curve of her fingers with the pad of his thumb, he brought them to his lips, brushed the backs with a gentle kiss. Her fingers went lax in his, fragile, trusting, and delicate. He turned her hand, feathered kisses into her palm, and brushed the tips of each of her fingers with his lips. He nibbled up the arch of her thumb, across the mound of tender flesh to the turn of her wrist. Her pulse beat fast beneath the milky, blue-veined skin. He marked the spot with a swirl of his tongue.

She drew a shaky breath.

"Do you want me to stop?" he asked as he raised his head. "Is there something I've done that frightens you?"

"No," she answered, her eyes gone huge. "I like what you are doing."

He let his fingers trail up her arm, his thumb raking slowly over the sensitive inner surface. The contact sent tingles coursing through his flesh, and he was amazed at how little it took to stir him where she was concerned.

He curled his palms around her shoulders, traced the neckline of her chemise with feather-light strokes. Her skin was like the petals of some exotic flower, exquisitely soft beneath his hands, deliciously smooth and velvety. The slow, repetitious strokes were compelling, hypnotic. They cast a spell on both of them.

He could see that the heat had begun to rise in her. A flush was blossoming in her cheeks. He could hear the cadence of her breathing escalate, feel the tension in her shoulders loosen.

Her resistance and fear were ebbing away. As hard as it was going to be, he must move carefully. The most dangerous territory was yet to be explored. He must fight his own impulses, fight his own needs. For while he was touching and seducing her, Burke was being seduced himself.

He bent his head to taste her skin, drizzling kisses from the lobe of her ear to the base of her throat. She was salty and sweet, vital and warm. He traced the curve of her collarbone with the tip of his tongue, nibbled upward to the turn of her jaw. She drew a hissing breath, tangled her fingers in the folds of his clothes.

"Celene," he whispered against her throat, his voice gone syrupy and soft. "Celene, I'm going to touch your breast. Is that all right?"

"Yes." Her reply was tremulous, breathy.

Burke fought to hide a smile as he raised his head.

He watched her as he curled his hand over the swell of her bodice, contoured her fullness to the arc of his palm. If he saw so much as a hint of reluctance, so much as a flicker of fear in the luminous silver-green depths of her eyes, he would stop, he promised himself. But there was wonder in them instead, incipient pleasure, the dawning of some understanding that had always eluded her. He savored her reactions, conscious of the blood running hot in his own veins, that the focus of his world had narrowed to the woman in his arms.

Celene gave a breathless sigh, and emboldened by the sound of her pleasure, he sought her nipple with his thumb. Through the fabric of her clothes, he stroked the puckered crest, circling it, rolling it gently between his fingertips. He could see the sensation take hold of her, move through her, drag her down. Her lips parted; her face went soft. A deepred flush moved up her neck.

Burke smiled into her widening eyes, satisfaction rife within him as he continued to touch and fondle her. She melted against him, and Burke could feel her trembling. She breathed his name, and the sound was like some soft elusive melody he'd been straining to hear. Garnering her response, gaining her trust, giving her pleasure, made him feel as if he'd won a victory, over her memories, over her hurts, over all the things that had made this kind of intimacy between them impossible.

He desperately wanted more. He wanted to kiss her long and deep. He wanted to slip the bow to her chemise and bare her breasts. He wanted to touch her naked flesh, tease and taste every inch of her with the tip of his tongue. But he knew he dared not. To give in to his desires would be disaster. It would lead them places she was not ready to go, jeopardize all that he had fought so hard to gain.

Slowly he withdrew, taking his hand from her breast, lifting it to stroke her cheek. Confusion slowly replaced the languor in her eyes.

"It's all right," he whispered, understanding how fragile and uncertain she must feel. He was feeling a little fragile and uncertain, too.

"Why did you stop?" she asked in a whisper.

"Because I want to make love to you."

"That's what I want, too."

"I've no intention of taking you here in the dirt. If you're sure, Celene, really sure, I'll come to you tonight. I'll come to you where we'll have privacy and all the time in the world."

"I do want you to come."

"There's far more to making love than what we've just done together," he warned her.

"Can you make the rest of it as wonderful as this?"

His heart slammed against his ribs. His head went light. She was looking up at him as if he had the power to bring her endless happiness, as if he was someone more far more selfless and tender than he knew himself to be.

Her blind faith in him made Burke steady her on her feet and step away. But the aura of trust, the legion of unfulfilled promises lingered between them.

The sun beat down from a blazing azure sky. The world around them was quiet, steamy, streaked gold and green. The cornstalks shuddered and whispered around them, giving hope for an evening breeze.

"Go back to the house," he told her softly. "Be with your son. And if you're sure, very sure of what you want, tonight I'll come and be with you."

He watched her as she turned to go, wondering if her resolve would hold, wondering if he could give her all she wanted and deserved. She said she loved him. She said she trusted him. But did she trust him and love him enough to overcome her fear? And if he had come to love her, too, could he claim her tonight in the dark and leave her with tomorrow's dawn?

She loved Burke. The moment she saw him standing in the cornfield, wet, bedraggled, mud-stained, and determined to apologize, Celene knew what he'd come to mean to her. If she'd lost Jean-Paul, she would have given up on life. If she'd lost Burke, there would have been no joy in going on.

Celene had never loved a man before, never felt capable of softer feelings where men were concerned. She had been disillusioned, betrayed, and hurt by her father and Henri. But the tenderness and the joy that Burke had showed her had changed everything. She loved him, and she had committed herself to act on what she felt. She would not let herself consider that Burke was leaving at first light, would not ask what the future held for her. Tonight was all that mattered, tonight when he would come to her, tonight when she would give herself to him completely.

It was getting through the evening ahead that seemed impossible. She had already stubbed her toe getting out of the bath, poked a finger through her stocking and found a stain on her best coif. The apples she was baking had stuck to the bottom of the pan. She'd spilled the buttermilk for the biscuits and dropped the plates on the way to the table. Fortunately Burke had made himself scarce, and she could only think that things would have been far worse if he had been about.

Pélagie kept her comments to herself, but from the smirk on the housekeeper's face, Celene guessed that the older woman knew what decision she'd made. Her father seemed blissfully unaware, and Jean-Paul was too caught up in regaling his friends with his exploits to take note of his mother at all.

Cardwell made his appearance just as supper was being served. He was freshly bathed, barbered, and dressed for travel in a new linen shirt, dark trousers, and knee-high boots. The meal was a companionable affair, eaten at the table Celene and Pélagie had moved to the gallery at the side of the house. Clouds had rolled in late in the day bringing a respite from the heat and the smell of an approaching storm. Sunset sent swirls of mauve and blue across the sky, giving a hazy pink glow to the festivities. The light reflected off the rims of the plates, shimmered in the wineglasses, cast a roseate warmth across all their faces. To Celene it seemed a magical time, a time when the people she loved were safe and together: her son, expansive and full of himself; Burke, laughing and exclaiming over the fare; Pélagie, her sallow face pinked by the wine and the sunlight; and her father . . .

Her father suddenly looked so old to her. He wasn't as tough and strong as he'd always seemed, as solid and indomitable as she'd always imagined him. There had been tears in his eyes today on the riverbank. Even through her distress that had shocked her, touched her, unnerved her. Until today she would have sworn Antoine was incapable of showing tender emotions. Perhaps it was seeing his unexpected vulnerability that cast her father in a whole new light. Was the change in him or in the way she looked at him? Was it that Antoine was showing his age or that she was growing up?

"Celene." Burke's voice cut through her thoughts. "Celene, would you like more wine. Monsieur Vallé sent over a second bottle so that we could celebrate properly."

As she raised her glass toward Burke, their gazes met. His eyes were full of tenderness, full of promises. She felt the warmth rise in her cheeks and glanced away. They feasted into the twilight, letting the bloom of the candles hover over the empty dishes and crumbled biscuits, the wrinkled napkins and half-filled glasses.

Celene's head was spinning with the excitement and the wine as she began to clear away the dishes. Sensing her impediment or her mood, Pélagie shooed her out of the kitchen. On the gallery Antoine had taken out his old harmonica and was sending soft, sweet music spilling into the dark. Burke sat smoking his pipe, and Jean-Paul was curled up in his lap as if it were the most natural place in the world for him to be. Cardwell motioned Celene to a place on the bench, and she settled in beside him. It felt right to be here with Burke, her father and Jean-Paul, the breeze ruffling through the leaves of the wisteria, the melody from her father's harmonica filling the night with music and contentment.

Jean-Paul drifted to sleep in the crook of Burke's arm, and Celene carried her son to his bed. Antoine and Pélagie excused themselves and retired soon after. That left only Celene and Burke sitting together on the porch at the side of the house.

The intimacy and the quiet intensified the buzz in her belly, her awareness of Burke. Though he did not move or say a word, every cell in her body tingled, alert to his presence beside her. She could smell the newness of his clothes, hear the cadence of his breathing, feel his warmth along her side. More than anything she wanted to give herself to him, to learn the secrets of love and life that he must know, but the trepidation was strong in her.

Her heart beat fast as she slid her palm along the seat between them, closed her icy fingers around his hand. He turned his head to look at her, searching her face. She did not want him to see how eager or how frightened she was, and she forced herself to stand. He came to his feet beside her. She led him behind her as she closed up the house, tightened her grip on his hand as they climbed the ladder.

His height seemed to fill the high-beamed loft, dwarf the rough-hewn bed she had slept in most of her life. It seemed unbearably close in the attic after the heat of the day, and, setting aside the candle she had brought to light their way, Celene went to the windows at the gable ends and swung open the wooden shutters. The sudden drift of breeze brought the scent of coming rain and stirred the film of mosquito netting that draped like a tent around her bed.

Drawing a calming breath, she turned to where Burke stood and began to remove her coif. She let down her hair and shook it free, then began to work the laces at the front of her bodice.

"You're sure this is what you want?" he asked.

"I am a woman who knows her mind, monsieur." Celene said the words with far more bravado than she felt, certain and uncertain, eager and afraid. "Surely you know that by now."

She trailed the laces onto the floor. Burke watched with glowing eyes. She pulled her bodice down her arms and dropped it to the floor. Unschooled in the ways of seduction, she wasn't quite sure what she should do. Did he want to watch as she removed her clothes? Would she have to strip naked before him?

As if sensing her uncertainty, he crossed the room and fumbled with the tapes at her waist, casting petticoats and pockets aside. And when she stood before him clad in only her chemise, Burke kissed her lingeringly on the mouth and pushed aside the drape of netting.

"Why don't you wait for me in bed?" he offered softly.

She complied with his request and settled in, turning back almost shyly to where he stood. The curtain of gauze that fell between them was like a haze, making him seem spectral and mysterious in the wavering semidarkness, making her feel invisible and safe in watching him. With surprisingly graceful movements he removed his boots, worked the ties at the neck of his shirt, and pulled the garment over his head. Something fluttered inside her at the sight of his naked chest, though she had seen him often in far less than this. The glow of the candle cast his musculature in sharp relief, gold overlaid with bronze, sinuous and malleable. When he lowered his hands to the buttons at the front of his pants, he turned away as if he was no more eager than she had been to show himself so flagrantly. The loosened trousers skimmed low, baring his narrow hips and his long, hard flanks. He stepped out of the pants and set them aside. Anticipation buzzed inside her as he turned toward where she lay. He was beautiful in the half-light, strong, well-formed, and masculine. Nor could he hide the evidence that he wanted her. The buzz of anticipation became a roar. Her mouth went dry. A trembling started inside of her.

Still, she sensed she could turn away even now, and Burke would not think less of her.

Slowly he pulled the drape of net aside. "Are you sure?" he asked.

"Perhaps it is you who is uncertain." That her voice was breathy and low made the words less of a challenge, more of a question.

"Perhaps I am," he answered settling on the edge of the bed. "Perhaps I am afraid that I will hurt you."

"I know you'd never hurt me deliberately."

"Or frighten you."

"Not if you give me the time I need."

He reached across to touch her face, smoothed the tangles from her hair. "I will give you as much time as you want, Celene. As much time as you need. We have all night to spend together."

All night. Were the words a promise or a benediction? Would he leave her in the dawn? The question of his intent crowded into her mind, but instead of letting herself think about things she could not change, she caught his wrist and pulled him down.

He came to lie beside her on the bed. His welcoming warmth brushed along her side. She turned into it, facing him, looking deep into his eyes.

"You're lovely," he said and leaned across to kiss her. His lips flickered against hers, lazy and light. "So very lovely," he amended and kissed her again.

The contact intensified by slow degrees, with each lingering brush of his mouth, with the longer and longer drafts he took of her. Her tension seeped slowly away, her muscles loosening, the knot in her belly uncoiling. She parted her lips, and his tongue slipped inside, exploring the smooth inner surface, sliding deeper in a slow, sweet penetration. Her mouth clung to his until the kisses flowed together, cresting and ebbing, rippling one into the next like the ceaseless rush of breaking waves. She expelled her breath on a sigh and had to fight to get it back. She arched against him and knew the thrill of deeper contact.

Shivers of sensation spilled through her body, fluttering in her throat, trickling through her chest, swirling low, eddying deep in the core of her. She stirred in the curl of his embrace, knowing, for the very first time in her life, what it meant to desire a man.

Burke's kisses grew deeper and more demanding, until

her senses were awash with him: the wine and tobacco tang of him on her tongue, his pine-fresh scent in her nostrils, his hushed endearments sweet as music in her ears. His height and breadth and strength overwhelmed her, yet he lay quiescent beneath her hands. She stroked over him in gentle exploration. She liked knowing him as intimately as this, liked learning the texture of his skin and hair, liked finding the places that made him quicken to her touch.

Burke was searching out the things that pleased her, too, though he seemed to have a far better idea where to find them. She melted against him when he kissed the corners of her eyes, shook with shivers when he nibbled at the lobe of her ear, gasped aloud when he swirled his tongue along the hollow above her collarbone.

Being bedded by a man had never been like this for her before, never this slow, never this tender, never this wonderful. It had never been something for her to savor and enjoy.

"Sweet girl," he whispered, drawing back to look down into her face. "Do you know how long I have wanted to see desire instead of fear in your eyes? Do you know how long I've wanted to touch you like this, wanted to help you learn what pleasure is?"

Smiling, he bent above her, pressing soft, drugging kisses into her mouth; lingering over her as if she were the source of some secret delight. He stroked her hair, her throat, her back, then curled his hand around her breast, finding her nipple beneath the drape of her chemise. He circled the nub with the pad of his thumb, each sinuous stroke stirring a maelstrom through her blood, each gentle brush spilling dizzying sensation through her. Lightning coursed along her nerves. Pleasure blossomed deep inside. She gave a desperate gasp, and Burke let his opposite hand trail down her spine, soothing her, enticing her, molding her body to his.

As his hand rose again, he skimmed beneath the flowing fabric of her gown, stroking her flank to the rise of her hip, sliding into the vale of her waist and across her ribs. He loosened the garment as he went and finally pulled it over her head.

Lying bared before him, she felt a rush of heat beneath her skin, tinting her flesh with dusty rose.

"You're beautiful," he whispered, letting his gaze roam over her. "So soft and delicate. So warm and lush. No man could want for more than this." Yet even as he whispered compliments, he tucked the sheet around her to preserve some semblance of her modesty.

She smiled and touched his face. He was such a good man, such an understanding man. She stroked his hair, let her fingers trail along his throat. She leaned across to kiss him as deeply as he had kissed her, savoring his mouth, letting her tongue dally at the seam of his lips, letting herself flow into him.

His breathing turned fast and harsh; a restlessness stirred beneath his skin. His body responded to her. She saw the pulse tripping at the side of his throat and lowered her head, feeling the rhythm of his body course beneath her lips. She splayed her palms against his chest, and when his nipples tightened beneath to press of her palms, she teased them with her thumbs. His hands tightened on her arms, and a growl of provocation and pleasure rumbled up his throat. She smiled softly to herself, intrigued by what she had discovered. Her power over him gave a pleasure of its own, the knowledge that while he sought to pleasure her, she could rouse and entice him, too.

With the dip of his head he claimed her breast, bared by the friction between them. His mouth curled over the puckered crest, drawing it into his mouth, circling the nipple with the tip of his tongue. Exquisite swirls of sensation wrapped around her.

"Oh, Burke," she murmured. "Burke." She had never known anything like this, never suspected a man could offer a woman such delight, never expected her body to respond with such wild, delicious abandon. Shudders racked her, shudders of gratitude and elation, of eagerness and joy. She melted into him, soft and pliable, willing and weak. She cried out as the pleasure intensified, seething and bubbling inside her.

As he drew her nipple deeper into his mouth, his hand slid down along her body, brushing over her waist, the rise of her hip, sliding across her stomach until it lay atop the vee of hair at the apex of her thighs.

Panic burned away some of the sensual haze, and Celene stirred in his embrace. Her mouth was dry. Her head slowed its spinning.

"Easy, love," he whispered, wooing her softly. "Trust me just a little more. All I want to do is give you pleasure."

She loved him and she trusted him, but this was the most difficult thing he had asked of her. Once she granted him access to her body, there would be no going back. She fought against her fear, knowing how patient and gentle he'd been with her, knowing he had earned her trust. As willing as she was to give herself, he was asking to breach her final defense.

Feeling trembly inside, she opened her legs, and his fingers slid gently against her most vulnerable flesh. He stroked tentatively, pressing deeper with each gliding stroke, awakening needs and sensations her body had never known. She rose against his hand, shivering with delight, took up the press and retreat of his fingers with the motion of her hips. He plied her with a skill that made her writhe, with a care and consideration that brought the sting of tears to her throat. As he touched her, he whispered endearments and watched her eyes. She knew he could see the wonder grow in her, the breathless surprise and wild elation, the soft, sweet ache and melting bliss.

She could see the need for her grow in him, hungry and fierce, bright and blinding in its intensity. But he tempered his need with a tenderness that stole her breath, a concern for her that passed all comprehension. And suddenly she knew he would never ask for more. The last bit of trust was hers to give; the final offering was hers to make. And deep within her heart she knew it was a gift she had been saving just for him.

She stroked his face and hair and looked into his eyes. "I love you, Burke. Please come to me. I want you with me now."

He nodded once in answer and began to move over her. He came into her as if she were something fragile and infinitely precious, as if she were some delicate, priceless treasure he was afraid he might despoil. But their union was sweet beyond all imaginings, steeped in pleasure, suffused with joy. He became part of her, part of the healing, part of the wonder, part of the delight she had begun to discover in herself. With his patience and understanding, his caring and his tenderness, he was giving her pleasure she'd never known, fulfilling her, making her whole.

"I love you," he murmured as he lowered his mouth to hers. "I love you, Celene. And now I know you love me, too."

His kiss became a dart of provocation and heat that seared its way to the core of her. Her body tightened around him, embracing him in a caress that was intimate and sensual. Her skin tingled. Shudders streaked along her spine. Her head went light.

She strained to rise against him, but he held her still, kissing her until her mind and body were filled with him: Burke's tenderness enfolding her. Burke's touch like satin on her skin. Burke's emotions in tune with her own. Burke's wisdom and concern protecting her.

"I love you," he breathed against her mouth, holding her as if she was the most precious and revered of women. "I love you. Love you. Love . . ."

He began to move inside her, circling and pressing, stroking and retreating. As he eased deep and deeper still, Celene was buffeted by waves of pure sensation, lifted on swells of utter delight. Each crest took her higher than the last, lifting her, compelling her to reach for some pinnacle she sensed but could not comprehend. With the sinuous movements of his body Burke urged her on, seeking something for her she could not find for herself. Then the glory burst inside her, and she understood the wondrous gift he'd given her.

Pleasure swelled through her, rushing in her blood, swirling through her consciousness, quivering in every cell. She twisted against him and called his name, clinging to him as the only solid thing in a world gone viscous and flowing, soft and unsubstantial. Then she felt the tumult take him, too, sending tremors racking through him, tearing a gasp of elation from his throat. Rising to undreamed-of heights, she shared in his release, gloried in their union as he filled her with his body, with his seed, with the essence of himself. As she shattered with new delight, Burke gathered her in, holding her, stroking her, taking her with him into the vast, sweet peace of utter completion that seemed intimate and infinite, all encompassing and soul-deep. They lay entwined as the passion ebbed away, echoing like a long, sweet note of music that lulled them into dreamless sleep.

It was full daylight when Celene awoke. Burke was still beside her in the bed, tousled and slumbering. With joy rising inside her, she watched his face. The sunbeams filtering through the netting touched it with gold, polarizing his brows and lashes, limning the curve of his cheek, falling full on his gently parted lips.

She loved this man and he loved her. Last night he had showed her what he felt, told her in words so eloquent and sweet that she ached with the memory. He had done things no man had ever done, given her things she had never thought to have. He had given her pleasure so wondrous she ached to experience it again, showed her consideration so tender that she could not fathom his selflessness, offered her a sense of herself she had never known she could feel. She had been renewed and reborn in the shelter of his arms. This morning she had awakened refreshed, happy, and utterly content. And she owed it all to Burke.

She didn't know what would happen after this. But even if he rose from her bed and went away forever, he had given her a gift, a knowledge of herself, a belief in love that would help and sustain her from this day on.

The murmur of voices and the clatter of dishes rising from the floor below awakened Burke a short time later. She saw him blink with drowsy confusion, get his bearings, and turn to her.

He reached across to touch her face, to trail his fingers the length of her throat. He smiled and seemed as hazily content as she was, as caught in the magic lingering between them. She smiled in return and reached across to touch him, too.

"So will you marry me now?" he asked her.

His eyes were heavy-lidded and warm, the color of the

summer sky. There was no hesitation in their turquoise depths, nor any in her answer.

"Yes," she told him. "Yes. If you want, I'll marry you today."

He hadn't meant for this to happen. He hadn't meant to love Celene, not this deeply, not this passionately, not this irrevocably. And certainly not in a way that would change his life.

Burke led the cow in the direction of the commons at the edge of the river. Taking the animal to graze was usually Jean-Paul's job, but Burke had offered to do it today, needing to escape the confines of the Peugeots' kitchen and the glowing faces around the breakfast table. When he and Celene had come down from the loft and announced they were going to be married after all, Jean-Paul had whooped like an Indian and launched himself into Cardwell's arms. Antoine had beamed with satisfaction. Even Pélagie had been grinning from ear to ear.

And Celene—Celene had been flushed, appropriately flustered, and ever so slightly abashed. But for the first time since he'd met her, Celene seemed truly happy.

Burke had to admit he hadn't meant to fall in love with her. Nebulous feelings of concern and tenderness and desire had been stirring around inside him for weeks. They were feelings he had tried to deny, tried to ignore. He'd almost convinced himself that he could go away and pretend he'd never met her, drive her memory from her mind and the longing from his heart. Then Celene had told him that she loved him.

Those three small words spoken in the midst of a cornfield had changed everything, clarified everything. When he'd gone to her last night, felt the emotion rise between them with a force too pure and elemental to resist, he had realized he loved her, too.

Still, he hadn't intended to marry her, hadn't intended to stay. It was just that awakening in her arms this morning felt so good, so incredibly right. It was like coming home after a dark and difficult journey, like finding the place where he'd always belonged. He felt sheltered and content, capable of accomplishing any task she gave him in the name of love. And the words that would make her his forever were on his lips almost as if fate, not Burke himself, had put them there.

He slipped the lead from the halter, and the cow lowered her head to graze. He stood for a moment, his hand resting on her brindle-brown haunches, and looked out at the river.

He was supposed to have left for England today. For months he had been planning his return: what he would say when he faced his grandfather, what he would do when he discovered who'd had him kidnapped into the wilds. Dreaming about going to England and wreaking revenge was all that had kept him sane in those last lonely months on the Athabasca. It had given him the fury and the drive to face another day when there was no other reason for living.

But now Celene had offered him something better, a part of her life in Ste. Genevieve. She had offered a home with the welcoming sweep of a wide front porch, the promise of children with golden hair and gray-green eyes, the security of loving and being loved. He could see the future stretch before him sweet with contentment, tart with adventure, warm with the knowledge that there would be someone with whom to share his joys and sorrows for the rest of his days. He could be happy here. He loved Celene with a depth and passion that were both oddly familiar yet strangely new.

It was only Morning Song's memory that cast a pall on what should have been a joyous day. Burke's decision to marry Celene and spend his life with her felt like a betrayal of all his first wife had meant to him.

It's just that I was so lonely without you, Morning Song, he thought. Marrying Celene would never erase the memories, the tenderness, the joy, or the communion he'd known with his Chippewa wife. It would never change his love for her. But Morning Song was part of his past. It was Celene who shared his hopes and his dreams for the future.

His mind filled with images from the night before, of Celene pulling him down beside her on the bed, of her gentle kisses, of her awakening passion, of the delight their union gave them both. In spite of his plans to go to England, in spite of his feelings for Morning Song, his life and his future were here in Ste. Genevieve with Celene and her son. He loved her and she loved him. That was all any man had a right to ask.

14

All brides were nervous before their weddings, Celene supposed. Surely there could be no other reason for her hands to be so clammy or for her insides to be tied in knots. The last month with Burke had been utter bliss. She had savored every moment, working together, laughing together, talking together long into the night. And making love. Warmth moved up her neck when she thought about the pleasures they had shared. Burke swept away her fears about married life as if they were so much smoke. After the ceremony today, her life would be settled, secure, wonderful.

Still, she couldn't seem to banish the snarl of uneasiness beneath her ribs. Angry at her own foolishness but giving way to it, she took the crude wooden carving Autumn Leaf had made of Burke from the birch bark box where Celene had kept it since they'd returned to Ste. Genevieve. It was a heathen charm, totally incompatible with the blessings she and Burke would receive from the priest today. Yet as she slipped the bit of wood into the tiny velvet pomander she wore around her neck, she felt immediately better.

"Ridiculous!" she scoffed aloud, but kept the bag around her neck as she began to dress. Her chemise was trimmed with crocheted lace, and Pélagie had embroidered the tops of her stockings and her garters with pink rosettes. Her first petticoat was of creamy linnette, her second of flowered chintz, and her last of the heavy blue-green silk that Burke had given her as a wedding gift. Marriage had proved to be an unexpectedly expensive undertaking for him, since Antoine had insisted that Burke grant a *douaire préfix* to support Celene should she have the need. Though she resented being dickered over by the two of them, she could not fault her father's concern. Had he been so scrupulous before her marriage to Henri, she and Jean-Paul might not have been left destitute when her husband died. As she tied the laces of the white silk bodice rimmed in thick gold braid, masculine voices drifted up from the hall below, and she knew it was time to leave for church. Adjusting her frilled lace coif atop her head and donning her matching apron, she drew a calming breath.

Below Antoine, Jean-Paul and Burke were waiting, decked out in satin frock coats, vests and breeches. Ruffles of lace spilled back from Burke's wrists as he guided her down the last rungs of the ladder.

She could hardly believe this was the same bear of a man whose proposal she had vehemently refused mere months ago. Then he had seemed homely and unkempt; today he shone like a golden Spanish *pistole*. His immaculate ruffled linen gleamed against the blue silk moiré of his frock coat and breeches. His vest of tan brocade closed with a row of silver buttons. His pale stockings showed off the contours of his muscled calves, and his shoes were of the finest leather. He washed up rather well, she thought, and she glowed with possessive pride when she so much as glanced at him.

"I've never seen you looking more beautiful," he told her quietly, though sparks snapped in his eyes. "If we weren't on our way to church, I could think of several other things I'd like to do with you."

"Perhaps later," Antoine intervened smoothly, offering his arm to his daughter.

Just as they were turning toward the door, Pélagie bustled toward them from the back of the house. No one had been more pleased by the news of this marriage than Pélagie. She had been cooking and baking for days, had used every spare moment to embroider a set of the fine linen sheets as a wedding gift, and had even done her part to ensure fair weather for the ceremony by hanging a rosary on the clothesline the previous evening. She had also single-handedly organized the celebration that would follow the service.

And they had so much to celebrate. Not only was Celene's new life with Burke beginning today, but the crops were in and the harvest had been one of the best in years. The entire town was in a festive mood, and the party was bound to be a memorable one. Even before the other women added their offerings, the kitchen had been overflowing with food. Monsieur LaVallier had sent over a full hogshead of wine. There was more tafia and cider and ale than the celebrants usually consumed in a month. Yet Celene was willing to wager that all of the spirits would be gone by morning, and her neighbors would have the headaches they richly deserved.

Stepping in time to the clanging bell, the wedding party walked north to the church at the head of the town, greeting friends along the way. Once they entered the tiny whitewashed building, they moved down the chancel and settled themselves in the family pew. To Celene the mass seemed interminable, an endless series of mumbled prayers and responses, of tinkling bells and drifting incense. But at last the blessing was spoken, and they were free to go into the yard.

Because Burke was Anglican by background, they were to be married on the steps of the church instead of in front of the altar. Though it was clear that Father Hilaire did not approve of one of his flock wedding outside the Catholic faith, it had not prevented him from paying a call on Cardwell and demanding that he do the honorable thing.

The sun shone down on them as they spoke their vows, their voices rippling over the heads of their friends and neighbors, carried on the crisp, light breeze. The ceremony was both moving and brief, the making of vows, the blessing and exchange of rings, a prayer for their happiness and fecundity. Then Father Hilaire pronounced them man and wife, and they were the center of a boisterous throng of well-wishers.

Holding Celene's hand and carrying Jean-Paul on his hip, Burke led the way back to the house. Some of the young men hooted and hollered as they approached and fired their muskets into the air by way of celebration. The crowd had hardly come inside before the fiddlers were tuning their instruments. Food and liquor were put out. Before Celene and Burke's marriage was an hour old, half the men were in their cups from the toasts that had been drunk to the new couple's health and happiness.

Gaiety flowed around Celene like honeyed wine. She laughed at the kissing and the foolery. She danced with every one of the young bucks in the territory and a few of the older ones, as well. Pélagie hugged her every time they passed. Her father sat back in one corner of the gallery with Monsieur LaVallier, looking flushed and proud and pleased with himself. Jean-Paul spent the day stealing madeleines from the table of sweets and tearing around the yard with the rest of the children.

Late in the afternoon Celene encountered Burke on the porch at the back of the house. "Are you having fun?" he asked, smiling down into her eyes.

"I'm having a wonderful time," she answered, helping herself to a drink of his wine.

"And are you happy?"

"Delighted. Happier than I ever dreamed I could be."

He kissed her then, right there where everyone could see. Heedless of the impropriety, Celene moved closer and kissed him back. "I love you," she whispered when he lifted his mouth from hers.

"Those are the three sweetest words you could ever say to me. I love you, too."

They circulated through the house together until the candles were lit and the fiddlers struck up a stately minuet. The others who had been dancing pressed back against the walls of the front room leaving Celene and Burke alone in the center of the floor. Bowing low, Cardwell came to take her hand, and with his touch a thrill of possession and possessiveness curled up her arm. This tall, strong, handsome man was her husband now. He was the man who would share her joys and tears, who would work beside her, lie with her, and give her the children she so longed to have. Life sparked in his turquoise eyes; his lightest touch was a caress. Even as they danced the precise, measured figures of the minuet, tingles of awareness flowed between them.

Applause and catcalls filled the room when they were done, and Pélagie brought out *la croquembouche* for them to cut and serve to their guests. The conical mound of cream puffs bound together with caramel and frosted with slivered almonds was the traditional wedding dessert and a delicacy to be savored by all. But before Celene and Burke could so much as take up a knife, Antoine came toward them across the floor, wine glass in hand.

"*Mesdames et messieurs, mes vieux amis*," he began. "It is not often that a man is as filled with joy as I am today. Though I have not always been the best of fathers to this girl, she has made me very happy. *Ma belle fille*, my beautiful daughter, has chosen to marry a man who has long been a friend. He is a fine man, an upstanding man, an honorable man. A man worthy of her in every way. Though I have not often told her how proud I am of her, I am telling her now. And I hope you will join me in a toast to Celene Peugeot Bernard Cardwell and her new husband. May they have many years of joy together."

Her father downed the glass of wine in a single draught, and while most of the wedding guests did the same, Celene crossed to where her father stood and embraced him. What he had said meant so much to her, and as they hugged, tears of happiness stung her eyes.

"I love you, Papa," she whispered.

"*Oui, ma chere. Je t'aime, aussi.*"

A cheer followed the toast, almost drowning out her father's words, but Celene had heard them clearly enough. Then abruptly the sound of the voices died away, and stepping out of her father's embrace, she searched the room for the cause of the sudden silence.

A stranger stood in the doorway, a large man, nearly as tall as Burke, but thinner, like a rapier instead of a broadsword. He was dressed in stark white and midnight black, a sharp contrast to the brilliant colors worn by the guests around him. He stood out like a raven in a flock of cardinals and jays.

Something about him made Celene's blood run cold, and she was glad when Burke stepped up beside her.

The man stalked toward them across the floor. *"Êtes-vous l'homme qui s'appelle Burke Cardwell?"*

Are you the man who calls himself Burke Cardwell? The words were spoken in proper French, but the weight of his English accent made them almost unintelligible.

"I am." As he spoke to the stranger in English, Burke's hand found and clasped Celene's in the flowing folds of her skirt. Though she knew he meant the gesture to be one of reassurance, dread roiled up inside her chest.

"Are you the man who is known in England as Frederick Andrew Burke Hammond-Cardwell?"

Celene could see Burke's face freeze up. "Yes."

"The Eighth Earl of Hammondsford?"

"What?" There was incredulity in Cardwell's tone.

Celene tried to read the expression on her husband's face. It was one of stunned surprise, of stark disbelief.

She turned to the stranger in their midst. "Surely you are mistaken, monsieur. My husband is a simple trapper, nothing more."

The stranger looked past her as if she were invisible, addressing Burke. "Your family sent me to America to find you and bring you home to claim your title. Or to provide irrefutable proof that you are dead."

"I am very much alive," Burke answered, "as you can see."

"Then allow me to offer my felicitations."

Was the news this man brought them true? Was Burke an English earl? And if he was, why hadn't he seen fit to tell her of his lineage?

A hum of whispered conversations went on around the room as those who understood English translated for their neighbors who did not. It was no louder than the buzz in Celene's own ears.

"And you are, sir?" Burke asked in a voice that crackled like melting ice.

The stranger executed a perfect throne-room bow. "Bayard Forrester at your service, my lord."

Sweet God in heaven! The Eighth Earl of Hammondsford.

How he'd gotten through the last few minutes, Burke would never know. Even after Antoine's warning that a man was searching for him, the last thing Cardwell had expected was someone bringing news of his elevation to the peerage. That he'd ascended to the title meant his grandfather was dead, and so were several other relatives, judging by the numeral he'd inherited.

Old Alarick had been the fifth earl, and the realization that his occasional champion and persistent nemesis had passed into oblivion filled Burke with a strange mixture of sadness and frustration. He had spent too many hours imagining the confrontation with his grandfather to be able to calmly accept the news of his passing. It had never occurred to Burke that his grandfather might have died in the ensuing years. He had been too autocratic and vital to be felled by something as mundane and inconvenient as death. It shook Burke's perceptions of the world to realize that life—and death—had gone on in England without him. Somehow he had expected everything to be the same when he returned. When he went back, as now he surely would, there would be new family to face—family who had sent a man like Bayard Forrester to find him and bring him home.

Of course informing him of his inheritance and bringing him home hadn't really been the reason for Forrester's trip. Forrester had wanted proof that Burke was dead and probably wouldn't mind doing the job himself, if it came to that.

Antoine had been right about the man. Forrester was an unscrupulous bastard if Burke had ever seen one. Calculating, sure of himself, cold as ice. The temperature in the room had dropped ten degrees when Forrester arrived.

But as stunned as Burke himself was by Forrester's announcement, it was Celene's reaction that worried him most. Her face had gone the color of tallow candles when the stranger arrived, paler still as the import and the implications of the Englishman's news began to dawn on her. Burke had done his best to reassure her, but with Forrester there and the wedding guests listening to every word, there had been no opportunity to do more than squeeze her hand. The crowd had pressed close around them, their eyes lit with speculation, their faces avid. This was undoubtedly the most entertaining scandal to shake the town in a decade: that a simple trapper who had come to live among them had become *un grand seigneur*. Still, their friends and neighbors had had the good grace to leave as soon as Forrester did, flowing out of the house like water from a broken bucket.

Nor was Burke looking forward to explaining all this to Celene, who had gone almost immediately to bed. She was bound to be angry, and he hardly blamed her. He should have told her about his family when she'd agreed to marry him. It was just that he hadn't thought it was necessary to embroil her in long-standing family intrigues when there seemed little likelihood of her ever being a part of them. Nor had he wanted anything to spoil the love and peace he'd found in Ste. Genevieve.

When he first met Celene at the rendezvous, he had planned to take her back to England with him. It was the reason he'd asked Antoine for her hand. Burke had wanted to flaunt her unsuitability in his family's faces, to use her to show them how little their status and their money meant to him. But once he came to understand her and to love her, he had refused to tell Celene about his other life because he wanted to protect her—and himself.

With the news of his inheritance, he would have to take her back to face his family's censure and their scorn, their hauteur and their mean-spiritedness. The irony of the situation did not escape him. This was exactly the situation he'd contemplated, exactly the situation he had decided to avoid. He had constructed his own private hell, and now he'd have to live in it. It was knowing that Celene was damned to share it that chilled the marrow of his bones.

Burke was just scraping together his courage to go in search of Celene when Antoine rounded the corner of the house, a wine bottle and glasses in hand. "Ah, there you are. I was looking for you so we could have a drink to celebrate your good fortune."

"Is it good fortune?"

"But of course. How could it not be good fortune to find that you are a man of wealth and influence?"

"How indeed?"

"Is it Forrester that worries you?" Antoine asked. "He can be dealt with. There are ways—"

"It's not Forrester; it's Celene."

Peugeot cast him a questioning glance. "Don't you think she will enjoy being a countess?"

"Do you think she will?" Burke hedged. The last thing he wanted to do was discuss the changes in his life with a man who was congratulating himself on marrying his only daughter to an earl. "There are things Celene and I need to talk about. Do you know where she is?"

"She's with Jean-Paul. He is sick. He's had too much excitement, I think. Too many madeleines."

"Then I believe I'll get some air," Burke told the older man, moving across the porch and down the steps.

It was late when he returned to the house, and the only light burning was the one in the loft. He closed the doors and climbed the ladder. The prospect of the confrontation awaiting him at the top tied his stomach into knots.

Celene was lying poker-stiff in the very center of the bed, the ridiculous bed Antoine had insisted buying at auction as their wedding gift. The dammed thing was huge. They'd had to bring it up to the loft in pieces, and fully assembled, with its tester wedged between the rafters, there was hardly an inch of floor space to be had among the piles of barrels and sacks.

"Is Jean-Paul all right?" he asked.

"He had a stomachache. By morning he'll be fine."

"That's good," Burke answered, laying his frock coat over one of the barrels and beginning to loosen the buttons on his vest.

Peering at him over the sheet, Celene watched him undress. "Don't think that you are sleeping here."

"Now, Celene," he began, determined to remain calm. "I know you have reason to be angry, but I'm your husband. This is where I belong."

"I married plain Burke Cardwell, not Frederick Andrew Burke Hammond-Cardwell, the Eighth Earl of Hammondsford."

The knot in his stomach jerked tighter. "I know you did.

The rest of this is as much of a surprise to me as it was to you.''

"Is it really? I think you knew and you didn't tell me.''

"I *didn't* know and I didn't tell you.''

"A fine distinction to be sure.''

Celene was going to be even more prickly about this than he had anticipated. Burke took a breath before he answered her. "I'm the second son of a fourth son. When I left England, there were five men between me and my grandfather's title.''

"You never told me anything about your family.''

"I haven't given them much thought in these last years.''

It was a lie and both of them knew it.

He was willing to admit that there were things he'd neglected to tell her in these past months, but Burke had never lied to Celene deliberately. That he was doing it so blatantly set panic bubbling inside him.

Celene sat up, her face flushed red. "Don't tell me that you haven't thought of them, Burke. You have been planning to go back to England for months.''

"Yes, I have.''

"To see your family.''

"In a way.''

"And you expected me to go with you—as your wife.''

Cardwell nodded. "You know I've been planning to stay here with you, to help you with the crops. We decided on that weeks ago. I did think that eventually we'd go to England for a visit, the three of us together.''

"And just when were you planning to tell me that your family is of the English nobility?''

"Before we left, I suppose. Does it matter that they are?'' It was a second lie by implication.

"Of course it matters. How could you expect they would accept me as your wife?''

"I don't give a damn if they accept you,'' Burke insisted. "It's what *I* think of you that counts.''

That, Burke thought, was the truth, at least.

"If your family doesn't matter to you, why were you going to travel all that way?''

"I wanted my revenge.''

"Revenge?"

"Remember Trouble's story, the one Belanger told at the rendezvous? Someone in my family had me kidnapped into the fur trade in the hope I'd never return. I want to find out who that was, and I want to make them pay."

"But Monsieur Forrester said—"

"Don't believe for a moment that Forrester was sent here by my benevolent family to take me home. He was sent for proof that I was dead."

"But why—"

"So that someone else could claim the title, the money, and the lands."

"Lands?" Her eyes widened, and he could see that she was beginning to understand what being the Eighth Earl of Hammondsford entailed. "Are there lands? And money? How much money?"

He reached for her. "Celene . . ."

She jerked away, rolling out the far side of the bed. "No, tell me," she demanded, glaring at him. "What exactly comes with being the earl?"

Knowing her tenacity and realizing he had no choice, Burke began to elaborate. "There's the estate at Longmeadow."

"Estate?"

"Most of the land in the county goes with that." Burke's stomach seemed to be tying itself into a hangman's noose as he went on. "There are shipping interests, a fur trade concern in Montreal, and banking shares. A stable, I suppose; my grandfather was raising racehorses when I left. A house in London. There may be other things—"

Her flushed face paled a shade with every asset he named.

"You're rich!" she accused.

"I didn't know you'd consider that an impediment."

"I don't want to be married to an English earl!"

An odd coincidence, since Burke didn't particularly want to be one.

"You won't have to call me 'my lord,' " he offered, trying to make light of the evening's revelations.

Celene was not amused. "Well, then, we'll just have our marriage annulled."

"The hell we will!"

She continued as if she had not heard. "The marriage hasn't been consummated, at least not since the ceremony was performed."

"A technicality, I'm sure." Burke's voice was terse.

"And perhaps I can convince Father Hilaire to file a petition in our behalf . . ."

Burke tried to make his way around the end of the bed and barked his shin against the corner.

"Damn it, Celene! Stop this foolishness. I don't want our marriage annulled!"

She turned to him, her eyes huge with accusation, suddenly wet with tears. "But it's what *I* want! You lied to me! You let me think you were something you were not."

Pain constricted Cardwell's chest, and he realized again how dire a mistake he'd made. Had he put their future in jeopardy by refusing to share his past with her?

"Henri may have done many things to me," she continued, fighting down a sob, "but *he never lied.*"

Burke went perilously short of breath. To be compared to Henri Bernard and come up short was the most damning thing she could have said. And how many more lies would he have to tell her in these next days? How many lies would it take before she began to hate him?

He had to get to her somehow, had to hold her. He had to make her understand that this wasn't something he'd done to hurt her.

"Celene, please," he whispered, clambering clumsily over the bed. "Celene, I love you."

She pressed against the barrels along her back. It ripped holes through his insides to see her shrink away from him.

"Why didn't you tell me who you were?"

"The time never seemed to be right. There was work to do, repairs to the house, crops to harvest. And it didn't seem all that important."

It was important. She knew that as well as he did.

"Not all that important to whom?" she demanded.

Panic turned him clammy. He loved Celene. He had to find a way to make her believe how much.

"To me, I guess. I've been so happy here with you. After

Morning Song died, I never thought anyone could make me feel so contented, so complete. I knew eventually we'd visit England, and I thought I'd tell you then.''

"Oh, Burke," she cried. "There's no place for me in your life, not now that you're a man of power and position.''

"I don't see why."

Another lie. His heart volleyed against the wall of his chest.

"You're an English lord; I'm a voyageur's daughter. You have estates and ships and bank shares. All I had when you met me was seventeen hams!''

"That doesn't change the fact that we love each other, that we have a life together.''

"What kind of a life?" she demanded, her eyes silver-green pools of anguish and mistrust. "Where will we spend it? What will we do?''

"I don't know anything except that I need you with me when I leave for England. Please, Celene, try to understand. This inheritance isn't something I can walk away from, but we'll find a way to work things out. I swear we will.''

He touched her then, for the first time since they'd danced, for the first time since Forrester and his news had forced a wedge of mistrust between Celene and him. He tightened his hands on her shoulders, and the feel of her flesh made an ache rise through him that filled both body and soul.

"Celene, please," he whispered, his voice as filled with misery as hers had been. "I need you with me now and always.''

At his stark, impassioned words she melted against him. He enfolded her in his arms, knowing full well this was only the first of many times when she would come to him with doubts and fears.

He knew it was selfish to want her by his side when he went home. But if he left and she stayed here, it would be the end of everything. And he couldn't bear to lose her— not now, not when they'd been through so much, not when he needed her so. He would need her strength, her loyalty, and her love as he did battle with his family. He would need her tenderness, her passion, and her succor every day.

But Burke also knew the trials Celene would face. What was worse, he couldn't protect her from the isolation, the loneliness, and the barbs his family were bound to set to hurt her. Though it was wrong to hold his peace, he couldn't bring himself to tell Celene what life in England would be like. Instead he buried his face in her soft, sweet-scented hair and prayed that she would forgive him for deceiving her, prayed that she wouldn't come to hate him in the months and years to come.

When her weeping finally shuddered to a halt, he raised her face to his. Even with her mottled nose and red-rimmed eyes, she had never looked more beautiful.

He kissed her then, a kiss that merged his needs and her fears, his regrets and her disbelief. He lingered over Celene, offering reassurance in the passion of his caress, in the constancy of his embrace. Physical solace and his love were really all he could offer her. But there was a promise beating in his mind and heart that he willed to flow into her: always, always, always . . .

And when she began to cling to the promise and to him, his mind elaborated. Always the sweet satin of your mouth. Always the mingling of our breath. Always the press of our bodies bound heart to heart. Always my love for you. The promises melded with the rhythm of his blood until each flicker of his pulse renewed the vow. Celene seemed to know, seemed to sense his commitment.

Their kisses deepened, and the intoxicating spill of her unleashed emotions washed through him. He was drowning in her, in her love and confusion and hope. It flowed through his chest in a cresting wave, swirled and eddied in his belly and his loins. In that moment he knew her as well as he knew himself, what she was feeling, what she wanted, what she needed. She sought union so complete that there would be no world but theirs, no future fraught with uncertainties, no lies that could insinuate themselves between them. It was what he wanted, too. And for now, for tonight, he needed to believe that he could give her all of that. He needed to believe he could give her more.

He tumbled her down beside him on the bed, heard the

straw mattress crackle beneath them, felt the snag of mosquito netting against his arm. He batted it away and rolled above her. Tangling his hands in her heavy, gold-streaked hair, he pressed his hips to the juncture of her legs. Desire rippled outward in scintillating waves.

They stared into each other's eyes. He could see the shimmers of pleasure in hers, the flickers of eagerness and hunger like silver sparks around the irises. He sucked down a ragged draft of air as if it were a rare and precious commodity. His head went light, and he wondered if he could ever tell her, show her how very much he cared for her.

Yet as their love play deepened, it was Celene who came to him, wrapping her arms around his neck, pulling him into her kiss. She drew against his lips, enticed him with the fluid slide of her tongue. He shuddered in reaction, his mouth savoring the essence of her, his chest teased by the crush of her softness, his manhood straining against the fabric of his clothes as she enticed him with the faint provocative movements of her hips.

As they kissed, her hands slid up his ribs beneath the fabrics of his shirt and vest. Quivery, tickly shivers flickered beneath his skin, and when she swirled over his paps with the pads of her thumbs, spirals of heat curled downward to his loins. He wanted her, bare and bountiful beside him. He wanted to slide his own unencumbered flesh along her body, press deep inside her, and share her joy.

Rolling slightly away, he flung off his clothes and stripped the lacy chemise over her head. He came back to her then, long-limbed and spare, fully roused and masculine. He hovered over her, kissing her nose, her lashes, her brows, and her chin. And as he delighted himself with sips of her, he clasped her breast in the curve of his palm. Her body was small but lush, her sweet voluptuousness so feminine and welcoming. He worshiped her with his eyes and hands and lips, delighted in the glow of her creamy skin, reveled in the supple flow of her flesh, gloried in the heat that bloomed beneath his lips as he kissed his way from her ear to her breast. She gasped when he took her nipple in his mouth. She arched her back, moved sinuously as her hands strayed over him. As he licked and sucked and savored the tightening bud, he was experiencing the same sensations, prickles of heat, waves of swelling excitement, a fullness that seemed to demand release.

As he swirled his tongue around the tip, his hands delved lower, stroking her inner thigh, finding the haven of her womanhood. She was slick and moist with her need for him, and he let his fingers slide from the furl of her ripening desire toward her core, plumbing the depths where his own straining body longed to go. She rose against his hand, sobbing not with fear or sorrow, but with eagerness and desire that matched his own.

She touched him, too, and as her palm encompassed him, lightning burst along his nerves. It sizzled up his spine, danced along his arms and legs, flickered behind his eyes. There was something sweet and unholy about such pleasure, even if he shared it with his wife.

Then she was rolling over him, kneeling across his hips, lowering herself onto his shaft. Delight exploded through him, shattering his senses until he shimmered like shards of glass in the noonday sun. He could not breathe; he could not think. He could do nothing but move beneath her, thrusting them both toward the sphere where they would savor perfect unity.

Above him Celene seemed luminous, her face and body glowing with pleasure, her eyes afire with love for him. He felt himself ignite with the same fearsome incandescence. The bliss rising between them flared brighter and brighter. They gloried in the stark, sweet heat it engendered in their blood, in the wild, dazzling brilliance of their joining. Completion swept over them and through them like a blinding light. It melted them together into something precious and new, an entity that encompassed them both—a marriage based in love.

Slowly sensation began to dim, flickering and fluttering like a candle in the wind. They sought each other with touches and caresses, too stunned by sensation to form coherent thoughts, too sated and spent to do more than cling together.

They lay curled in a tender embrace for a very long time, drifting in and out of sleep, touching, holding, touching.

Burke finally stirred enough to drag the covers over them and tug the mosquito netting in place. He settled back into the pillows beside his wife.

The candle had long since guttered out, but he could see the pale oval of her face and the glitter of her eyes. "I love you, Celene," he whispered. "Nothing will change that as long as I live."

He saw her smile, felt her touch his face. "I love you, Burke," she answered him.

Yet he knew that in spite of his pledge of love, in spite of his reassurances, in spite of the pleasure they'd shared, Celene was still afraid. And while she slept beside him, Burke lay awake, knowing full well what the future would hold for them—for Frederick Andrew Burke Hammond-Cardwell, the Eighth Earl of Hammondsford, and his lovely bride.

"I can't bear the man," Celene confided to Pélagie as she folded a pair of Jean-Paul's freshly mended breeches into the small wooden trunk sitting open on the floor of her father's bedchamber. "Forrester is an arrogant bully, and I can't understand why Burke is letting him disrupt our lives."

They were leaving for New Orleans the very next morning, less than a week after the wedding, mere days after the Englishman had arrived in Ste. Genevieve with word of Burke's inheritance.

"He's polite enough. I grant you that," she continued, thinking of Forrester's courtly bows and charming smiles. "But there's something unsettling about him, as if he has some hold on Burke, as if he's manipulated things to his own ends."

Though he'd found lodgings in Kaskaskia, Forrester had attached himself to their household with the tenacity of a river leech. Underfoot from daylight to dark, he invited himself to meals, lounged on the gallery, dogged Burke's steps. Celene resented his intrusion, resented the news he'd brought, resented that Burke had charted a new course for their lives without once consulting her. That Burke would make a place for himself in Ste. Genevieve was a decision they'd made together in the weeks before they'd said their vows. With the Englishman's arrival, her husband seemed to have forgotten that she had an equal stake in how they lived their lives.

While he claimed to be no more pleased with Forrester's constant presence than she was, Burke seemed fascinated by the man. The two talked for hours: about England, about Burke's family, about people her husband had known in his other life. The subject and Forrester's forbidding mien excluded Celene from most of the conversations, but Burke seemed almost as eager to shut her out.

It was bad enough that Burke had turned out to be an English earl, but to be expected to accept his decisions and accommodate herself to her new role without so much as a by-your-leave left Celene feeling compromised, impotent. She had spent the last year regaining control of her life. Now that she had married Burke, she was as much prey to her husband's whims—and to Bayard Forrester's machinations—as she had been to Henri Bernard's.

As if conjured by her thoughts, Bayard Forrester came to the doorway of the bedchamber. The stir of gooseflesh along her arms alerted her to his presence even before he spoke. "Packing, I see," he observed with a condescending smile. "Of course you know those things will never do in England. They're hopelessly outmoded, too shabby by half."

Celene bristled at his words and glared up at his trim, impeccably tailored figure. "Unless you want us to arrive in *la Ville* as naked as the day we were born, you will have to put up with our *déshabillé*, I'm afraid."

One dark eyebrow lifted in response to the vinegar in her tone. "We'll see that you get some proper clothes once we reach New Orleans. Though you'll never have the style and flare to be a proper countess, with your face washed and your hair combed, you might be pretty enough to turn some heads."

She wanted to slap Forrester for his impudence, rail at him, shout down curses on his head. It was only Pélagie's restraining hand that prevented Celene from following the Englishman down the hall.

What made his insults more venomous was that Forrester had given voice to Celene's own fears. She was afraid that she would prove unworthy of the new Earl of Hammondsford, that his family would disapprove of her, that going with Burke to England would change everything between them. She longed to run to her new husband and seek reassurance in his arms. But even as she pushed aside the clothes on her lap to go in search of him, she heard Forrester greet Burke at the back of the house.

"You've been out seeing to the estate, I see," Forrester drawled. "Have the chickens laid an egg or two? Has the cow offered up her milk today?"

Burke's voice was cool and crisp. "If you'd ever done so much as a lick of honest work in your life, Forrester, you might be able to understand the satisfaction it gives a man."

"You're thoroughly rusticated, aren't you, Hammondsford? Thoroughly caught up in these peasant concerns. But then, it's important, I suppose, for a man with your vast holdings to have a feel for the land."

"And my first act as master of Longmeadow will be to throw you bodily off my estate."

Celene's stomach quivered at the contentiousness in the two men's tones. Perhaps she was just as glad that they had seen fit to exclude her from their conversations. It was only that now, when she was filled with doubts, Forrester's presence in the kitchen made it impossible to go to Burke. There was nothing to do but to continue with her packing, though her resentment of Forrester and everything he stood for rose another notch.

The following morning Celene stood with her husband and son on the front gallery of the house, well within sight of the bateau that would take them to *la Ville*. Though she had steeled herself to say goodbye to her father and Pélagie, she was not prepared for the lost, hollow feeling inside her. Her chest ached and tears stung at the backs of her eyes. She would give up almost anything to be staying here with the people she loved, here in these safe and familiar surroundings. She would give up anything—except her love for Burke.

He stood beside her as silent as a grave, realizing at last, she thought, just what his inheritance was costing her. Pélagie had been teary-eyed since they'd finished packing the night before, and with her own vision beginning to blur, Celene rose on tiptoe to hug the older woman. The housekeeper had been a trusted friend and confidante. Celene was the daughter Pélagie never had. They would each miss the other terribly in the days to come; no words could make the parting easier.

Antoine seemed dwarfed by the older woman's bulk, and when Celene turned to him, she realized again how stooped and frail he had become. His worn face was as gray and solemn as the cloud-strewn sky, and there was terrible resignation in his eyes. It was as if he never expected to see them again, as if he had given up all hope of their return. Celene could not accept this parting as anything so final and felt compelled to reassure him.

"We will be back in time for planting in the spring," she told him. Burke had not been willing to agree to that when they'd discussed it, but Celene needed to make the promise to her father for all their sakes.

"We will be back for planting. I give my word."

She stepped closer and hugged him hard, clutching Antoine's bony shoulders as if she could not bear to let him go.

"I pray that it is so," he answered. "I will do my best to wait for your return. No matter what I've said or done, Celene, I've always loved you. Please, *ma chére*, remember that."

She clung to him a moment longer, then laid a hand on her son's arm.

"Jean-Paul," she prompted, swallowing her tears. "Say goodbye to your *grandpère*. We need to go."

Instead of moving into his grandfather's open arms, Jean-Paul turned on her. "But I don't want to go to England!" he insisted, voicing the words in his mother's stead. "I want to stay here!"

"Jean-Paul, please," she whispered. "I've explained why this trip is necessary."

"But I won't like England. I'm sure of it. They all speak

English there, and Monsieur Forrester says everyone is told what to do by a king!''

''Well, yes, that's true,'' Celene began, hardly knowing what to say to calm her son when her own fears were every bit as overwhelming as his.

''Let me talk to him,'' Burke offered, ushering his young *beau-fils* around the corner of the house. From where she stood, Celene could not see the two of them, but their words drifted back to her on the crisp fall breeze.

''Jean-Paul,'' Burke began. ''You're happy that your mother and I are married now, and that we've become a family.''

''Yes.''

''And you want to live with both of us and be our son.''

''Yes.''

''You believe me when I tell you that that's what I want, too. But I have business in England that just can't wait. I don't want to go alone. You can understand that, can't you?''

Jean-Paul must have nodded, for Burke went on. ''I want my family with me, you and your mother both. I want to take you places I used to go, show you things that pleased me when I was a boy. I understand how hard it is to leave the things you know, to go away where things will certainly be new and strange. But your mother and I are going, too. We'll do our best to make things easier.''

''But I don't speak English very well,'' Jean-Paul blurted out.

''We'll practice on the ship.''

''And I don't want a king telling me what to do.''

''You won't have to do anything he says unless I agree,'' Burke reassured him.

''Will *Maman* have to do what the king says, too?''

Celene could hear the laughter in Burke's voice. ''Your *Maman* does pretty much what she wants, and I'd hate to see even the King of England try to stop her.''

There was a pause, as if Jean-Paul was considering what Burke had said.

''So—will you come to England with your mother and me?''

"We'll be coming back here, won't we, to see *Grand-père* and Pélagie?"

"We'll come back as soon as we can."

"Then I'll go," the boy conceded, "if you promise we'll be back."

"I promise you, Jean-Paul." Burke's voice was thick and low. "I give my word."

Burke returned from around the corner of the house with Jean-Paul riding the crest of his hip. He held the boy as he hugged his *grandpère* and Pélagie, then scooped Celene into the curl of his opposite arm.

"Take care of them, Cardwell, *mon ami*," Antoine said as they made their way down the steps. "And of yourself."

"I'll do my very best," Burke vowed. "My thoughts will be with you, Antoine, while we are gone."

The old man nodded, his eyes on Burke.

From the bow of the bateau, Forrester watched them board. Celene shivered when she saw him there, her sense of foreboding instinctive and bone-deep. This man, this arrogant, contemptuous man, was part of a future she did not want to face, part of a life that threatened all she held dear. She knew it as surely as she knew her name, and she sensed Bayard Forrester knew it, too.

Noting the Englishman's presence at the front of the bateau, Burke ushered Celene and Jean-Paul toward the stern, tightening his hold on both of them. He stood like a bulwark at their backs, like a tower of stone. There was determination in his face and a coldness in his eyes that Celene had never seen in them. But how could Burke, how could any man protect them from the myriad uncertainties that lay ahead? He would do his very best, she knew, but would even his best be good enough?

The bateau moved out from the shore and was caught by the rushing river's flow. As the current drew them away, Celene waved to her father and Pélagie. She waved until the people she loved and the town where she had known such happiness had faded from her sight. She stood looking back for a very long time, preferring to watch the places she'd been than look to the future that sprawled vast and forbidding ahead of her in the river's widening channel.

15

The sun seemed to pour its brightness down onto the open sea; the breeze seemed sharper, clearer, and more bracing. Without the encroachment of hills and trees, the sky took on a whole new dimension, a whole new magnitude. Stretching unbroken from horizon to horizon, it dominated the world with its changing colors and shifting moods. The water gave a rhythm to every phase of life, a new lilting gate to every passenger, a constant sway that lulled and unsettled all perceptions, a rush of sound from beneath the keel.

They had been aboard a ship bound for Bristol for more than a week, long enough to get their sea legs, long enough to find pleasure in strolling the deck, long enough for Celene to discover she enjoyed the unaccustomed indolence.

A few yards from where she sat reading in the sun, Jean-Paul was prattling to Burke about his visit to the crew's quarters earlier in the day. Her son's English was improving at a rapid rate, and with the constant use required of her, Celene's was becoming more eloquent and fluid, too. The leisure afforded by the voyage had been pleasant for all of them, and though he often seemed preoccupied, she liked spending time with Burke. She was learning to play chess under his rusty but competent tutelage, was putting her skills as a needle woman to use on delicate and impractical embroideries, and was systematically indulging her curiosity about the variety of passengers onboard their ship.

Their stay in New Orleans had passed in a blur, filled with sightseeing, meetings and dinners with traders from

Burke's trapping days, and visits to the tailor and the dressmaker. Celene was still accustoming herself to the constricting whalebone corsets, rattan panniers, and flowing skirts that the seamstress assured her were the latest English style. The dresses Burke and Bayard Forrester insisted she order for the trip to England were by far the fanciest she'd ever owned. There were a full dozen of them made of damask and brocade and satin, some with quilted underskirts, some with ruffled or embroidered petticoats. Some had lowcut bodices trimmed in lace; others were thick with bows or braid. To go with the gowns were shoes with gleaming buckles and fluted heels; stockings in a score of different hues; hats with flowers, trimmed in gauze; scarves and shawls; gloves and chemises. She was amazed by their elegance, their beauty—and appalled by their expense. And for every sou Burke spent on her, he spent another on himself and a third outfitting Jean-Paul like a proper English gentleman. Her son was no more comfortable in his new clothes than Celene, but the two of them bore the burden well, eager for Burke to be proud of them.

The only blot on their stay in *la Ville* was the runaway coach-and-four that had nearly struck Burke down as he crossed the street. Frightened, wild-eyed, driven by some unseen goad, the team of horses had thundered toward him. How they had gotten up to such a speed on a city street, she did not know. But with her heart fluttering against her ribs, Celene watched helplessly from the narrow banquette as the team bore down on Burke. In the second when Burke's life wavered before her eyes, she realized what a fragile thread bound her to this man, to his future and her own. Cardwell had dived out of the way at the very last moment. But even now when Celene thought of how close she'd come to losing him, a chill ran down her spine.

Jean-Paul shouted excitedly, breaking into her thoughts. "*Maman*, look at the fish!"

"They're dolphins," Burke told him as Celene joined the two of them at the rail. More than a dozen huge silver animals were leaping high into the air apace with the coursing ship. The sun glinted on their sleek gray skins, and they seemed almost to be smiling at the people who came crowding to the side to watch them cavort. They darted through the blue-green waves like a seamstress's needle through some rich translucent cloth. Gracefully they leaped and dived, like acrobats, like dancers eager to please and entertain. Jean-Paul, Celene, and Burke laughed and exclaimed over their antics, while around them other passengers shared their delight.

"It's the refuse the cook dumps overboard that brings them in such numbers," someone said. "They'll circle the ship and eat their fill and will be gone as suddenly as they came."

Celene glanced up to find Bayard Forrester had joined them, and she hastily turned away. She was no fonder of the Englishman now than she was when they had left Ste. Genevieve. His mere presence set her teeth on edge, his arrogance and his menace disconcerting her. For reasons of his own Burke was willing to tolerate the man, and she often found the two of them together, sparring in a veiled, oblique way that sent apprehension dancing across her skin.

She especially resented Forrester's intrusion today, resented that his derision had spoiled the magic of the dolphins' sudden appearance. But as Forrester said, the fish were falling away behind the ship. As they did, the number of passengers at the rail began to thin.

When she and her family turned away, too, Forrester was waiting. Dressed in an open-necked shirt, close-fitting breeches, and brown suede boots, he carried a pair of short swords beneath his arm.

"Planning on doing a little fencing?" Burke asked.

"If I can find someone to partner me."

"I thought one of the ship's junior officers usually put you through your paces," Cardwell observed.

"Usually, yes. But he is busy with his duties this afternoon. I thought perhaps you would fence with me."

"Oh, no." Burke shook his head. "It has been ten years and more since I've even held a sword in my hand."

"But you learned the skill."

"I took instructions once. All gentlemen did, but that was long ago."

"Surely you remember some of what you learned,

enough, at least, for us to get a little exercise.''

Celene could feel the excitement wound tight in Forrester today. At the best of times an aura of energy radiated from him like heat from glowing coals. It was one of the things that made her so uncomfortable. But the tension in him now was something else, something more focused, something more dangerous, something directed at Burke.

"You promised we'd play chess this afternoon," Celene put in, trying to divert her husband, to lure Burke away.

"Both chess and fencing are games of strategy and skill," Forrester observed. "Perhaps your wife's challenge is more intriguing than mine."

"There's no question," Burke answered with a lift of one brow, "that you are far more versed in intrigue than she."

Forrester's blue eyes sparked. "Then accept my challenge. Fence with me."

"I've been fencing with you from the moment we met."

Burke's words hung in the air between the two men, a challenge issued or a clever riposte.

"Yes, Burke, please," Jean-Paul piped up, breaking into the tension twisting taut between them. "Show me how men fight with swords."

Celene saw her husband's capitulation in the squaring of his chin and the glint in his eyes. Dread crackled through her like trails of flame.

"All right, Forrester. I'll see if I can give you some sport."

"Burke, no—"

"The weapons are blunted, Your Ladyship," the Englishman put in. "Your husband has nothing to fear."

She could see that the tips of the swords had been bent back to form a small curved loop. That bit of protection seemed inadequate somehow, and Celene took no comfort in the precaution.

"If you prefer not to watch, Celene, I suggest you go below."

The imperiousness in Burke was something new. Though his commands were always couched in terms of concern, there was something about them that rankled her. Bristling slightly at his tone, Celene determinedly stood her ground.

"No, I'll stay," she offered. "You'll need someone to hold your clothes."

With a shrug of indifference, Burke slipped out of his rich blue coat, unbuttoned his hip-length vest, and unwrapped the length of his stark-white stock. Though his actions were casual, almost mundane, Celene could see his concentration narrowing, focusing on the other man. As he handed the garments off to her, Celene felt as if she'd slipped to the very periphery of his senses, that Forrester and his challenge had taken preeminence over her presence and her concerns. It was not a pleasant realization.

Smiling, Forrester extended the hilts of the gleaming swords. "Your choice of weapons, my lord."

Burke took one to test its weight and grip. He moved with it, flexing his arm and wrist, shuffling forward and back. As he did, Celene could see some latent memory in his body respond to what once must have been familiar, almost unconscious movements. The muscles in his thighs bulged beneath his tight-fitting breeches. The wind pulled the shirt taut against his shoulders and chest, so that the contours of his body stood out in stark relief. He was graceful, strong, and beautifully formed. In other circumstances Celene might well have enjoyed the display.

But what was about to happen was more than posturing, more than exercise, more than a game. She didn't understand the subtle animosity between the two men or the stakes for which they played. It was the very fact that they had decided to play that frightened her.

They moved to an open space in the center of the deck and took their positions. They saluted each other and assumed the *en garde* pose, swords crossed and pointed slightly down, feet planted, bodies turned, back arms raised for balance. A look passed between them that should have sent off sparks.

"May the best man win," Forrester taunted, his face alight. He was planning to enjoy himself.

"I doubt very much that that will happen," Cardwell countered. "But we shall see."

The blades clattered and disengaged. Burke stepped

backward, his movements awkward, uncharacteristically clumsy. Forrester followed, thrusting with his arm. At the very last instant, Cardwell deflected the lunge with the lift of the bell-shaped guard that cupped his hand. Forrester's sword scraped harmlessly past and off to the right. Forrester retreated a step, and Burke forced him back another. The swords clanged together as the slighter man raised his arm to protect himself.

"You remember more than you let on."

"Perhaps," Burke answered, pressing forward again.

Forrester parried with a raise of his wrist. Fumbling, Burke let his weapon slip to the side. A screech of steel ripped through the air. The other man lunged inside Burke's guard, thumping him soundly on the chest.

"*Touché!*" Forrester cried with undisguised glee.

Celene sucked in a draft of air and realized she had been holding her breath.

They assumed the *en garde* position again, circling this time, shuffling slightly. In this tactic, she could see Burke's lack of recent training in swordsmanship. His movements were uncertain, almost bumbling. Forrester's were practiced, as graceful as a dancer's. Forrester was agile and quick where Burke was strong; Forrester's tactics were subtle and sly where Burke's were obvious, direct. The breadth of his body worked against Burke, too, slowing him down, providing a larger target for his opponent to hit. The other man was slim and lithe, elusive as a wisp of smoke.

Forrester's studied response to the probing of Burke's sword point turned each of the attempted attacks aside. Then the more skillful swordsman went on the offensive, forcing Burke back. As he shuffled to get out of the way, Burke's feet got tangled up. He stumbled and went down hard, thudding to the deck with bone-rattling force.

"Surely you've had enough," Celene hissed as Burke was struggling to rise.

He ignored her as if he had not heard. As he fought to regain his balance on the shifting deck, something came into Burke's eyes that Celene had never seen in them before. It was incipient outrage, utter scorn, sudden imperiousness. Bayard Forrester seemed to sense the subtle shift in Burke's demeanor, too. A smile lifted one corner of his mouth. Acknowledgment sparked in his cold blue eyes, as if Forrester was satisfied by whatever he read in her husband's face.

The two men shifted forward, glaring across their two crossed swords.

Celene balled her fists in the fabric of Burke's clothes. Her breath wavered and caught in her throat. There was something happening here she did not understand.

The fencer's blades squealed as they disengaged, a shiver of sound that curled the hairs at the nape of her neck. Forrester moved in slowly, on the attack. He thrust; Burke parried. Forrester marched forward; Cardwell gave ground. Forrester's blade trailed gold in the sunlight like a shooting star through a midnight sky. Burke raised his own weapon in determined but hasty defense. With easy grace, Forrester beat aside Burke's sword, forcing him back and back again. Cardwell came up short against the far rail.

Forrester pushed in to claim his victory. The two men crashed together, their bodies tangled, their swords held high. Burke straightened slowly, his muscles tightening. As he did, there was a subtle shift in his bearing, a transformation from a posture of defense to one of attack. He glared into the other man's eyes, an aggressive tactic of intimidation, as if Burke's position were the stronger one.

From across the deck Celene could feel the clash of wills, the enmity crackling between the two men, focused and strong as tensile steel. Burke fought for dominion by strength of will, though Forrester outclassed him in cunning and skill. They seemed frozen in the pose, poised, hovering, waiting for resolution, for one of them to break the contact or give ground.

Then Forrester began to move. With the finesse of a fine violinist drawing back his bow to prolong a single, resonant note, he raised his arm, scoring his blade against the taut, vulnerable skin of Cardwell's throat. Though the points of the swords were blunted the edges were not, and a thin, red line split the flesh at the side of Burke's neck. Blood swelled from the edges of the wound, pearled dark against Burke's skin and trickled toward his collar.

A sick, stark dread clutching her insides, Celene stood quivering and helpless on the far side of the deck. She took a step toward, as if to intervene. But the two men were oblivious, cloaked in the fervor of single combat like two ancient, mythical lords.

Though she prayed he would, Burke did not flinch away. He did not break his stance, did not acknowledge the wound, did not succumb to Forrester's intimidation. Burke stood his ground as if he were rooted there, still glaring into the other man's eyes.

Then all at once, Cardwell pushed off the bloodstained blade and rammed his fist into Forrester's ribs. Air whooshed out of Forrester's battered chest. He reeled backward, doubled over, and sat down. Burke stood over him like an avenging god, bloodied but unbowed. In that moment there was something in Burke that Celene had never expected to see, something primal, something indomitable, something unspeakably arrogant.

Her blood froze up in her veins.

Forrester must have seen the change in Cardwell, too. His head came up; his expression changed.

And then, he laughed. He sucked in a raspy breath and filled the air with booming mirth. He howled with wicked jubilation. Clutching his stomach with his free hand, Forrester roared like one demented, seeing something in the situation that Celene could not.

Forrester's outburst broke the mood, and no matter what had caused his hilarity, Celene was glad. Shaking with pure relief, she crossed to where Burke stood over the fallen man.

The clench of Burke's shoulders loosened as he reached for Forrester's extended arm. Hauling him to his feet, Cardwell relieved him of his sword.

"Well done, my lord," the other man gasped as he gave up his grip on the weapon. "Doing the unexpected will always win the day. For once I played with honor and you did not. How very entertaining."

"A man does what he must," Burke answered grimly, choosing not to elaborate.

"And indeed, you've taught me a valuable lesson where

Your Lordship is concerned. Doubtless it will hold me in good stead in the days to come.''

There was more to what had passed between these two in the last few moments, Celene well knew, but she chose to ignore Forrester's double meanings and obscure threats. It was enough that Burke was safe, enough to know that the only damage done in the encounter was the graze at the side of his throat. Seeing that the blood from the cut was seeping into his collar, Celene stepped closer to tend the wound.

She was surprised when her husband shooed her away. "The cut is nothing," he told her gruffly. "It will heal."

Celene could feel Forrester's interest, his speculation as he watched the exchange. His scrutiny, as always, fired her anger and mistrust.

Before she could manage to drag Burke away, Forrester spoke. "Our fencing has given me a mighty thirst, my lord. Will you allow me to offer you some refreshment? I've a fine bottle of brandy in my cabin, and I've been longing for an excuse to draw the cork."

Burke gave a quick assenting nod. "A bit of brandy sounds just the thing."

When Celene opened her mouth to protest his leaving her and Jean-Paul to fend for themselves, Burke cut her off. "Celene, I believe it's best if you take Jean-Paul below. The wind is whipping up, and you'll both be better off in the stateroom if the weather turns. I'll join you in a little while."

Burke's preemptory tone put starch in Celene's spine. All her life, men had been ordering her about, and she'd be damned if she'd do Burke's bidding now. She'd be damned if she'd scuttle off to their cabin like a meek, obliging wife while he was giving his attention and his time to Forrester and a bit of brandy. She'd stay on deck as long as she liked. And to hell with her husband's orders, to hell with him.

But as she watched Burke disappear down the companionway in Forrester's wake, it was more than her husband's high-handed manner, more than her own sudden need to resist that made dread snarl tight inside her. Forrester, the world he represented, and Burke's own past had claimed another bit of influence on her husband. Burke's subtle arrogance in dealing with her, his unexpected rebuff, and his unlikely camaraderie with Forrester gave testimony that he was changing before her eyes.

The Burke she'd loved and married in Ste. Genevieve was crumbling away like a clump of sugar in a cup of tea. He was being absorbed into another life, into a life she did not understand, a life she could not share. She did not know how to fight what was happening to Burke, did not know how to combat the fears for the future that were rising inside her. She had pledged her future to this man; it was too late to change that now. But for the first time since their wedding night, she began to wish she could. As she and Jean-Paul stood at the rail watching the sun ignite copper spangles at the crests of the waves, she wondered just how much of the Burke she'd known would be left when they reached the shores of England, just how much of the wonder and magic would still exist between them when they reached his family home.

16

They could have been the gates to heaven or to hell. They were tall and made of iron, with spear-shaped points along the top. In the center of each one was a coat of arms with gilded sabers and a crown. Celene was impressed and more than a little intimidated that gates as grand as these would guard the entry to Burke's estate.

But then, she had been impressed and intimidated by everything she'd seen since they'd landed in Bristol early this morning. All the ships in all the world seemed to have converged on the harbor city, filling the sky with masts and spars and the air with the scent of coffee, spices, and salted fish. The number of barrels and crates being loaded and unloaded dwarfed anything she'd ever seen going down the river from Ste. Genevieve, and there were more people bustling about the docks than there were in her entire town. The buildings that faced the harbor rose nearly as high as the masts, with three and four rows of windows stacked sill to sill. In the streets beyond them were more closely packed buildings, and several church spires seemed to prod the heavens above.

Waiting at the end of the gangway when they disembarked was a sleek, blue coach, a separate wagon for their trunks, and a squadron of outriders who would accompany them on their journey to the Hammond-Cardwell family home. Burke ushered her inside the carriage and settled himself on the seat beside her, leaving Jean-Paul and Bayard Forrester to claim the facing seat. As they moved through the city streets, Celene stared out the open window in fascination and awe. Nothing she'd seen in New Orleans prepared her for the density of the houses and shops, for the masses of humanity, for the horses and carts clogging the narrow thoroughfares. She had never heard such a din of clanging bells and jingling harnesses, such a clamor of people talking and vendors crying their wares. The town seemed to go on forever, and every street they passed seemed to branch into half a dozen others. Gradually the central town had given way to quieter residential drives, to sprawling gardens that in summer must be thick with produce, and finally to rolling countryside.

They had been under way for several hours when they reached the imposing gates. They were the only break in the high stone wall that had run for more than a league at the side of the road. Could all this land be part of Longmeadow, Burke's family home? Celene wondered. Never in her life had she seen fields so vast, hedgerows and woodlots so well-disciplined, nature so sternly repressed.

Celene drew a shaky breath as they waited for one of the outriders to open the gates. Inside her leather gloves her hands were damp. She wished she were anywhere on earth but here, waiting like an urchin before the high, imposing gates. She nearly jumped out of her skin when Burke shifted beside her.

She turned to him for reassurance, but he was oblivious to everything but the view beyond the coach's window. He was deaf to Jean-Paul's questions, blind to Forrester's inquiring glances, unaware of Celene beside him in the coach. What might have been eagerness or apprehension showed in the narrowing of his lips and the granite set of his jaw. An undefinable tension seemed to radiate from him to her. Was he as wary of what awaited them at the end of the drive as she was, Celene wondered, as nervous about being accepted? But if Burke felt such ambivalence, why on earth had he brought them here?

Moving under the cover of his sleeve, Celene slipped her hand into his. Burke started at her touch and jerked around. There was such distance in his eyes that she felt as if he were regarding her through the wrong end of a telescope, such coldness that she was not certain he remembered who she was. New panic churned inside her.

Then suddenly Burke smiled and crushed her fingers in his own. His handclasp must have been meant to calm and reassure her, but in some strange, inexplicable way Celene felt as if it was she who was reassuring him. It was an odd sensation, one that played havoc with her perception of her husband, their relationship, and her insides.

Celene had no time to contemplate the change, for the carriage was moving again, down a long paved drive, through carefully manicured parkland and a row of ancient trees. Across a long vista she caught sight of a house at the top of the rise. It was massive, immense, a mansion built of the local, pale-gray stone. Beneath an expanse of steeply peaked roofs and ornate chimney pots, it rose three stories tall, as stately as a castle but with screens of windows across the front. There was a broad, low-walled forecourt in the L-shaped angle between the main building and the wing to the left. As they rolled through the gatehouse that guarded its interior, she could see Burke's coat of arms carved into the stone high above the peaked front door. That her husband might once have lived in any house so grand shocked her, appalled her. How could he have seemed so content with their bed tucked under the eaves after he'd grown used to all of this?

Feeling weightless and sick inside, Celene held her breath as they came to a stop in front of the entrance. She would have welcomed a word of encouragement, if Burke had been capable of giving it. But in spite of the flush rising in his face, his hand had gone suddenly cold. Jean-Paul seemed every bit as unsettled by their arrival at the house as his mother was, and Bayard Forrester's sharp-eyed scrutiny exacerbated the tension in each of them.

The house steward stepped forward as they clambered out of the coach. "Welcome back to Longmeadow, my lord. It is good to have you home after so very many years."

"Thank you, Marshall," Burke replied, his voice clipped and formal. "Lady Hammondsford and I are very pleased to be here at last."

The steward nodded and ushered them into a towering,

slate-floored foyer, where the servants had gathered to welcome them. As Marshall went through the introductions that set each of what seemed like dozens of servants bobbing in turn, Celene stared in awe at her surroundings. The dark-paneled entry rose the full height of the house and was overhung on three sides with ornate wooden balconies. A tall newel post stood sentry at the foot of the stairs, a long hallway hung with tapestries lay ahead, and huge double doors led off to the right and left. The house was enormous, magisterial, and utterly overwhelming.

Jean-Paul seemed to be as intimidated by the grandeur as she, and Celene reached across to take his hand. In her own need to assimilate her new surroundings and act the proper wife, she knew she must not cast her son in a subordinate role.

With the introductions to the staff complete, the small army of servants scurried off, and Marshall led them to the tall double doors to the right of the foyer. "The family awaits you in the drawing room, my lord."

Burke slowly straightened his stance in a way that bespoke generations of noble breeding, of bone-deep arrogance. In his dove-gray frock coat, black breeches, and wine-colored brocade vest, with his features sketched sharp and tightly drawn, he looked every inch the Earl of Hammondsford, haughty, cool, imperious.

He belongs here, Celene realized suddenly, a flutter of apprehension moving through her veins. He belongs here in these high-vaulted rooms and these richly appointed halls, here amid the sweeping vistas of his country estate. *He belongs here, and I do not.*

The knowledge clutched her in its vicious grip, crushing her chest, closing like talons around her heart. She was unworthy of the man who had taken her for his bride. There was no escaping either the truth or the inevitable humiliation of facing his family's disdain. She should never have come here.

"Very well, Marshall," Burke was saying. "I would like you to announce us please."

The steward did as he was bidden, opening the doors and

stepping inside. "The Earl and Countess of Hammondsford," Marshall intoned.

"And Jean-Paul Bernard," Burke prompted him.

"And Jean-Paul Bernard."

With her heart pounding in her ears, Celene moved into the drawing room on her husband's arm, the fingers of her opposite hand clutched around her son's. The drawing room was even more grand than the foyer had been, with hundreds of diamond-shaped windowpanes glinting in the sunlight, with thick, dark carpets and heavy, expensive furnishings. But it was the people gathered there that drew Celene's attention. There were a full dozen of them, all staring, all curious, all hostile. She felt the bite of their instantaneous disapproval all the way to her bones.

A middle-aged man dressed in shades of mauve came toward them, his face crinkling in a smile that defined the limits of insincerity. "May I offer you greetings, Cousin," he said, "and tell you how very much you've surprised us all by turning up on our doorstep after so many years."

"I just hope, Randolph," Burke answered him coolly, "that our arrival has not inconvenienced you in any way."

"Inconvenienced us?" One eyebrow lifted as Randolph answered. "Oh, how could you think that? Longmeadow is your home, after all."

"Yes," Burke acknowledged. "Yes, indeed, it is."

Celene saw the man's shoulders twitch ever so slightly as he turned from Burke to make the introductions.

"Surely, Burke, you remember Aunt Sophy, Uncle Andrew's wife, the dowager countess."

"Of course I was not aware that I *was* the dowager countess," a tiny, white-haired woman intoned from where she was settled in a wing-backed chair, "until we received Mr. Forrester's missive a week ago."

Burke moved toward where she sat robed in mourning black, and lifted one beringed hand to his lips. "Aunt Sophy, it is a pleasure to see you looking so well."

"Well!" she snorted, "Well? I have not been truly well in years, you young scalawag. But then, you have been off having adventures, I'll warrant, without giving those of us here a passing thought. This place has been like a tomb since you've been gone. Your grandfather missed you and so have I. Now you may kiss my cheek in proper greeting.''

An odd look of what might have been surprise or disbelief passed over Burke's face, but he was quick to comply with her request.

''And who is this you've brought with you?'' she demanded.

''This is my wife, Celene, and her son, Jean-Paul.''

''Well, come here, girl,'' the dowager countess croaked. ''Let me get a look at you.''

Celene moved toward where the older woman sat and suffered a full minute of her scrutiny.

''Well, you're comely enough. Have you the spirit to match a man like Burke?''

Celene sent Burke a questioning glance, wondering how she should answer the woman's question. ''I'd like to think I do, Your Ladyship.''

''Don't you 'Your Ladyship' any of us,'' Sophy scolded. ''You're the Countess of Hammondsford now. Remember that.''

''*Oui, madame*, I will.'' Celene liked the old harridan in spite of her bruskness.

''Of French extraction, are you?''

''My father was a fur trader from Montreal.''

''And you met our Burke there?''

''No, madame. I met him at a fur trade rendezvous.''

''That sounds like a fascinating story. You must tell me the whole of it in the days to come.''

''Fascinating, indeed,'' one of the women said, though there was hardly agreement in her tone.

Introductions to the rest of the family came next: to Randolph's wife, Cecily, robed in matching shades of mauve, to their son Phillip and their daughter-in-law Felicia.

''How lovely it is to meet such a sweet blossom from the wilds of America,'' Phillip oozed, stepping forward.

''Yes, but is she a flower or is she a weed?'' Celene heard Felicia whisper to the woman beside her.

That woman, Burke's beautiful, red-haired cousin Elizabeth, and her husband, the Viscount Langford, were presented to them next.

"Indeed," the viscount lisped in a voice that all but sloshed when he spoke. "We hope your stay with us is most propinquitous. We relish our opportunity to further our acquaintance with you."

Portly Lord Chillingham was next to make his bow, though his wife, another of Burke's cousins, Susannah, sent them both a look that could have turned fire to ice. Beside the fashionable viscountess and the icy baroness, Celene felt small and drab, utterly insignificant in such exalted company.

Sarah and the Vicar Trowbridge were introduced next. "Surely only God's mercy could have brought you home to Longmeadow after so many years," the vicar intoned in his fruity baritone.

"Or God's folly." The whisper came again.

Celene glanced at Burke to see if he had heard. There was an almost imperceptible tightening at one corner of his mouth, a stoniness in his eyes that made her think he had. But Burke said nothing in response.

As Felicity and Elizabeth laughed softly together, Randolph presented his youngest daughter, Margaret. She ducked her head in mute acknowledgment, though the frown she cast on the newcomers confirmed just how inauspiciously their arrival was viewed.

As Celene was struggling to put the people and the names together, Burke spoke up. "Since Mr. Forrester lacked precise information about the family, I have some questions about exactly how I came to be the new earl. When I left England, there were several others in far closer proximity to grandfather's title than I was."

Randolph launched into an explanation. "Uncle William became the Sixth Earl of Hammondsford when the old earl died. That was back in sixty-seven."

"And William's son Edward?" Burke asked.

"Don't you remember how sickly Edward always was? He predeceased his father. When William died, Uncle Andrew assumed the title. Then my father was struck down with apoplexy."

"I'm sorry," Burke offered, but Randolph brushed aside his condolences.

"Cousin Alarick, who would have been the first in line from our generation, was killed in a very nasty hunting accident. And when the Seventh Earl passed on two years ago, the title fell to you. We've been looking for you ever since. If Forrester hadn't been able to find you, we would have had no choice but to ask that you be declared legally dead."

"And you would have been forced to assume the earldom, I suppose," Burke finished for his cousin.

Randolph regarded Burke through half-closed eyes. "But you're remarkably hale and hardy for someone who was supposed to have passed to his maker some years hence."

There was something in Randolph's voice that made Celene study the man more closely, seeing the calculation in his face, an underlying cruelty in the curve of his lips. Was it anger at being displaced by Burke's return that she sensed in him, or was it something more? It would take a diagram for her to understand the interconnecting family relationships, but she knew malice when she heard it. In that instant, fear for Burke's safety invaded her heart.

"Well, then, it's a very good thing that I came home." Burke's mouth lifted in a superior smile, and his words fell like a gauntlet between the two men.

"A very good thing indeed," the dowager countess piped up unexpectedly. "But now, isn't it time for luncheon? You can see me into the dining room, Burke, and tell us about your travels while we have a bit to eat."

"Certainly the new countess needs time before luncheon to change into more suitable clothes, and to meet her son's new governess," Randolph's wife Cecily suggested, her harsh, appraising gaze sluicing over Celene and her son. "I'll have Marshall show them to the children's wing."

Governess? Children's wing? Burke had said nothing to Celene about being separated from Jean-Paul. It was unthinkable, intolerable. Celene was about to demur, when Burke slashed her a glance that froze the words of refusal on her lips.

"Once you've left the child in Miss Winthrop's care," Cecily went on, "you can join us in the dining room. Any of the servants can show you where it is."

Did the English hide children away in some far-flung part of the house? Celene wondered. Did they turn their offspring over to a stranger to raise? Panic sprouted in Celene's chest, and she could see the same emotion in her son's bright eyes. Everything was different here, and she wanted Jean-Paul close at hand until they managed to acclimate themselves. Yet she was Burke's wife, the new countess, and she knew that bowing to the conventions these people embraced was an important part of gaining acceptance.

"I would like to see Jean-Paul settled," she said with as much aplomb as she could muster.

"A good idea to be sure," Burke agreed. "Stay with him as long as you like."

In a matter of moments the steward was leading Celene and Jean-Paul out of the drawing room, through a maze of halls and up two flights of stairs. The children's wing was tucked beneath the rafters on the third floor of the adjoining building. It consisted of a gloomy schoolroom, a common bedchamber, and a tiny separate room that was clearly all the frazzled governess could call her own. There were three other children in Miss Winthrop's charge, Randolph's grandsons and granddaughter—Alarick, Louise, and Randolph by name. They greeted Jean-Paul no more cordially than their elders had greeted Celene and Burke, for all that Miss Winthrop had them make their curtsy and their bows. The three eyed Jean-Paul with marked contempt, an unwelcome stranger in their midst, an inferior worthy of nothing but their disdain, a younger child to torment in his new surroundings.

Celene saw their sly superiority for what it was and knew exactly who had fostered it. It mirrored the underlying currents she had sensed in the drawing room, and she staunchly refused to abandon her son. She ate luncheon amidst the bedlam at the nursery table and spent the afternoon listening to lessons in the schoolroom. Her opinion of Miss Winthrop plummeted as the afternoon advanced. The woman's discipline was lax, and her ability as a teacher came into question when she misspelled several English words and added a column of figures incorrectly. What kind of education would Jean-Paul receive at this woman's hands? Celene wondered and stayed with the children far longer than she'd intended to.

It was late afternoon when one of the maids showed her to the bedchamber adjoining Burke's, and she found when she arrived that her clothes had been unpacked and put away in the dressing room. Instead of going in search of her husband, Celene explored their suite of rooms, angry and distressed that she and Burke would not be sleeping together. She knew he had no part in arranging their accommodations, but she felt as if giving them separate rooms was another way to show her how unsuitable she was to share his bed.

The chambers themselves were extremely comfortable, even more richly furnished than the rest of the house. Her own room was done in shades of spring green and pink, with a pale, flowered carpet on the floor and heavily embroidered bed hangings on the mahogany tester bed. There was a writing console before the window and a pair of bow-fronted commodes standing opposite the marble fireplace. A lounging chair was upholstered in a rich pink damask that matched the room's flowing, tasseled draperies. Beyond the connecting door, Burke's room was decorated in blue and gold, the half tester hung with velvet that matched the thick blue counterpane. Burke had a desk of his own, two high-chests, and a shaving stand. The entire house in Ste. Genevieve could have fit in these two rooms.

There was a fire burning brightly on the hearth, and Celene curled up in the gold velvet chair beside it to wait for Burke's return. She must have dozed, for when she awoke, Burke was standing over her. "I wondered where you'd gone," he said, settling himself on the arm of the chair. "Did my relatives scare you off?"

Celene smiled up at him in wry acknowledgment. "I stayed with Jean-Paul for luncheon. I hope you don't mind."

"I know all this is as unsettling for him as it is for you. Is he all right?"

"Is this really how they raise children here in England," she asked, asperity rife in her tone, "by hiding them away in an attic with some stranger hired to care for them?"

"It's how Randolph and I were raised," he answered with a shrug. "I saw my father once a day when he was on the estate and spent the rest of the time with a governess or a tutor."

His bland acceptance of the situation made her angry. "Why didn't you explain before we arrived that Jean-Paul would be sent off alone like this? Surely you knew. Surely there was time on the ship for you to prepare us both. I did my best to soothe Jean-Paul, but I know he feels as if I've abandoned him."

"I'm sorry, Celene," Burke apologized, unwilling to meet her gaze. "I guess I never thought of it."

There was much he had not thought to divulge about what life would be like in England. She wondered what other omissions he had made.

"And why didn't you tell me we wouldn't be sleeping together?"

"What ever gave you that absurd—"

"They've given us separate bedrooms!"

Burke laughed for what seemed like the first time in days. "You know as well as I do that not every couple marries for love. This is the way the English go about assuring the partners their privacy. You and I can make far better use of the bedrooms, though. First we'll make love in my bed; then we'll make love in yours. Then we can make love on the floor, and then in—"

"Burke!"

"—this very chair." Her husband leaned over her as he spoke, his eyes gleaming wickedly through the furl of his lashes, a heavy sensuality settling over his face. He lowered his head and sought her lips, in a long, dark, seeking kiss that made her body tingle and her pulses throb. Pressing her back into the cushions, he took possession of her mouth as if she was his salvation as well as his right. His tongue plundered deep to mate with hers, teasing her, taunting her, tempting her.

She met his advance with a thrust of her own, seeking the taste and texture of him, too long denied. Sharing the cabin on the ship with Jean-Paul had given them few opportunities for physical communion, and Celene yearned for the sweet release of their mingled passion.

Burke curled one hand around her throat, compellingly, possessively. He drew her deeper into his kiss. She kissed him back, arching into his tightening embrace, slipping the ribbon from his queue and tangling her fingers in the soft, thick strands of honey hair. His kiss grew deeper still. Burke ravished her with nothing more than his lips and tongue, possessed her with a totality that she had never been possessed.

She whimpered into his mouth, so breathless and dizzy she could hardly think, so helpless with pleasure she never wanted the kissing to stop. She shuddered and moaned when he lowered his hand to cup her breast, the heat of him penetrating through the stiff, tight layers of her clothes, burning deep into her flesh. He sought the puckering bud of her nipple with the pad of his thumb, sending sensations licking through her like tongues of flame. And still he continued to kiss her, with fierce and focused deliberation, with reckless and intemperate abandon, until she was trembling, melting, lost to him.

Lifting his mouth from hers, Burke shifted into the chair and positioned Celene across his loins. Beneath the drape of her flowing skirts, she could feel the press of his straining body at the apex of her thighs. It made weakness run down her legs, intensified the harsh, sweet ache at the core of her.

"I need you," he whispered. There was desperation in his face, tension coiled inside him that seemed separate from his need for union with her. Celene tried to look past the smoky intensity of his eyes, past the flush of pleasure in his cheeks. But her mind was too fogged with desire to discern the strange and subtle emotions astir in him.

"I need you," he breathed again. "Will you come to me?"

She nodded once, and, making short work of the impediment of his breeches, lowered herself onto the fullness of his shaft.

He shivered and clutched her hands, clinging to her as if she were life. "I love you," he murmured.

He was deep, so deep inside of her, filling her body and

her mind with delicious possibilities, helpless pleasure.

"I love you," he repeated and began to move beneath her. Circling her hips, he brought the thrust of his body into her. The sinuous strokes were like a question asked softly and slowly, again and again. She gasped, arching toward him, cleaving to him with body and soul.

As she began to sway in answer to his movements, he fixed his gaze on hers in fierce concentration as if he were afraid of losing her—or perhaps himself.

Satisfaction shimmered at the periphery of their senses like the sun cresting the lip of some far horizon. It flared brighter with every moment that passed, rippling through their senses, pulsing where their bodies joined.

His breathing was so ragged he could barely speak. "Oh, God, Celene. I—love you. Please don't ever—"

"I won't, Burke. I won't. I love you."

Spangles danced along her nerves. Her body tightened, and the world exploded in a flare of light and pleasure. Sensation burst along their nerves with incandescent intensity, with the unleashed abandon of desires too long denied. Ecstasy rolled through them in escalating waves, each cresting, each sweeping them to new, undreamed-of heights. They cried out as one in the turmoil of fierce completion, clung together as reality shattered and shimmered around them. Celene had Burke to cling to in this strange new place, and that was all that mattered.

They sprawled backward in the chair, awash in the quivering aftermath of making love. As Celene curled herself into Burke's embrace, he clutched her as if he never meant to let her go and buried his face in her white-gold hair.

Burke Cardwell smiled a beatific smile and drained his fifth—or was it his sixth—glass of port. He was drunk. There was no question about that; his eyebrows had long-since gone numb, just as they always did when he overindulged.

Surely he had to be drunk to smile so kindly at the ne'er-do-wells and vipers gathered around his dinner table. There was Viscount Langford, as addlepated a lout as he'd ever met, dressed like a fop in his high-flap collars and cutaway coat, a man with no more wit than your average flea. Beside him sat Lord Chillingham, even more glassy-eyed than Burke was himself, mumbling endlessly about King George's leniency toward the American colonies, though no one seemed to be listening. Randolph's son Phillip came next in the circuit of the table; Phillip, who had grown in these past years from a sly and sneaky boy to a thoroughly despicable man.

Bayard Forrester had a place at the far end of the mahogany expanse. Burke wished to God he understood Forrester's role in all of this. It was clear he was more than Randolph's henchman, yet less than an equal to the others in this house. Though he was doubtless a man of action, he was an astute observer, too. And he seemed to consider the machinations here at Longmeadow some form of delicious entertainment only he could truly appreciate.

Vicar Trowbridge sat to Forrester's left, dour, priggish, and mean-spirited, guarding his single glass of port as if it were a delicacy he was both eager and loathe to enjoy. And then there was Randolph, seated to Burke's right, handsome in his overblown way, his stiff gray wig set firmly in place, his jacket cut impeccably to disguise his growing corpulence, his staid and proper demeanor concealing the greed and corruption within him.

The ladies had left the table for the drawing room more than an hour before, and Burke wondered if Celene had joined them there. When the children had come in to say their good-nights, she had chosen to eschew her dessert in favor of seeing her son put safely to bed. Burke understood her need to see to Jean-Paul's welfare and was sympathetic to the difficulties both his wife and son were going to have adjusting to their new environment. Still, when Celene had left the dining room to go upstairs, it had felt very much like defection.

He supposed he should excuse himself and join the ladies. If Celene had ventured into the drawing room after putting Jean-Paul to bed, she would be in no more congenial company than he was himself. Burke knew English society well enough to realize that Celene would prove a tasty morsel for the women of Longmeadow. He should go and offer his wife what protection he could. Though in his current state, Burke realized, it was questionable if he could fend off more than the most meager attack. At least Sophy was there; Sophy, who had pronounced Burke's meeting with Celene at the rendezvous daring and romantic. Sophy would champion Celene even if he could not.

He drained his glass and was gathering himself to rise when Randolph reached out and caught his arm. "Surely you're not depriving us of your company so soon, Cousin. Tell us your impressions of the estate after being away so long."

Burke fumbled for a reply. He had hardly seen more than the drive and a bit of the house. "It seems to have been well-tended in my absence," he acknowledged carefully, wondering what it was Randolph wanted him to say.

"Then you'll want me to continue with my stewardship?"

Burke's numbed brows knotted as he tried to discern if there was more to the question than what there seemed. "For the moment, I suppose."

"Then let's drink to father's continued administration of the estate," Phillip suggested.

The glass at Burke's place was filled again, as if by magic. He took a swallow to be polite and set the port aside. "Tell me, Randolph, just what you've done," he suggested.

As Randolph prattled on about the yield of rye and wheat, the husbandry and the crofts, Burke's mind began to wander. In spite of the mob of relatives hanging about, the house seemed empty without his grandfather's presence. Old Alarick had filled the rooms with his contentiousness, his demands, and his vitality. He was a man who had shaken the walls of this old house with his rages and his laughter. There had been energy here when he was alive, something compelling about awakening every day. With his pranks and misbehavior, Burke had drawn more than his share of the old man's fire, but there had been camaraderie between them, too. That was why it hurt so much when his grandfather sent him away.

What would you think, old man, he wondered, now that I have the earldom after all?

But there was no victory for Burke in coming home. Even assuming the title gave him no real satisfaction. It had been too easy somehow; it wasn't something he had earned. It was anticlimactic being here, almost claustrophobic for a man like him—the difference between a satisfying bout of fisticuffs and a softly murmured apology. He'd been looking forward to making his accusations, to facing his grandfather man to man. There was no way to discover if his grandfather had had him kidnapped all those years ago, and that deprived him of his sense of purpose.

Then there was the question of Randolph's ambition. His cousin wanted the earldom, the money, and the property, and there was only one way for him to achieve that goal. Burke had grown far too fond of living to let Randolph get the best of him. If Phillip's alliance with his father was not threat enough, there was Bayard Forrester lurking on the perimeter of their lives, hired for who-knew-what sinister reason. The duel on the ship had left Burke with a scar at the side of his throat as a reminder of Forrester's ruthlessness. He would have to keep his wits about him in the days to come.

Nor would it be wise to underestimate any of the others in this house. After the introductions in the drawing room and the jibes at luncheon, Burke realized they'd walked into a hornet's nest. One glance at the estate's books and the complex records for the other family concerns told him how far beyond his depth he was. One taste of his relative's hostility convinced him that for a time, at least, Longmeadow was going to be a living hell. The responsibilities it was his duty to embrace tightened like a noose around his throat. His relatives' enmity and his concern for Celene and her son dragged him down. It almost made him wish Forrester had never found him.

But for tonight there was wine aplenty, and at the expense of those who owed him their begrudging fealty, he meant to revel in the twists of fate that had brought him here. It's what his grandfather would have done. As he downed the port Randolph had poured before he had excused himself and called for more, Burke could almost hear the old man laughing.

* * *

Celene had absolutely no desire to learn what Burke's relatives thought of her. But her untimely arrival outside the drawing room doors, gave her no other choice.

" . . . no idea that the French pampered their children so," Elizabeth was saying. "Imagine leaving her dinner to go cold when the governess could just as well have put the brat to bed."

Celene had known she was risking censure by going upstairs, but Jean-Paul had looked so forlorn when Miss Winthrop brought the children in to say their good-nights, that she had made her excuses and gone with them. In the end she was glad she had. As she'd tuck her son into his narrow bed, Jean-Paul had clasped her fingers in his own.

"Do you know when we'll be going home?" he asked.

There was wistfulness in his words that made Celene's throat go tight. "But, Jean-Paul, we've only just arrived. Tomorrow we'll have a chance to look around, and I think you'll find some things you'll like."

"Are there horses, do you suppose?"

"I'm sure there are."

"Do you think Burke will let me ride them?"

"Why don't you ask him in the morning?"

She sat with Jean-Paul until he slept, thinking how little it took to please a child, how little it took to make one happy. Why didn't these Englishwomen understand a mother's need to care for her son?

"I'm only glad *my* children behave so well," Felicia agreed, settling back in one of the drawing room's graceful tapestried chairs.

"Still," Sophy spoke up in Celene's defense, "all this must seem very strange to the little tyke. Surely Celene was only trying to make him comfortable here."

"How could they ever hope to be comfortable here?" Cecily sniffed. "Burke said himself that they'd been living at the edge of the wilderness. They're little more than savages, both mother and son."

"I shudder to think of my dear, sweet babies having contact with a such a child," Felicity agreed.

"And what possessed Burke to bring them here?" Elizabeth asked. "She's positively the most unsuitable wife he could have chosen. She's not even pretty."

"How could she be pretty with that ghastly yellow tint to her skin and all that unruly hair?" Margaret sneered.

"She had no style, no proper clothes—"

"She looks like she's been dressed on Monmouth Street."

"Oh, no," Susannah laughed. "She looks even worse than that. And did you see her wrestling with her panniers when she sat down to dinner? My dear, it was all I could do to keep from kicking you under the table!"

"Well, she certainly has no poise, no manners," Cecily went on, "no intelligence, and no wit. Who is she, I ask you, to be married to an earl?"

The women's censure was worse than Celene had ever dreamed it would be. She wasn't good enough for Burke; she wasn't worthy of a place at his side. And these brittle, careless women had set themselves against Jean-Paul, as well as her. How could she and her son make a life with Burke if all his relatives hated them?

As Celene stood huddled in the shadow of the door, the small hard kernels of doubt Henri had planted deep inside her sprouted again. They flourished and grew in the residue of the women's caustic words, filling Celene with hopelessness and dread.

"She's even less prepared to be a countess than Burke is to be an earl," Elizabeth pointed out.

"It's just a shame that he turned up alive after all this time," Susannah said, "especially when Randolph has so much to offer the earldom."

"And Celene is certainly young enough to breed. In no time she'll be whelping brats for Burke, and where will we all be then?"

"And, too, there's the family pride at stake," Felicia sniffed, helping herself to a cake and another cup of tea.

"I think Burke is more than capable of upholding the honor of the Hammond-Cardwell name," the dowager countess answered.

"Oh, he's impressive to look at, I'll give you that," Margaret said, "but will he be up to the responsibilities of managing the holdings and the estate? He's been living in the wilds. What can he possibly know about handling money?''

"He seems to have grown into a good, responsible man,'' Sophy said, staunchly defending him. ''I think he'll do his best.''

Celene was trying to decide if she should burst into the drawing room and confront their detractors or take the coward's course and slink upstairs, when the dining room door opened abruptly. She turned, hoping it was Burke come to rescue her. Instead it was Randolph who stepped into the hall.

He crossed the expanse of foyer at a measured pace. "Are you about to join the ladies, or have you a moment to spend with me?''

It was a dismal choice: throwing herself into a den of vipers or spending time with a man she'd already decided she could not abide. Still, facing a single adversary seemed preferable to consigning herself to a roomful. ''I've a moment to speak with you if you like.''

Taking her arm, Randolph led her down the center hall and around the corner. Settling her on a couch in a secluded alcove, he lowered himself beside her.

"So, my dear, what do you think about all this?'' he asked, indicating the estate with a sweep of his hand.

"I think it's very lovely,'' she answered carefully, ''very grand.''

"Is it different from what you're used to?''

"More different than you'll ever know.''

He shifted forward until his knees brushed the slope of her skirt. Celene shifted slightly away.

"Do you think you can be happy here, you and your son?''

Uneasiness washed through Celene; there was more to Randolph's questions than he let on. ''We will do our best, monsieur, for my husband's sake.''

"Well, I expect you'll grow used to the differences''— he settled closer—''in your good time.''

"I'm sure we will. And I thank you for your concern.''

Thinking their conversation was over, she made as if to

leave. But Randolph reached out and grasped her hand.

"Well, if there is ever anything I can do to make your stay more pleasant, you need only ask. I'd like to be your friend, you see."

The feel of his fingers on her flesh sent a chill racing up her arm. "That's a very generous offer for you to make. But I am sure Burke will see to all my needs."

With her fingers still in his grasp, Randolph leaned toward her. "I am prepared to be very generous with you, Celene. You're a beautiful woman, and we could become very good friends, indeed." As he murmured the last four words, his lips grazed the skin at the side of her throat.

Celene jerked back as if she'd been burned, but his grip tightened, holding her fast.

"You're so young and lovely, and you smell so sweet," he murmured, nuzzling against her. "I would so enjoy getting to know you better."

Celene braced her free hand against his chest, but her resistance against a man so much bigger than she was ineffective at best.

"Please, monsieur! Burke would not take kindly to the propositions you are making. Nor do I."

"Then we will not tell him what I propose. It would only make him angry and perhaps bring on a duel. Surely you're not eager to take up widow's weeds so soon again."

Celene struggled harder as Randolph closed his hand around her breast. As she twisted against his hold, a tall, dark shape loomed out of the shadows at the head of the hall.

"Getting to know your new kinswoman a little better, my lord?"

If it had been the devil himself, Celene would have been every bit as glad to see him. Instead it was Bayard Forrester.

"Go away, damn you. This is none of your concern."

Randolph shifted slightly away in deference to the other man's appearance, and Celene took advantage of his withdrawal. She leaped to her feet and fled to Forrester's side.

"If a woman has no desire for a man's attentions," Bayard drawled, "can a gallant do less than offer his protection?"

"You're no gallant, sir, as well I know. Give Celene the chance to know me better, and there will be no cause for you to interfere."

"Indeed, monsieur, you mistake me if you think that," Celene spoke up. "I am faithful to the man I've married."

"But will he be as faithful to you?" Randolph asked as he rose to leave. "Things are different here in England, and Burke has never been immune to a pretty woman's charms. But then, I suspect you'll learn that soon enough."

Dread stirred up inside of her. Was casual infidelity among the aristocracy something else Burke had neglected to tell her about?

Still, as unlikely a rescuer as Forrester was, Celene pressed close against his side as the older man brushed past them and disappeared down the hall.

"Stay away from him," Bayard Forrester advised as they watched him go. "Randolph won't let a single interruption deter him if he's intent on seducing you. In a house as big as this, you can't count on someone happening by if he manages to corner you again."

"Nonetheless," Celene answered, "I'm grateful for your help."

"Don't thank me, Your Ladyship," Forrester murmured. "You've no idea how this game is played, and I'll not see your virtue forfeited before you've had a chance to learn the rules."

"I will be careful of Randolph. I had no idea what he was about when he asked to have a word with me."

"He's about a good deal more than this," Forrester prophesied darkly. "Be aware of that in the weeks to come. Now get yourself off to bed, and take your husband with you. When I left him in the dining room, he was lapping up port as if he'd just had news of a shortage. And mind the stairs. There's a broken tread three short of the top."

When she opened her mouth to thank him again, Forrester stayed her with a gesture. "For your sake, Your Ladyship, I hope your husband realizes what he's up against."

Then, as silently as he'd come, Bayard Forrester was gone, and Celene stood alone in the hall pondering his warnings.

17

Mon Cher Papa et Pélagie,
 *I am so pleased to hear that it has not been terribly cold
in Ste. Genevieve so far this year. Though we have had no
more than a dusting of snow, the weather is quite unpleasant. It is the dampness and the heavy skies that make it so.*
 *We are all fine here. The black eye young Alarick gave
Jean-Paul has faded, and the dowager countess and Miss
Winthrop have recovered from la grippe. Caring for four
children instead of one was far more difficult than I thought
it would be, and I am glad to be relieved from my duties
in the nursery. I do still spend part of every day with Jean-
Paul. We wander through the grounds of the estate, on foot
or on horseback. You would be so pleased to see how well
he rides now that he has a pony of his own. It was a most
thoughtful gift for Burke to give him.*

Burke had been very generous since they'd come to
Longmeadow. He had not complained about the expense
when Phillip's wife Cecily had insisted on calling her dressmaker to the house so Celene would have some "proper
clothes," and Burke had brought her a cameo necklace and
a silver music box when he returned from a trip to London
on business.

But if she'd had a choice, Celene would rather have had
more of his time and attention. During their first week at
Longmeadow, her husband had been closeted in the study
with Randolph and Phillip, where they instructed him on

310

the extent of his holdings and responsibilities. Burke spent
most of the second week touring the estate, meeting tenants,
and looking over the vast acreage. But rather than being
pleased with his new wealth and position, he seemed tense,
dispirited, and he had snarled at her when she asked him
what he'd seen. The racing stables did seem to hold a certain fascination, and since Burke often took Jean-Paul, Celene did not complain about time he spent there. It was just
that she was seeing less and less of Burke, sometimes only
in their bedchamber, and then usually after he'd consumed
a fair quantity of port.

Only during the four days he had been convalescing after
wrenching his knee in a fall was she able to get her fill of
him. Though at first she did not mention it to Burke, the
incident worried her. Her husband was a superb rider, and
it had been the cinch on his saddle breaking that had
dumped him down the steep ravine. It occurred while he
was out for a morning gallop with Phillip, and Celene could
not help wondering if Randolph's son had somehow engi-
neered the accident. Bayard Forrester's warnings rang in
her ears every time she thought about it, but she had no
proof. When she went to the stables to examine the faulty
cinch, the saddle had disappeared. With suspicion niggling
inside her, she had finally spoken to Burke. He had laughed
when she told him her concerns and drawn her up on the
bed beside him so that he could put his head in her lap
while she read to him.

But even while he convalesced, while they played chess
and cards, while they applauded Jean-Paul's antics, Burke
did not ask her about her days. And she did not tell him
how empty they seemed after the bustle of life in Ste. Genevieve. Burke did not want to hear that she was unhappy
as the Countess of Hammondsford, and so they communi-
cated more and more with their bodies and less with words.
Every night Burke made love to her with a single-minded
desperation that left her breathless and weak—though in an
odd way, unsatisfied. She wanted and needed so much more
from him, but the gifts he brought her and the passion they
shared seemed all Burke had to give.

Celene sighed and took a moment to sharpen her quill

before turning her attention back to her letter.

Burke's relatives continue to treat us ... like creatures from another world, something to be gawked at, derided, and criticized.

She rethought what she meant to say and wrote: ... *kindly. Just last week the dowager countess bundled me into her carriage with a pile of blankets and a flask of hot tea, and we toured the estate.*

It was an excursion Burke had been promising Celene, but was always too busy to take.

It was a delight to spend the afternoon with the dowager countess. Sophy has lived at or near Longmeadow all her life, and she knows everyone for miles around: who married whom, all the children's names, the bits of history that made touring the countryside in her company so interesting. She even told me the tale of a ghostly figure who stalks the church graveyard late at night with saber rattling, seeking his lost, lamented love. The trip around the estate was a most pleasant way to pass the day.

Other days passed far less pleasantly. Celene especially hated the ones she spent with Cecily, Felicia, Elizabeth, Margaret, and Susannah, days where the women gave equal time to needlework and character assassination. And Celene's was most often the character they chose to assassinate. They advised her—for her own good, mind you—just how she should walk and dress and comport herself. They instructed, in dulcet tones laced with hemlock, on which topics were appropriate for conversation in polite society, on how to pour tea, on which stitches to use in her new embroidery, and on how to raise her son. Celene would leave the cozy sewing parlor at the end of the afternoon feeling as if they had been picking away parts of her, like fluff off a length of fabric. She felt smaller after an afternoon spent in their company, as if one day there might be nothing left of her when they were done.

The library became her haven, and she read until her eyes stung and the pages blurred. Occasionally Burke took refuge in there, too, since it was one bastion none of the rest of the family seemed inclined to breach. He had cut a wide swath through the collection of books in his youth, and the time they passed discussing what she'd read were the benchmarks she measured her days against.

She soon learned that there were places in the house where she was safe and places she never dared venture alone. The conservatory became one of the latter when Randolph came upon her while she was cutting flowers for the suite she and her husband shared. It was a luxury to have fresh flowers when the ground outside was flecked with snow. The flowers made Celene believe that spring would eventually come—spring, when she would return home to plant her fields and visit her family.

"Goodness, Celene, one of the servants will bring you flowers if you want them," her husband's cousin admonished her.

"I don't mind cutting them myself, and sometimes I pick the colors to match my mood."

"You've picked mostly blue ones today. Does that mean you're feeling sad?"

Mindful of the warning Bayard Forrester had given her, Celene kept her distance as she answered. "Even in the winter, the skies are blue at home. I think I picked these flowers to remind me of that."

"If you're feeling sad and in need of a friend," Randolph suggested, "I am sure there is something I could do to lighten your mood."

"Somehow, monsieur, you don't strike me as a man who is given to singing songs or telling amusing stories," she demurred.

The distance she had managed to maintain was somehow not enough, and Randolph was suddenly at her elbow. "Let me make you happy, sweet Celene. Let me kiss your soft mouth. Let me touch you luscious breasts."

When he tried to suit his action to his words, Celene jammed the sharp, long-bladed scissors she had been using on the plants into the swell of his paunch. With them pressed between two buttons of his waistcoat, she backed him across the flagstone path.

"If you ever try to touch me, if you ever insult me with your propositions again," she threatened, "I will cut out your gizzard and laugh while I'm doing it."

The part of her that had faced down Rivard and Arnaud that morning at the rendezvous had come unexpectedly to the fore, and Randolph simply gaped at her.

Shifting toward the door, preparing to make good her escape, Celene thrust the scissors a little deeper. As Randolph shuffled backward, he caught his heels on the rim of brick at the edge of the flowerbed and toppled ingloriously into a bank of hothouse ferns.

Though it amused Celene to see Randolph sprawled in the dirt, she never went back to the conservatory unless she was in the company of someone else.

Of course she could not write to her father and Pélagie about Randolph's advances and her narrow escapes. She nibbled at her lower lip and tried to think of other news.

The children continue to squabble, but Jean-Paul is beginning to hold his own, even though he is a year younger than Phillip and Felicity's youngest son. Still, it is the older boy, Alarick, who gives him the most trouble. After one of his pranks, Jean-Paul and I searched the grounds until we found a patch of burrs. I suppose it was wrong for me to help him put them in Alarick's bed, but it seems to have made the boy realize that Jean-Paul is not a child to be trifled with. Things are better, for the moment, though I am not sure how long it will be before Alarick finds some new way to torment Jean-Paul. But he seems willing to stand his ground against the odds, and I think you would be proud of him.

Celene was also doing her best to stand against the odds, against Burke's family, against her own loneliness, against Burke himself. But the cost was desperately high. She paid it in tokens of infinite value, in loss of her independence, in destruction of her confidence, in forfeit of her most deeply held beliefs. She and Jean-Paul had been to neither mass nor communion since they'd reached England, and she knew she was willfully endangering their immortal souls by forfeiting contact with a priest. But what left her sleepless long into the night, what was far more tangible and real than the threat of eternal damnation, was the fear that she was losing Burke.

The man she'd known, the man she loved, the man she'd married for better or worse, was gradually slipping away. He still told her he loved her and made it clear how much he needed her. But Burke seemed to be as preoccupied and discontented as she was. It was as if he had lost the thread of who he had been in Ste. Genevieve, and a staid English gentleman was taking his place. His grandfather's death had robbed him of his mission, of his quest, and he filled that void with long hours of riding the estate and with vices he'd turned from long ago. He was driving himself toward a goal she could not completely comprehend, a goal he would not let her share. He was narrowing his aims and his interests in a way that completely excluded her. As Celene stood helpless watching, she feared that soon nothing would bridge the gulf widening between them.

Unhappiness fed unhappiness, Celene well knew, and she hoarded the last vestiges of her hope and her self-respect. If she could hold out until spring, she could return to Ste. Genevieve with Burke and Jean-Paul, and life would be good again.

She picked up her quill and began to write, forcing the possibility that Burke might refuse to leave England to the back of her mind. She couldn't think about that now—not when the promise of home was all that got her through the days.

Though there is much of the winter still ahead of us, my thoughts are constantly filled with the promise of spring. They are filled with the knowledge that I will be with you when the dogwood and redbuds blossom, and the woods are filled with wildflowers. I long for the scent of fresh-turned earth, for the whisper of peepers, for the sight of the river and the trees. I long for the sight of both of you, for the sound of Papa's harmonica on a soft spring evening, for the contentment of home.

As I promised, I will be in Ste. Genevieve in time for planting. I long to be there with you now. Home with the people I love is where I belong.

Je t'aime,
Celene

* * *

Longmeadow
15 January 1775

Dear Antoine,

I am sorry it has taken so long for me to write to you. There have been concerns here at Longmeadow that have taken much of my time.

As Celene must have told you by now, we have arrived safely at my family's estate. The voyage was an uneventful one, and the weather was remarkably fair for so late in the shipping season. Longmeadow is even more grand than I remembered it, the house and grounds taking in nearly five hundred acres. I believe Celene and Jean-Paul were both a bit overwhelmed by the place.

Burke himself had not been quite as sanguine about his homecoming as he might have wished. After his years in the wilderness, he, too, had been taken aback by the estate, by its grandeur, by its majesty. It seemed to go on forever, the lawn and gardens, the outbuildings and the crofts, the fields and hunting preserve. And all of it was his, his land, his animals, his tenants. The realization had made his stomach roil.

He had never looked on the estate in quite this way, knowing the sense of ownership, the sense of responsibility. In the days that followed their arrival, he had begun to understand what becoming the Eighth Earl of Hammondsford really meant. He supposed he should consider each new obligation a challenge, each decision an opportunity to prove himself. But instead, he felt shackled to the dusty ledgers, intimidated by the columns of figures. Every time he sat down with Phillip and Randolph, he became distracted, restless. It was almost as if his grandfather were standing over him, looking for mistakes, for some sign that Burke was unworthy of all that had been entrusted to him. It was almost as if old Alarick was watching for some confirmation that he had been right to send Burke away all those years ago.

Instead of being cooped up in the study for hours on end, Burke wanted to be outside, overseeing what needed to be overseen. He was a man of action, not a goddamned clerk. He hated being hemmed in by boring meetings with bailiffs

and solicitors, railed at the need to write endless letters and
keep the meticulous records his predecessors had. When he
suggested that there must be another way to handle the
mundane matters, both Randolph and Phillip had looked at
him as if he'd lost his mind. The welfare of the vast Hammond-Cardwell fortune rested squarely on his shoulders,
and Burke found that he resented the weight of the duty
that had fallen to him.

Burke sighed and dipped his quill in the inkwell, returning to the letter before him.

Both Celene and Jean-Paul seem to have . . . settled in
very well here at Longmeadow, Burke wanted to write, but
he knew the words would be far less than the truth. He
raised his quill and frowned down at the page.

. . . *found things to keep them occupied here. Celene has
taken up reading and embroidery. She spends much of her
time in the library. When he is not busy with his lessons,
Jean-Paul can always be found in the stables. I have bought
him a pony, and in no time he will be a proficient rider.
My grandfather kept racehorses, and Jean-Paul and I took
several of them to a race meeting at the county seat some
days ago. Three of the four horses we took won handily,
and your grandson was excited by our victories.*

Watching Longmeadow's horses thunder toward the finish line and cross it in the lead had set Burke whooping
and hollering as loudly as Jean-Paul. He had gladly accepted the other men's congratulations, feeling for the first
time since they'd arrived in England as if he might belong
here, after all. Not only had Longmeadow's horses won,
but his bets on other races left his pockets well-lined with
coin when the day was over. Feeling ebullient, he bought
Celene a bauble in one of the shops with his winnings, an
emerald and diamond bracelet someone had pawned. After
sending Jean-Paul back to the estate with one of the
grooms, Burke retired to the local tavern with his newfound
friends. Joviality and liquor flowed half the night, and when
he reeled into his bedchamber just before dawn, Celene had
been waiting for him.

Consumed by bleary lust, he'd tumbled her onto the bed,

but she'd lain beneath him as cold and unresponsive as stone.

"What's the matter?" he slurred against the soft, lavender-scented skin of her throat.

"Where have you been?" she demanded, pushing him off her.

"We went to the race meeting."

"Yes, I know. You sent Jean-Paul back with one of the grooms last evening. Where have you been since then?"

He knew he was foxed. She knew he was foxed, and there didn't seem much point in denying something so obvious. It was then he remembered the bauble in his pocket.

"Brought you something," he told her, fumbling through his clothes. After a haphazard search, he produced the bracelet and coiled it around her wrist. It glimmered in the candlelight, the emeralds cool and dark, and the diamonds winking silver fire.

Disappointed and confused, he watched her face. "Don't you like it?" He thought the gift would please her, thought it might buy a little conciliation since she seemed angry about his condition and his absence.

She ran her fingers over the sparkling stones. "It's very nice."

"Nice?" It was more than nice. He'd paid three hundred quid for the bloody thing.

"It's lovely really. But I'd rather have had you home with me—home and sober."

When Burke could think of nothing to say in his own defense, at least nothing that would make any sense to her, Celene went on.

"I didn't know where you were. I didn't know if you'd fallen off your horse in a gully somewhere. I didn't know if you were hurt. I was worried, Burke, and with good cause."

Even in his fuddled state, Burke knew what she meant. There had been several incidents in these last weeks that unnerved them both. His horse's cinch had snapped unexpectedly, and he'd been shot at one evening riding home through the woods. The ball had slammed into the tree mere inches above his head. As he'd lain on his belly in the dirt, he was sure his cousin Randolph would come rustling out of the brush to check his body. When no one came, Burke searched the woods himself. But whoever his assailant had been, he had long since scuttled away. It was most likely a poacher whose shot had gone awry, Randolph assured him the next morning when he mentioned what had happened. But Burke was not so sure.

He realized Celene was right to be concerned. As he'd taken her in his arms, he'd vowed to be more careful. But by the time he dropped off to sleep, her warnings and his promises had slipped his mind.

He'd come home alone and drunk on three occasions since then, Burke realized when he thought about it, and nothing untoward had happened. Perhaps Celene was being overcautious. Perhaps Randolph had decided Burke wasn't the threat he'd originally seemed.

He sat for a moment more, staring at the letter before him, then dipped his quill and began to write.

The Yule season is just recently past, and we indulged in the usual English traditions. We cut a Yule log in the woodlot big enough to burn until Twelfth Night. We decorated the house with evergreens, mistletoe, and holly. Carolers came to serenade us, and we greeted them with wassail and cakes.

We went to Christmas services, he'd almost written, but that was not true. Everyone but Celene and Jean-Paul had gone, and Vicar Trowbridge had commented on their absence. His mouth had dropped open with shock when he discovered that Burke's wife and son were—of all things—Papists. In the vicar's eyes it was the next worst thing to convening a coven in the garden. Trowbridge had taken Celene to task for her beliefs later in the day. Didn't she realize that she and her son were headed straight to hell if they didn't renounce their faith immediately? Didn't she know that Catholics had no place in the English aristocracy these days? The vicar would be more than pleased to offer them instructions in King Henry's church.

Burke had been drinking wassail and talking horses with one of their neighbors when Trowbridge began his harangue. By the time he realized what the vicar was up to,

Celene's face was pale as whey. Because of the general intolerance for Catholicism and her position in the community, Celene and Jean-Paul had had no contact with a priest since they'd come to England. Only Burke knew how much that worried his wife, and Trowbridge's diatribe didn't make things any better.

Stealing the victim of the vicar's fervent evangelism from under his nose, Burke had hustled Celene into the hall. But it had taken him far too long to intervene.

"I don't belong here," she told him with tears in her eyes. "Your family doesn't approve of me. I don't fit in. And now even my beliefs are being called into question."

"It doesn't matter what they think; it doesn't matter what they say." Did the words really count as a lie, Burke wondered, if he said them to comfort someone he loved? "Celene, I want you here with me. I need you beside me every day."

"I don't know if that's enough anymore."

It was the first time she had voiced the sentiment, though he suspected she'd thought it more than once. The realization that their marriage might fail, that she might leave him, that she might return to Ste. Genevieve without him, chilled Burke to the marrow of his bones.

"I'll find you a priest. I'll see to it that you can meet with him in private," he promised. "Will that be all right?"

Celene shook her head in a sad resignation that had nothing to do with answering him.

It was more than this single incident that made her want to leave, and he didn't know how to protect her. What was happening here in England was dismantling her confidence bit by bit. It was bringing back all the doubts from her childhood, all the pain from her years with Henri. The confusion he saw in her eyes was destroying her, and that was killing him.

"I love you, Celene." The words were stark and clear. His love was really all he had ever had to offer her.

But was his love for her enough to keep her here?

The question lay unspoken between them as they stood in the hall. The Yule gaiety flowed around them, the carols and the laughter.

When she did not reply in kind, Burke spun away. He'd needed to know Celene loved him as much as he loved her. He'd needed answers, affirmations, reassurance. He'd needed a drink.

Burke sat with his head in his hands, his elbows propped up on the top of his desk. There must be something he could do to make things right between Celene and him, something he could say to keep her with him.

And certainly he could find something to tell Antoine that would disguise what was happening here. Picking up the thread of the previous paragraph, he began to write.

Though our Christmas festivities are different from yours in Ste. Genevieve, they are every bit as filled with laughter and celebration. This year I managed to give Jean-Paul a special gift. On a trip to London, I found a box of small tin soldiers. Though they were made in Germany, they are painted with the colors of the King's Horseguards. Your grandson was very pleased with them.

Jean-Paul's eyes had gone round as dinner plates when he'd received the gift. He'd thrown his arms around Burke's neck, and within moments, the two of them were hunkered down on the drawing room floor, fighting mock battles, lining up the soldiers as if on parade. This was a special gift, a special time between Jean-Paul and him. If Burke could not make Celene happy, he'd thought, at least he could please her son. He had deliberately excluded the other children from their play, but in the end that proved to be a mistake.

The adults had just settled in for another cup of wassail and a few more Christmas cakes when Jean-Paul began to wail. Four of his six precious soldiers had disappeared. They searched the drawing room from one end to the other, moving furniture, scouring every inch of the carpet. It was Bayard Forrester who spotted the toys in the fireplace. Working with shovel and tongs, the two men managed to rescue what was left of the soldiers from the coals, four clumps of melted tin. What had been glorious and new earlier in the day was ruined, and Jean-Paul was inconsolable. Clutching the remaining soldiers in his fists, he had sobbed against his mother's shoulder until she had taken him upstairs.

Under the fury of Burke's temper and his persistent questioning, young Alarick finally confessed. He had thrown the soldiers into the fire. Though Burke would have caned the child for such a malicious act, Phillip merely sent his son to bed and offered to replace the ruined toys.

It was an unsatisfactory ending to the episode as far as Burke was concerned, but Jean-Paul had taken his own revenge. The scamp put burrs in Alarick's bed, and that seemed, to the children at least, to end the matter.

Burke looked down at the letter again, wondering what else there was to say. Peugeot had entrusted Celene and Jean-Paul to him. How could he tell Antoine that his daughter and grandson were desperately unhappy here? How could Burke admit to a man who was dying that he was failing in the most important request anyone had ever made of him?

The answer was that Burke could not. Though he hated himself as he penned the words, there was nothing else to do.

But with the Yule season behind us now, there is the new year to think about, new challenges to face. There will be repairs to the crofts, the plantings in the spring, new colts and lambs and calves and piglets. Celene and Jean-Paul are as excited as I am about what lies ahead. I have done my best to make them happy here, and you must believe me when I tell you that they are.

> *Your devoted friend,*
> *Burke Hammond-Cardwell*

He folded the paper quickly and affixed his seal. He had ended the letter not with a gentle distortion of the truth, but with an outright lie, one more in the series that seemed suddenly to dominate his life. Lies to Antoine; lies to Celene. Lies to himself. And he didn't know how to change that.

He was caught, ensnared by his title and his holdings, enmeshed in responsibilities he neither wanted nor cared about, hamstrung by his need to prove his grandfather had been wrong to send him away all those years ago. There wasn't any escape. The only joy he had was in Celene and Jean-Paul, and he wondered how long even they would stand by him.

Desperation rose in him, a hot, terrifying, familiar clot at the base of his throat, a pain beneath his ribs that almost never went away. He knew from recent experience that only a drink could offer ease. He left the letter on the desk and went in search of a bottle to comfort him.

18

Since ten o'clock this morning, Celene had pummeled Randolph with her umbrella to fend him off, exchanged heated words with Felicity, and broken up a fight between Jean-Paul and Alarick. But it was jabbing her finger as she stitched the bit of frippery stretched on her embroidery frame that made her realize how intolerable her life had become, how desperate she was to leave this place. That single, simple pinprick sent her fleeing the small parlor where the women gathered, in search of her husband.

She found him by the fire in the library, a book open in his lap and a half-empty decanter of claret at his elbow.

"I promised my father we'd be home for planting in the spring," she announced as she crossed the expanse of Turkish carpets toward where he sat. "And since there are arrangements to be made, we need be about them."

Burke straightened in his chair as if she'd shoved a shiv against his back. "God in heaven, Celene! What's brought all this up?"

It was the strangeness and the hostility, the loneliness and the disillusionment, the antipathy and the hopelessness. It was that she was losing herself, that she was losing him. She thought he understood that, in his way.

"It's everything, Burke," she said simply. "I want to go home."

As she watched, his expression changed. But instead of his features contracting with anger, the planes of his face seemed to elongate, solidify. What she saw in him was more harsh than anger, more devastating than fury, though she couldn't seem to give it a name.

Yet when Burke spoke, his voice was deceptively mild. "I realize there have been difficulties here at Longmeadow that neither of us anticipated, but I was hoping you'd give this a little more time. Consider all you'd be giving up if you went back. Here you have comforts you never dreamed of in Ste. Genevieve, a grand house, beautiful clothes, servants to see to every need. Why should you want to exchange all that for the hardships of the frontier?"

Burke's arguments were rational, reasonable. They were the arguments of a man who would not be moved.

"I don't care what I'll be giving up," she told him. "Longmeadow is not my home, and I'm needed in Ste. Genevieve."

"You are my wife," Burke reminded her as if she might have somehow forgotten. "Where I choose to live, you must set yourself to be content."

Resentment flared up as he mouthed the platitude. "But I'm not content, and neither is Jean-Paul."

"And it doesn't matter that I need you?"

She looked down into his face, seeing the compelling cast of Burke's features, the breadth of his clean-shaven jaw, the blade-straight nose, the tender curve of his lips. But there were new lines sketched deep between his brows, weary creases at the corners of his mouth. There was a faintly diminished clarity to his turquoise eyes, as if both the color and his perceptions were slightly blurred. Those subtle changes bothered her, made her even more certain that she was right in insisting they leave.

Returning to Ste. Genevieve for planting time was a promise she'd made to her father, a promise she'd made to herself. But it suddenly seemed too important a vow to break—too important to all of them.

"Please, Burke," she said, coming to her knees beside his chair, "come home with me to Ste. Genevieve. Once we're there, we can plant our fields, tend our animals, work together side by side. We can start a family of our own. We can build a life for ourselves in Ste. Genevieve—the kind of life we dreamed about before Bayard Forrester came, before we knew about all of this."

She took his hand, trying to bridge the distance that had grown between them in these last weeks.

"I feel so lost here, Burke. I look in the mirror, and I don't know who I am. I say things a voyageur's daughter would never say, do things Celene Peugeot would never do. I dress in silks and satins. I sit idle drinking tea. I try to fill my days with gossip and needlework. I want to behave as a proper countess should, but that's not who I am. I need more than this. I need fields to plant, a house to keep, people I love to care for."

His grip tightened on her hand, tender and conciliatory, compelling and desperate.

"I love you, Burke, but this life is changing both of us. I don't recognize myself anymore. You're turning into someone I hardly know. I realize things have been more difficult for you here than you let on. I can see how the responsibilities weigh on you. I know how hard you're trying to do things right. I love you, Burke. I want to help. But you won't tell me what you want, what you need. You exclude me from your life a little more every day."

"If you love me, as you say, you'll stay at my side. *That* is what I need from you." His words were stark and unconditional, as petulant as a child's.

Anger surged through her blinding and bright, anger at his stubbornness, frustration at her inability to make him see, fury at the choice he was forcing her to make.

Unthinking, she lashed out at him. "Shall I stay at your side and watch you drink and gamble away your life and your inheritance? Shall I stay and watch you turn into a man I can't respect, a man I cannot love? You can't see your own worth when it's measured against what these people prize. You can't tell what you're accomplishing in endless columns of figures in endless books. You're losing track of who you are. You're as dissatisfied with your life here as I am with mine, but you won't admit it. And that's undermining everything."

When he said nothing, she went on. "I have Jean-Paul to think about in all of this. I have my own life to think about. And as hard as it is to admit, the future I want for myself and my son isn't the one you're offering me!"

Burke's face was set, his lips compressed. "If that's how you feel, Celene," he offered quietly, "then by all means, go. But realize, if you do, you will have to leave without me."

Celene fought the urge to weep, swallowed around the lump of frustration and fear lodged deep in her throat. "But I need you with me in Ste. Genevieve!" she cried.

"*And I need you here.*" His voice was colder than the winter wind that whipped around the corners of the house, colder than a challenge met at sunrise. As final as an early grave.

"Oh, Burke," she whispered, "Oh, Burke, please. If you don't come with me now, it will be the end of everything."

He had the look of an animal caught in a trap, frightened, resentful, resigned. "Don't you think I know that? Don't you think it matters?"

"Then show me that it matters. Come with me."

"Damn it, Celene!" he shouted at her. "Don't you understand? I *can't* go with you."

Knowing the kind of man he was, the dangers he'd braved, the things he'd done, his refusal made no sense to her.

"But why? For God's sake why?"

He paused. There was weariness in his tone. "Because I'm the Eighth Earl of Hammondsford, because all of this belongs to me. There are things I must do here, things I must prove, things I can't run away from even if I wanted to."

She stared at him, unable to comprehend, unable to see what was driving him so mercilessly. It was as if he expected these few words to explain why he'd chosen to stay when she must go, explain why their life and their love was crumbling around them. And in a way, she supposed they did.

Or perhaps he was like her father and Henri after all, Celene found herself thinking. Perhaps he meant to win his way by intimidation, by force of will, by playing on her weaknesses. The realization that he might well be turning her love for him against her tore at her heart. How could he bear to do that to her? How could he have changed so much in these few months?

She knelt before him, trembling with the knowledge that what she said and did in the next few moments would decide the future for both of them. If she played the only card in her hand, gambled on the only threat that might convince Burke to leave, she could lose the only true happiness she'd ever known. She could lose the marriage that had taught her what true communion of spirit meant, lose the man she loved to the depths of her soul. But if she held her peace, if she chose to stay, she would sacrifice the most vital parts of herself. She would sacrifice her son. She would sacrifice Burke to needs and wants and aspirations that would not matter in the end.

Tears rose in her eyes and terror flooded through her as she spoke the words. "If I thought it would make a difference, I would do as you ask. But I can't stay and watch what's happening to you, and you won't let me help you stop it. With you or without you, I'm going home. It's where I belong, where I can live and work and worship and raise my son as I see fit. I love you, Burke, but I have no choice. It's the decision that is right for Jean-Paul and me. I only pray that you'll come to understand my reasons, and be with us when we sail."

Burke's eyes flared lapis-dark. With an oath he rose to go. "Indeed, madam, I know you've done what you think is right. But don't expect me to condone this foolishness or become party to your plans. If you choose to leave Longmeadow and decry your vows, it's the last you'll ever see of me."

He slammed the library door as he took his leave, the sound reverberating through the house with the resonance of a thunderclap.

She had not meant for it to come to ultimatums and threats between them. Yet she had made the only decision she could make. The conviction that she was right was strong in her. She must leave England, for herself and for her son. They must leave before they lost their way, before the corruption of this house and the people in it destroyed them—as those things were destroying Burke.

Knowing all she'd gained and all she'd lost, all she forfeited in the name of truth and self-respect, Celene curled
into the upholstered chair. She curled into Burke's faint,
lingering warmth, into the elusive, woodsy scent that still
clung to the velvet cushions. Enveloped by the remnants of
the man she loved, the husband she was giving up, Celene
pressed her hands to her mouth to muffle the sounds of her
terrible grief.

Frederick Andrew Burke Hammond-Cardwell, the
Eighth Earl of Hammondsford, bent low over his black gelding's neck and urged the horse to greater speed. As they
blazed along the frozen road, the cold wind slashed his
cheeks and brought the sting of tears to his eyes. The world
to the right and left blew past in a blur, and he fancied it
was time flashing past him as he rode.

His lifetime seemed to flicker by, his boyhood ruled by
his grandfather's loving aggravation, his adolescence spent
in schools only slightly warmer than the January day, his
youth fueled by deviltry and indolent excess, the end of
that tempestuous time coming on the voyage to the American wilderness in the bow of a canoe. Only then did time
seem to slow its wild careening, as thoughts of Morning
Song filled the visions in his head. Those memories were
warm and bright, as if the sun had risen in his life to chase
the gloom away. Song was there as she had always been,
filling him with hope, offering him help and understanding,
touching him with love.

Then Morning Song was gone and swirling into her place
was a tiny, determined Frenchwoman, her hair like a flickering silver-gold flame. Celene was as tart as Morning Song
was sweet, as astringent as Morning Song was soothing.
Yet the light of the love he felt shining down upon his head
had never wavered. That love had changed from mellow to
fierce, from constant to flaring bright. He had basked in
Celene's fiery glow. There was real passion in her heart,
real power behind her love, real independence in what she
offered him. But now that light had begun to fade, and the
cold, bleak world was his again.

He drove the gelding onward, hoping for a glimpse of

some future yet to come, but the fancies left him alone on the narrow, frozen road to who-knew-where with only the promise of some impersonal, distant fire to take the chill of loneliness from his bones.

It was not a compelling picture of what was to come, and he reined in the gelding's headlong flight. He needed a drink to help him think through what was happening. Far across the stubble of his rutted fields, he could see the smoke from the chimney of his favorite tavern beckoning him. He pulled the horse's head sharply to the right, guiding him toward the local haven of masculine strength and solitude.

He left the gelding with the ostler in the tavern yard, then made his way through the smoky taproom. The innkeeper came at once to see to his needs.

"The usual, my lord?" the fellow asked.

"The usual?" Burke echoed, wondering just how often he'd taken refuge here in these last weeks. More often than he realized, he supposed.

"A bottle of our best brandy and a single glass."

A bottle of brandy and a single glass. That spoke of a solitude and an excess he had not quite realized he'd been indulging in. Celene was right; he had been drinking far too much. He didn't want to think what else had she been right about.

"That will do nicely, I am sure."

As the man bustled off to do his bidding, Burke settled back in his chair and considered what had transpired between Celene and him. She was leaving, going home. He had known all along that this is how it would end between them: with Celene in Ste. Genevieve and him here. He had known it the night Forrester burst into their wedding celebration with the news that Burke was the new Earl of Hammondsford. It had played out exactly as he had thought it would, and none of his explanations, none of his promises, none of his declarations had made any difference.

Just then the brandy arrived at his table, and Burke drained a glass in a single draft, hoping to fend off the resignation and the hopelessness stalking him.

That first day in Longmeadow's drawing room, Celene

had stood out from the rest like a wild, bright daisy in a bouquet of hothouse flowers; a crisp, tart apple on a tray of marzipan. In that moment he had chosen to see the promise of what could be instead of the grinding inevitability of what was. He had hoped that in this world of sophistication and pretense Celene might prove his touchstone to reality, the one sweet haven of quiet and contentment in his life.

But as much as he needed her, it had become almost immediately apparent that he could not protect her, that living here would ultimately destroy Celene and her son. He had done his best to fend that off, but when the confusion and humiliation in her eyes had become too much for him to bear, he had withdrawn. He had left her with nothing but his passion to blunt the harsh edges of her life, had refused to share his burdens because he could offer no help with the ones that she was carrying. He had put Celene through hell because he was a selfish bastard and because he had needed something to call his own in all of this. He had failed her, and he had failed himself.

He poured another glass of brandy, trying to drown the bitter taste of that failure in the fiery glow. But he could not.

Celene said she was leaving. With another woman, those words might have been an empty threat, but the pain of parting would slice as deep for her as it would for him. She would never have come to him, never have spoken the words that would end their marriage, if she felt she had another choice. There was nothing he could do to bend her to his will. He had sworn devotion, told her lies, made her promises. He had said all there was to say. The only course left to him was to let her go.

She wanted him with her in Ste. Genevieve, and the prospect lured him like a Siren's song. He had imagined himself living out his days in her house and in her bed. He had wanted to work at her side, hold her when the nights were cold, comfort her when she birthed their children, share her sorrows and her joys. He craved that simple domesticity, the peace only Celene could give. But how could he share her life when he couldn't go back?

Impending doom weighed on him, Celene's ultimatum,

the demands the earldom made. He felt trapped, resentful. If she chose to leave without him, their love would not survive the separation. Nor, he supposed, would it survive the life they were living if she stayed.

But his future was here, shackled to his grandfather's legacy, ensnared with Burke's own need for the approval of a man who was long since dead. He'd often wondered in these last days how the old man who had sent him away—perhaps forever—would feel knowing the holdings and the land had come to Burke. Would he be amused by the twists of fate? Horrified that all he had worked so hard to amass had come to his wastrel grandson? In the end it was those two questions that kept Burke at Longmeadow. He had to prove his grandfather had been wrong about him. He had to prove that he was worthy, now that he had the chance. But if he forfeited his life with Celene to appease the old man's spirit, to allay the doubts he had buried inside him for eleven long years, how would he live with himself?

He slammed down another glass of brandy and spilled coins across the table to pay his bill.

If Celene was leaving, at least there would be time before she went away. It would take a few weeks to secure passage on a ship, perhaps longer if Burke used his newfound influence. He would have at least a score of precious days in her company; some long, lingering hours to spend making love to her. He would have time to store up the sound of her laughter, the taste of her tears, the balm of every murmured endearment. He would have an opportunity to ride with Jean-Paul, to coddle and spoil the boy who had so briefly been his son.

The time would be heart-wrenching, bittersweet. But then, every day of a man's life could be his last. At least Burke would know enough to savor every moment, every heartbeat. It was more than some men had. He only hoped it was enough.

He passed back through the tavern and reclaimed his horse. He needed to get back to Longmeadow, back to Celene, back to the woman who would be taking all of his heart with her when she left his life forever.

* * *

"Do I sense trouble in paradise?"

Celene dashed the tears from her eyes and started, looking up to find Randolph Hammond-Cardwell leaning against the shuttered library door.

"And if there is, are you the serpent come to gloat?"

"Perhaps I've come to offer sympathy."

"A new role for the serpent, to be sure," Celene answered tartly, rising from her chair. Randolph's mere presence in the unoccupied library turned her queasy. Since the family had never trespassed here, she had thought she would be safe.

"I can be most sympathetic to a lady in distress," Randolph told her, "and there's no question that you qualify. What has my cousin done to make you cry?"

"It's really none of your concern."

"Everything that happens in this house is my concern," he answered, moving toward her.

"It's not as if you're master here." As Celene issued the challenge, she sidestepped the chair, putting its bulk between her and the older man.

He stalked a few steps nearer, frowning either at the impediment she'd put in his path or the tenor of her words.

"Surely you don't cast your husband in that role. He's too easily diverted with his race meetings and his drinking to even realize what being master means."

"I think he's trying to do his best," Celene answered, instinctively defending her husband. "Perhaps he has a different idea of how to run Longmeadow and the other holdings."

"He has no idea at all, and that's the rub. He's done nothing to deserve the earldom. I am the one who has overseen the property these last few years."

"And you've gotten very used to it, I'll warrant." She continued moving to her left, being careful to keep the table and chairs between them. "But it's hardly Burke's fault he wasn't here to do his share."

"Yes," Randolph drawled, a bemused smile on his lips, "hardly his fault. But returning to Longmeadow is going to be his downfall, I'm afraid."

She eyed him, sensing again, as she had from the first,

that there was intrigue afoot where the earldom was concerned. Bayard Forrester's continued presence here proved that, Forrester's presence and her husband's spate of "accidents." If Burke stayed on, he would have to be far more careful than he'd been thus far.

"Are you threatening Burke?" As she spoke, Celene reached the last chair in the row and spared a glance for the library door. It seemed impossibly far away.

"Threatening my dear cousin? Goodness, no. But sooner or later he'll be called out over a game of cards—or by some irate husband angry at his wife's indiscretions."

Her head came up sharply, Randolph's words freezing her where she stood. He had made the same assertion that first night in the hall, and Celene was certain her husband had been true to her since then. "Burke wouldn't trifle with other women! Burke loves me!"

Of course, she couldn't answer for her husband's behavior once she was gone.

"Poor naive girl," Randolph said with a shake of his head. "Such an unsophisticated country mouse. All men cheat on their wives, and many wives on their husbands. I'd wager a quarter of the second sons in England are not legitimate issue."

Shocked and unconvinced, Celene stood her ground. "That can't be true!"

"Indeed it is," he replied as he maneuvered closer, cutting off her path to the door. "So you see, the favors I want from you are hardly something worthy of the protests you've lodged. You're a pretty little thing, and I've had an urge to taste your charms since I first saw you in the drawing room."

"Then you're destined to be disappointed in your quest, monsieur. For I have no intention of—"

Before the words were out of her mouth, Randolph sprang across the space that separated them. She took refuge behind the chair. With a thrust of one arm, he cast it aside. It wobbled and overturned, sending the gate-leg table and decanter crashing to the floor. The yeasty smell of claret filled the air.

Panic spiked inside her as Randolph sidestepped

the mess. His fingers closed around her upper arms. He drew her to him with a jerk and crushed his lips across her mouth.

Celene fought to get away. Pushing hard against his chest, she tried to twist free of his imprisoning grip. But he was so much larger than she, so much stronger than she, and she had no weapon to hold him off.

He held her fast and forced his tongue between her teeth. When her struggles did not cease, he swept her up in his arms and carried her toward the settee on the far side of the room. Randolph deposited her roughly on the seat. Before she could wriggle away, he threw himself on top of her.

The weight of him pinning her down sent her memories spiraling, of Henri's heinous demands, of being held down while her husband forced himself on her, of being overcome and helpless. Her chest heaved as she fought for breath. The only thought that reverberated through her brain was the desperate need to get away. She writhed and bucked beneath him, twisted and fought.

"Here now," Randolph panted above her. "There's no need for all of this. All I want is a tumble. Surely you can give me that."

His belly pressed hard against her ribs. His hips molded to her. Even through the fullness of her skirts she could feel the jab of his arousal. She tried to kick away. He jammed his knee against the juncture of her legs, pinning her skirts to the seat of the couch. She flailed against him, catching him with a hard but glancing blow beneath his eye. He gathered her hands together in a punishing grip, pinning them above her head. She spat into his lowering face.

Randolph gave a moan of rage and tangled the fingers of his free hand in the neckline of her bodice. She cried out as he ripped the fabric aside, baring the corset and chemise beneath. Her scream was lost against his mouth as he clamped his wet lips over hers.

His hand dropped to the swirl of her skirts, jerking them upward in a series of violent, hasty snags. What had begun as unwilling seduction was swiftly moving toward something infinitely more dangerous and degrading. Randolph coveted what Burke had: his earldom, his property, and his wife. Was this about despoiling something that belonged to his cousin? Had Randolph's advances always been based on his need for power?

She cried out again as Randolph's fingers bit deep into her thigh, forcing her legs apart, positioning her to receive the thrust of his body. As one hand retreated to open the buttons on his pants, Celene went totally still. Revulsion and the swarm of memories his treatment roused held her immobile. Tears coursed down her cheeks. Soft, desperate mews rose in her throat.

Then rage flared in her head, overcoming the panic, shattering the memories. She fought free of the hopelessness, the resignation that might well have made her Randolph's helpless victim. Desperation gave her strength.

She shifted on the couch, bracing her foot against the seat, shifting toward the open edge. In the moment when Randolph was poised to enter her, she threw her full weight against him, and pushed away from the cushions.

Taken full of lust and unaware, Randolph lost his balance, teetered, and went over the edge of the couch, landing on his back. Celene spilled herself on top of him, driving her elbows into his stomach and her knee into his groin. A howl of pain ripped from his throat, and he lay dazed for the one brief moment Celene needed to roll away.

She scrambled to her feet and staggered out of the library. With tears of fury and humiliation scoring her cheeks and her bodice clutched together at the front, she made good her escape. After racing up the stairs and down the hall, she locked the door of her bedchamber.

She'd not stay in this house another night, she vowed as she braced back against the oaken door. There was nothing for her here but pain and degradation, nothing for her but hurt and disillusionment. She would pack her bags, gather up Jean-Paul, and be away before Burke came back. It was all there was left for her to do.

Celene was packing. Burke went short of breath when he saw her leather-bound trunk standing open in the center of the bedroom floor. A neatly folded pile of clothes lay beside it, a pair of leather shoes, the silver-backed hairbrush he'd given her for Christmas, her lavender pomander bag. Celene was doing exactly what she'd threatened. She was leaving, going away.

But not now. Please, God, not yet.

As he stood staring, Celene came out of the dressing room, a blue-gray gown across her arm. She hesitated when she saw him there, then went to kneel beside the trunk.

"I'm only taking the simplest things," she told him. "Most of this finery would be useless in Ste. Genevieve. You'll see someone makes use of it, won't you?"

Burke closed the door behind him. "I didn't realize you'd be leaving so soon."

Celene nodded her head. "There's no sense putting it off."

Panic swelled thick and hot inside his chest. "Please, Celene, I love you. I need you with me."

He hadn't meant to plead with her for a second chance, but he couldn't seem to help himself. He was desperate enough to beg her, order her, or bribe her to stay if he thought it would do any good.

She folded a chemise across her lap and smoothed it into the trunk. "If I matter so much, come with me to Ste. Genevieve."

"Damn it, Celene, you know I can't."

"You're the Eighth Earl of Hammondsford." Her gaze rose to his, her eyes clear and green, swimming with silver sparks. "It seems to me that you can jolly well do whatever you please."

"It's not that simple."

"Well, I'm sorry that it's not." She slapped the silver-backed brush into the trunk. "In any case, I'm leaving today."

"Are you so eager to have it quits between us? Don't you want a few more hours, a few more days—"

"A few more hours or days for what? So that every time I look at you I'll be reminded of what I'm giving up? So that every time I touched you or kissed you I would think, 'Is this the last time, the very last time?' Maybe you could stand that, but I never could. Nor could Jean-Paul. As eager as he is to leave England, he doesn't understand why you're not coming with us. And neither do I.''

He wished he could make her understand the things that held him here, the pride, the anger, the compulsion to prove that his grandfather had been wrong to send him away.

She raised her gaze to his, her eyes beseeching, filled with tears. ''Please, Burke, come away with me. Come be my husband, be my love. I swear I'll make you happy. I'll cook for you and clean for you, tend your fields, and bear your children. Come home to Ste. Geneviève with me.''

It seemed as if she couldn't stop asking for second chances, either.

He looked down at where she sat before him on the floor. She was so small, but so determined. She fought so hard for the things she wanted, gave so much to those she loved. For these last months they had shared something fierce and sweet, something brief and incomparably special. But there was no middle ground between them now, no room for compromises. She could not stay; he could not go. Further debate was useless; it could only make their parting more difficult. With terrible resignation, Burke realized there was nothing left between them but to say goodbye.

He came to his knees beside her and touched her face, stroked his fingers through her tumbled hair. He kissed her tenderly, lingeringly, letting her essence seep around him, through him. He felt the warmth of her tears on his cheeks; the clutch of her fingers on the front of his frock coat; the soft, simple pleasure of her mouth. The intimacy between them sent a current of misery rushing through him. Blackness fell over his world like twilight.

At length he drew away. ''If ever there's anything you need . . .''

''Only that you be careful once I'm gone.''

''If there's anything at all I can ever do . . .''

She shook her head, unable to speak.

He clasped her hand in his one last time before he turned to go. He crossed the room and closed the door behind him, the click of the latch echoing through him like the last notes of a requiem.

Leaning back against it, he wondered, for the second time in his life, if a man could die from losing the woman he loved. Yet this was worse than Morning Song's death. That had been irrevocable, finite. He had grieved, but in time he had put his loss away. He would never forget Morning Song, but he had been able to go on.

Losing Celene was not irrevocable, only inevitable. It implied a choice, a choice there was no way for him to make. Because there would never be closure, real resolution in his decision, losing Celene would always be a raw, fresh wound inside of him. The promise of another world, another life would always taunt him. For the rest of his days, he would be tortured with the knowledge that it was still possible to turn to her, if honor ceased to matter, if he forgave himself for what he'd put her through, if he could somehow prove that he was worthy of both her love and his grandfather's trust.

He pushed away from the door and wandered through the house like a living ghost, searching for something that was not there, searching for something that could never be.

The coach that would take Celene and her son to Bristol rolled up to the front door an hour later. Burke had said his goodbye to Jean-Paul by taking him to the stable. They had patted the boy's pony, fed it an apple and some carrots.

"Why can't you come with us to Ste. Genevieve?" Jean-Paul had asked as the pony swished his tail and turned away.

"I just can't. That's all," Burke said, too empty and battered to try to explain things that went far beyond the boy's comprehension.

"But I want you to come."

Instead of answering, Burke squatted down to hug the child. "You'll take care of your mother for me, won't you?"

"Yes."

"And give my best wishes to your *grandpère* and Pélagie."

"*Oui.*" Jean-Paul nodded as his arms tightened around Burke's neck. Cardwell hugged him back. "I love you, Burke. I wish you could always be my papa."

The words couldn't have sliced any deeper if the child had been born of his own flesh. Burke closed his eyes against the sudden sting of tears. "I wish I could always be your papa, too."

Loosening his hold with an effort, he had sent Jean-Paul to his mother, watching him run back through the garden toward the house. It had taken Burke a good deal longer to compose himself and follow his *beau-fils*.

Now he stood in the drawing room window, watching the two most important people in his life go away forever. He saw the servants hand up Celene and Jean-Paul's three small trunks, saw Celene embrace the steward and his wife, saw her look back at the house one last time before climbing into the coach. There was a pain around his heart that might well last his whole life long. Still, he stood silent and unmoving, unable to change either the future or the past.

His regrets were legion as the coach rolled out of the courtyard and down the lane. But there was no help for what was happening; Celene had seen that far more clearly than he. Her life was in Ste. Genevieve and his was here. His inheritance had made him a man of property and responsibility, and now he had to find a way to live up to all of that. It was really all he had left.

The sound of the drawing room door opening drew him away from the window. Sophy stood in the doorway, hunched on her cane.

"She's leaving for good, isn't she?" she said, her face lined with concern.

For good, no. Forever. "Yes."

"Your grandfather would never have let someone he loved go like that," she admonished him.

Burke drew an unsteady breath, eleven years of bitterness suddenly rife inside him. "No, my grandfather never let the people he loved go. He sent them away. He made sure they never returned."

Sophy closed the door behind her and crossed to where he stood. "Is that what you think happened?"

She'd touched him on the raw, and Burke turned on her. He had held his peace as long as he'd been at Longmeadow, tamped down his questions, tried to put away the past. He hadn't dared let anyone see how vulnerable he was when it came to this. But Sophy seemed to be baiting him, and he gave his anger sway.

"Of course that's what happened," he answered. "Old Alarick sent me away."

"For God's sake, Burke. You dueled with Jason Hargrave, the son of one of his oldest friends, so Alarick packed you off to Montreal until things cooled down. It was never anything more than that. He thought you might even enjoy seeing America."

"And once my goddamned grandfather sent me there, he had me kidnapped into the fur trade!" The accusation had festered inside him so long, it was a relief to speak it aloud. It was just that he had always imagined saying it to the man himself, not to this small, wizened woman who had set herself up as his grandfather's champion. "He thought I'd die out there in the wilds. God knows, I almost did."

Sophy's eyes went steely. "You're a fool, Burke, if you believe Alarick meant you harm. Your grandfather loved you. He never had any idea how you'd ended up at Fort Mackinac. When word came back that you'd been there at the time of the massacre, he was nearly beside himself. He sent men to find you, but there was no sign, nothing at all to lead us to believe that you'd survived. We all thought you were dead, and your grandfather blamed himself."

"As well he should."

Sophy rapped him sharply on the arm with the head of her cane. "You young dolt," she huffed. "Losing you was the beginning of the end for him. Alarick had plans for you, not the earldom, to be sure. He couldn't give you that. But there were other things he wanted you to do and have. He loved you, Burke. He respected you. He would have been very proud of the man you've become, of what you've accomplished on your own. You proved him right about your abilities. And it would have pleased him to know that all he'd amassed eventually came to you."

Burke simply stared. Was Sophy telling him the truth? Had his grandfather loved him after all?

But there were other questions to be asked now that the

subject had been broached. "Then who did have me kidnapped?"

Sophy shrugged. "Who had the most to lose if you stayed here?"

"But I wasn't in line for the earldom."

"No, but there were many other things your grandfather could have given you, enough to make others fear for their position, for their livelihood."

The memory of the broken cinch and the shot in the woods rippled through his mind. Had Celene been right to be concerned for his safety?

"And do they fear for them now?" Burke asked with a twist to his lips.

"You're referring to your 'accidents,' I presume. The attempts on your life."

"Is that really what they are?" He needed to know what Sophy thought.

"You're being naive, Burke, if you don't realize how inconvenient your return to Longmeadow has been for everyone here. By just being alive you've upset their plans. And what's worse, you've managed the estates and the holdings far better than anyone expected you would. If you'd left things as they've always been, they might have tolerated your presence. But you're taking an active role, making changes. The tenants are happier than they've been in years. If you choose to stay, I predict that things will continue to improve. But you'll also run the risk of finding yourself in an early grave."

"So you're saying that I have reason to fear for my life—just as I should have eleven years ago."

Sophy's thin brows lifted above piercing slate-gray eyes. "And I'd wager the source of the threat is still the same."

"Randolph, you mean? But he was only in his early twenties when Grandfather sent me away."

"Is that too early an age for a man to know jealousy and ambition? Or perhaps his father was involved," the dowager countess suggested.

"But there were no threats in all the intervening years."

"Because they thought they had succeeded; they thought you were dead. It was only a little more than four years ago that word came to us through the trading company in Montreal that there was a trapper in the Northwest who called himself Burke Cardwell,'' Sophy went on. ''But Alarick was gone then, and it didn't seem to matter what had become of you. It was only when both Randolph's father and Andrew died that we began to search for you in earnest. It was then you became a threat.''

Burke nodded, thinking how perceptive a woman his aunt really was.

''And Forrester brought me home''—he raised one hand in a gesture of contempt—''brought me home to all of this.''

She must have heard the bitterness in his voice, for she looked at him long and hard. ''The title and the holdings have been more of a curse than a blessing to you, haven't they, boy? You were happy there, weren't you? You'd proved yourself. You'd found the place where you belonged.''

Burke took a long, slow breath as a new realization settled over him. Administering the earldom was not the test of his worth. He had proved it far away and long ago. He had proved it by surviving in the wilds, by learning to love and respect the people in his life. That's what made him the man he had become.

''Coming here has cost you all of it, hasn't it?'' Sophy offered gently. ''You home, your stepson, and your wife?''

Burke nodded as his thoughts turned again to all he'd given up. Understanding what he really needed to define his life made Celene's leaving even more difficult, even more tragic. He had lost what mattered most.

''Then why don't you go after her?'' his aunt prodded him. ''Why don't you go and bring them back?''

Burke sighed and shook his head. ''Celene hasn't been happy here. I haven't been able to make her happy.'' It was a hard thing to admit aloud, a harder thing to accept. A burst of shame came with the words, a fearsome sense of failure. ''She finally decided she couldn't stay.''

''Then it's more than what Randolph did?''

''What Randolph did?'' Even through the pain, Sophy's

question raised a burr of curiosity. "What did Randolph do?"

Sophy looked at Burke as if he'd lost his mind. "Why, he forced himself on Celene this afternoon. He manhandled her and tore her dress. The whole household has been abuzz with it. The servants can hardly talk of anything else. And it's not the only time he's tried to have his way with her. He's been after her like a rutting hound since the day you arrived."

Burke stared at his aunt in utter disbelief. Randolph and Celene? Randolph forcing his attentions on Burke's own wife? Images blossomed in his mind: of his cousin's hands on Celene's soft skin, of Randolph's body crushing hers. Bile rose in Burke's throat. Fury thundered in his brain. Why hadn't Celene told him?

It was the grip of Sophy's fingers around his arm that sent the kaleidoscope of horrifying images swirling away.

"Oh, Burke," she whispered in deepest understanding and sympathy. "You mean you really didn't know?"

19

"You goddamn son of a bitch!" With a haze of wild, red rage swimming before his eyes, Burke burst into the estate office at the back of the house. Forrester and Phillip were there, but Burke thrust past them, intent on Randolph behind the desk. He reached across and dragged his cousin from his chair. With his hands twisted in Randolph's coat, Burke shook him like a terrier does a rat.

"You vile bastard! You worthless swine! You tried to force your attentions on my wife!" Death would be too good for any man who harmed Celene, and Burke adjusted his grip to close around Randolph's throat. He meant to wring the life from this useless bastard, to feel the crush of his windpipe beneath his thumbs.

Randolph cackled as Burke's fingers flexed. The other men leaped to intervene. Before he could accomplish his goal, Forrester and Phillip broke Burke's hold and dragged him off. He fought as they hauled him back, punching and flailing, bloodying Phillip's nose. The younger man quailed at the well-placed blow, but Forrester persisted, slamming Burke against the wall. Forrester pinned him there with his weight and strength, holding him until Burke's raging bloodlust dropped to a boil, until his muscles stopped quivering.

Glaring past Forrester's shoulder to where Randolph had collapsed in his leather chair, Cardwell waited for his cousin to get his breath. There was a certain satisfaction to seeing Randolph flushed the color of pickled beets, with his wig shaken ridiculously askew. He looked exactly like what he was, Burke suddenly realized, a corrupt, decadent aristocrat, preying on those who were weaker than he. Though the realization filled him with repulsion and disgust, fury still seethed and bubbled in his veins.

"Vile ruffian," Randolph croaked. "Found out—what I'd done—did you?"

Burke stiffened, and Forrester went instantly on the defensive.

"Glad she decided—to leave. Silly little—trollop. Didn't understand—all I wanted was—a tumble."

"Goddamn you, Randolph!" New fury spun through Burke's brain, and he strained against Forrester's hold. "Goddamn you for touching her, for hurting her, for believing you could rape my wife. But it's not the first time you've tampered with my life, is it, Randolph? Not the first time you tried to deprive me of something that's rightfully mine."

Randolph snorted and raised his head, a smile playing at the rubbery curve of his lips. "Pity my father's plans—went awry. Would have saved—us all—good deal of trouble."

"What are you saying, Randolph?" Burke demanded, pushing for confirmation that Sophy's suspicions were correct. "Was it your father who had me taken into the wilds?"

"Old earl—too fond of you by half," Randolph answered, still fighting for air. "Father's instructions to the lawyer in Montreal—see you never—came back to England. Signing you on with the voyageurs—a stroke of genius. Who could expect a dandy—to survive such a journey and come back—to bedevil us?"

And there it was, what had haunted Burke for years, what he had come all this way to avenge. It had been Randolph's father, not old Alarick, who had wanted him dead. Sophy had been right; his grandfather had not set out to hurt him.

"But it's not just the past you have to answer for, is it?" Burke went on. "You're responsible for someone shooting at me in the woods. You were behind the skittish horse, the broken cinch. What else did you have planned for me, some strychnine in my brandy? A fall from one of the balconies?

A knife in my back as I slept? Well, it hardly matters, because now *I* want *you* dead. You tried to hurt Celene, and for that I mean to send you to hell!''

As the threat was spoken, silence descended on the room, a silence with an air of calculation about it, an air of satisfaction. Burke was instantly wary.

"Are you challenging Randolph to a duel?" Bayard Forrester asked softly, still blocking Burke's body with his own.

So that was what they'd planned, Burke thought, to do away with him in the guise of a challenge. Well, so be it. A duel would suit his purposes perfectly.

"I am indeed. I'll meet him at any time and place he cares to choose. But let's decide it now. I have no stomach for waiting so much as another day."

Randolph nodded. "Dawn?"

"In the meadow by the brook," Burke stipulated.

"Web'ons?" Phillip asked around the handkerchief he had pressed to his bleeding nose. "I b'lieve d'ey are my fadd'er's choice."

Either short swords or pistols were the traditional choices. Burke waited, holding his breath. With the latter, they might be equally matched; with the former, he would be at a distinct disadvantage, as his duel with Forrester on the ship had proved. Still Burke stood his ground, his determination to see this through undiminished by whatever choice his cousin made.

"Pistols," Randolph rasped, and for a moment a faint, smug smile seemed to play at the corners of his mouth.

"I'll sta'd my fadd'er's second," Phillip volunteered immediately.

So the three of them were indeed prepared for this eventuality, Burke thought fleetingly. The duel was to be another attempt on his life, wrapped in honor's guise. It hardly mattered if it was. Burke was getting what he wanted, too.

"That you're your father's second will help immeasurably, Phillip, when it comes time to find his burial plot. Unfortunately, I have no friendships to call on here."

"I'll stand second for you," Forrester offered.

Burke shifted his gaze to the other man, as another layer of the plot against him fell into place. "How very comforting it will be to know that while I square off against one enemy on the field, I'll have another at my back. But you'll do well enough, I suppose. I don't plan on having need of you."

Though he saw the fire come up in Forrester's face, Burke straightened, adjusted his clothes and stepped away.

"Then I'll see you in the morning, gentlemen. In the meadow by the brook at dawn."

Though still blanketed in shrouds of fog, Bristol's docks were stirring to life. The filmy glow of lighted lamps blossomed in the windows of some of the buildings along the waterfront. A cart rattled down a cobbled street. There was the stutter of footsteps shuffling along the pier, the dip of oars, and the occasional ring of voices as sailors made their way toward ships that would leave on the morning tide.

Celene shivered inside her cloak and pressed close to the rail of the vessel that would take her and Jean-Paul to New Orleans. She had kept her vigil all night long, standing alone on the open deck while her son slept in their cabin below, peering into the shifting darkness, praying that Burke would appear at the edge of the dock.

But he had not come.

In the graying half-light of a new day, her icy fingers curled around the Chippewa carving clutched tightly in her palm, hoping to conjure up some spark of magic left in the tiny scrap of wood. Once this charm had given Autumn Leaf mesmerizing power over Burke, and though Celene had fought to break that spell, she wished it still possessed some faint, mystical hold on him. Though she might endanger her immortal soul by calling up that heathen magic, Celene would have made a pact with the devil himself if Burke had agreed to come with her. But as tightly as she clutched the carving, Burke did not appear.

Around her the ship was coming awake. Sailors were gliding across the decks, moving silently through the filmy tatters of fog, preparing the ship for departure. That a vessel bound for Bermuda and New Orleans had been in port was a bit of serendipity Celene had not counted on, though their imminent departure gave Burke very little chance to change his mind.

Still, she was sure of the decision she had made. She was doing what was right for Jean-Paul and herself. Had the two of them remained at Longmeadow, they would have succumbed to the hostility and the loneliness, the viciousness and the intolerance. Their only chance to survive was to return to Ste. Genevieve where they belonged. And the only chance to save Burke from himself was if he chose to accompany them.

That the charm lay inert and lifeless in her hand convinced Celene, as logic could not, that Burke would not be there to sail with them.

Standing alone at the rail, Celene finally accepted what his refusal meant. It was an end to her marriage, an end to the tenderness and caring she and Burke had briefly shared, an end to all her dreams. The emptiness of being forever without him echoed through every cell. She ached with the devastation of blighted hopes, with the knowledge of all she'd given up, with the terrible weight of resignation. It was over, ended. There was no hope.

The activity around her intensified as she stared out at the brightening sky. The sailors cast off the lines that bound them to the dock, unfurled the sails to slap in the crisp dawn breeze. She felt the ship move beneath her, straining for the freedom of the open sea.

Far beyond the town, across the woods and countryside, in a formidable stone house at the head of a rise, Burke must be greeting the dawn of a brand-new day. He must be looking across the fields and woodlands that meant so much more to him than she did. He must be secure, if not in the man he had been with her, in the man he had become.

She had made her choice and Burke had made his. She must accept that each of them had the right to do that. She must accept that the small, scorched carving gripped tightly in her hand was her very last link to the man she'd loved.

The dueling pistols were as beautiful as they were deadly. Their blued barrels and lock plates were finely engraved, the satiny rosewood gun butts inlaid with scrolls of silver wire. Gleaming and cold, they lay in their mahogany box which was set up on the portable table in the meadow by the stream.

Six men clustered around the guns: the duelists; their seconds; an impartial third party, in this case one of the local squires; and a doctor, ready to offer his services. The men's breath pooled in a cloud of vapor, rose white and dense into the frigid morning air. Behind them stood the coachmen and the carriages that had brought the combatants to the appointed place.

"Are you ready," Squire Stratham asked, "or is there some way to resolve this disagreement short of bloodshed?"

With his anger still molten within him, Burke glared across at Randolph. He could never excuse what his cousin had done to Celene, could never back down. Nor did the older man show any sign of remorse. They had been moving toward this confrontation since the day Burke had returned to England, and it would be a relief to have things settled between them once and for all. In a few minute's time the Earl of Hammondsford would be standing alone on the field, a new one or the old one. Only the fates knew which.

"Ready the pistols," Burke said quietly.

Randolph nodded in agreement.

Each of the seconds stepped forward. Bayard Forrester took one of the pistols from the box, sighted down the barrel, and nodded his head. It was the gun that Burke would use in the duel. Phillip took the other pistol from the box and began loading it. Forrester did the same, measuring powder down the barrel and into the pan, inserting the patch and ball, and ramming it home. Burke watched the process for any sign of tampering. A duelist without a properly loaded pistol was as good as dead. Since Forrester was clearly in Randolph's employ, it would be to his advantage to send Burke insufficiently armed into the field.

With this aspect of their duties completed, each second offered his loaded pistol to the appropriate duelist.

"Take your places, then," the squire instructed.

Burke and Randolph strode to the center of the meadow, and stood back to back.

"On the count of ten you will turn and fire," Squire Stratham continued, "and may God have mercy on your souls."

Burke drew in an uneven draft of air. His heart was tripping wildly inside his chest. It was not the first time he had faced his own mortality. In the wilderness he'd had plenty of opportunities to contemplate his end. But in all those times he had never faced it with such regret. There was too much left unfinished in his life for him to stoically accept what might well happen here. But even if he died on this cold, wintry field, he had done what he must to avenge Celene's honor, and his own.

"One," the squire called out, his voice crisp and clear on the morning breeze.

Burke and Randolph each took a step away.

During his long, sleepless night, Burke had made his will. Much of his property was encumbered, part of his title holdings. But the money he'd made trading furs was his to distribute as he wished, and he wanted to make sure Celene and Jean-Paul were provided for.

"Two."

Sophy and Marshall had witnessed his signature on the will before he left the house, so his life was in order where his wealth and his property were concerned.

"Three."

It was that there was so much he'd left unsaid and undone. Though he'd tried to make Celene understand how much he loved her, he was not sure she had believed him. If he died, she would have the money as proof of his concern. If he lived—

"Four."

If he lived, he would follow her to Bristol, try one last time to explain the unexplainable.

He wished he could blame her leaving on what Randolph had done, wished he could believe that killing Randolph would enable Celene to return. But Burke was more honest with himself than that.

"Five."

The fault of it lay with him, and while Randolph's attack the previous afternoon might have hastened her departure, it was not what convinced her to go.

"Six."

He had failed Celene. He had failed himself. Bringing her here had been a terrible mistake. Being here had changed him; he could see that now. If he lived to see the dawn of another day, he would put his house in order.

"Seven."

He only wished that he could make Celene understand, make her realize how encumbered he'd felt by the responsibility and the need to prove himself.

"Eight."

He was free of that now, liberated at last. But Celene was gone. He had made too many mistakes, learned the truth too late to change the inevitable.

"Nine."

With an effort Burke cleared his mind of all regrets. In an instant he would turn and face Randolph. His destiny would be decided by a pistol ball.

"Ten."

Time seemed to slow as Burke wheeled to face his cousin. Two dozen yards away across the frozen earth, Randolph was doing the same. Both men braced their feet, turning sideways to present the narrowest possible target, raising their right arms to sight their guns. They fired simultaneously. Burke saw the orange flare of fire from his cousin's pistol, felt the recoil of his own. The acrid smell of powder singed his nostrils.

The sting of his cousin's ball burned past his left arm. He could feel the searing pain, the warmth of his own blood starting to flow.

At the other end of the field, Randolph was reeling, staggering, sprawling backward onto the ground.

Elation lit inside of Burke. He had bested the man who hurt Celene, defended her honor as his wife.

He stood where he was, watching as Phillip and the doctor ran toward where Randolph had fallen, watching as Bayard Forrester joined them a moment later. There were hurried consultations, muttered curses, shaking heads. Ser-

vants from the carriages came forward bearing a basin and
bandages.

Burke waited, standing alone. As the doctor worked over
his cousin, the blood coursed from Burke's own wound,
darkening his shirt with red, dripping off his fingers, steaming as it fell onto the snow-flecked earth.

At length, Bayard Forrester came toward him across the
field, his face hard and unreadable. Burke could hear the
thud of his footfalls on the frozen ground as he approached.

"He's dead," Forrester said.

"Dead," Burke answered.

"Your shot was true."

Burke nodded, trembling a little with reaction and relief.
He was unprepared for the rush of remorse that washed
through him with the news, the sudden regret that his difficulties with his cousin had ended with one of them lying
dead. Burke had killed men before; he had accepted long
ago that he was capable of taking life. But in the wilderness
it had always been in the heat of a fight, when there had
been no choice, no time to think. There was a calculation
about this morning's confrontation that sickened him.

"He had every intention of killing you," Forrester went
on. "There's no sense condemning yourself on that account. He wanted the title and lands. He would have done
anything to get control of them. Including murder."

Forrester spoke the truth. Burke recognized that, but it
didn't seem to help the clutch at the base of his throat, the
hollowness inside him. At the far end of the field they were
bearing Randolph's body away.

Burke shifted his gaze to the tall man before him, meeting his cold, dark eyes. "And what about you?"

"You have nothing more to fear from me. My employer
has—no further need of my services. And Phillip lacks
the—initiative his father had."

"It was you who shot at me that day in the woods."

"And arranged for the runaway team in New Orleans. I
cut the cinch on your saddle, too. You're a very hard man
to kill, my lord. But it's what I was hired to do. It was
nothing personal."

It was nothing personal, only what Forrester was hired

to do. The man was a mercenary through and through.

"And now, my lord, I'll take my leave. I have another very interesting offer up in Yorkshire to consider." Forrester bowed and turned away, moving toward the carriage he had hired to bring him to the duel.

"Forrester," Burke called after him.

The mercenary paused, breaking stride.

"When Randolph had the choice of weapons, why did he choose pistols instead of short swords?"

It was something Burke needed to know, something he needed to understand. Both men knew why he was asking.

Forrester laughed and kept on walking.

"Why, Forrester?" Burke shouted. "Why?"

The man stopped at the door to the coach and looked back with a smile on his lips.

"Because I told Randolph," the mercenary's words drifted to Burke on the frigid wind, "what a very fine swordsman you are."

20

She'd been right to come home; Celene knew it the moment she saw Pélagie's face. The older woman's countenance was dour at the best of times, but now it was lined with weariness, scored with pain. As they stared at each other through the half-open door, the housekeeper's eyes lit with a quick, unexpected joy that was swiftly doused by tears.

"Is it Papa?" Celene asked, pushing into the hall.

Swallowing hard, Pélagie nodded.

"Is he very bad?"

Celene did not wait for an answer, but tugged off her cape and bonnet and crossed the hall to her father's bed-chamber. With the curtains drawn, it was dark inside. The room smelled stale, of sickness, sweat, and eucalyptus. But neither the depth of Pélagie's misery and concern, nor the pervasive sense of impending death prepared Celene for what she found inside.

By the light of a single candle, she could see that Antoine lay in the very center of the tall tester bed, a thin, emaciated form Celene hardly recognized. As she moved closer, she could see his ghastly pallor, hear the rasp of his labored breathing. His face was skeletal. He looked so old, more like a hundred than his fifty-some-odd years. With tears burning a path up the back of her throat, Celene stepped closer and reached out to stroke his hair. It was wispy and sparse across his pate. His skin was the texture of onion skins.

At her touch, he opened his eyes. The life that had

burned so brightly in their gray-green depths was all but extinguished.

"I am glad you are back, Celene," he said, his voice as brittle as tinderbox char. "I have prayed so hard for your return."

"Oh, Papa, you have never prayed," Celene admonished him, taking his hand.

"I have prayed for your mother's soul, and for Emile's. And I prayed that you would come to be with me at the end."

"Then, Papa, I am glad I'm here."

"A man should have some of his prayers answered," he told her with finality. "God should be willing to grant a man one last favor, no matter how sinful a life he may have lived."

She did not argue, did not lie. She knew as well as he did that he had little time left, and to use it in denials seemed unnecessarily cruel.

"Is Burke with you? Is Jean-Paul?"

Celene had heard her son come into the house some moments before and was glad that Pélagie had headed him off. Celene would need time to prepare him for the change in his grandfather so that the sight of Antoine would neither disturb nor frighten the boy.

"Burke's business in England was more time-consuming and complicated than he expected," Celene lied to spare her father worry, "so he sent Jean-Paul and me ahead. There will soon be planting to do and Burke knew I wanted to be here to make certain it went well."

"He's a rich man now, your Burke. I can't imagine that a few fields here in Ste. Genevieve would concern him so."

The clutch of uncertainty inside her did not change her tone. "It's me those fields concern. They're mine, my property, my livelihood."

When Antoine nodded, accepting her husband's absence, Celene breathed a good deal easier. "You love the land— as your mother did. You're very like her, you know."

Relieved to be able to show a bit of what she was feeling, Celene spoke, regret rife in her tone. "I wish I remembered her more clearly."

"She was lovely, as are you. She would be very proud of the woman you've become."

The press of grief against her breastbone nearly cut off her air. "I'm glad you think she would."

"I will tell her how well you turned out," he assured her, "when I see her next. But I must rest. There is more I want to say to you, and I seem to tire so easily."

Celene squeezed her father's hand and moved from the bed to the door, closing it softly behind her. She stood silently in the narrow hall, letting the tears that had been threatening overtake her. She wept freely, but without making a sound, the ache in her breast all but unbearable. She cursed herself for going away with Burke when her father was in such desperate need of her, wished with all her heart that there was something she could do to change what was clearly inevitable. Regret and futility lay heavy on her, bowing her shoulders, making it hard to get her breath.

But there was no sense repenting things she could not alter, could not rectify. She was here now, and she would see to her father's comfort, see that he was buried properly with people who loved him to mourn his passing. There were things to do, comfort to give, people who needed her strength and compassion. Mopping her cheeks with the corner of her handkerchief, she headed toward the kitchen to explain her father's illness to her son and to see how she could lighten the burden Pélagie had been carrying alone.

It was late afternoon when Antoine next awoke. Celene was sitting by the bed, a bit of mending in her lap.

"Light another candle, Celene," her father scolded her. "You'll ruin your eyes stitching in such dim light."

Celene smiled a little at his tone. "I didn't want to disturb you."

"There is very little that can disturb me now."

She moved to light the cluster of candles on the table beside the bed. "There's some medicine here for you to take."

Antoine shook his head. "That vile stuff; something Pélagie boiled up to plague me."

"She says it helps the pain."

"It dulls my mind as well, and I would spend the rest of my time upon this earth without such addled wits."

"There is broth in the kitchen if you like," she offered.

"I would take a sip of water if it does not trouble you to get it."

Her father's unaccustomed meekness brought a knot to her throat, and she turned away, pouring water from the pitcher on the table into a cup. She raised him and helped him drink.

Antoine grimaced as she laid him back. "Perhaps God sends us illness and pain so that we do not mind leaving this life behind when it is time to go."

"I don't know why God sends illness and pain, or grief and unhappiness. But He seems to send us pleasure and joy to lighten the burdens He asks us to bear."

Was that true, Celene wondered as she resumed her seat, or merely words she'd conjured up to comfort a dying man?

"I do not regret the life I've lived," Antoine went on around another rasping breath, "only those I've lost and those I leave behind. I've had more blessings than many men, excitement, adventures, friendship . . ."

A vision from the rendezvous flashed across her memory as he spoke: of her father dancing around the fire with the other voyageurs. She could see the flare of vitality in his eyes, hear his uninhibited bursts of laughter, feel the admiration and camaraderie flowing from the men around him. She saw him then as she had never been able to see him before, without the veil of her conflicting emotions to cloud her sight. And Celene knew suddenly that the way he had been at the rendezvous was how she wanted to remember him, wild and free and full of life.

"I've had two good women to love me," he continued. "Three strong children, and a grandson who bears my blood. Your other children will carry my seed as well, carry it beyond the turn of the century."

His words made Celene think, for the first time since they'd arrived, of the thing she had begun to suspect in these last days. She was carrying Burke's child, and in spite of the way she and her husband had parted, she was glad. Their child was a tie with Burke that could never be broken, a part of him she would always have. He had chosen his life, and she had chosen hers. Through the child she carried inside her, she would always have a bit of Burke's love, a bit of his laughter, a bit of his tenderness to claim as her own.

Bending close, she whispered her secret to her father. It was her promise to the future, her promise of life to the old man who lay dying. She saw his eyes light with pleasure, felt the press of his wrinkled hand. With his touch, it was as if a spark had been passed from him to her, and on to the child that was growing inside her. It was life, endless and sweet, moving through generations; love, fragile and warm, spanning the breadth of time.

They sat in silence with their fingers linked on the coverlet, hers strong and hard and competent, his knotted, gnarled and cold. It was the symbol of a bond they had never been able to make in life. It seemed to pass for all the conversations they'd never had, all the feelings they had never been able to express. But time was passing, Celene well knew, and Antoine's strength was waning.

"Jean-Paul has been eager to see you since we arrived. May I bring him in to speak to you?"

"Will it frighten him to see me like this, so different from how he remembers me?"

"I have told him you are very ill. I think he understands the sickness has made a change in you."

Antoine nodded and fought valiantly to prop himself up in bed. Celene helped him, adjusting the bolster at his back and straightening his hair. With her heart fluttering in her throat, she went to the door and called her son.

Jean-Paul entered the room on tiptoes, his usual rush through life sternly subdued. He came to stand by Antoine's bed and looked into his grandfather's face. Celene held her breath, wondering what her son saw when he looked at his grandfather.

"You've let your whiskers grow," he said solemnly.

Celene pressed her hand to her mouth to hide a smile, tears burning like acid in her eyes. Pélagie, who had been standing in the door behind her, rustled swiftly away.

"I thought a man of my advancing years would look

better with a beard,'' Antoine answered.

"Will it scratch when I kiss you?'' Jean-Paul asked.

"Why don't you come up and try it?''

Jean-Paul did as he was bid, clambering carefully over the covers to press his cheek to his grandfather's face. "It's not so very itchy,'' he reported, hugging the old man fiercely, then sliding down.

"But you have returned from England so suddenly,'' Antoine said with regret in his tone, "and I had intended to have a gift to give you to mark your return.''

"It's all right,'' the child replied. "I'm glad to be home. I didn't like England, anyway.''

But Antoine was not to be put off. "Celene,'' he ordered imperiously, sounding remarkably like himself, "get my harmonica from the box on the top of the chest. I'll give that to Jean-Paul instead of some other present I might have bought for him.''

Celene moved to obey. She took down the battered, silvery instrument, her father's most prized possession, and gave it to Antoine. He held it in his hand for one long, bittersweet moment as if remembering better days. Then he gave it to his grandson.

Jean-Paul blew on the harmonica, two sharp, discordant notes. "Will you teach me to play when you are well?''

"Someone will teach you, I am sure.''

"Can I play it in when we walk in the woods, like you used to? Can I play it on the porch at night? And when I've learned some tunes, will you and *Maman* dance for me?''

"I am sure your mother can find a more suitable partner than this old man.''

"Tell your *grandpère* thank you,'' Celene admonished her son. "And then it is time for you to go.''

"*Merci, Grandpère*. I like the harmonica very much.''

Jean-Paul left the room, and Celene stepped outside to hug her son. "You are a good boy, Jean-Paul,'' she said, lifting him in her arms, "and I love you very much.''

Jean-Paul hugged her back and blew a note from the harmonica in her ear. She chuckled and settled him on the floor again, ruffling his hair as he raced past her toward the kitchen, waving the gift his grandfather had given him and calling Pélagie's name.

Antoine must have heard the exchange through the open bedroom door, for when Celene returned to her chair beside the bed, he was smiling his approval.

Celene awoke with a start, stiff and vaguely disoriented. Blinking in the light, she rose from her chair and glanced around. Antoine was sleeping peacefully, just as he had been since midnight when Father Hilaire had come to offer absolution and administer last rites. The only sound that disturbed the quiet was the rhythmic ruffle of Pélagie's snoring.

Sparing a glance for the older woman who sat crumpled in a chair at the opposite side of the bed, Celene paced to the window and peered out into the misty night. As she did, inexplicable prickles rose across her skin, and she clasped her hands around her arms to rub away the chill.

Restless, strangely on edge, she looked back to where father lay. He was neither better nor worse, and she crept out of the room and down the hall. The house was steeped in stillness, muffled in fog. These soft, silent hours should be a time of grieving and acceptance, she told herself, a time of reflection and peace. Instead some instinct was astir in her. Taking refuge in mundane tasks, she added logs to the fire, dippered water from the keg, put the kettle on to boil. She climbed the ladder to the loft to check on her son and looked in on her father again.

Even after she'd made a circuit of the house, the anticipation remained, nestled tight and hot beneath her ribs. Thinking a breath of air might help, Celene took her cloak from the peg in the hall and let herself out the kitchen door. The feeling grew stronger as stepped onto the porch, as if the walls of the house had protected her from whatever was stirring in the night.

Alone in the dark, she could feel the pull of some mysterious magnetism. It drew her down the steps, across the yard and into the lane behind the house. The air was damp and chill against her skin; the buildings and the fences around her seemed spectral and indistinct. Barely able to see a yard ahead in the dimness and the fog, she entered *le Grand Champ* and began to cross the expanse of crusty, crumbled earth. Guided by some unseen hand, she stumbled forward, her footsteps faltering on the uneven ground. Her heavy breathing was the only sound in the stillness, the knot inside her jerking tighter with every step.

Then a figure rose up before her, looming out of the mist. It was a man, tall and lean with a fan of feathers in his hair.

"Darkening Sky!" she gasped, recognition muffling the cry that had been rising in her throat. "Darkening Sky."

She reached to clutch his outstretched hand. It was broad and hard, warm and reassuring. Comfort flowed from him to her, mystical, healing power that only he seemed able to give.

"I knew you'd come," he whispered, tightening his fingers around her palm. "I knew you'd understand."

She was desperately glad to see him. "Papa's dying . . ."

"Yes, I know. That is why I came."

She had learned not to question how he knew the things he did. Darkening Sky's prescience was part of who he was.

"Then quickly, come back to the house. Father was sleeping when I left, but I know he'd want to see you."

Her half brother shook his head. "There is no need. Our spirits have touched. Our father knows that I am here."

"But surely there are thing to settle between you."

"Nothing will change what has been between us, nothing can be altered in his last hours on earth."

She stared at him, a kind of comprehension settling in. "You love him, don't you?"

"All the days of my life. But I have always understood that our father can be no different than the man he is. I have learned to forgive his mistakes and accept his weaknesses."

"I love him, too," she admitted softly. But her own acceptance of Antoine had come far more recently than Darkening Sky's and with terrible, heart-wrenching difficulty. It had come bit by bit, on the day she'd married Burke, on the day they'd left for England, and as her father lay dying.

The things she'd finally begun to understand about Antoine had come too late to make to make a difference in the way she and her father had lived their lives. But they had come. Thank God they had come.

"I came out of respect for the man who gave me life," Darkening Sky continued, "and because I knew you needed me."

Celene swallowed hard and looked away. "I'll get through this as I have through all the rest."

She could feel his gaze upon her, hear the compassion in his voice. "Alone, you mean. You'll get through this alone, with your silence and your strength."

"I've had no choice but to stand alone."

"You do it because you have had to, not because you know you can."

It seemed a fine distinction; but one she understood. Relying only on herself, she had faced losing her mother and Emile, faced her nightmare marriage to Henri and more recently her estrangement from Burke. In each circumstance she had drawn on reserves of pride and determination to see her through. Yet she had always feared she would fail, always wondered if her persistence would be enough. And again she was afraid.

"Don't you know you have nothing to fear?"

It was as if he'd read her mind, as if he knew her far better than she knew herself. Tears burned in her eyes. They were tears not of grief, but of frustration and self-doubt.

"Then why am I afraid?" she asked in a whisper.

"What are you afraid of?"

"I—I'm afraid I won't be strong enough to stand alone. I'm afraid I won't be able to do what I must. I'm afraid happiness will always elude me."

"You will find what you seek when you have conquered your own doubt." His words had the ring of prophecy.

Even through the dimness she could see his eyes had gone flat, unfocused, as if he were seeing far beyond this moment, far beyond her. His head was cocked slightly to one side as if he were listening to voices she could not hear.

"You will learn the future," he continued, "when you

escape the past. You will find happiness when you are a woman complete, not a daughter, not a widow, not a wife.''

His words were like a riddle she did not know how to solve. Her hand clamped tight around his arm. ''Darkening Sky. Please, Darkening Sky, tell me what you mean.''

He blinked once and she could see the mystical link was broken. The moments of prophecy were gone.

''This is something you must learn for yourself, I think. But it is time for you to go. Our father will soon have need of you.''

Celene took a shaky breath. ''Please come back to the house. Please stay with me.''

Slowly, sadly, he shook his head. ''I will always be with you in my spirit, Celene, but I will never return to this place. Men like our father come farther west with every passing year. As they come they destroy the lives of the Chippewa, the Shawnee, the Osage, all the many bands. One day all this wilderness will be gone, the trees cut for homes, the animals killed for food, the ground broken for many farms. It will be the end of the life my people know. Though I doubt we will succeed, I must join with others who see the danger. I must try to prevent my people from being destroyed.''

Darkening Sky's fingers closed tight around her hand. ''Doing what I must will take me far from this place, far from you. That is my only regret.''

She raised her opposite hand to cover his. She would regret his leaving, too. He allowed her a single moment of comfort, then broke the bond.

''Now hurry, *ma soeur*. Soon you will be needed back at the house.''

When she hesitated, he pushed her in the direction he wanted her to go. ''Hurry!'' he whispered. ''Hurry!''

Celene did as she was bid, moving away. When she paused to look back, Darkening Sky was gone, and there was nothing but heavy, drifting fog to mark where he had stood.

When she reached the house, it was as if she had never left. The kettle was bubbling over the kitchen fire, and Pélagie was asleep in her chair. Only Antoine's condition had changed. His breathing was so shallow that it barely moved the wall of his chest. His skin was faintly tinged with gray. She resumed her seat beside the bed and took his hand. His eyelids fluttered, and he seemed to smile, as if he knew that she was there.

She sat still and silent beside her father. She watched him for what seemed like a very long time, remembering the good times, forgiving the bad. She stayed with him as his life slipped quietly away. She stayed with him until the essence of the man she had lately learned to love was gone.

And from out where the night was turning to dawn, she could hear an Indian keening.

The church bell clanged loud and long. Celene sat bundled in her cloak at the top of the steps, listening to the slow, resonant peals that announced her father's passing. A man's death was always signaled by a longer ringing of the bell, as if the lives men lived required more prayers to be raised to heaven in their behalf, as if their sins were far more important than a woman's were.

But her father did not repent his life, the people he'd known, the places he'd been, the things he'd done. He had lived it on his own terms, just as Celene herself had chosen to do. She only hoped that when she left this world, she could have as few regrets.

The door opened behind her, and Jean-Paul came to sit beside her at the edge of the porch.

"Is the bell ringing for *Grandpère*?" he asked, his brow puckered and his eyes suspiciously bright.

Celene curled an arm around her son and gathered him into her warmth. "*Oui, mon cher*, it is. Your *grandpère* has gone to heaven now."

"Are they ringing the bell so God will know?"

Celene blinked back the sudden sting of tears. She wasn't sure how to explain death to a child, didn't know how to spare him the grief of losing one of the most important people in his world.

"Your *grandpère* had gone to live with *Grandmère* and with God. Although we will miss him very much, we must be happy that is where he's gone."

The child beside her nodded as if he understood at least a bit of what she was telling him.

"I wanted him to take me fishing," Jean-Paul said around a sniff. "I wanted him to teach me to play the harmonica."

"You will learn," she assured him. "And every time I hear you play a tune, a bit of *Grandpère* will live again."

Jean-Paul screwed up his face. "What do you mean?"

She snuggled closer to her son and nuzzled his thick, dark hair. "It means that every time you play a tune your *grandpère* knew, I will think of him. That he will live in my memory, and in yours, for years to come. It means that because *Grandpère* is my father a bit of him was passed to me. With your father's help, a bit of *Grandpère* came to you. In turn, you will pass on a bit of him to your children through your wife, and on and on for endless generations."

Celene found unexpected comfort in knowing she was part of that unending chain: father and daughter, mother and son. It made life seem less futile, less solitary, less fleeting.

Her thoughts drifted to the unborn child she carried beneath her heart. That child renewed the link between her father and her, but it was also a bond of another sort. Through this child, she would have Burke with her always, a part of the past they'd shared, a promise to the future yet to come. Knowing that gave her purpose, gave her strength.

She sat with Jean-Paul for a few minutes more, talking softly, stroking his hair. But there were things to do, preparations for Antoine's burial to be made. It was the last act of respect she could offer the man who had given her life, and she meant to carry it out with tenderness and love.

The funeral cortege left the house at midafternoon. With the processional cross held high, Father Hilaire led the mourners up *la Grand Rue* toward the church. Celene, Jean-Paul and Pélagie walked behind the bier, borne by six of her father's closest friends. As they moved up the street, people from Ste. Genevieve and Kaskaskia fell in behind. Superstition held that to pause for even a moment before any house would precipitate a death before the end of the year, so the growing throng moved sedately but steadily northward.

Celene was surprised by the number and diversity of people who had come to pay their respects. There were traders and merchants, soldiers and laborers, whole families from settlements along the river. Even a few Osage Indians put in an appearance, braves Antoine had hunted with and traded with over the years. It surprised her and comforted her to see how well-liked her father had been.

The requiem mass was long and solemn, the droning of Father Hilaire's words a backdrop for Celene's own memories. She recalled how her father had carried her high on his shoulders when she was a child so she could see over the heads of the crowds that gathered in Kaskaskia on market days. There had always been something wonderful in his packs for her when he returned from a rendezvous, a doeskin vest thick with embroidery and beads; a delicate carving of a bird; a necklace of trade silver in the shape of a turtle. She remembered summer nights when she'd lain in her bed, listening to the soft, sweet music of his harmonica stealing through the air. They were warm memories, things she could treasure all her life, things she wanted to remember her father by.

When the mass was over, the mourners filed into the plot of land beside the church where a grave had been hacked open in the raw, hard earth. "*Et cum Lazaro quondam paupere aeternam habeas requiem,*" Father Hilaire intoned, sprinkling holy water over the lid of the coffin. As Celene feathered a handful of the cold, rich soil of the Mississippi Valley into the open grave, she realized that though it had been difficult to put aside her anger at her father, she was glad she had. She was sending Antoine to his final rest knowing both of them were at peace.

Others of the party paused to offer their condolences before going silently on their way, until only Celene, Jean-Paul and Pélagie stood together beneath the dense, gray sky. There would be a gathering back at the house, but Celene was not yet ready to face her neighbors' reminiscences.

"Please," she asked Pélagie, "take Jean-Paul home. I will be along directly."

The housekeeper nodded and turned away.

Celene waited until the men who had stayed to fill the grave and plant the stout wooden cross at the head of it had finished their work. When they paused to express their regrets, she pressed coins into their hands and thanked them for their service. As they gathered up their tools and went away, Celene stood alone, her eyes misting as she looked at the freshly mounded earth.

There were no blossoms of pink or white to strew on the grave so early in the spring. Instead she took a red ribbon from deep within one of her pockets and looped it around the base of the cross. It was one of the ribbons Burke had given her at the rendezvous. It seemed right that he should be here in this small way to mourn the passing of a friend.

"Goodbye, Papa," Celene whispered as she stood small and straight beside the grave. "Tell *Maman* I love her, too."

Though it had been a long, difficult time since Antoine had offered her his shelter, his guidance, or his protection, Celene felt as if it was only now that the last remnants of her girlhood were slipping away. She was no longer her father's daughter, no longer a child. Through the years she had fought and struggled to make her own way in the world, but until now she had never sensed her own independence as a woman grown. With Antoine's passing, she knew she was all of that and more. She was not a daughter not a widow not a wife. She was Celene Peugeot, herself, alone.

Life stretched ahead, an untraveled road, full of twists and turns, hills and valleys. For the first time she felt strong enough to face its challenges, solitary, unbowed, and unafraid. Tempered by the past, eager for what was to come, Celene belonged to herself at last. And in a way he would never have understood, Antoine Peugeot had given her all of that.

21

It was the kind of stark spring day when the blues and greens and browns of earth and sky were especially vivid, when the air was sharp and crystalline as heady wine, when the delineation between sun and shadow cast the landscape in deep relief. The cloudless sky seemed to resonate with a force of its own, and sunlight spiked off the river's shifting surface, winking in starbursts of silver and gold.

The wind was cool and soft with the promise of good planting weather to come as Celene Peugeot Bernard Hammond-Cardwell stepped out onto the porch. She was headed across the channel to Kaskaskia to sign the papers that would transfer her father's land and holdings to her. It would make her truly independent, truly the mistress of her fate, and she was filled with plans.

Soon she would sow her three arpents of land in *le Grand Champ*. Then, in partnership with Monsieur LaVallier, she would use the funds from her *douaire préfix* to buy a mill site on *La Petite Rivière*. As the spring and summer advanced, there would be the construction of the mill to oversee in the hope that it would be ready to turn Ste. Genevieve's grain into flour at harvest time. It would be a busy few months, but Celene was sure of herself and eager to face the challenges that lay ahead.

But as she came to the top of the steps, she noticed a single, heavily loaded canoe fighting its way upriver. It was a bit too early in the season for traders to be headed north, nor was this one of the large bateaux that came from New Orleans with supplies. She paused to watch the boat's progress as it veered closer to the western bank, its occupants paddling furiously against the current. Their business must be pressing indeed, she thought, for traders to venture this far upstream before the river's heavy springtime flow had completely subsided. But as the two men pulled toward the town, she recognized one of them.

No apparition from beyond the grave could have shocked her more. Celene went weightless, trembly, short of breath. Hope soared through her insides. Then confusion and anger wiped it away. The tall man in the stern of the canoe was her husband, the Eighth Earl of Hammondsford.

What possible reason could Burke have for coming to Ste. Genevieve? His life, he'd told her, was in England. Her life and her lands were here. They had said their good-byes at Longmeadow months ago.

Things had changed since that morning in Bristol when she'd clung to the wooden charm and prayed that Burke would come to her. The months had changed her, tempered her, enlightened her. Celene was no longer Antoine's daughter, no longer Cardwell's wife. She was a woman on her own, a woman who had discovered new determination and strength within herself. She would stand her ground no matter why he'd come, no matter what he wanted. Still, at the thought of seeing him again, of talking to him, of being within the potent lure of his presence, powerful emotions swirled through her.

She waited silently at the top of the steps while the two men beached the canoe, while Burke gathered up his gear and climbed the slight rise to the street. He strode in the direction of the house, his movements measured, determined. It was seeing her waiting on the porch that stopped him in his tracks. For an instant, he simply stared across the fence at her.

His face was burned ruddy by the sun, his features sharper, more tightly drawn than she'd remembered. He was dressed in a buckskin waistcoat and brown woolen trousers that were tucked into the tops of knee-high moccasins. His honey-colored hair hung thick and long, dark as molasses against the pale tan leather of his thigh-length vest. She resisted the urge to meet his gaze, knowing that the light in those turquoise eyes had been her undoing more than once.

When he finally raised his hand to lift the latch, she broke the silence hovering between them. "Don't expect me to go back to England," she warned. "My life is here. I won't leave it for you or anyone."

He stopped, frowned. "Damn it, Celene. I don't know who is more inhospitable, you or Jean-Paul. At least he let me in the gate before he tried to throw me out."

He suited his actions to his words, coming in the gate and stopping at the bottom of the steps. Instead of the square-shouldered arrogance she'd expected in his stance, there was the sag of bone-deep weariness, a hint of odd uncertainty. Something twisted tight beneath her ribs.

"You're even more lovely than I remembered," he said, lowering his musket and pack to the ground.

She knotted her arms across her chest. "Is that what you came all this distance to say?"

"And if it was?" A smile tugged at one corner of his lips.

"I wouldn't believe your blandishments."

Burke's smile faded, and he nodded his head. "How is Jean-Paul?" he wanted to know.

"He is fine. He's in school just now. I've enrolled him in classes with a priest who decided to winter here before pressing farther west."

"And Antoine?"

"My father is dead. The illness took him some weeks ago."

"I'm sorry," Burke offered, his voice thick with grief and sincerity. "Your father was a good man and a faithful friend. I just wish I had been here to say goodbye, to help and comfort you at what must have been a difficult time."

"The need for comfort isn't something that goes away," she answered softly, half to herself.

His head came up sharply at her words, and though she had spoken the truth, she wished she could bite back the sentiment, the undeniable wistfulness in her tone. Though she and Antoine had resolved their differences at the end of his life, the truce had come too late for either of them to truly enjoy the peace they had finally found. With that knowledge heavy inside her, it would have been wonderful to accept the comfort Burke could give.

"And Pélagie?"

They were running out of neutral topics. Unless he meant to ask about the weather, the crops to be planted, and the health of the rest of the town, she would soon learn his reason for coming here.

"Pélagie is fine."

"Good," he said. "Good." He pursed his lips, looked down at his hands. "Aren't you going to invite me into the house?"

"No, I'm not."

To see him sitting at the table in the kitchen drinking tea and eating tarts, to hear his voice ripple through the house again, to have his presence fill the empty rooms would reinforce the memories she'd been trying so hard to erase.

"Oh," he said in answer. "Yes, I see."

"Really, Burke," she prodded him, " why don't you just tell me why you've come. If it isn't to take me back to England, what has brought you all this way?"

He settled back on his heels, took a long, slow breath. "I've come to apologize."

"Apologize?" Hope lifted inside her like a kite in the wind. Hastily she reeled it in. "Whatever for?"

"You were right."

"Was I? About what?"

"You were right about England. You were right about me."

Her heart snagged somewhere north of her breastbone, beating so hard it seemed ready to leap up her throat.

"And you were right about leaving when you did."

She bit down hard on her lower lip, determined to let him have his say. If Burke had really come to apologize, she meant to hear him out.

"Sophy told me after you'd gone what Randolph tried to do." When Celene said nothing, Burke went on. "I don't know why you didn't come to me, why you didn't feel you could tell me he was bothering you."

"Randolph isn't why I left."

"But he was part of it, wasn't he?" The hopefulness in his tone was hard to ignore.

Celene wearily nodded her head. "I suppose. But there were other reasons that were far more important. It was the way the children were treating Jean-Paul. It was not being able to visit a priest. It was the wasted days and the decadence. It was the viciousness and the hopelessness."

"And it was me."

"Yes. And me." She had felt like a lump of coal in a strand of pearls. But what was worse, what had damned her completely where life in England was concerned was that she hadn't aspired to more than that.

"I knew where I belonged," she told him simply, "and I came home."

Pain came fresh and hot in her chest once more. Futile tears seared beneath her downcast lashes. Why had he come halfway across the world, to stir up things that should have been settled long ago? Why was he ripping open wounds that had only begun to heal?

She wanted to tell him to go away. She wanted to tell him never to leave. She wanted to touch him and hold him just once more. She wanted to push him away. She wanted a life with him on her own terms. And in the end, how fair was that?

"When we went to England," Burke said, "I knew full well what you would face. I knew exactly how intolerant my family would be, how impossible it was going to be for you to gain acceptance there. That was what I was counting on when I asked for your hand at the rendezvous. I wanted a completely unsuitable wife to flaunt in my family's very proper English faces. I wanted to use you to show them how little their money and position meant to me. I'm not proud of what I originally intended to do. But in truth, I meant to make it worth your while."

Celene felt a little breathless at Burke's confession. She had always wondered what prompted him to ask for her hand, but she would gladly have gone the rest of her life without knowing all of this.

When Celene said nothing, Burke continued. "When Forrester came, when I saw I had no choice about going back, I knew full well how difficult it was going to be for you and Jean-Paul. I didn't tell you because by then I needed you, because I couldn't bear to leave you behind. But in taking you with me I was asking things of you I had no right to ask, expecting concessions from you I had no right to expect. I loved you, and I hoped we'd find a way to make things work. I should have known they never would; I should have spared us both.''

His lips compressed a little before he went on, ''And what is worse, while we were at Longmeadow, I lost myself. I thought I had things to prove that didn't matter in the end. I felt I had things to find out that weren't all that important. When I saw how unhappy you were, I felt guilty and drew away instead of trying to make things better. I let the work and the drinking fill the time I should have spent with you. I'm not proud of how I behaved, and I've come to say I'm sorry. I'm sorry for the lies, sorry for the way I treated you. I'm sorry I didn't spare you all of it. I should have left you here when I had to go back, but somehow I couldn't do that.''

Celene swallowed hard, wondering what she should say. She knew how difficult these admissions must be for him, what it must have cost to face himself and acknowledge all of this. Coming here and admitting the truth took a kind of courage she wasn't sure she had. But Burke had done it, boldly, unflinchingly. Was it forgiveness he was after or something else?

''Things have changed at Longmeadow since you've been gone,'' he went on. ''I've sent all the relatives away: Elizabeth and her viscount to stay with his father the marquis, Susannah and Lord Chillingham back to his estate in Northumberland. Vicar Trowbridge and Sarah were packing for Ireland when I left; somehow the bishop heard about his evangelistic zeal and means to make the most of it. Phillip, Felicity, and the children are gone for an extended visit to her parents' home. Cecily and Margaret have moved into the townhouse in London, under Sophy's watchful eye—''

''What about Randolph?''

Burke paused before he answered her, his eyes gone

hard. "I killed Randolph in a duel. I avenged your honor and my own."

A duel? Oh, God, a duel! Burke might have been killed because of her. Her knees went wobbly at the thought of it. How could she have lived with herself if Burke had died in such a useless, senseless way?

"That's why I never told you," she admitted. "I didn't want you killed, especially on my account."

"I understand that now. But everyone in the house knew what Randolph was doing—except for me."

It was a small rebuke, but one Celene felt all the way down to her bones.

"Well," she said around a long-drawn breath. "None of that matters. I won't go back."

Burke straightened slightly; his chin came up. "I don't recall I've asked you to."

Her stomach dropped toward her shoes and confusion swarmed in her head. She'd been stoking righteous anger, steeling herself to send him away. She was strong enough to do that now. She had her land, her plans for the future, and her independence. Yet because he didn't want her, she felt like curling up at the top of the steps and sobbing like a disappointed child.

"You don't want me to go back to England?" she asked a bit unsteadily.

"I've put the money and the property into Aunt Sophy's control. I imagine overseeing that will keep her alive another twenty years. And I've come to Ste. Genevieve to stay—if you still want me here."

It was as unencumbered a declaration as a man could make. It wasn't trussed up with love words or smothered in promises. It was her choice, simple and plain.

For an instant pure, intemperate joy singed through every cell. Burke wanted to be a part of her life again. It was what she'd hoped for, prayed for, wanted more than anything.

Then why was she afraid?

"I didn't think I could do it," he went on, "but I walked away. I realized I didn't need to prove myself to anyone. I didn't care about the earldom, the power, and the riches.

What I care about is you. What I care about is the two of us having a life together.''

She wanted to throw her arms around him and take him back. She wanted to tell him about the baby and her plans. But could she believe him, trust him with her love a second time? If she let him into her life, would he be happy? Would he stay?

She knew men's perfidy, their trickery, their need to dominate and control. She'd had experiences enough to destroy her faith where men were concerned. But Burke was not her father, she argued with herself. He had rescued her from Rivard and Arnaud, saved Jean-Paul from the river, taught her the joys of being a woman, and given her a child. He was not Henri. Burke had offered her help and support and respect. He had been patient and kind, unfailingly gentle.

She sucked a draft of air into her lungs and fought to put the past behind her. Burke was his own man with his own faults and weaknesses, his own power and strength. He had made mistakes, but so had she. He had grown and changed, and she had, too.

. God knows, there were reasons enough to take him back. He had proved his worth a dozen times over. He had proved his devotion by coming here. But the strongest reason for taking him back was that she cared for him beyond all men. It was the easiest argument to refute, the hardest truth to accept.

"I love you, Celene," he said so softly that his words were nearly lost in the rush of the wind. "I wouldn't be here if I wasn't sure."

She knew she loved him, too. She loved his tenderness, his compassion, his ability to understand her when no one else could. She was finally strong enough to reach out to him as an equal. He was strong enough now to accept her as one. Knowing that did not eradicate the fear, but it made reconciliation possible.

She smiled in welcome and offered her hand.

He was up the steps in two quick bounds, standing over her with adoration bright as flame in those clear, compelling eyes. He trailed rough, cool fingers over her face and lowered his head to claim her mouth. The kiss was ravenous and gentle, desperate and soft. She curled her arms around his neck and unrestrainedly kissed him back.

At length he raised his head. "Are you sure this is what you want? I won't give you another chance to change your mind."

She nodded once and touched his cheek. "Yes," was all she said in answer.

Sweeping her up in his arms, he kicked open the wooden door. The sound of it banging back on its hinges brought Pélagie rushing out of the kitchen. She jerked to a halt halfway down the hall.

"Burke has come home to stay!" Celene announced.

" 'Bout time," the housekeeper huffed and brushed past them to close the gaping door.

Without another word Celene and Burke scrambled up the ladder to the loft. They each knew what they wanted, what they needed to seal the bond between them, to make their reunion vital and real.

Standing on the landing at the top, they kissed, loneliness mingling with longing, desperation with desire. He dwelled over her mouth as if he could hardly believe she was here beside him now, as if every taste of her, every brush of her lips was something to be savored, something he'd never thought to experience again. His fingers curled into the folds of her clothes, clutching her to him, clinging as if he never meant let her go.

"Oh, God, Celene," he whispered, pressing his face into the curve of her throat. "I was so afraid, so afraid you wouldn't take me back, so afraid I'd never have a chance to make things right."

The raw misery in his voice, the ferocity of his grip told her as words could not that he, too, had felt the agony of loss, that he had ached with desolation and regret.

"I know," she whispered, holding him as hard as he was holding her.

"I love you, Celene. I love you."

"I know." Her eyes burned and blurred with tears. Her throat was so tight she could hardly breathe.

"And you must say you love me, too," he instructed her.

His need for reassurance tore at her. For as much as she'd been disillusioned and hurt, he had felt the pain of parting as deeply as she. How could she have doubted it?

"Yes, I love you, Burke. Oh, yes, I do."

Moving blindly, she turned her head and sought his mouth. She kissed him with all the passion she'd repressed, with all the joy and wonder beating through her veins. She relished the texture of his lips, the lingering tang of tobacco, the sinuous slide of his tongue. She clung to him more tightly than before, raking her fingers through his hair, curling her hands around his nape. She held him—simply held him—as tears of elation and relief and welcome ran down her face.

With a murmur of distress, he half dragged, half carried her the few scant feet to the edge of their bed. He tumbled her onto the blankets and took up his place beside her. Cursing softly he fished in his pockets for a handkerchief, and finally sopped up her tears with the pads of his thumbs.

"I didn't mean to make you cry. I've never wanted to make you cry. I won't ever make you cry again."

It felt so good to have his broad, rugged body sheltering her; his strong, rough-skinned hands moving soft as down against her skin. She laughed softly and touched his face. "Oh, doubtless you will. You're not perfect, and neither am I. Besides, women cry for hundreds of reasons, and tears are not a bad thing when there's someone to hold you and wipe them away."

Urging him closer, she offered him her mouth again, parting her lips to welcome him, to draw him in. He came ravenous and eager, holding her, caressing her, pressing hot, soulful kisses into her mouth. The taste of tears and passion mingled thick and sweet upon her tongue. She had never expected this to happen, never imagined they would have another chance, never dreamed they would share this magic again.

Even through the layers of their clothes, she could feel the press of his maleness against her legs. It made the want-ing rise in her, a need for union sharp and keen. She shuddered with eagerness and raised her hands to push aside the panels of his vest. As she did, Burke began to undress her, too. Soon their clothes were cast on the floor: Celene's bodice, skirt, and petticoats, Burke's jerkin and shirt, and moccasins.

"It's cold up here," Celene whispered as he stripped off her chemise.

"Then get under the covers and I'll do everything I can to make you warm," he promised her.

The sheets were chill against her back, but when he joined her between them a moment later, the feel of his skin against her flesh kindled more than adequate heat inside of her. It invaded every cell, melted her bones, left her languid and trembling. Whispering endearments, he gathered her in, stroking her body as if to reacquaint himself with every curve, kissing her with a delicious thoroughness that left her weak. He ravished her with the tenderness of his touch, spilling shudders down her body with the stroke of his hand, swirling anticipation through her belly with the graze of his thumbs. She flowed against him as his kisses deepened, as his caresses became ever more compelling, ever more intimate.

Celene sought the same with him, skimming her fingers over his flesh, the breadth of his shoulders, the length of his back. Her nails raked up his buttocks, around the curve of his hip. She heard his breath snag in his throat as she dipped down across the rough, soft hair to the shaft between his thighs. He reached across to touch her, too. Lying barely a handspan apart, they stared into each other's eyes, pleasuring and pleasured, wanting and wanted, loving and loved. Together they watched the hunger grow, felt the desire swell, shared joy and commitment so wondrous that they could scarcely take it in.

She breathed his name, awash in him, in them, in what they'd found together. She ached for the ultimate sharing of body and life, of soul and consciousness. They needed this joining, the solace and the welcoming, the passion and the forgetfulness, the sweetness and elation.

Burke seemed to understand that, too. As he rolled above her, pinned her gently with his weight, delight ruffled through her in scintillating waves.

"Be gentle," she warned him, her mind so fuzzy with desire she'd only now remembered the reason for caution.

"I'm always gentle with you, sweet girl," he murmured, stroking into her, pressing deep.

Sensation flared inside her. "If not for me, then for our child. . . ."

She needn't have worried; his entry was so gentle and tender it took her breath. She shivered with the wonder of having him part of her again, reveled in the unutterable sweetness of the intimacy. Tingles raked her. Her heart beat fast. The forces in her body were already gathering, focusing.

Above her Burke went utterly still, his body buried deep within her flesh. "Child?" he panted. "Child?"

His words came to her from far away. Her eyelids fluttered, and she raised her hips, offering and wanting something more.

"Celene!" His voice was harsh, his breathing as thick and unsteady as hers. "Tell me."

Her head went light as dizziness swamped her. Delight beckoned stronger than before. "In the fall," she whispered. "Our baby is coming in the fall."

Confusion drew his brows together. "How did that . . ."

She chuckled, breathless and soft. "Oh, Burke, I think you know."

He buried his face in the fall of her hair. "A baby, Celene? A child of our own?"

She nodded, trembling, her thoughts more on the beginning of the process than the end.

"Oh, God, Celene! I love you. I love you so . . ."

Then the need for words, the ability to form coherent thoughts moved beyond them as the magic their bodies wove together deepened, carrying them away. The slide of heat into heat spawned pleasure beyond all imaginings.

Rippling with awareness, ripe and full and blossoming, Celene sought Burke's gaze and held it with her own. His eyes were smoky, heavy-lidded, dark as the blue of winter twilight. She smiled, already lost in them, in him, in the wonder hovering at the edge of her consciousness. He pressed deeper and she took him in, into her body, into her life, into her heart.

Their world began to blur in a swirl of light and heat and sensation so intense that perceptions merged. Caught in the glow of his eyes, she could feel the delight course through his body, feel the last of his uncertainty melt away, feel the stunning totality of his release. He flowed into her, and she dissolved in her own pleasure, holding nothing back, letting him share her ecstasy, her elation, and her love. They held each other, united on a plane of pure sensation, complete, sated in body and spirit. When there was no part of themselves that had not mingled, had not merged, they clung together, spent, trembling, helpless, whole in a way they had never been before. Whole, united, one. Forever and ever inseparable.

It was late afternoon when Celene awoke, muddleheaded and languorous in Burke's embrace. She turned and touched his face. His breathing did not alter; he did not stir. She could see the exhaustion in him now, the shadows beneath his eyes, the heaviness around his mouth. He must have spared no effort, no expense to reach her in Ste. Genevieve as quickly as he had. But he was here now, here to stay. He could rest and recover and be with her. They had the rest of their lives ahead of them.

Moving slowly to the edge of the bed, she reached for some bit of clothing to cover herself. Burke's shirt was the first thing to come under her hand, and she worked it down her body as best she could before slipping from beneath the covers. Behind her, Burke slept on, his face half-buried in the fullness of the bolster, his hair tumbled about him in tawny disarray.

Celene smiled and turned away, slinking toward the trunk that stood by the wall. She opened it slowly, with exaggerated stealth and took out a birch bark box. Her mother's silver needle case, Emile's tin whistle, and her father's favorite beaded garters were inside.

Drawing the ribbon of the calico pomander over her head from where the tiny bag still hung between her breasts, she carefully loosened the drawstrings and dumped the contents into her palm. She blew the crushed lavender blossoms away and looked down at the small wooden carving in her hand. It was warm from her body, sweet-scented by contact with the flowers. She had carried it with her all these months, needing, hoping, praying. She looked down at the charm and across at Burke, then closed her fingers around the tiny bit of wood one last time. The charm had brought her good and bad, happiness and misery, pain and elation. Or perhaps it had brought her nothing more than what fate had had in store for her. What mattered was that Burke was here with her now, that he was pleased about the child, that he intended to stay.

Gently she lay the carving in the box with the rest of her treasures, the rest of her remembrances. Slowly she settled the cover in place and tucked the box away.

The hinges on the trunk groaned as she lowered the lid, and behind her, she heard Burke stir. "Celene? What are you doing, Celene?"

She turned back to where he sat at the edge of the bed, tousled and sleepy. With a smile on her lips and a glow in her eyes, she crossed the room to where her husband and her future awaited her.